HUNTER'S MOON

HUNTER'S MOON

A Hunter Buchanon Black Hills Western

WILLIAM W. JOHNSTONE

AND J.A. JOHNSTONE

PINNACLE BOOKS

Kensington Publishing Corp.

www.kensingtonbooks.com

PINNACLE BOOKS are published by

Kensington Publishing Corp.
119 West 40th Street
New York, NY 10018

All Kensington titles, imprints, and distributed lines are available at special quantity discounts for bulk purchases for sales promotion, premiums, fund-raising, educational, or institutional use.

Special book excerpts or customized printings can also be created to fit specific needs. For details, write or phone the office of the Kensington Sales Manager: Attn.: Sales Department. Kensington Publishing Corp., 119 West 40th Street, New York, NY 10018. Phone: 1-800-221-2647.

PINNACLE BOOKS, the Pinnacle logo, and the WWJ steer head logo are Reg. U.S. Pat. & TM Off.

First Printing: August 2021
ISBN-13: 978-0-7860-4866-3
ISBN-10: 0-7860-4866-2

ISBN-13: 978-0-7860-4867-0 (eBook)
ISBN-10: 0-7860-4867-0 (eBook)

10 9 8 7 6 5 4 3 2 1

Printed in the United States of America

Chapter 1

Bullets crackled like miniature lightning bolts around Hunter Buchanon's head. They were followed by the screaming reports of at least two, maybe three rifles.

"Whoa!"

Trotting along to his left, Hunter's pet coyote, Bobby Lee, gave a yelp and jerked to one side as a bullet tore up sod in front of him.

Hunter looked around quickly, saw a low rise off to the south, the opposite direction the lead was coming from, and put spurs to his fleet grullo Nasty Pete's flanks.

"Sudden lead storm, Bobby Lee!" he told the coyote. "Time to split the wind!"

Nasty Pete put his head down, laid his ears back, and stretched his long legs into a ground-consuming gallop. Hunter hunkered low, the wind bending the brim of his high-crowned gray Stetson against his forehead. He whipped a quick glance over his right shoulder as more bullets caromed around him, some plunking into the ground to each side of him or behind him. One spanged shrilly off a rock inches to his left, then severed a sage brush branch, flipping it high in the air.

Maybe forty yards to the north—way too close for comfort—smoke puffed from the top of a long, shelf-like rise. Three sets of intermittent smoke puffs lined up maybe ten feet apart. Three rifles, all right. The shooters were close, but Nasty Pete was pulling away from them fast.

However, as Hunter turned his head back forward, one of those bullets sliced a burn across the outside of his right cheek to ricochet off a rock ten feet ahead of the galloping grullo. He swept a hand across his cheek, saw the blood streaking his fingers. Hot rage rose in the big ex-Confederate as he approached the knoll he'd been heading for.

He'd been ambushed before, but not on his own range and doing something as innocent as riding out to check the graze along Sweetwater Creek. The bushwhack really put a bee in his bonnet. The only good thing he could see about the situation was that the three ambushers, while way too close for comfort, were lousy shots.

They seemed overly determined to snuff his wick, firing too quickly, not taking the time to line up their sights, firing as though in desperation. If they'd have waited a minute or two, he'd have ridden up to the very front of that shelf, and at six-feet-four-inches tall and broad of shoulder and chest, he'd have been a hard target to miss.

Rustlers, most likely. Raggedy-heeled broad-looping sons of Satan who had spotted Hunter riding toward them. Knowing the penalty for rustling in beef country was a necktie party, they'd panicked and started firing without taking the time to aim.

Jumpy sons of bucks.

"Hurry up, Bobby!" he called to the coyote streaking along in a gray-brown blur beside him.

Hunter put the grullo around behind the knoll and drew back on the reins. Nasty Pete skidded to a halt, kicking up dust and needle grass, snorting and blowing. Hunter leaped out of the saddle, grabbed his Henry repeating rifle from the saddle boot, and ran up the back side of the knoll, fleet of foot for a man his size. He gritted his teeth and flared his blue eyes in fury.

Behind him, Bobby Lee stood, copper eyes bright with anxiety, tongue drooping down over his lower jaw as he panted.

Ten feet from the top of the hill, Hunter dropped to his knees, shucked away his hat, and crawled, his long, blond hair bouncing down his back and across his shoulders. He swept it back from his eyes with his gloved right hand, cocked the Henry, and laid the barrel over the top of the knoll, gazing over the octagonal barrel toward the shelf from which the shooters had flung lead at him.

They were no longer firing, and they were hunkered low, but he could catch glimpses of the men and their rifles as they glanced up from behind the shelf's lip from time to time, jerking their heads sharply this way and that, likely conferring in frustration over having lost their quarry when they should have had him dead to rights. The ambusher left of the other two from Hunter's perspective poked his hatted head out from behind a thumb of ground he'd been hunkered behind and started to extend his rifle in Hunter's direction.

Hunter snarled an oath as he quickly but carefully lined

up the Henry's sights, steadied the rifle, and squeezed the trigger.

Boom!

The man jerked back with a yelp, dropping his rifle and falling away out of sight.

The other two jerked their rifles up over the lip of the shelf and hastily resumed firing, rifle maws stabbing smoke and orange flames, the rifles cackling shrilly. Hunter pulled his head down beneath the crest of the knoll as bullets plundered dirt and gravel from the hill's far side. He rolled to his right. When the shooting tapered off, he quickly lifted his head and rifle again, lined up his sights on the black hat of one of the bushwhackers, and fired a hair too late.

As he pulled the trigger, the bushwhacker saw him and jerked his head down behind a juniper root. Hunter's slug tore up dirt and grass just beyond where the man's head had been a second before.

Hunter pulled his head down as the other shooter opened up on him again, the rifle belching across the distance of ninety yards or so, the slugs pluming dirt at the knoll's crest. He fired only two rounds before silence descended once more. Hunter raised his head and rifle again, but they were waiting for him.

He pulled his head and the Henry back down as two slugs hammered the side of the knoll well wide of where his head had been. He gave a dry chuckle and wagged his head. "Just because they can't shoot for mule fritters don't mean they ain't gonna continue to throw lead. They might even get *lucky*!"

He turned his head to one side and up a little, encircled his mouth with his gloved hands, and yelled, "Why don't you two tinhorns give it up and throw your rifles out before you end up wolf bait like your friend!"

Two seconds passed before one of the bushwhackers returned with: "Go to hell, Buchanon!"

Hunter frowned. The voice had been familiar. Nasally but familiar.

His mind shuffled through a deck of faces and recent encounters until he stopped at the leering, long-nosed face of Rolly Piper. A small-time outlaw from Missouri, Rolly was one of a small clan of brothers and cousins who haunted the Black Hills, rustling stock and selling it to corrupt ranchers, pulling occasional stagecoach holdups, and rolling drunk miners for their pokes in dark alleys behind grog shops and hurdy-gurdy houses in Hot Springs, Tigerville, and Deadwood.

Just last week, Hunter had bent Piper's nose sideways against his face when Hunter had caught him pestering a young lady on a side street in Tigerville. The girl had been walking toward the main drag to sell eggs to a local grocer when a drunken Piper grabbed her skirts from where he'd been lounging with a mug of beer on a loafer's bench in front of one of Tigerville's seamier side-street grog shops.

Hunter had been buying feed next door, and intervened. Piper had told him to mind his own business and to cart "his big, Confederate grayback self" off to hell where he and his "old man and that saloon girl" he'd married belonged. Then he'd continued to paw the girl with the egg basket, who'd been all of fourteen. That, and what he'd said about Hunter's father, Angus, and his new bride, the former Annabelle Ludlow, had cost Rolly Piper a broken nose with one vicious swing of Hunter's right fist.

Hunter had dried the egg girl's tears with his hankie,

sent her back on her way without so much as a single broken egg. He finished loading the feed sacks into his wagon, climbed aboard, clucked to his horse, and clattered off down the street, leaving Piper lolling back against the saloon, clutching his nose and wailing.

So here he was on Hunter and his father's—and, more recently, his wife Annabelle's—4-Box-B range, likely rustling cattle as his cowardly way of getting even for that busted beak. He couldn't have known Hunter himself would be riding out this way today, to check the grass along Sweetwater Creek to which, now after roundup and having sold five hundred steers to a packer in Belle Fourche, he intended to settle his remaining herd. The creek, here in the low country near the ranch headquarters, was the perfect place for these remainders over the long Black Hills winter.

No, Piper hadn't been expecting Hunter. But when he'd seen him heading his way, he'd seen a chance for an even more satisfying revenge than merely rustling a few head of 4-Box-B beef. But he'd gotten his nerves up, lost his patience, and he and his partners in rustling, likely as nervous as Piper was about turning to cold-blooded murder, or maybe knowing Buchanon's renegade Confederate war record and remembering how he'd handled the men who'd burned his ranch two years ago, had been too quick to throw lead.

Now they had a pretty good idea they were going to die, and they were even more nervous than before.

Hunter halfway hoped they'd run. He didn't want to kill. He'd had enough killing during the War for Southern Independence. When his father, Angus, had hauled him and his two brothers, Shep and Tyrell, out here from Georgia, leaving their mother behind in a grave—she'd died during the war when Hunter and his father had been off fighting it—Angus had wanted him and his boys to leave bloodshed behind.

But two years ago, they'd run into another war, albeit a smaller one, after Hunter had met a pretty Yankee girl, his now-wife Annabelle Ludlow, the daughter of a rich area rancher and proud, Confederate-hating Yankee, to boot. To show how much he'd disapproved of the notion of his daughter marrying a lowly Southern hillbilly, Graham Ludlow, with the backing of the crooked county sheriff and help from his thuggish business partner, Max Chaney, had sent their henchmen to sack the 4-Box-B. Many men had died that day, including Shep and Tye.

Also on that day, Hunter had learned that there was likely nowhere on earth a man could go to flee the trouble of other men.

He was looking at that again now.

At least he was armed. Before his ranch had been attacked, he'd been naïve enough to believe he could walk among other men unarmed. Max Chaney's son, Luke, a deputy sheriff every bit as crooked and loutish as his father, had taught him he couldn't. Luke, wanting Hunter out of the way so he could pursue Annabelle, had ambushed the unarmed Hunter one day when Hunter had been on his way to town to deliver his father's locally famous Scottish ale to several saloons in Tigerville. Luke hadn't lived to learn the lesson that you never messed with a Buchanon, even an unarmed one.

Hunter, however, had learned his.

Today, he had his Henry repeating rifle, which had belonged to his older brother Shep, and the pretty LeMat revolver, a gift from a Confederate general whose life Hunter had saved and which he wore in a black leather holster thonged on his right thigh. The bowie knife he'd made himself was sheathed on his left hip, opposite the French-made LeMat, which fired five .44-caliber rounds from the secondary barrel under the main one, and a twenty-gauge shotgun shell from the stouter, longer barrel above.

Now it was time to teach a lesson to Rolly Piper, who likely wouldn't run. He was a coward, but he was too afraid of his own cowardice to run. He'd stay and try to finish the business he'd started in order to save some semblance of his pride.

That was all right with Hunter. If he didn't finish Piper off now, he'd only have to do it later. Besides, he couldn't let the man get away with rustling. That would only encourage him to try it again, and encourage others to do the same. The 4-Box-B could never be seen as an easy target.

Hunter looked around, pondering the situation. He glanced over the top of his covering knoll once more. They'd been waiting for him to do just that. He saw the two rifles extending over the lip of Piper's shelf, and just as he jerked his head back down behind his own covering knoll, flames and smoke stabbed from each barrel at nearly the same time.

The bullets plunked into the lip of the knoll, spraying Hunter with dirt and grass.

He cursed and shook the debris from his hair.

A man laughed jeeringly.

Another one yelled, "Give you a close shave there, Buchanon?"

The other man laughed again.

Hunter cursed again. They had him pinned down and outnumbered. He could sit up here and swap lead with them all day, but it would likely take a lucky shot to grease Piper or the other fellow, staying low as they were now since the third man had taken a pill he couldn't digest and was likely shaking hands with old Scratch.

Hunter had to figure something else out.

He looked down the long slope of the knoll he was on. A wash slithered along the base of it, running generally from south to north. It cut through the sagebrush prairie back toward Piper's shelf and then, maybe another hundred yards farther north, it swung around behind the shelf, angling east. That was Juniper Creek, though it was dry most of the year and was good only for watering cattle during the spring snowmelt.

The cut of the creek was sharply gouged and maybe six feet deep. Deep enough to conceal Hunter if he kept his head down.

"Hey, Buchanon!" Piper called from the north. "Why don't you throw that rifle down? We'll throw ours down, too, shake hands, and call it a day? Yeah, you'll lose a few beeves, but that's better than your life, ain't it? I mean, you wanna go back to that purty saloon girl you married, don't you?"

The man's voice rose a few jeering pitches as he added, "I sure know I would! All that long, red hair! In fact, if we have to kill you out here, I might just ride over to the 4-Box-B and introduce myself—*if you know what I mean!*"

Piper cackled a goatish laugh.

The other man howled.

Hunter's heart burned again with anger. Annabelle was *not* a saloon girl. She might have worked in a saloon for a few months in Tigerville, prancing around in skimpy outfits and fishnet stockings, but that had been only to make Hunter jealous.

She'd wanted her prospective husband to see the error of his ways in postponing their marriage until he could relocate the gold he'd dug up to secure his and Anna's future in the ranching trade, and to rebuild the 4-Box-B. The gold had been stolen from his secret stash by Annabelle's own brother Cass, who'd returned it after he'd realized just how deeply in love Hunter and Annabelle were.

No, Anna was not a saloon girl. She was Hunter's wife. Rolly Piper, on the other hand, was a gutless cur who was going to die a gutless cur's death.

Squeezing the Henry in his gloved hands, Hunter gained his feet and walked down to where Bobby Lee stood near Nasty Pete, both animals looking anxious.

Hunter leaned down and patted the coyote's head. "You stay with Pete, Bobby Lee. If you were armed, it'd be a different story. But since you ain't, you stay."

Bobby lifted his snout and gave a low yapping whine.

Hunter turned and began jogging down the long slope toward the creek at the bottom, ready despite his war-weary self, to draw some blood.

Chapter 2

Hunter leaped into the creek's dry bed, both boots sinking into the alluvial sand pocked here and there by chunks of driftwood washed down the previous spring. There were also the bleached bones of a dead deer and something he noted in passing, though it did linger in his mind for a second or two, troubling him vaguely—a large pile of bear scat bristling with fur and bits of undigested bone.

Hunter swung to his left and began jogging north.

He stopped suddenly, looked down at his boots, and shook his head.

He leaned his rifle against the cutbank, then sat down in the sand and removed his boots and socks. He'd fought most of the war barefoot, moving fast as a deer behind enemy lines. A fellow couldn't run in boots that were made for toeing stirrups, not speed.

He lined the boots up neatly against the creek bank, each sock stuffed into each well, then took off running again, moving more fluidly now, faster, easier. During the war his feet had acquired thick, leathery soles, the product of many callouses. His feet had grown a little more tender since the war, since he didn't go barefoot nearly as much, but a good, thick skin remained on the soles, and the sharp bits of gravel and burrs didn't bother him overmuch.

He ran to the north.

When he moved out into the open ground between his knoll and the shelf on which Piper and his fellow rustler and bushwhacker perched sixty yards beyond, both formations on his right now, he crouched low, grateful for the fringe of brush growing along the embankment, offering good cover in most places, though there were still some open patches he had to be wary of. Piper and his cohort might spy him and shoot through one of those open patches and just might, even poor marksmen as they were, land a lucky shot.

As he ran, wending his way around obstacles, keeping his head low, the big ex-Confederate, on the lee side of his twenties now, glanced often to his right, noting his progress in closing the ground between his knoll and Piper's shelf. He was roughly halfway between them . . . then two-thirds . . . then he was at the west end of the shelf so that he could see the erosions and rocks and twisted cedars and the autumn-red leaves of the shadbark shrubs peppering the shelf's steep western slope.

A deer trail angled up the side to the crest, starting at a gap in the brush fringing the cut to Hunter's right.

Hunter jogged around a bend in the wash and stopped suddenly.

So did Rolly Piper and Otis Lowery.

They'd seen him at the same time he'd seen them, and both men's eyes widened in shock. Lowery, a thickset, suety man in a sweaty shirt and funnel-brimmed, badly weathered Stetson, took one leaping step back, as though he'd just seen a coiled rattlesnake. He held an old Spencer repeater on his right shoulder. Now he lowered the stock and angled the barrel up, wanting like hell to take the gun in two hands but too wary to do so . . . yet.

His washed-out blue eyes rolled nervously around in their sockets.

Piper froze, chin down, elbows out, crouched slightly, eyeing Hunter sharply from his badly swollen black eyes above his bandaged nose and shaded by the brim of his flat-crowned, black Stetson. He was holding a saddle ring Winchester carbine low in his right hand. Keeping his shocked eyes on Hunter, he angled the rifle up slowly now, a leering grin shaping itself on his thick-lipped mouth mantled by three days' worth of dirty brown stubble.

He was a skinny man of average height, sort of coyote-faced and patch-bearded, his pasty skin mottled red from sun and windburn. His nose, bruised black and yellow and with a little inky green around the edges, looked sore as hell. He wore a shabby wool coat over a sweaty, wash-faded longhandle top, canvas trousers, and mule-eared boots. Always having fancied himself a gunman against the evidence, he wore two Schofield revolvers in low-slung, tied-down holsters, both for the cross-draw.

Both men looked at the Henry in Hunter's right hand, held as low as Piper's.

Their eyes kindled darkly. Sweat glistened on their brows.

They glanced in silent conferral at each other, then shifted their gazes back to Hunter, who grinned despite the anger-burn in his chest.

He remembered what Piper had said about Annabelle.

Damn his crazy Rebel heart, anyway, he wanted Piper to raise that rifle so he could blow him back to the hell the man had come from. Otis Lowery was Piper's cousin, so Lowery too.

The third man, now presumably dead, had likely been the Tigerville ne'er-do-well and close pard of Piper and Lowery, Titus Wilcox, who'd once worked for Max Chaney and Graham Ludlow until Chaney, whom Hunter had shot through his mouth, had cashed in his chips at the local sawbones' office, and Ludlow, having lost his daughter as well as the war, and with a bad ticker, was holed up and likely sulking at his appropriately named Broken Heart Ranch to live a life of brooding seclusion with his son, Cass, awaiting the end which he likely did not dread.

Yeah, Piper and Lowery needed to go the way of Wilcox. Yeah, Hunter would have more blood on his hands. But he'd be making the world a better place.

He quirked his mouth corners with a smile at the thought. That seemed to rattle Piper and Lowery a little more than they'd been rattled before. They stared at him, tensely, both men sweating profusely now, their foreheads glistening. Dark sweat crescents streaked the armpits of their jackets.

Piper did not like the mocking smile on Hunter's lips. The man flared his nostrils angrily. He bunched his mouth, and the skin wrinkled across the bridge of his nose and forehead as he suddenly raised the Winchester in his hands, straightening as he snapped the butt plate to his right side.

Hunter raised his faster and shot Piper in the belly.

The man squealed, crouched, and stumbled backward. Hunter cocked the Henry quickly, the ejected casing arcing back behind him as he slid the Henry slightly right. His own eyes widened in surprise when he found that Lowery had gotten the drop on him and was twisting a wicked smile as he drew his index finger back against the Spencer's trigger.

Hunter flung himself to his left as the Spencer roared. He hit the ground on his left hip and shoulder, rolled once, brought the Henry up again, and shot Lowery just as the man was ramming a fresh .56 cartridge into the Spencer's action. Hunter's bullet took the man through the dead center of his forehead.

The man lifted his chin and dropped the Spencer. He gaped at Hunter, shocked and horrified. His chin came up as his head settled back and both eyes rolled up in their sockets. Lowery stepped back stiffly, dying fast on his feet, then fell straight back against the ground, doing nothing to break his fall.

He struck with a loud thump and a grunt and lay there, still, showing only the whites of his eyes through half-closed lids.

Piper was on his knees, crouched forward, arms crossed on his bullet-torn belly, wailing.

Hunter walked up to him and stood staring down at him. "Where are the cattle?"

Piper lifted his head and cast a glassy-eyed glare at Hunter. "*You go to hell!*"

Hunter lowered his rifle and turned and headed for the wash's east bank.

"Wait!" Piper screeched at him. "You can't leave me here to die like this! Like a damn *dog*!"

Hunter climbed the bank and began moving off to find the cattle.

"Please!" Piper cried.

Hunter stopped, wheeled, cocking a live cartridge into the Henry's breech, and fired. The bullet tore through Piper's left temple, silencing the man forever. Piper flopped back, as still now as Lowery in death.

Hunter cursed. He shouldn't have wasted the lead on the man. He ejected the spent shell and racked a live one into the Henry's breech. He held the rifle out from his right hip as he strode forward, looking around for the cattle. Piper, Lowery, and Wilcox might not have been the only ones out here. He'd taken only a few steps before he heard muffled lowing off to his left.

He moved between two low buttes, crossed Juniper Creek where it swung to the east, then followed the gradually loudening lowing into a broken canyon area filled with scrub and rocks and burr oaks whose leaves were turning brown now in the early fall. He bottomed out on the twisting canyon floor, stepped around a bend in its meandering course, and stopped.

Ahead, lay the cattle. They'd been herded into a small box canyon. A makeshift fence of oak and aspen logs had been erected across the canyon mouth as a gate. The restlessly milling cattle stared out at Hunter from between the rails, kicking up their nervous lowing.

A boy stood near the makeshift gate. He was a small, narrow-faced, sandy-headed boy, maybe ten or eleven years old, clad in wash-faded blue overalls and sack shirt under a shabby black coat, and a floppy-brimmed black hat. The boy stood watching Hunter, scowling skeptically.

Hunter removed his finger from the Henry's trigger and dropped the barrel.

He looked around quickly, making sure no other men were around. Seeing no one but the boy out here, he returned his gaze to the child.

The boy lifted his chin and said with a strange indifference, "Uncle Rolly dead?"

Hunter winced. Damn the luck, finding a child out here. One related to a man he'd killed. "Yes."

If he felt any emotion, the boy did not betray it. He continued to regard Hunter flatly from his deep-set, brown eyes beneath the floppy brim of his hat.

Hunter strode slowly forward, partly afraid that if he moved too quickly, the boy would run. As he approached, however, the boy held his ground. If he was afraid, he did not show it. The boy's right eye was swollen, mottled purple and yellow. The boy had a few crusted cuts on his lips, as well, another two-inch, scabbed gash on his jaw.

Hunter squatted before the child, rested the Henry across his thighs, and thumbed his Stetson up off his forehead.

Again, regretfully, he said, "They didn't give me much choice. Lowery's dead too."

"Wilcox too?"

"Titus Wilcox?"

"Yes."

"He's dead too." When the boy did not respond but continued staring at him flatly, Hunter said, "Does that mean anything to you?"

The boy frowned. "What do you mean?"

"Do you feel bad?"

"Bad?" The boy looked off speculatively, then turned

back to Hunter. He shrugged a shoulder and said, "No. You Buchanon?"

"Yes."

"Uncle Rolly had it in for you, for what you did to his nose."

"What's your name?" Hunter asked him.

"Nathaniel P. Jones," the boy announced flatly, though his eyes said he was proud of that middle initial.

Hunter nodded. "I'm Hunter Buchanon." He canted his head toward the cattle staring out at him from between the rails in the makeshift gate. "Those are my beeves."

"I know."

"Why are you out here?"

"Rolly made me come. I cook and clean the dishes when they camp, so they can drink an' howl an' such. You ain't gonna arrest me, are ya?"

Hunter shrugged. "I believe a man deserves a second chance." He frowned. "Where's your ma?"

"She died last year in Deadwood."

"No pa?"

"None that I know about."

"Is Rolly the only kin you got?"

"Him an' his brothers an' cousins, but I don't know them. Only Rolly and Lowery and Wilcox."

"Did he give you that black eye?"

"No, he busted my jaw for me for kickin' up too much dust when I swept out the cabin. Wilcox blackened my eye. I woke him when I got up to use the privy."

"I see." Hunter scraped a thumb along his jaw, pondering the child. "You got anywhere to go?"

"I'll go back to Rolly's cabin." Nathaniel jerked his chin. "Our horses are back in the trees."

"You'd be alone at Uncle Rolly's now, since he's passed?"

"Don't worry about me," said Nathaniel P. Jones, lifting his chin a little and puffing his chest out, though keeping the same flat expression as before. "I'll do just fine on my own. A whole lot better than with Uncle Rolly and them two polecat pards of his kickin' me around and makin' me do all the work. Maybe I can go fishin' for a change."

Hunter smiled at that. He considered the boy once more. He was a tough kid. Hunter could see it in his eyes. But there was hesitation in those eyes as well. Fear. Far back in them. Hunter didn't blame him a bit. It was tough being a man alone on the frontier west. Even tougher for a boy.

"You wouldn't be needin' a job, would you?"

The boy frowned. "At the 4-Box-B?"

"That's right."

"I don't ride."

"Do you want to learn?"

"Hell, yeah."

"In the meantime, we always need help around the ranch. Nothin' glamorous like ridin' an' ropin', but gatherin' wood, feedin' the hosses, an' such. My old man could use a hand in his brew shed."

The boy looked at him for a long time, scowling skeptically, as though he suspected he might be being teased. Finally, he toed a rock with his boot, stuck his tongue in a corner of his mouth, and said, "Heck . . . yeah."

"A roof over your head and three squares a day. Good, proper cookin' includin' steaks and roasts with all the trimmin's, and pie or cake for dessert."

The boy's eyes widened and an eager flush crept into his sunburned cheeks.

"Sound fair?"

"I ain't a stranger to hard work, Mister Buchanon."

"I can tell you are not." Indeed, the boy's hands were large for his age, brown from weathering and thick with callouses.

"Three squares a day, and I don't have to cook?"

"No, but you might have to split some wood for the stove."

The boy opened his mouth again and his eyes grew expressive, but he checked his boyish enthusiasm—he was among men now—and looked down again, shrugged, and toed the rock again. "Sure. If you're needin' someone, I can help out."

"All right, then." Hunter rose and extended his hand to the boy, who shook it. "Welcome to the 4-Box-B."

Just then, the soft thumps of four padded feet sounded to Hunter's right. He turned to see Bobby Lee running toward him.

"Coyote!" Nathaniel exclaimed, pointing.

Bobby Lee leaped into Hunter's arms. Laughing, Hunter wrapped his arms around the coyote and endured the face laps and whines as Bobby Lee demonstrated how happy he was to see his master unharmed. Hunter laughed as Bobby squirmed in his arms, giving his face a bath with his long, rough tongue.

"What in tarnation . . . ?" Nathaniel exclaimed, looking at the big brawny frontiersman and the coyote in his arms.

Hunter laughed. "This here is Bobby Lee, Nathan. Can I call you Nathan?"

"Sure."

"Bobby and I have been glued to the hip ever since I found him, a poor little orphan coyote, all alone and afraid, only a few months old. I figure his parents and maybe the litter he came from got killed by ranchers, so I took him home and raised him up, and here he is. Best friend I ever had!" Hunter leaned down and patted the head of the coyote who sat close beside him, gazing up at him admiringly, eyes half-closed.

Gradually, Nathan's face lost its shocked expression. As he studied Bobby Lee, he said, "Can I pet him?"

"Go on over and let Nathan pet you, Bobby Lee. I just added him to the payroll."

Bobby Lee walked over and sat before the boy, who reached tentatively down to stroke the coyote's thick, gray-brown coat. Bobby Lee slid his nose up close to Nathan, sniffing, familiarizing himself with the boy's scent.

"I've never heard of a pet coyote before," he said.

"I reckon I hadn't neither till Bobby Lee wandered into my life."

The coyote looked away, saw a rabbit, and gave chase. He could chase a rabbit for an hour, or give up on one, see another, and chase that one before likely spying even another one, or maybe a mouse. Somehow, though, he always kept track of Hunter, his lord and master.

Nathan turned to Hunter. "I heard about the 4-Box-B. You're the outfit that got burned out by Ludlow, Chaney, and Sheriff Stillwell."

"That's right, boy," Hunter said grimly. "It took me, my wife, and my pa and a handful of neighbors almost two years, but we built the place back up from the ground, and we're stompin' with our tails up, in full operation again. I have four top hands. You'll be my fifth."

The boy almost smiled that time.

Hunter glanced at the cattle penned up in the box canyon. "Today too early to start work?"

"Heck, no," said Nathaniel P. Jones with another shrug. He gave the rock a resolute kick.

Chapter 3

Hunter and Nathan dismantled the gate across the box canyon, then stepped out of the way as the herd of nine or so, mostly young steers with a couple of brindle heifers among them, bolted out of the canyon and up a twisting trail to the grassy tableland above, buck-kicking, the steers trying to jump over each other in their haste to be free.

Nathan led Hunter over to where the dead men's horses were tied in an aspen grove up a side canyon. The next task Hunter chose to do alone. Leaving the boy in the canyon with a canteen, he rode one of the dead men's horses, leading the two others up out of the canyon and over to where Piper and Lowery lay dead in the wash. He rolled each man in his bedroll and tied the blanket-shrouded bodies over two of the horses.

After retrieving his boots and socks, he rode up to the top of the shelf from which the rustlers had ambushed him. He found Titus Wilcox sprawled on his back, head down-slope, feet upslope, arms flung wide, staring skyward with a startled expression. A puckered blue, .44-caliber hole shone in his left cheek, just above his patchy beard, an inch left of a large wart growing up from the side of his broad, pitted nose.

Hunter wrapped Wilcox in the man's own blanket roll, lashed him to the third horse, then left the horses on the side of the shelf as he rode back into the canyon to retrieve the boy. He hadn't wanted the boy to see the dead men's faces. He didn't know if Nathan had seen a dead man before. Most had by his age. Just the same, he didn't want to put him through it.

When he'd helped Nathan onto Nasty Pete's back, Hunter told him to hold on tight and then retraced his own path to where the three horses stood ground-reined, grazing contentedly. Hunter swung down and gathered up the horses' reins. He glanced at Nathan.

The boy regarded the three horses speculatively. "That them?"

"Yep." Hunter walked over and placed his hand on the boy's thigh. "You all right, boy?"

Nathan looked down at him in his flat, passionless way and said, "I've seen dead men before. Plenty of 'em in Deadwood. They were always cartin' 'em out of the Dancin' Bear. Sometimes they'd haul 'em up to Boot Hill in a wheelbarrow."

"What's the Dancin' Bear?"

"Saloon where Ma worked. I emptied the spittoons an' slop buckets."

Hunter suppressed a wince. The boy's short life had been no picnic. Holding the reins of the three packhorses, he swung up onto the grullo's back and settled himself in the saddle before the boy.

"Here we go, son. Close to an hour's ride to headquarters. You hungry?"

"I'm always hungry."

"We got that in common."

"Where's Bobby Lee?"

"Don't worry about Bobby. He comes and goes, Bobby does. But he'll be back for supper, an' you can count on it!"

Hunter laughed and spurred the grullo down around the side of the shelf and south in the direction of the 4-Box-B. He followed the old cattle trail he'd taken out here between Windy Butte and Spur Ridge and then along the east bank of Sandy Wash.

He'd ridden only a mile or so along the wash when a sour stench touched his nostrils.

"Peeee-YOU!" he exclaimed, drawing back on the grullo's reins. "What in tarnation . . . ?"

Hunter glanced into the wash. Right away he saw it lying sprawled on the wash's far side—dead cow with its entrails trailing out away from it, like a long, tattered red guidon. Flies formed a black cloud over and around it.

Hunter swung down from the saddle, then lifted the boy down to the ground. "Here, hold Nasty Pete's reins for me, will you? I'm going to check it out."

Hunter followed a game path into the wash and walked over to the cow. He had to hold his arm over his nose to muffle the death stench.

There wasn't much left of the cow, but he could see enough of the brand to know it was his 4-Box-B. The poor creature had nearly had its head ripped off and was gutted tail to neck, its ribs split open and resembling a ship with timbers ripped from stern to prow.

Nothing left inside but some stray guts and sinew. Flies filled the cavity, a roiling black mass, buzzing loudly and monotonously. Whatever the bear hadn't taken, carrion-eaters had finished off, including the eyes. Judging by the stench, the beast had been dead between two and three days.

Looking around, Hunter saw the sign of at least a dozen more cattle having passed through here recently. The heifer had likely been with the herd that Hunter had been pasturing on Blue Meadow, on the slopes of Crow's Nest Peak. It appeared the entire herd had lit a shuck, and a fast one, down from Blue Meadow to the northwest and down here into the draw and off down the draw, probably scattered from hell to breakfast in the aspens farther along down the wash where the banks flattened out around Easter Gulch.

The culprit was a bear, all right. Hunter had seen what nearly every predator in these hills left behind when it had taken down one of his cows, and the blunt, thorough, and aggressive work here was surely due to a grizzly. A black bear will rarely kill a cow and even more rarely devour the whole thing. Same with a cat. Same with wolves, who usually hunted in packs.

This looked to Hunter like the work of one animal working alone.

A lone griz.

He rode on away from the smelly carcass and scoured the draw to the north. He spotted a paw print—way too large for a wildcat and even a wolf. It didn't have the roundness or toe and pad alignment of a black bear print.

As Hunter looked around some more, his heart quickening at the prospect of a bear problem—he and his father and brothers had had a grizzly problem before, and while they'd run down and killed the venal bruin within a few weeks—it had cost them twenty prime animals worth a good sixty dollars a head. The bear had killed some for food, devouring the entire carcass. But most he'd killed for fun, left to lie on the range, only partly eaten and perfuming the air around them with the smell of rot.

As Hunter continued looking around for more prints he could track, the drumming of galloping hooves grew on the quiet mid-day air. Standing on the lip of the draw, the boy said matter-of-factly, "Riders." He jerked his head to indicate behind him.

Hunter walked back up out of the draw to stand beside the boy holding Nasty Pete's reins and cast his gaze to the southeast. Five riders galloped toward him through the grass and sage. The rider on the far right was a woman. Hunter could tell that even from a distance, and he couldn't help lifting his mouth corners a little in a contented smile— the contentment he always felt whenever he saw his beloved.

The former Annabelle Ludlow rode toward him now with the four men garbed for the range, her thick red hair bouncing on her shoulders clad in a red calico blouse under a black vest, a gray Stetson on her head that nicely contrasted the jade of her wide, sparkling eyes.

She came up fast and reined up hard along with the four others—Hunter's foreman, the lean and dragoon-mustached Kentucky Wade; the Mexican from Arizona, Noble Sanchez; Hunter's contrary old wrangler, Hec Prather; and the full-blood Teton Sioux who was still lean and hard despite his sixty years, Chief Red Otter.

Red Otter had once headed up a small band of Teton Sioux who'd roamed these hills before the white invaders came. Most of his people had been wiped out by smallpox. One of the few survivors, and a practical man who'd been able to put his bitterness behind him, Red Otter had adapted to the white man's ways. Hunter and Angus had known him for years; even at sixty, he was still the best horseman and puncher in the Hills.

"Hunter!" Annabelle said, her jade eyes cast with worry, dust billowing around her and the others. "We heard shooting from the headquarters, thought for sure you were in trouble out here." She hadn't finished the sentence before her eyes, which had already taken in the boy, flicked toward the three horses over which the blanket-wrapped bodies of the rustlers were tied.

She returned her gaze to Hunter, and lines of befuddlement cut across her forehead.

Hunter held up his right hand, palm out. "All's well, honey."

"You have a nasty cut across your cheek!" Annabelle pointed out.

Hunter had forgotten about the bullet burn and now swiped his hand across the cut to remind himself. "Not nasty at all. Just a little stinger. Got ambushed." He canted his head toward the packhorses. "By them."

"Anyone I know?" Kentucky Wade asked, booting his fine steeldust gelding over to the dead men.

He swung his long, lean body clad in a crisp checked shirt, brown vest, and denim jeans, and a handsome pair of tooled leather chaps, down from his steeldust's back. An ivory-gripped Russian revolver rode high on his left hip, in the cross-draw position. A high-crowned, broad-brimmed Stetson with a horsehair neck thong shaded his handsome face with earnest, light brown eyes.

Wade was a good, affable man, easy to work with, one who commanded respect among others, and he knew the range. Having been born in Kentucky, he'd cowboyed in Wyoming since he was "knee-high to a grasshopper" before coming to the Black Hills when everyone else had, after gold was discovered and the beef men moved in to feed the gold seekers. Hunter had considered himself lucky to hire the man, who spoke much like Hunter, with a soft, rolling Southern accent.

"Rolly Piper," Hunter said. "Otis Lowery and Titus Wilcox."

"Figures," Annabelle said, nodding slowly. "It figures they'd get to us sooner or later. Especially since you turned Piper's nose sideways."

Beside her, Hec Prather grinned. So did Noble Sanchez. Even the customarily stoic Red Otter.

Hunter placed his hands on his hips and frowned up at his pretty wife. "Now, who told you that?"

Annabelle slid her eyes toward Hec Prather sitting a piebald gelding to her left. "A little bird told me from the windowsill one morning."

Hunter glanced at Hec, scowling. "Hec," he said, cutting his eyes at the others, all of whom had been with him in the saloon the day he'd rearranged Piper's facial features, "didn't I tell you boys I didn't want Annabelle to know about that?"

Kentucky Wade, checking out the bodies, merely flushed.

"Boss," Noble Sanchez said, raising his black-gloved hands and smiling winningly from beneath the brim of his dusty, sweat-stained palm leaf *sombrero*. He was short and lean, slightly potbellied but otherwise in good shape, and with thick, dark brown hair curling down from his hat. Long, mare's tale mustaches drooped down over the corners of his broad mouth. He wore a red shirt with Spanish-style embroidering, wash-worn denims, and brush-scarred chaps that had a hole on the outside of one leg, courtesy of a long-looper who'd tried to bushwhack him early last spring. Sometimes there was a lot of bushwhacking around here.

Crossing his arms and leaning forward on his saddle horn, he canted his insinuating smile at Hec Prather and said, "Who among us has the worst reputation for keeping secrets?"

He glanced at Red Otter, who gave a wry, crooked smile.

"Gosh-darn it   I tried!" Hec said, "But when she came askin' me what happened in town that caused you to bruise your knuckles, I tried to . . . I tried to . . ."

"He tried to keep mum but I could tell by the way his ears turned red"—Annabelle reached over and with her left, doeskin-gloved hand gave Hec's right earlobe a play-ful flick—"he was hiding something. All it took was the small bribe of a piece of my famous peach pie, fresh out of the oven, and slathered with whipped cream, to get the old fella to spill the beans."

Hec waved his hand across his ear as though at a fly, then scowled sheepishly at Hunter. "Ah, beans! You know I can't turn down a piece of Annabelle's pie, Hunter! I mean, what man can?" He turned his admiring eyes to the young woman sitting her calico mare, Ruthie, beside him.

Annabelle smiled insouciantly at her husband.

Wade and Sanchez chuckled.

Annabelle switched her gaze to the boy standing beside Hunter. "Who's your new friend?" she asked her husband.

Hunter placed his hand on the boy's shoulder. "This here is Nathaniel P. Jones." He added the next bit of information grimly, furling his brows, "Piper's nephew."

All four men looked at the boy with renewed interest.

"Oh," Annabelle said, sitting up straight in her saddle and nodding once, slowly, at the gravity of the information she'd been given. Hunter saw her eyes go to the boy's swollen eye and then to the cracked lips. She glanced at Hunter again, meaningfully. "I see."

Hunter smiled as he squeezed the boy's shoulder and said, "Nathan, I'd like you to meet my lovely wife, Annabelle."

"Pleased to meet you, Nathan," Annabelle said, smiling warmly.

Hunter looked down to see the boy flush under the pretty woman's gaze. Annabelle's rare beauty and charm tended to tongue-tie men of all ages. Nathan averted his gaze and toed a rock.

Hunter chuckled and said, "Sitting beside Annabelle there is a mean old cuss whose bark is worse than his bite, Hec Prather."

"Loudest snorer in the bunkhouse," Noble Sanchez said, cutting a mock accusing look at the old man.

Hec beetled his brows at him.

"And sitting beside Hec is Noble Sanchez. All you got to know about Noble is never play poker with him."

"You can say that again!" said Hec Prather.

"Beside Noble is Chief Red Otter. He was, indeed, a Sioux chief at one time."

"Once a chief, always a chief," Red Otter returned with

a brief flare of his flat, taciturn humor, leaning forward against his saddle horn. "Hello, young man. Welcome."

Hunter turned to regard his top hand, Kentucky Wade, who now stood by his horse, holding its reins. "And last but not least is my foreman, Kentucky Wade. He's my top hand."

"Top hand, my behind!" Hec Prather carped. "I am!"

"Oh, be quiet, you old rattlesnake!" Kentucky said.

"Kentucky," Hunter said, "since Nathan here has no family now that his uncle's gone, I offered him a job at the 4-Box-B."

"You did?"

"I did."

"Well, in that case . . ." Kentucky walked up to Nathan and extended his hand. "Mister Jones, welcome to the roll!"

Nathan shook the foreman's hand, smiling up at him now, shyly narrowing one eye, another flush burning up into his cheeks.

Hunter and Annabelle shared a glance. Annabelle winked and smiled affectionately at her husband, giving her silent approval of his offering a home to the orphan child.

Chapter 4

"What were you doing down in the draw yonder, Hunter?" Annabelle asked.

Hunter winced, then jerked his chin toward the draw. "Dead heifer. Bear kill, I think."

"Not grizzly kill though," Kentucky Wade said with more dread than hope in his voice.

"Pretty sure it is."

"Oh no," Anna said darkly. Having grown up on a ranch herself, she was all too aware of the threat as well as the cost of having a grizzly run loose on a range.

She swung down from her saddle and walked up to the edge of the draw. Hunter hadn't smelled the stench up here on this side of the wash since he'd climbed out of it. The wind had switched direction and was blowing it west.

"I was about to head farther up the draw to the north and see if I couldn't track it, find out where it was headed." Hunter turned to Anna, placed his hands on her shoulders. "Honey, would you escort our new hand, Nathan Jones, back to headquarters? Maybe show him around, give him a bite to eat? Looks like he could use some fattening."

"Why, sure I would," Annabelle said, affectionately

nudging his chin with her finger and then turning to the boy with a warm smile. "What do you say, Nathan? You hungry?"

Nathan gave a crooked smile, shrugged a shoulder, and looked away. The boy was still tongue-knotted in front of Annabelle and maybe in front of the other men, too, since they were all strangers to him. It had taken him a while to open up to Hunter after they'd first met.

Hunter chuckled and said, "Don't ruin your appetite for supper though. You wouldn't wanna miss one of my lovely wife's pot roasts with all the trimmings!"

"Boy, now I'm hungry!" said Kentucky Wade in his soft-spoken way and with his shyly glinting smile.

When Annabelle and Nathan had mounted up on Annabelle's mare, she turned to her husband and said, "You boys be careful. See you back at the ranch."

That's what her words had said, but her eyes, riveted on her husband, wide and lustrous, said so much more than that. Hunter knew his own eyes returned every bit of his pretty young wife's affection, because his heart was fairly brimming with it. If the other men hadn't been here, he'd have swept her up in his arms and planted a sweet, long, loving, lusty kiss on her bee-stung lips and maybe even touched her in places he'd never dream of doing in public.

His smile told her that.

She returned his smile with a wide, knowing one of her own, a faint flush rising in her cheeks. She'd gotten the message loud and clear.

"See ya, fellas," Annabelle told the others with a wave, turning the mare toward home.

Hunter watched Anna and the mare and Nathan Jones

trot away to the southeast. When he turned to the other men, he saw that Kentucky Wade was mounted now, and that all their eyes were on him, vaguely jeering, good-natured grins on their mugs. Even on the usually stoic, copper, severely chiseled face of Chief Red Otter.

"Newlyweds," said Hec Prather, shaking his head in mock disgust. "Can't keep their blasted hands off each other for two minutes!"

"Oh," Hunter said, laughing and grabbing Nasty Pete's reins, "I thought we did a pretty good job." He swung up into the leather and turned the horse toward the draw. He'd leave the dead men where they were—on their horses, which he'd tied to a picket pin. "Come on you lobos. Let's see if we can follow that bear to his hidey-hole."

He put the grullo down the bank and into the draw. The other men gave the cow a quick inspection from behind the neckerchiefs they lifted to their noses to muffle the stench, then Hunter showed them the scat.

"At least he ate the whole thing," Red Otter said from behind his own raised neckerchief. "He or she is not just on a killing spree."

"What's that look like to you, Hec?" Hunter asked old Prather, who'd once hunted bear in Colorado and Wyoming back in the days he'd been fur-trapping in the high country. Nothing like a grizzly robe to cut the high-mountain chill when the brittle snows and winds of winter came howling down from the Never Summers.

Kentucky Wade and Noble Sanchez watched the man, waiting for the older, more knowledgeable hand's assessment. Chief Red Otter nodded slowly, as though he'd already made up his mind about the track.

"Hold on a minute," Hec said, and swung heavily down

from his saddle, wincing against the aches in his aging bones.

He stepped up to the scat pile, hitched his canvas trousers up his thighs, then dropped to both knees with a grunt, doffed his hat, and leaned forward to sniff the scat.

He needed only one sniff. He straightened, making a face. He set his hat back on his head and cast Hunter a dark glance. "Griz."

"How can you tell from smelling it?" asked Sanchez, owning the skepticism of a much younger man.

Hec heaved himself to his feet with another wince, flushing with the effort. "Griz scat smells like chili peppers. Don't know if it's somethin' they eat, or if it just naturally smells like pepper, but it does, all right. Yep, that's a grizzly. A big one, too, judgin' by that track over there."

Heart quickening now with anxiousness and urgency, Hunter booted Pete on up the draw. "Let's see if we can pick up his trail."

Sitting on his horse, wrists crossed on the horn, Red Otter said, "You know, boss, this could be a onetime kill. Grizzlies move in a broad range. This one could have come all the way from Wyoming two days ago, maybe attracted to the Black Hills because the miners and prospectors up in the Bighorns have shot out all the game."

"That's right," Hec said, swinging up onto his horse. "Red Otter's got it right."

"Just the same," Hunter said, "I want to track him. If his trail leads off 4-Box-B range, I'll sleep well tonight." He stopped Pete and curvetted the horse to stare back at the others now riding toward him. "I don't begrudge a bear a beef now an' then. I just want to make sure this bruin hasn't set store by the 4-Box-B and decided to call it home for a while, to fatten himself up on my dime."

He booted Pete ahead.

He knew that Red Otter was likely right, and that he was probably over-reacting. But, doggone it, he and Annabelle and old Angus had worked too hard to rebuild their ranch after the fire to have their herd thinned by a bruin looking to expand his territory.

It wasn't that Hunter didn't sympathize with the bear. He'd always tried to live in harmony with his natural surroundings, never begrudging a coyote for being a coyote, or a wolf for being a wolf. He never hunted the beasts or, worse, poisoned them the way some ranchers did. Hell, they had to eat, too, and they were here before Hunter was.

Hunter wouldn't begrudge the bear a cow or two, but if the bruin had a mind to move in and dine at its leisure, well, then, Hunter would have something to say about it.

He and the others quickly picked up the bear's trail and followed it for a mile along the wash. When the creek bed swung toward the east, the bear had climbed up out of the wash and headed northeast, toward the massive toothy peak of Eagle's Nest rising in that direction. That's likely where he'd come from, since the heifer had come from the grassy range along the base of the ridge.

If he was returning the same way he'd come, he might not be widely ranging but maybe calling Eagle's Nest home and intending to fill his larder on Hunter's herds before holing up for the winter. The thought plagued Hunter as he and the others rode into the high country.

"Come on, fella," he silently willed the bruin, catching another glimpse of its print in the forest duff below. "Keep movin', will ya?"

When they'd ridden up out of the dense pine forest and come to a talus field spread broadly across the mountain's rocky slope, the tracks disappeared.

"Damn," Hunter said, stepping down from his saddle and casting his gaze along the ground.

No sign of the bear. Somewhere around here, though, they'd find spoor.

He shucked his Henry from his saddle scabbard and said to the others, "Let's spread out and walk ahead slow, see if we can't pick him up again." He glanced at Hec Prather who climbed heavily down from his saddle, a little flushed from the long ride. "You can stay with the horses if you want to, Hec."

Hec scowled at him, narrow-eyed. "Hell, how old do I look, anyways? I can walk as well as you young sons of devils." He patted his behind and winced. "It's ridin' that cankers my poor backside!"

"It's them whores you let ride you bareback in Tigerville of a Friday night that stoves up your backside, old man!" jeered Noble Sanchez. Hunter knew he loved the crotchety old geezer, though they rarely said a kind word to each other.

Hec turned to him with a mock venomous look. "If I want any bull dung out of you, you tequila-swillin', chili-chompin' bean eater, I'll—"

"All right, all right," Hunter said, cutting the older man off. "Let's get a move on. Shadows are growing long; we're gonna lose good light soon."

He moved slowly up the talus slide, weaving his way around wagon-size boulders. He scoured the flat talus for spoor while keeping one eye skinned on the bulging crag of granite that topped the ridge roughly a hundred yards farther up the grade. The sun was angling back behind the mountain, so the shadow sliding down from the base of the crag grew deeper, heavier, making it harder to give the ground a close inspection.

The others had spread out around him, keeping roughly twenty feet apart, moving slowly with their heads down, rifles cradled in their arms, the building breeze bending their hat brims and whipping Sanchez's red neckerchief back behind him.

"I have something," said Red Otter.

Hunter stopped and turned to the man to his right and a few feet back down the grade. Red Otter was six feet tall, broad in the chest and shoulders, his belly still relatively flat. He wore buckskin pants, a blue work shirt, suspenders, and a light wool jacket.

He did not wear a sidearm but was handy with the Winchester carbine, boasting a bear pattern of rivets on both sides of its rear stock, which he held now. His salt-and-pepper hair fell in twin braids down his back, angling down from his high-crowned, black Stetson sporting an eagle feather in its band. He pointed his high-cheeked, severely featured face with deep-set, slanted dark eyes toward Hunter now, pointing at the ground before him.

"Paw print in the dirt between rocks. Fresh. Real fresh." Red Otter turned his head to gaze up the slope toward the stone crag capping it. "He's up here . . . somewhere."

The words had no sooner passed his lips than a guttural grunt sounded from atop the slope. Hunter swung his gaze up the slope to see the undefinable movement of some murky figure, partly concealed by the shade of the crag itself. Then he saw a round boulder lurch forward and

begin rolling down the slope, in nearly a straight line toward
Red Otter.

A rumbling sounded, growing louder as the boulder
picked up speed.

Hunter shot his gaze from the boulder to Red Otter,
who had also turned his head toward the top of the slope.
He was directly in the boulder's path.

"Chief!" he cried.

Red Otter shuffled uncertainly sideways along the slope.
A chunk of shale slipped out from beneath his moccasin-
clad left foot, and he dropped to a knee.

Hunter had instinctively started running toward the Indian
as soon as he'd seen the boulder rolling down the slope.
Holding the Henry in one hand, having trouble keeping his
own footing on the appropriately named sliderock himself,
he ran as hard as he could.

He could see the boulder caroming toward Red Otter
now as the man struggled to right himself, one hand on
the ground, the other thrown up for leverage. He, too,
saw the boulder hurling toward him, thirty feet away . . .
twenty . . . the Indian's dark eyes growing wider.

Hunter closed on the chief only seconds ahead of the
rock, each bounce of the boulder as deafening as the roar
of a near thunderclap. Keeping his feet moving, Hunter
grabbed the man under his arms and hurled both himself
and Red Otter forward. They struck the ground at the
same time, Red Otter partly on top of Hunter, groaning
and making a face. On his back, Hunter glanced up as the
boulder caromed through the air where he and the chief
had been one second before.

The boulder bounced again, just beyond where they'd

been, cracking and shedding pieces of itself, and continued thundering on down the slope.

Beneath the boulder's thunder, the other men were shouting. They had all dropped to one knee, gazing anxiously toward where Hunter and the chief lay entangled.

Heart still pounding, Hunter looked at the chief. "You all right, Ch—"

He stopped. On one knee beside Hunter, hatless, the chief had turned his granite-like head to stare ominously toward the top of the slope, his eyes glistening with anxiousness, lips slightly parted, showing a glimpse of his teeth.

"No," Hunter heard him mutter.

Hunter turned to follow the chief's gaze to the base of the granite crag. A stone dropped in his belly. A dark figure stepped out of the shadows of the ridge. Ambient light shone in the beast's black eyes and rippling, cinnamon fur as it rose onto its back feet, standing straight and tall—all one ton of a giant grizzly the likes of which—the size and symmetry and otherworldly beastliness—Hunter had never seen before.

A word came to him: majestic. Another one followed close on its heels: killer.

The bear pounded its chest with its massive paws sporting claws the size of knives. It tipped its head back and opened its mouth, showing long, curving white teeth made for slashing and tearing and grinding prey to pulp.

A roar even louder than the roar of the plunging boulder filled the canyon.

It echoed, each echo making the ground beneath Hunter tremble nearly as much as the initial roar.

The cry was filled with a beastly rage so keen and unnerving that for stretched seconds, Hunter's knees turned to putty. He'd never felt such fear even during the war.

Atop the ridge, the beast dropped back down to all fours, swung around, and ambled back into the ridge's stygian shadows.

Gone.

Behind it, the last echo of its roar dwindled skyward.

Silence settled over the canyon, heavier than before.

Hunter returned his gaze to Red Otter. The chief was down on both knees, head bowed, arms raised high above his head. Softly, the sounds of a desperate chant, almost like Lakhota war chants he'd heard from a distance while riding the remote parts of the Black Hills, touched Hunter's ears.

Again, that dread he'd felt a moment ago placed its cold hand against his back.

Chapter 5

"So, Mister Nathaniel P. Jones," Annabelle said as she and the boy rode back toward the ranch together. "How long did you live in Deadwood?"

No response.

Hmm.

That was the third time she'd tried to make polite conversation. The boy had ignored both former attempts.

Anna was growing perplexed. Was the boy just shy or didn't he like her for some reason? Maybe he was just more of a man's boy. He seemed to have done fine with Hunter and Kentucky.

"Okay," she said, raising her voice ironically. "Let's try this one on for size—what do you like to do for fun?"

For a long time, only silence rode behind her. Then, his voice, weak and small, "Didn't have much time for fun, ma'am."

"I see."

He didn't seem overly eager to expound on his answer, so she gave up, quit trying. He was just shy, that's all, she told herself. It wasn't that he didn't like her. She couldn't help thinking so, however, because in the past she'd always taken to kids right away, and they'd always taken to her.

Oh well. He'd come around eventually, she told herself. Maybe he was feeling bad about his uncle, though from what Annabelle knew of Rolly Piper, the vile man's demise was nothing to feel bad about. Especially when the boy carried the scars of the man's temper. At least, she assumed Piper had been the cause of the bruising around Nathan's eye and mouth, the poor kid.

When she came to the last hill before the 4-Box-B, she reined in the calico and gazed down into the broad bowl between two forested peaks before her—the cradle that held the newly rebuilt compound of Hunter's ranch. No, she corrected herself. *Hunter's and her* ranch. And Angus, of course, since he'd been the one who'd founded it, with the help of his three sons, back in the years just after the war.

The headquarters appeared much as before. Angus had wanted it to look the way it had before Shep and Tyrell had died. The main house sat off to the right, the barns, stables, corrals, and the small, box-like blacksmith shop off to the left. A Weatherford windmill stood in the middle of the yard, its tin paddles turning slowly now in the late-afternoon breeze, filling the mortared stone tub ringing its base.

One of the few differences in the current headquarters was that Hunter and Anna had added a third half-story to the sturdy, log, peak-roofed main lodge, and they'd put a slightly larger front porch on it as well. They'd added the extra footage because some day they hoped to have a passel of young'uns bouncing about the place, and they, being Buchanons, would certainly need room to bounce.

Anna smiled at the thought, and in appreciation at her and her husband's and father-in-law's accomplishment. What a simple but handsome place lay before her, the house with its large stone chimney climbing the north side, and several wicker chairs set out on the porch where Angus and Hunter usually sat and sipped Angus's ale before supper . . . and occasionally after supper with, in Angus's case, a doctor-proscribed cigar or two.

Another point of difference was that Hunter had added a small bunkhouse, a low, rectangular log, shake-roofed structure facing the compound from its far end, flanked by a wash house, a privy, and line for drying clothes. A man of great ambition and pride, Hunter intended to expand his herd and his holdings over the years to come, and since his brothers were no longer here to help run the place, and his father was getting too old to do much but brew beer, he needed a few hands.

The third and last point of difference was that Angus had insisted his brew shed be slightly larger, with an ice house extending off to one side. Angus used the ice to cool the wert before adding the yeast. The brewery sat between the stable and the blacksmith shop, a small L-shaped building with two large front, stable-like doors that stood open now. Smoke curled from the brew shed's brick hearth, which meant that Angus was likely hard at work, brewing up another batch of his locally famous ale.

"There it is, Nathaniel," Annabelle said, gesturing to the compound before her. "Your new home for the time being." She turned her head to one side. "What do you think?"

Again, he didn't say anything. Consarn it, anyway— what was wrong with the child? Was he suddenly overcome with grief at his uncle's fate? Or was it her, Annabelle? She didn't want to, but she was beginning to take his silence personally.

"Oh well," she said with a sigh. "Let's go down and whip up a snack. I made a peach pie this morning. What do you say to that?"

"That's fine," came the weak response. She felt his shoulder shrug against her back.

At least it was a response, she told herself, and booted the mare on down the hill toward the yard. They rode through the ranch entrance portal, two cottonwood posts straddling the trail holding up a cottonwood plank that proudly announced BUCHANON RANCH, with the 4-Box-B brand burned into each end.

As they trotted into the yard, old Angus stepped out of the brew shed up beyond the barn and stables and walked quickly toward Annabelle and the boy, leaning on his hickory walking stick. He was a small man, clad in a checked shirt and baggy dungarees held up over his skinny hips with snakeskin suspenders. Annabelle had heard he'd been a much larger man at one time. The weight of the years, as well as the war, a dead wife, and two dead sons, had whittled him down to gristle.

His face was long and craggy, half covered in a thick, gray beard that drooped nearly to his chest. The left sleeve of his checked shirt was pinned up over the stump of that arm. Despite the pain he'd endured, both physically and emotionally, he usually seemed a contented soul, his blue eyes—the same blue as his only living son's—owning a near-constant glint of wry humor.

Now, however, having heard the shots but being too

chewed up with arthritis to fork a saddle anymore, his weathered features were a mask of dread.

He'd just barely survived the death of Shep and Tye. If anything happened to Hunter . . .

Anna rode over to him, holding up a placating hand, palm out, calling, "It's all right, Angus. Hunter's fine."

Angus stopped and leaned on the cane. "What happened? What was all the shootin' about?" His eyes flicked to the boy peeking out from behind Anna, and acquired a curious cast.

"Rustlers," Annabelle said, not wanting to go into detail until she and the old man were alone. "Hunter's fine, Angus—I assure you. He and the others will be along soon."

Angus gave a heavy sigh of relief and wagged his head. "I declare . . ."

"Angus, I'd like you to meet my new friend, Nathaniel P. Jones. Nathan, this is Hunter's father, Angus."

"Hello," Nathan said softly.

"Well, hello there, son," Angus said, glancing at Annabelle again, curiously, then stepping up to the horse, leaning his cane against his hip, and extending his right hand to the boy. "Put her there."

Nathan looked away.

Annabelle and Angus shared a puzzled frown. Angus lowered his hand.

Annabelle feigned a smile and said, "Nathan lost his uncle today," she said with a little added emphasis to Angus, trying to convey that the uncle had been one of the rustlers. "We've invited him to stay at the 4-Box-B for a time. Some awfully big changes came on so suddenly for Nathan that he's not feeling too good right now. What he needs is a piece of peach pie and a little time to wander around by himself, get the lay of the land."

"I see, I see," Angus said, gazing solemnly up at Anna, nodding slowly, telling her with his eyes that he understood that the boy's father had been one of the bushwhackers, and that Hunter had turned him toe-down. "Indeed, a piece of Annabelle's pie will make you feel a whole world better, son," he added to Nathan, patting the boy's shoulder.

Still, Nathan kept his head turned away from the man.

Annabelle turned the mare around and rode over to the corral. She helped Nathan down and he stood solemnly by, watching her as she stripped the tack off the calico's back, set the saddle and blanket on the corral's top rail, and turned the horse into the corral. When Anna turned back to the boy, her heart sank.

His head was down. Tears dribbled down his cheeks and into the dirt at his scuffed stockman's boots.

"Oh dear," she said, dropping to a knee. She reached up to place a hand on the boy's shoulder. "Don't cry, Nathan. Everything's going to be just fine. You're going to love it here with Hunter and the other men. I know you've lost your uncle, but—"

"No!" the boy said, choking back a sob. He shook his head adamantly and closed his eyes. "It ain't that!"

"What is it, then?"

Nathan opened his eyes and gazed at her through a sheen of building tears. He didn't say anything, but his eyes were so cast with anguish that Annabelle thought that she was going to break down as well.

Swallowing down a knot in her throat, she removed the boy's hat and ran her hands gently through his hair. "Please, Nathan. You can tell me. What has you so upset?"

"You'll think I'm a sissy."

"I will absolutely not. Please, Nathan—tell me what's bothering you so." Again, she ran her hand through his hair, gently caressing his head. "Please, tell me. Maybe I can help."

He looked down suddenly as though in shame. "I miss my mom. She was purty an' sweet an' kind . . . just like you." He looked up at Annabelle. "She even had hair like you." His lips fluttered with emotion. "I miss her. I didn't realize how much till I saw you!"

"Oh, dear child." Annabelle wrapped her arms around him and pulled him close, hugging him tight against her. He did not resist. In fact, she was surprised to feel his arms snake around her and hold her as tight as she was holding him.

Annabelle cooed to him, rocking him gently. "I'm sorry I remind you of your mother."

"I'm not," he grunted, pulling away enough that he could look up at her. "I like it." He almost smiled, and there was a glint in his eye.

Annabelle choked out a sob now herself, and drew the boy taut against her once more. He trembled in her arms. It was the sorrow welling up out of his heart.

No, not welling.

Exploding.

He'd probably tucked it away there ever since his mother had died, not wanting to express his grief out of fear of being ridiculed by his uncle and the cretins Rolly Piper had ridden with. No, Nathan had never had a chance to express his sorrow. But he'd felt comfortable doing so in front of Annabelle.

That made her feel warm and . . . what? It made her feel downright motherly. It was a good feeling, indeed.

She rocked Nathan for a long time. Gradually, his trembling abated, his sorrow, having been released, diminishing.

Finally, he pulled away from Annabelle. He sleeved the tears from his eyes.

"Do you feel better now, son?" she asked him. He did feel like a son to her now. That was a good feeling too.

He nodded, smiling a little sheepishly but smiling just the same. It was a pleasant sight, like seeing the sun come out after a storm.

"You know, Nathan—you can tell me about your mom anytime."

"She was a whore," he said as though giving a long-overdue confession.

"I suspected but I didn't want to ask. She may have worked as a whore, but she was first and foremost your mother.

"You can cry about her any old time you want. Heck, I find myself crying over one thing or another two or three times a day. I just let myself go ahead and cry, and I always feel better afterwards."

He smiled, cleared his throat, stepped back. He turned his gaze to the corral behind Annabelle. Annabelle's mare, Ruthie, had come over and extended her long snoot over the top of the corral, regarding the boy, her large, light brown eyes cast with sympathy.

Nathan smiled at Annabelle. "She remembers me."

"She likes you."

"She's a nice horse."

"Do you know how to ride?"

Nathan shook his head.

"How 'bout tomorrow I start teaching you how to ride?"

He looked at her in surprise, small lines burrowing into the skin above his nose. "I'd love nothin' better, ma'am!"

"Annabelle."

"I mean, Annabelle."

"A hired hand isn't much good without a horse, now, is he?"

"No, I guess not."

Annabelle gave him his hat, and he put it on. She straightened and held out her hand to him. "Now, how about we go and cut you a piece of peach pie?"

"Might spoil my supper," he warned, smiling up at her.

"I have a feeling you'll eat supper just fine." She winked.

Nathan placed his hand in hers. Annabelle glanced over to see old Angus standing in his brew shed's open doorway, leaning against the frame, smiling around the pipe he was puffing. He raised the pipe to his temple in salute.

Annabelle smiled. Together, she and Nathan headed over to the lodge for pie.

Chapter 6

His heart still pounding, Hunter turned to Red Otter.

Still on his knees, the Sioux slowly lowered his head and pressed his forehead against the ground. He stopped chanting but just lay there, his big hands and thickly muscled arms stretched out to both sides.

Hunter bent down to place his hand on the man's shoulder. "You all right, Chief?"

Keeping his forehead pressed against the ground, the chief moved his head up and down.

Hunter took his Henry in both hands and ran straight up the slope, slipping and sliding and several times nearly falling on the loose shale. He breathed in and out, his lungs working like a bellows, heart thundering against his breastbone. It was a long, hard, precarious climb. By the time he reached the base of the crag, he was covered in sweat.

He looked around.

There were several cave-like gaps at the bottom of the crag. The gaps were tunnels that showed daylight at their far ends, maybe a hundred feet inside the crag. The tunnels were natural arches likely carved by wind over the past eons. Hunter had never seen them before because he'd never been up here before. He'd had no reason to be. But now he saw that the bear had escaped through one of these tunnels.

He tracked the beast into one of the four tunnels—the second one from the right. He moved quickly, watching his footing, as the floor of the arch was littered with rock that had fallen out of the ceiling, and there wasn't much light in here.

He could smell the wild, sour, feral odor of the bear. The stench hung thick around him, almost as strong as mink musk. It burned in his nostrils.

He came to the far end of the tunnel and stopped at the edge of the opening. Before him, the ground dropped steeply away to a pine-choked valley below peppered with the bright orange of turning aspens. The pines were turning dark now at the end of the day, with here and there a dapple of sunlight on the highest crowns.

A dark figure moved below.

Hunter raised the Henry, squeezing it in his gloved hands, his heart picking up speed again.

The bear—a chunky black figure—jostled as it moved down to the bottom of the slope and entered the forest, where it quickly disappeared. Hunter heard the distance-muffled snaps of breaking branches and thrashing brush. He could also hear the guttural growls and low roars. The sounds dwindled to silence.

Quick footsteps sounded behind him. He turned to see Kentucky Wade's tall, slender silhouette take shape before him inside the natural arch, the man's chaps flapping against his legs. Wade held his Winchester up high across his chest.

He stepped out of the cavern's shadows, the weak, late sunlight sliding over the crown of his cream Stetson and glinting in the man's tan eyes above his straight nose and bushy mustache.

"You see him, boss?"

Hunter turned to stare down the steep slope into the darkening forest beyond. "Just a glimpse. He's gone."

Kentucky's eyes were wide. He was flushed and breathing hard from the climb. "Did you see the size of that thing?"

Hunter nodded. "I saw."

"We gonna hunt him?"

Hunter shook his head. "I think it best if you and the boys move that last herd down to the number two meadow, while I deliver those three bushwhackers to the sheriff in town. Maybe the heifer below is the only cow he killed. If so, I won't begrudge him. But if you see more dead cattle tomorrow, let me know."

"Will do."

"How's the chief?"

Hunter started back into the tunnel. Kentucky fell into step beside him. "I think he's comin' around." He glanced at Hunter. "What do you suppose came over him? I thought maybe a seizure . . ."

Hunter shrugged.

When they came to the far end of the tunnel, Hunter paused and stared down the slope. The chief was on his feet now, Hec Prather standing close beside him as though giving counsel. The two men were speaking in low tones.

Noble Sanchez was climbing the slope from below. He held a small whiskey flask in his hand as he made his quick but unsteady way toward Red Otter and the old man. The Mexican's red shirt glowed in the weak light down there but darkened as soon as he moved into the shade of the crag.

Hunter and his top hand shared a dubious look, then

started making their careful way down the talus slide. Going down was almost harder than going up. Several times, the flat rocks slipped out from beneath them, nearly laying them out.

When they finally reached the three others, Red Otter was taking a pull from Sanchez's flask. His face was unusually pale and haggard, the skin around his mouth sagging down around his chin. His broad chest rose and fell heavily as he breathed.

Hec Prather was holding the man's high-crowned black hat with the eagle feather in the band. As Hunter and Wade approached them, Red Otter and Prather stopped talking and turned toward them.

Hunter placed a hand on the Sioux's shoulder. "How you doing, Chief?"

Red Otter's severely sculpted face shaped a manufactured smile, one corner of his mouth hooking. "I'm fine, just fine."

"What was that all about?"

The chief and Prather shared a quick, almost furtive glance.

Red Otter smiled again. "Just a silly old Indian's superstitions is all. It's nothing. Nothing at all." He took another pull from the flask, then handed it back to Sanchez. As he accepted the flask, Hunter saw Sanchez looking at him pensively, black brows beetled above his dark brown eyes.

"What is it?" Hunter said.

"Oh," Sanchez said, jerking with a start and then shrugging and glancing away. "Nothing, boss."

As though wanting to change the subject, Prather quickly turned to Hunter and said, "You goin' after him, boss?"

"No," Hunter said. "We'll wait and see what he does

next." Hunter scowled suddenly, his suspicions aroused. He glanced from Prather to Red Otter and said, "What the hell were you two palaverin' about all serious as ladies from the Sobriety League?"

Red Otter did not respond. He took his hat from Prather, set it on his head, and started making his careful way down the slope.

Hec turned to Hunter, shaping a grin. "Who? *Us?*" He feigned a laugh. "Just old man stuff. Can we go home now, boss? My belly's so empty my brain's got to thinkin' that grizzly done ripped it out!" He rubbed the potbelly bulging out his dusty, sweaty shirt.

Hunter glanced at Kentucky Wade again, then gave a caustic chuff and started making his way down the slope.

Late that night after supper, Hunter had one more conference with Kentucky Wade on the house's front porch, then said good night and turned to head upstairs to bed.

Only, his father, old Angus, stood in the doorway, clad in a ratty red robe over wash-worn longhandles. He had a cigar drooping from one corner of his mouth, smoke slithering up from the tip. In his lone hand he held two filled whiskey goblets and another cigar. His walking stick was clamped under that arm.

"Not so fast," Angus said in his gravelly voice around the cigar.

"I'm awful tired, Pa. Been a long day."

"So long you can't have a drink and a cigar with your poor, long-suffering father who obviously spared the rod and spoiled the son?"

Hunter laughed. "You did at that, Pa." He took the drink and the cigar, then leaned forward to peck the old man's bearded, craggy cheek. "Sure, I'll have a drink with you. Let's chin a spell."

Hunter walked over and slacked into one of the wicker chairs parked on the porch. Angus came over and eased his spindly frame into the one beside him. Hunter set his drink on the table between them and dug a match out of his shirt pocket.

He dragged the match across his belt buckle. It flared in the heavy darkness that had settled over the ranch now in the unusually mild autumn evening. The only light in the yard were the lit windows of the bunkhouse nearly straight across the yard from the house. The velvet sky was awash with flickering stars.

Very slowly and quietly, the windmill blades creaked as they ever so slowly turned, the swivel screeching softly.

Hunter lit the cigar, blew out a long smoke plume, and turned to his father. "What's on your mind, Pa? If it's about the boy, I know it's an inconvenience, but I did kill Nathan's uncle and—"

"Oh, it ain't about the boy. He's a good kid, and Annabelle's already taken a shine to him, him to her. As far as I'm concerned, he can stay as long as he wants. You two sure don't seem to be in much hurry to fill the house with shavers of your own!"

Hunter chuckled. "In time, Pa. In time. In case you hadn't noticed, we've been a might busy these past two years."

Angus sipped his whiskey, lowered the glass, and turned to his son. "What's on yours?"

"Huh?"

"What's on your mind tonight? You've been broodin' ever since you an' the fellas rode into the yard. Is it the men you killed? Remember, they tried to—"

"I'm not brooding about Rolly Piper and them other

miscreants, Pa. They tried to trim my wick and got theirs trimmed for their trouble. I know how it goes out here. I finally learned. I hate it, but I've learned."

"What, then? Out with it?"

Dammit, he thought. Had it been that obvious? He'd tried not to let on that the bruin was bothering him. He hadn't wanted Angus to know about the bear, because Angus was a worrier, and Hunter saw no reason for him to worry unless Hunter knew they actually did have something to worry about.

Hunter sipped his drink, took another puff off the cigar. "I found a dead heifer in Sandy Creek."

Angus turned his grizzled features sharply toward him. "Cat?"

Hunter grimaced and shook his head.

"Wolf?"

Again, Hunter shook his head.

"Bear."

Hunter looked at him.

"Black?" Angus asked, raising his gray brows hopefully.

Hunter didn't say anything.

"You sure?"

"We saw it."

"Where?"

"Atop that talus slide beneath Devil's Rock."

"You didn't kill it or you wouldn't be brooding about it." Angus took another sip of his drink, sat back in his chair, and nodded slowly. "How many others has it taken?"

"None that we found. I'm sending the boys up tomorrow to move the last herd to the number two meadow, closer to home where we can keep an eye on 'em."

"Could be a traveler."

"That's what I'm hoping."

Angus winced, shook his head. "If he's claiming territory—"

"We don't know that, Pa."

"No, but that's what's got your drawers too tight." Angus stared out into the yard from the handsome porch that he and his son had built together with their own hands. "All the work we put into this place. Now, to have a bruin preying on the herd."

"We don't know it's preying. Like you said, it could be a traveler."

"Let's hope so."

Angus picked up his drink, took another sip, and sat back in his chair again, this time with a fateful sigh. "You goin' to town tomorrow?"

"Have to."

"You don't owe Piper an' them other dry-gulchin' wide-loopers a damn thing."

"I'm not just gonna dump their bodies and not report it to the law."

"Why not? That's what they would have done to you."

Hunter gave his father a pointed look. "I'm not them."

Angus studied him in the light that pushed through the curtained window behind them. His thin, cracked lips shaped an admiring grin. "No, you're not." He patted his son's arm resting on the arm of the chair. "I raised you right."

"You're not either, you know," Hunter told him.

Angus frowned as though puzzled. "Ain't I? Hmm. I thought I was." He turned his head away as though deep in thought.

"Well, you ain't." Hunter threw back the rest of his drink, peeled off the cigar's coal to save the stogie for later, then rose from his chair. He leaned down and pressed his lips to the old man's forehead. "Good night, Pa. I'm off to bed."

He walked to the door but stopped when Angus said, "Hunt?"

Hunter turned back to him, brow arched.

Staring off into the night, Angus said, "Do you miss 'em? Shep an' Tye." He turned to his sole surviving son. "Do you miss 'em?"

"Every day, Pa. Every minute of every damn day."

Angus croaked a sob, and his head bobbed with emotion. "Me too," he said, his vice sounding half caught in his throat.

Hunter walked over, patted the old man's shoulder with deep sympathy and affection, choking back a sob of his own, then turned and walked into the house. He climbed the stairs to the second story.

As he walked down the hall toward his and Annabelle's room, he heard voices behind the partly closed door just ahead and on his left. That was the room that Annabelle had bedded Nathan down in. He could hear them talking softly, Anna's voice sounding gentle and motherly.

"All right," she said, suddenly louder. There was a creak of bedsprings. "Good night, Nathan. Do you want me to turn the lamp all the way down or leave some flame?"

"You can turn it all the way down, ma'am—I mean, Annabelle!"

"How 'bout the door?" she said as she opened the door, her eyes finding Hunter standing a few feet away.

"You can close it all the way," came Nathan's bold voice. "I ain't scared."

"All right, then. Good night," she said, smiling at Hunter as she drew the door closed behind her and quietly latched it. She was ready for bed in a spruce green wrap over her white nightgown, deerskin slippers on her feet. Her copper hair spilled down over her shoulders, framing her cameo-pretty face with its long, straight nose and wide, full mouth and flashing jade eyes.

She stepped into her and Hunter's bedroom, lit by a single burning amber lamp on the dresser. Hunter followed her in and closed the door, saying, "You're good with him, Anna."

"It's easy to be good with the boy, Hunt," she said as she walked around the far side of their bed covered in a star quilt given to them by one of their neighbors.

Since all of their furnishings had burned in the fire, they'd had to start from scratch. The house was still only about half furnished, but it was livable and comfortable, everyone having at least a bed and a dresser.

She picked up her brush from the night table on her side of the bed and began brushing her hair. "He's a good boy from a very bad situation." Keeping her voice low, she said, "Did you know his mother was a whore in Deadwood?"

Hunter kicked out of his boots. "No, but I suspected. Not much else for a single woman to do. And since she had a child an' all. Yeah, I pretty much figured."

"I hate that Rolly Piper abused him so!"

"Well, he won't abuse him anymore."

In fact, Piper and his two demonic cohorts were laid out in the barn, ready for their trip to Tigerville in the morning.

Hunter pulled out his shirttails and walked to the

room's single window, sliding the curtain aside with his hand. The room looked out into the backyard, where Angus had transplanted several apple trees. An unusually large, full moon was rising, blood-red, limning the edges of the twisted, leafless branches of the apple trees and the arrowhead pines standing tall beyond them.

He opened the window to feel the cool autumn, cinnamon-scented air push against him, and stared out. He was so deep in thought, he hadn't realized that Anna had come up behind him until she snaked her arms around his waist, pressing close against him, rubbing her cheek against his left shoulder blade.

Very softly and intimately, she said, "I'd like to start a family, Hunt."

Hunter smiled as he turned to her, wrapped his arms around her, drawing her head against his chest. "I've wanted nothing more, Anna."

She looked up at him, smiling a little devilishly, jade eyes showing a little of the red, flickering light of the lamp behind her. "Are you ready to get started? Say, tonight . . . ?"

Hunter chuckled, kissed the top of her head. "How 'bout if you hold that thought? I'm dead dog tired and I'm feelin' a little off my feed tonight."

She frowned suddenly. "Are you criticizing my cooking?"

Hunter laughed and hugged her again. "No, no, no! The roast was wonderful as usual. And I'm gonna dream about that pie."

"You've been brooding all evening. It's about the bear, isn't it?"

"Yeah, I reckon it is."

Anna reached up to place a hand on the side of his cheek, directing his gaze at hers. "Hunter, grizzlies come in and take a cow once in a while. And then they move on. Rarely does one stay."

"I know, but this one gave me a strange feeling up there. Somehow, it seemed different. And then the way the chief carried on."

"What do you mean? What did Red Otter do?"

"It's almost like he had a seizure of some kind. Sorta reminded me of a medicine man trying to purge an evil spirit—you know, the way they do. Angus knew one such man who'd ride around the hills in beaded buckskins and full headdress, singing and chanting. Angus said the man was a Teton shaman, and he rode around the hills once a year, praying to the Sioux gods to purge the white eyes from their land and return it to them once more."

"Did you ask him what he was doing?"

"I sure did, and he laughed it off as crazy old Indian stuff." Hunter ran his hand absently through his wife's silky hair. "Strange. Left me with a strange sort of feelin'."

"I reckon I don't blame you." Anna took his hand. "Come on, I'll help you get undressed. I'll rub your back, make you feel all peaceful and happy, back to the Hunter I've come to know and love."

Hunter chuckled, then sat down on the bed and let his lovely wife undress him down to his longhandles. As she did, he swept her long, red hair back behind her head, held it there as he cupped the back of her head in his hand, taking a good, long, close look at her lovely face.

How much they'd already been through together! Yet they'd remained inseparable in spirit if it was not always possible to be side by side, which it never is on a working ranch.

"God, I love you, woman!"

Annabelle sandwiched his face in her hands and slid her face down to within inches of his, eyes boring into his own with a hard intensity, a flush rising in her cheeks. "God, how I love you back, you big grayback scalawag!"

She groaned as she pressed her lips to his. He kissed her back with every bit as much passion until . . .

"Oh no, no," she said, and laughed, scuttling back away from him. "We're not going to start tonight, remember?"

"I might be havin' second thoughts."

"Lay down there and roll onto your belly and let me go to work on that back!"

"Oh, all right . . ."

Laughing, she climbed up and knelt beside him and ran her hands down his back. "All knotted up. You're all knotted up tonight, my love. You need to forget about that ole bruin and—"

A horse's squealing whinny, issuing through the crack in the window, rose in the otherwise silent night. It was as startling as a glass being smashed against a wall in a previously silent room.

It was followed by a man's shrill yell. *"Bear! It's the damn bear!"*

A rifle crashed . . . again . . . again . . .

"Bear!" the man cried again.

"Bear!" Hunter yelled.

He shot up off the bed like a bull through a chute.

Chapter 7

By the man's second yell, Hunter was already on his feet bounding across the room to where his Henry leaned against the wall. He glanced at his wife, who knelt on the bed, hands raised to her temples in wordless shock.

"Stay here, Anna!"

Hunter cocked the Henry and for some automatic reason grabbed his hat off a wall peg and set it on his head, then ran out the door clad in only the hat and longhandles.

A door opened on the right side of the hall, and the diminutive, bearded Angus appeared clad in his night-gown and holding a lit candle lamp, looking as though he might have just gone to sleep before the cacophony had awakened him. Bobby Lee ran out from behind the old man—he'd probably been asleep under Angus's cot—then bolted out the door and down the stairs.

"What in holy blazes?" Angus roared, his eyes wide as china saucers.

Hunter was too intent on getting outside to answer him. He knew no more than Angus did. He leaped down the stairs in three long strides, his foot sliding off the last step and slamming onto the one below it. Hunter nearly fired the Henry into the ceiling as, draping his left foot around the railing, his butt hit the oak steps hard.

Bobby Lee, who'd been clawing at the door, ran over to Hunter, whining and licking his face.

Hunter shoved the coyote away. "I'm all right, I'm all right!"

He heaved himself back to his feet and, gritting his teeth, his butt aching like a spike had been driven into it, unbarred the door and ran out onto the stoop. Bobby Lee leaped off the porch steps and ran out into the yard so quickly that in only seconds the darkness consumed him.

Hunter paused, looking around, listening, already bathed in a cold sweat.

Rifles were cracking and men were yelling behind the bunkhouse.

Presently, Bobby Lee yipped wildly. Hunter saw the coyote's slender silhouette shoot off into the northern darkness.

"Hold your fire! Hold your fire!" a man yelled. "He's gone!" Hunter thought it was Kentucky Wade.

Hunter leaped down the steps and ran hard around the bunkhouse's west end to the back, where three of his hands—Kentucky Wade, Noble Sanchez, and Chief Red Otter—were holding smoking rifles as they gazed toward the north, from about twenty feet out from the bunkhouse's rear wall. All were clad in longhandles and not much else, though Red Otter was also wearing his bullet-crowned hat.

Smoking rifles sagged in their arms.

Kentucky turned to Hunter, who strode slowly, numbly forward, gazing into the darkness where Bobby Lee had disappeared. "Not *our* bear!"

"Sure as hell!" The crow-like voice had issued from off Hunter's right flank.

Hunter whipped around to see Hec Prather, clad in longhandles and stovepipe boots, his own battered hat on his bearded head, leaning against the bunkhouse, sort of crouched forward, feet spread at an awkward angle.

"It was him, all right," Hec said. His voice was strained and he was breathing hard. "There ain't two bruins that size in these parts. There ain't two like that!"

"Hec, are you sure?" Hunter asked, walking toward the old man.

"I'm certain-sure. I heard the horses stirrin' in the corral yonder. I was sittin' in the privy. I walked over to see what was goin' on, expectin' to see coyotes or maybe a fox. But first I went back in the bunkhouse to get my pistol."

He raised his old Remington .44.

"Lucky thing I did too. I'd no sooner walked up to the corral than two big red eyes appeared in the darkness just beyond it. They grew and grew. And then the bruin roared and ran toward me. Holy hell clad in a bear fur coat runnin' *right at me*, sure as the devil! I shot him full in the head from six feet away. That startled him and he only brushed me aside and went runnin' off in the night."

Hec held his left hand against his side. Blood oozed from between his fingers. His longhandle top was shredded— four foot-long slashes down the poor man's left side, starting from up near his pouchy left breast.

"Lordy, Hec!" Hunter exclaimed, blood quickening once more. "You're hurt. You're hurt bad!"

The old man looked at his side. "Oh . . ." He dropped the pistol, and his knees buckled. He was slumping fast.

Hunter rushed forward and caught him just before he would have hit the ground, and swept him up in his arms.

The others hurried toward them.

"We have to get him inside!" Hunter exclaimed.

"Hec," Noble Sanchez said, walking along behind Hunter and the oldster, staring at the old man with grave concern. "You all right, Hec?"

"Do I *look* all right, you ninny?" the old man barked.

Hunter hurried around to the front of the bunkhouse and ducked through the low door. No one had taken the time to light a lamp, so it was nearly as dark as the inside of a glove.

"We need light!"

He lay Hec on the first cot he came to and looked at the bloody claw marks extending down the man's left side. He turned to glance at the others gathering around him while Noble Sanchez lit a lamp and carried it over. Now Hunter could see the crimson blood oozing from the deep scratches.

"Someone fetch Annabelle!"

"I'm here," she said as she stepped through the door, clad in her nightgown and robe and with a shawl wrapped around her shoulders. She was flanked by old Angus, also dressed in his robe, and young Nathan, who'd wrapped his booted and longhandle-clad body in a blanket, his hair poking out from around his hat still mussed from sleep.

Hunter stepped aside as Annabelle approached the cot on which poor Hec lay grunting and groaning.

"How bad?" she said, crouching over the man to inspect the wounds in the light from the lamp that Noble Sanchez now hung from a ceiling support post near the cot.

Annabelle sucked a sharp breath through gritted teeth,

then placed her hand over Hec's forehead. She glanced at Hunter, her eyes round with gravity. "We need hot water and many towels. Someone bring me a bottle of whiskey."

"I'll get the fire going," said Red Otter, and hurried to the potbellied stove in the middle of the room.

Annabelle glanced at young Nathan staring down at the bloody claw marks.

"Nathan, would you please take that washbasin over there outside and fill it from the rain barrel? Then place it on the stove that the chief's stoking."

The boy nodded and hurried over to the door, grabbed the porcelain bowl from the zinc-topped washstand, and slipped outside. Meanwhile, Annabelle probed the cuts through Hec's blood-soaked longhandle top, then turned and said, "Someone, hand me a knife."

A folding barlow knife was produced and placed in Annabelle's right hand.

Reconsidering, she gave it back to Kentucky, saying, "Pour some whiskey over the blade."

Kentucky picked up the whiskey bottle that he'd placed on the floor by the cot, popped the cork with his teeth, and poured a stream of the whiskey over both sides of the blade. He gave the knife back to Annabelle.

With two fingers of her left hand, she gently pinched up the sodden longhandle top away from Hec's skin, poked the barlow's blade through the material, and began cutting. To Hunter hovering nearby, she said without looking at him but keeping her attention on her delicate work, "Was this the same bear you fellas saw?"

"Unless there's two grizzlies on the place," Hunter said. He didn't know which would be worse—having been tracked by the same bear they'd seen yesterday or having another one haunting the range.

Standing near Hunter, Kentucky said, "You think he actually tracked us from Devil's Rock?"

"Or followed you," said old Angus, sitting at a small table near the washstand, filling his pipe.

Hunter suppressed a shudder at the thought. He'd never been stalked by a bear before. He'd heard of it happening, but it had never happened to him.

Anna glanced up at Hunter, reading the perplexity in his mind. She glanced at the other three men— Sanchez, Wade, and Red Otter standing around watching her anxiously—and said, "Why don't you men either go back to bed or otherwise occupy yourselves? You're making me nervous. Nathan and I will take good care of Hec."

She glanced at Nathan sitting on the edge of a chair on the other side of the cot.

"Yep," the boy said, customarily taciturn.

"You got it, honey," Hunter said. "Let us know if you need anything."

While the other men turned away a little sheepishly, as though suddenly realizing they were only in their long-handles and socks with a lady present, and began dressing, Hunter walked over to where Angus smoked his pipe at the table.

"What're you gonna do, Pa?"

Angus blew smoke out his nostrils. "I'm gonna fetch me a drink. I'll never be able to sleep."

"I'll send the men after that griz first thing tomorrow. After I take the dead men to town, I'll join them."

"No, you git after 'em first thing, boy," Angus said slowly, broodingly, puffing his pipe. "I'll take the dead men to town. You just load 'em in the wagon for me, have it hitched and ready to ride before you leave."

Hunter shook his head. "No, Pa. I killed them. I'll take 'em to Sheriff Lodge."

Angus looked up at Hunter with fire in his rheumy, red-rimmed eyes. "I'll take 'em to town, son. I'll explain how it happened and that you would have brought them in yourself if not for a bear matter. That's how it's going to be, you understand? You're the bear hunter in the family. Named you proper, your ma an' me. You get after that bruin and kill the damn thing before it comes back."

Hunter opened his mouth to object, but Angus cut him off with: "That's my final say on the matter." He pointed his pipe stem at Hunter, narrowed one eye, and the old hard-headed and not-so-vaguely threatening Angus Buchanon revealed himself. "As long as I'm still suckin' air, I'm still the boss out here—understand?"

Hunter knew his father well enough to know when it was time to backwater. He didn't like Angus's idea at all; it was downright dangerous. But it warmed him to know his father still had enough pluck to voice it.

Hunter nodded. "If that's how you want it, Pa. I'll have the wagon ready at first light."

Hunter glanced around the room. All eyes were on him. Including Anna's. She held his gaze for a few seconds, with a wary one of her own, then continued dabbing a cloth at Hec's torn side. Anna had sent Nathan to check the water on the stove and to add more wood. Now even the boy stood near the stove's open firebox, staring silently at the two Buchanons, as though watching two bull buffalo, one old, one young, go head-to-head.

Hunter smiled, squeezed his father's shoulder. As long

as Angus was still alive, he'd have the final say. By merely being Hunter's father, he'd earned that right.

Hunter stepped outside, and the other men, fully dressed and wearing wool coats against the autumn chill and packing their cigarette makings, followed him out. Red Otter stepped up to Hunter. He wore a three-point capote and a red wool cap pulled down over his ears.

"Boss, can I have a word?"

Hunter looked at him. He studied him closely, pensive, then jerked his chin toward the house. "Come on. I'll set a pot of coffee to boil."

Chapter 8

Hunter poured the thick, black, smoking brew into the stone mug sitting on the kitchen table before the grim-faced Red Otter.

The man sat back in his chair, watching the coffee bubble up to the rim, the fragrant steam wafting around his face. One of his large, brown, thickly calloused hands, curled into a loose fist, rested on the table's edge, near the cup.

Hunter filled his own cup at his customary place at the end of the table. As he did, Angus shuffled into the kitchen in his robe and elk skin slippers. "Spare a cup for the old man?"

"Sure, Pa." Hunter grabbed another cup from a shelf, set it on the table, at Angus's usual place, and filled it.

Angus held a speculative gaze on Red Otter, who sat as before—stone-faced, gazing down at his coffee, one hand on the table's edge. Angus sat down across from the Indian. Hunter sat down at his place, slid his chair in, and set his elbows on the table, entwining his fingers, waiting.

Red Otter looked at him. "That is no ordinary bear, boss."

"No, it's not."

"It's an *otshee-monetoo.*"

"A what?"

"A bad spirit. Some might say a *waka sica*—a demon."

Hunter glanced at Angus, his lips quirking a grin. Angus didn't look back at his son. Angus kept his sober gaze on Red Otter, apparently waiting for the chief to continue.

Hunter sipped his coffee and decided to give the Indian his head. He sat back in his chair, keeping his right index finger curled through the cup handle. "I'm listening."

"I believe it is the Curse of the Grizzly Moon."

"Oh, come on!"

Angus turned to him now. "Hear him out, son."

Hunter frowned, puzzled. Angus didn't believe in all that Indian mumbo jumbo, did he?

Hunter turned back to Red Otter, who was as stoic as ever and said, "According to the ancient ones, whose home the hills were before the white man's invasion, when a grizzly attacks a man or his property during a blue moon, it is a sign that the bear might not be a bear at all, but a demon in bear form—the earthly embodiment of a curse that someone on the other side has placed on the man and those he loves."

Hunter stared at the Sioux in stone-faced disbelief. He didn't say anything for a time, but then he swept his hand across the table, as though brushing invisible crumbs to the floor. "Look, Chief, I have nothing but respect for the old Sioux legends. I know your people believe in them the way the white man believes in his own God. But, while your story is right entertaining, you can't expect me to believe—"

Angus cut in with: "Who would have put a curse like that on my son, Red Otter?"

"Someone he's killed," Red Otter said bluntly and without hesitation.

Angus looked at Hunter. "There's plenty enough of them, both during the war and after."

Hunter scowled his exasperation. "Pa, do you really believe that stuff?"

"Son, I've lived long enough to know that we can't know everything. I've seen some things back in Appalachia that would turn your hair white—ghosts of old red-coat soldiers come to life again, toothless old women killing their men with spirit powders. Then you throw in the Indian stuff, and you have a whole lot more that can't be explained. At least in no way we can understand it.

"A Ute medicine man from Colorado once told me about a man in the San Juan Mountains who was stalked by a rogue griz. The man, a wealthy ranch owner, and his family had been cursed by the grizzly moon when a bear attacked and killed their mules and several hired hands on a blue-moon night. The bear came back later, after harassing and terrorizing the family for weeks, and attacked them in their cabin, killing them all.

"Turned out the man had killed another man, a rival ranch owner, in a duel over a woman, a forbidden love, the week before. The medicine man believed that was the man who'd sent a curse from the other side."

"Well, I'm sorry, Pa, but I just don't believe that." Hunter slid back his chair and rose. "You two can sit here the rest of the night and swap big windies about Indian demons and old hoodoo legends, but if you'll excuse me, I'm going to go check on Hec and head to bed. I aim to get after that bear—just a regular old griz like any other, this one just a might more colicky than most—at first light."

Hunter walked down the hall to the front door. He

slipped into his buckskin coat, then opened the door and stepped out in time to see Bobby Lee race across the yard and dash up the porch steps.

"Bobby!"

The coyote sat before him, mewling and yammering as though moon-crazed.

"Bobby, what is it?"

Hunter knelt down beside the coyote, placed his hands on him. Bobby was quivering as though he'd been struck by lightning. He scratched desperately at the door and looked up at Hunter with pleading in his fear-bright eyes.

"Here you go, Bobby; here you go—go on upstairs to bed," he said as the coyote dashed through the door. Bobby Lee disappeared in the darkness at the end of the hall. Hunter heard his toenails clicking as he frantically climbed the steps to the second story.

Frowning, Hunter turned to stare out into the night beyond the bunkhouse, at the blood-red moon quartering low now as it approached three a.m.

What had gotten Bobby Lee so riled?

What had the coyote seen out there on this blue-moon night? Despite what Red Otter had said, a bear was just a bear.

Gazing off, a cloying chill rippled through Hunter. He shivered.

"Get a grip on yourself," he growled, suddenly angry for apparently having let the Sioux's words get under his skin.

He gave a caustic chuff, then dropped down the porch steps and crossed the yard to the bunkhouse.

* * *

The next morning, Angus excused himself from the breakfast table and walked to the door. He was dressed in dungarees and cowhide vest over a plaid work shirt, snake-skin suspenders pulled up over his age-bowed shoulders.

He hacked phlegm from his throat and called, "I'll be heading out, Annabelle!" Hunter had left the house earlier, at the first crack of dawn, and he and Kentucky Wade, Noble Sanchez, and Chief Red Otter had headed north to track the grizzly, which shouldn't be too hard. A light dusting of snow had fallen during the night.

"Hold on," came the young woman's response from the kitchen behind him.

As Angus pulled on his striped wool blanket coat, Anna stepped out of the kitchen carrying a small bundle wrapped in waxed paper.

"I made you an extra breakfast sandwich for the road back from town, in case you get hungry."

Angus smiled and accepted the sandwich. He shoved it into a coat pocket and leaned forward to kiss his daughter-in-law's cheek. "You're always lookin' out for this old man."

"Someone has to. Lord knows you don't do it yourself." She returned his kiss with a warm one to his own cheek carpeted in his untrimmed, gray-brown beard. "You be careful in town. I'm going to be worried about you."

Angus set his old gray, broad-brimmed Confederate campaigner on his head. "Don't worry about me. I'm too old and worthless for anyone to pester."

"Rolly Piper has family."

Angus smiled at her. "So do I. Besides . . ." He picked up his big, double-bore shotgun from where it leaned against the pine-paneled wall in the foyer. He stroked the long barrels lovingly. "I got my bird gun loaded with double-aught buck. Got extry shells in my pocket, and, look here . . ." He turned so she could see the grips of the old Colt pistol poking up out of his left coat pocket. "The Great Equalizer."

Annabelle frowned suddenly with renewed concern. "Are you expecting trouble, Angus?"

"I been through one of the bloodiest wars known to man, sweetheart. I always expect trouble. I don't figure there's a sizable chance I'm gonna run into any today in Tigerville, but, if so, I'm prepared."

He winked and squeezed the shotgun. "Have a good day with the boy."

"I'm going to get him familiar with horses, teach him how to ride."

"He'll like that." Angus's smile broadened. "I got a feelin' you will too. Nice havin' young blood around the place, ain't it?"

Annabelle felt a flush rise into her cheeks. "You'll get those grandkids soon enough. Now, skedaddle. Off with you, old man—I have a kitchen to clean and dishes to wash, and I have to rebandage Hec's wounds!"

Chuckling, Angus opened the door and stepped out onto the porch. He stopped abruptly and turned back. "Uh, Anna," he said just as she'd turned to walk back into the kitchen. She turned back to face him, and he canted his head to indicate the yard fronting the house.

"What is it?"

He didn't say anything, just gave her a dark look before swinging around and walking down the porch steps and into the yard.

* * *

Annabelle stepped outside into the cool air of morning as Angus made his way over to the wagon that Hunter had hitched to a gray gelding and laid out the dead men in, for their trip back to Tigerville.

Annabelle felt a slight tug in her throat as she stood regarding the masked rider sitting a large claybank stallion near the rear of Angus's makeshift hearse. The mask was a flour sack with the eyes and mouth cut out. The man wore a quilted leather coat against the chill, and a low-crowned black hat studded with silver conchos sat on his head. A yellow silk neckerchief fluttered in the breeze. He sat there with the fine horse turned sideways to the house and craning its neck to probe a patch of hide on its left hip with its teeth.

"Hello, Cass," Annabelle said, stepping forward and crossing her arms against the chill. "You're out early."

"Pa kept me up all night."

Of course, she was curious, but Anna feigned disinterest. She wanted nothing to do with her father. She waved at Angus as he pinched his hat brim to her and shook the reins over the gray's back, heading for the trail to Tigerville.

"Who're the stiffs in the back?" Cass asked, following the wagon with his gaze.

"Rolly Piper and friends."

"Ah. Rustling?"

"What else?"

"Right."

"Why don't you light and sit a spell? I just made a fresh pot of coffee, and I'll even rustle you up some breakfast."

"I don't want to be any trouble."

"No trouble. You're my brother. I'm glad to see you. I wish you'd come around more often."

"Only one hand left on the ranch. Pa's gone kinda loco, run everybody else off. I'm actually having to do an honest day's work at the Broken Heart—can you believe it?"

Anna smiled. "You? No, I can't believe it. Who's keeping the Tigerville saloons in business?"

Cass laughed at that. Anna's older brother was a known drinker and carouser. That had pretty much ceased, however, when the barn fire had destroyed his face. Anna felt guilty about the fire. Trying to defend herself against him—when, drunk and enraged, he'd threatened to bull-whip her in the Broken Heart barn for her intention of marrying Hunter Buchanon— she'd smashed a lantern over his head. The fire had spread from Cass to the hay-littered barn floor to the dry, timbered walls.

That had been a former Cass. He'd changed two years ago, after he'd returned Hunter's gold to Hunter and Annabelle. Now he was a much more serious young man, mostly staying home and working hard and tending his and Annabelle's father, who'd taken ill after a heart stroke he'd suffered during the old trouble he'd instigated himself, when he'd tried to block Anna from marrying Hunter.

"Don't you wanna know why he kept me up all night?" Cass asked her now.

Anna shook her head. "Not really."

"He's dying. Every night he leaves his head and becomes a raging madman. I don't know what to do with him sometimes when he gets like that. Mostly, I feed him whiskey till he drifts back asleep."

"I'm sorry you have to endure that, Cass. But you don't need to. I've told you that you can leave the Broken Heart and come live here with us whenever you want."

"The Broken Heart is my home, Anna. I wish I would

have realized that a long time ago, and not wasted so much time running around whoring and drinking, getting crossways with Pa." Cass paused and glanced around at the ranch buildings. The bunkhouse windows still glowed with lamplight; the men must have left it burning for Hec.

The windmill's blades turned lazily, the swivel squeaking faintly. The birds were chirping and piping wildly.

Turning back to Anna, Cass said, "You have a home here now. A nice one. You and Hunter did a good job."

"Thank you."

"My only home is the Broken Heart. I'm gonna need to stay on there after Pa's gone. I'm gonna have to work to keep the place up."

"You'll manage, Cass. You seem to have come a long way since . . ." Annabelle stopped and shook her head. No point in finishing the thought.

"Since I tried to bullwhip you in the barn?" Cass said with a wry, crooked smile.

Anna stepped forward, wringing her hands now. "Cass, I'm so sorry for what happened. For what I did . . . your face. I was only trying to free my—"

"Uh-uh." Cass held up a placating hand. "No, Anna. What's done is done. What's more"—and now he pinned her with a direct gaze from behind the mask—"it was my own damn fault." He paused, then said, "I rode out here to tell you about Pa in case you had any interest in seeing him one last time."

"I don't—no," Anna said without hesitation.

"I think he regrets what he did, Anna. I think part of his insane spells come from guilt. Sometimes he yells out, begging you to forgive him."

Anna tucked her mouth corners down and shook her head. "I don't. I can't. He burned this place, Cass. He burned it to the ground and shot Shep and Tyrell!"

It was Cass's turn to avert his eyes, sheepishly.

When he raised them again, he said, "Well, all right—I reckon I'll be riding on, then."

"I wish you'd stay for coffee, at least."

"Best get back to Pa." Cass booted his horse toward the main trail, glancing over his shoulder at his sister and giving a two-fingered salute. "So long, Anna."

"So long, Cass."

Then he was gone.

Despite the chill nibbling at her ears, Anna stood staring after her brother for a long time, more troubled than she wanted to admit.

Chapter 9

As Angus rattled along Tigerville's main drag in the old buckboard wagon, one of the few things that had survived the fire though it wore the fire's kiss in the form of scorch marks along both side panels and tailgate, he glanced along both sides of the street.

He was mildly surprised to see only a few sets of wooly eyeballs cast his way, these mainly from shop owners glancing up as they swept the boardwalks fronting their establishments, or from miners still celebrating the end of their night shift, with soapy beer mugs clenched in their big, red fists.

The shop owners mostly didn't care for the Buchanons because they'd fought for the Confederacy. Union-sympathizers outnumbered ex-Rebels two to one in and around Tigerville, and there was still a good bit of animosity left over from that bloody contest. That animosity, however, drew the ex-graybacks closer together, which was their way, anyway, most of them hailing from hoots and hollers in the Blue Ridge Mountains and being naturally colicky against outsiders as well as clannish.

That was another thing the Union folks didn't like

about the ex-Confederates. They stuck together, like family. Only with the help of their fellow ex-Confederate neighbors had it been possible for Angus, Hunter, and Annabelle to rebuild the ranch and get it up and running again so quickly, with a fresh inoculation of breeder cows and a seed bull from England. The money from Hunter's gold had gone a long way.

As far as Angus's fellow Southerners, several called or hooted playfully at him from either side of the street.

The miners, on the other hand, didn't like the Buchanons for fresher reasons than the war. When Hunter had essentially killed Max Chaney and the man's sons, Chaney's mine had been closed down, putting nearly sixty men out of work. Those men who'd been left without jobs were the ones eyeing Angus the coldest now as he passed another several saloons, a parlor house, a grocery store in front of which the big, beefy grocer, Liam Duberhaun, was butchering a fresh antelope hanging upside down from a hay hook; he was just now peeling the skin away from the blood-red hide, like a banana.

His long apron over buckskins was caked with blood and bristling with vanilla fur.

He was from Chattanooga, Duberhaun was. He'd fought in Hunter's regiment. He smiled through his thick, black beard and tipped his big bowie knife to his temple in salute as Angus passed him. Puffing his pipe, Angus smiled and dipped his chin to the gent.

He pulled the wagon up in front of the low, log county sheriff's office that had an addition in back, behind the jail block, which served as the county courthouse. Trials were usually held in saloons that could hold a larger crowd of onlookers, however, for court trials and hangings were big entertainment. The last time Angus had visited the sheriff's office had been when he and Shep and Tye had backed Hunter's play against the corrupt Sheriff Stillwell and several friends of Luke Chaney, whose body Hunter had hauled to town to deliver to this very building. He'd wanted then, like he wanted today, to come clean on a self-defense killing.

He'd had no idea, of course, that that move would not only be under-appreciated by Frank Stillwell, but would lead, in addition to his plans to elope with Annabelle Ludlow, Chaney's business partner's daughter, to the old trouble and the burning of the 4-Box-B.

And, of course, the death of Stillwell himself.

No loss there.

Angus chuckled at that. A couple of boys had spotted the three corpses in the back of the wagon and were slinking in, wily as coyotes, to get a better look. One of them probed one of the bodies in the box with a long stick.

Angus rose from the driver's seat, crouched low, and screwed up his face to hiss, "You get out of there, boys, or I'll take you home and make boy-stew out of all three of yas!"

They yelped and scattered. Angus slapped his thigh, laughing.

They were kids from Yankee families. So they naturally had a fear of the one-armed, bib-bearded old grayback already. In his gray campaign hat and greatcoat, they probably thought he was the ghost of some long-dead Southern general. Now they'd be even more scared, and that was as it should be.

Damn Yankees.

Harumph!

As he started to climb down the front wheel, the sheriff

ducked out of his office and placed his Texas-creased Stetson on his blond-gray head. "That wasn't very nice, now, Angus—scarin' those kids like that!"

Snorting a devilish laugh, Angus walked up around the big gray in the traces, running a gentle hand along the horse's left wither, then down its long, fine snout. "I love nothin' better than frightenin' them Yankee brats, I tell you, Ben!"

He slapped his thigh again.

"I see that." Ben Lodge was a good-natured, friendly faced man in his late forties, a former rancher whose first wife, Em, had died. Lodge wanted to give his second wife, Syvvie, an easier life. She had been a hard worker on the ranch, too, but Ben wanted a simpler life for her now and had moved them to town. He'd been a lawman before, so he ran for sheriff in the special election after Frank Stillwell had bought a pill he couldn't digest from Graham Ludlow's prissy almost-son-in-law.

Fitting end for the son of a buck—shot by an Eastern, four-eyed popinjay with a quivering hand!

Lodge was originally from Ohio, but he'd never shown any special sympathy for either the Confederate side or Union side. At least, not any around here. The Buchanons had gotten to know him because he'd ranched not far from the 4-Box-B, and they'd bought eggs from Lodge's dear first wife, Em, and they'd ridden roundup together, cutting cattle from the free-range herds that mixed every spring.

Lodge was an easygoing, congenial man with a bulging belly to go with his forty-some-odd years, though over the past two years he'd shown himself to be an effective sheriff. Law-dogging was not easy in these parts, the area being as violent as it was, what with the polyglot of greedy men teeming the hills now during the gold and land rush.

Now he cast his gaze to the buckboard behind the gray, and said, "What had those boys so attracted to the back of your wagon, Angus?"

"Gimme a minute."

Angus walked around to the back of the wagon, dropped the tailgate, and pulled the blanket away to reveal the deathly glaring countenance of Rolly Piper. He pulled the blankets away from the faces of the other two men and stepped aside to let Lodge get a look at them.

Lodge turned to Angus. "Rustling?"

Angus nodded, hard-faced. "Not only rustling, but they bushwhacked me, the sons of evil owls! Had to take 'em all down. It was either them or me, Ben."

Lodge studied Angus, lower jaw hanging. "*You* took them down?"

"Of course. Why's that so damn surprising?"

Angus noticed several men now approaching the wagon—beer-wielding miners, mostly, who'd been drinking outside of the two nearby saloons.

Lodge canted his head to one side, skeptically, and said, "Angus, you shot these men out on the range? After they ambushed you."

"That's right. They got ants in their bloomers an' started shootin' too soon. I swung around behind 'em and got the drop. *Bang! Bang! Bang!*" Angus swatted his thigh, then raised his right hand and blew on the barrel of the gun he was shaping with his thumb and index finger.

Lodge poked his hat brim up off his forehead and folded his arms on his lumpy chest. "Angus, I haven't seen you on a horse in years."

"You haven't? Well, that's because when I come to town I'm usually haulin' beer. Not today, though. Maybe tomorrow. Didn't have room today."

"I haven't seen you on a horse in years, Angus, because you haven't been on a horse in years. You told me once how frustrated you were because arthritis was keepin' you out of the saddle."

"I got better. I bought an elixir from a travelin' medicine man. A couple drops of that every night in a beer, and, hell, I'm greased lightning out there on the range now, sure enough! I can ride like I'm twenty again. All the boys are amazed!"

"Hunter shot these men."

"Who?"

"Hunter. You know your son?"

"Of course, I know Hunter's my son. An' no, he didn't. I did!" Angus thumbed himself in the chest. "They bushwhacked me, an' I rode around 'em, got the drop, and shot 'em all down!" He made his hand into a gun again and extended it straight out from his shoulder. "*Bang! Bang! Bang!*"

Lodge made a face, probed a lower tooth for a chunk of meat as he scrutinized the old man carefully. "You'd be willing to sign an affidavit attesting to that? Lying in a court of law, and that's what that would be, is a federal crime, Angus."

Angus studied the growing number of men approaching the wagon warily, curiously, muttering among themselves. Word that Piper, Lowery, and Wilcox were dead would soon get back to the rest of Rolly Piper's family, and Angus wanted to make sure that if Piper's kin went after anyone, it would be him instead of Hunter.

He gritted his teeth angrily at Ben Lodge, and said, "Dammit, Ben—I shot 'em. I did! Hunter didn't have nothin' to do with it. I'll swear on a whole stack of Bibles. Now let's go in and I'll put my mark on that affy-david of yours!" He nudged the lawman's arm. "Oh, by the way, Ben—Hunter an' Annabelle an' me, we took in Piper's nephew. He was there with Piper, see, an' he said he had nowhere else to go, so we took him in. If no place better comes up for him to go to, he'll be just fine out at the 4-Box-B. Kind of nice havin' a young'un around again, and Annabelle has been mother-hennin' him just awful!"

"I didn't know Piper had a boy living with him."

"'Bout ten years old, yay high. Sandy-headed. Kinda serious. I doubt anybody knew about him, the poor kid. Piper probably kept him locked up in that cabin, doin' chores. Annabelle said his mother, God rest her soul, was a whore in Deadwood."

"I see." Lodge thought it over. "Well, I can't think of better foster parents to the boy than Hunter and Annabelle."

"Me neither."

Lodge shook a mock admonishing finger at him. "Just don't you go corrupting the child!"

Angus laughed and hitched his trousers up higher on his lean hips. "We all done here? I'd just as soon make my mark and head back to the ranch. I got beer to tend. Almost done keggin' the last batch."

Lodge glanced at the small crowd that had gathered around Angus's wagon. He turned to Angus, a wary expression building in his eyes, and said, "I tell you what—I'll ride out later with the affidavit. It might be wise for you to—"

A man's belligerent voice cut the sheriff off: "Is what I'm hearin' true, Buchanon?"

Angus and Lodge followed the shout to its source on the other side of the street. A short, stocky, red-bearded man in buckskins stood out front of the Lucky Devil Saloon, several others of his ilk gathered around him. This was Royce Piper, another of the no-good Piper clan. He was a market hunter who sold his meat to the local grocery stores and saloons.

Mostly, however, he drank. That's what he was doing now. He held a nearly empty beer glass in one hand and a filled shot glass in his other hand, almost daintily between his fat thumb and fat index finger. A floppy-brimmed, cream leather hat shaded his broad cheeks, the nubs of which above his ginger beard were as red as apples.

Sheriff Lodge held a placating hand out to Piper. "Stay out of this, Royce. None of your affair."

"The hell it ain't!"

Royce Piper, who wore a big revolver wedged down over his belly and a big bowie knife on his right hip, threw the whiskey shot back, slammed the empty shot glass onto the railing of the saloon's front stoop, then threw back all the rest of his beer. He scrubbed a big fleshy hand across his mouth, hitched his pants up his broad hips, and walked forthrightly down the porch steps and into the street.

The crowd of onlookers parted for him. Most were Piper sympathizers, it appeared—raggedy-heeled miners like the Pipers once had been themselves before being fired for fighting or general sloth. As Piper moved toward Angus and Lodge, Angus saw in the corner of his eye the sheriff close his hand down over the grips of his holstered six-shooter and heard him mutter under his breath, "Dammit all."

Chapter 10

"Get your hand off your gun, Royce!" Ben Lodge ordered as the big, ginger-bearded man strode angrily up to him and Angus. "I won't tell you again!"

"Are you gonna stand between me an' this old, one-armed polecat?" Royce barked back at the sheriff.

"Yes, I am. Angus says he killed these men on his own range. They were rustling. You and Rolly and all the rest of you Pipers are known stock thieves. Now, since I only have Angus's word on the matter, I believe him. What other reason would he have for killing your cousin?"

Royce turned his enraged face to Angus, looked Angus up and down quickly, and curled his nose. "This broken-down old scudder with one foot in the grave didn't kill my cousin."

"You believe what you want to believe, you big, fat, Yankee blowhard!" Angus barked through a taut, proud smile.

"Angus, you're not helping!" Lodge said, cutting a quick, reprimanding look at the old man.

To Lodge, Royce said, "His son killed my cousin. Now, stand back, Lodge. I'm gonna beat it out of him." Royce glanced at three men standing close behind him—close friends and partners-in-crime of Royce's. "Right, boys?"

"We'll back you all the way, Royce!" said a one-eyed man in a shabby beaver hat and broadcloth coat over a ragged buckskin shirt. His eyes were bright with drink. In fact, all four, including Royce, smelled as though they'd been drinking steadily since midnight.

Royce tightened his grip on his gun handles.

"Don't do it, Royce!" Lodge warned, tightening his hold in the walnut grips of his own revolver.

"I'm faster'n you, Lodge!"

"Don't bet on it!"

Royce grinned and jerked his right arm. Just as he did, Angus stomped down hard on Royce's left foot. Royce yelped. As his gun cleared its holster, Angus stepped forward and swung his arm up and back, smashing his elbow into Royce's throat.

Royce gave a strangled wail, dropped his gun, and flew straight back off his feet to land in the ground horse manure and dirt of the street. Dust wafted. Royce lay groaning.

Lodge had jerked up his own revolver and held it straight out before him, hammer cocked. Maybe two seconds had passed since Angus had stomped on Royce's foot, and the sheriff was still trying to work his mind around what had just happened. It appeared the three men backing Royce's play and the rest of the small crowd behind them were as well.

There wasn't a set of eyes in the bunch smaller than silver dollars as all gazes flicked between the down and groaning Royce to the frail, one-armed Angus.

"Dammit, Angus!" Lodge said, keeping his own revolver aimed at the three men now crouched over Royce.

Chuckling with satisfaction, Angus had turned and walked back to the driver's seat of his wagon. He pulled out his double-barrel and walked back toward where Royce lay clutching his throat and making strangling sounds, his face puffy and red.

Angus peeled both of the double-bore's hammers back to full cock and aimed generally at Royce and the three men behind him, still staring down at the big man in shock, hands on their guns but appearing too preoccupied with Royce's precarious condition to jerk them up.

"Now what do you think, Royce?" Angus crowed over the double-bores of his side-by-side barrels. "Still think this broken-down old scudder with one foot in the grave didn't kill your cousin and them polecats he ran with?"

Still clutching his throat but appearing to be finally able to suck some air into his lungs, Royce turned his own stunned gaze to Angus.

"Throw those guns down," Lodge ordered the three men around Royce. "Do it now, or you bought a bullet!"

"And double-aught buck," warned Angus, tightening his grip on the double-bore and grinning from ear to ear. He hadn't thought he'd had that move in him anymore. But he did, all right, sure enough. Lodge wasn't known as a particularly fast draw, and Angus hadn't wanted to take the chance of Royce killing the sheriff and leaving Angus to face the four men alone. Not until he'd had time to fetch his double-bore, anyway.

Besides, he hadn't come to town to get Lodge, a good man and a good friend to him and Hunter, killed.

Reluctantly, switching their gazes between Lodge's aimed six-shooter and Angus's twelve-gauge, all three men pulled their pistols from their holsters and tossed them into the dirt. Royce was sitting up now, one hand still wrapped around his throat. His little pig eyes were casting bayonets of raw fury at Angus, who grinned back at him.

"You three, haul those bodies over to the undertaker, then you, along with Royce, drag your raggedy asses out of town. I don't want to see you back in Tigerville for a month."

"*What?*" Royce croaked, his voice sounding like that of a little bird.

"You heard me. It's either that or thirty days behind bars and a five-hundred-dollar fine each for threatening a lawman. Which is it gonna be?"

Royce's gaze softened a little, grew resigned. They quickly shifted back to rage, though, when he returned his gaze to Angus.

Sullen as schoolboys caught peeking through the half-moon in the girls' privy door, Royce's three accomplices pulled the dead men out of the wagon and draped them over their shoulders, grunting and cursing sourly with the effort. When they turned and slogged off in the direction of the undertaker, Royce pushed himself to his feet, grabbed his hat up off the ground, and glanced again at Angus.

His gaze was more befuddled than threatening. Maybe even apprehensive. He hadn't had any inkling the old codger had had that move in him either. He shifted his eyes to the double-bore Angus aimed at his head, winced a little, narrowing one eye, then swung around, kicked a rock, and tramped off after his cohorts.

As they retreated, the rest of the small crowd slowly dispersed, the onlookers returning to their respective saloons but not before casting more than a few awestruck glances over their shoulders at the proudly grinning Angus.

Lodge holstered his Colt and turned to Angus, who lowered his shotgun and depressed both hammers. "What am I gonna do with you?" the sheriff asked in disgust, though a faint grin reluctantly pulled at the man's mouth corners, beneath his shaggy, blond-gray mustache.

"What do you mean?" Angus said, feigning incredulity. "You oughtta make me an honorary deputy. Hell, Ben, I think I just saved your life!"

He walked back to the front of the wagon, slid the shotgun under the seat, and climbed aboard. He swung the big gray out into the street, then full around to head back the way he'd come.

As he did, he pinched his hat brim at Ben Lodge staring up at him skeptically, both fists on the man's stout hips holding his broadcloth coat back behind him, one booted foot cocked forward. He regarded Angus uncertainly.

"Have a good day, Ben," Angus said.

Lodge only snorted and shook his head.

Steam rose from the dung pile that resembled a German chocolate cake dropped here on the snow-dusted floor of the mountain meadow. The warm bear scat had melted the snow for several inches around the pile, showing dirt, bits of dead brown grass, dead brown leaves, and part of a flat, white stone.

Down on one knee, leaning on his Henry rifle, Hunter could smell the peppery aroma rising from the dung, confirming that it had, in fact, been left by a grizzly. The same bruin that had left its calling card at the 4-Box-B last night in the form of Hec Prather's torn side.

Hunter, Kentucky Wade, Noble Sanchez, and Chief Red Otter had picked up the bear's trail easily despite the light dusting of snow that had partly concealed it until it had led them here on the broad, forested eastern slope of Crow's Nest. The snow had continued here roughly a thousand feet above the ranch until an hour ago, easily accepting the bruin's tracks, which had led the party to the scat pile still steaming and issuing its pungent aroma.

"Fresh," Noble Sanchez said, standing to Hunter's right, cradling his own Winchester in his arms. His brown eyes were cast with wariness as he slid them from the scat to Hunter and arched a brow.

Hunter rose slowly, looking around. "He passed through here within the hour."

"They stop at the water." This from Red Otter, who stood at the edge of the lake that lay twenty feet beyond Hunter and Sanchez.

Red Otter stood with his back to Hunter and Sanchez, facing the iron-flat lake that perfectly mirrored the sky and a few remaining, high, rag-like gray clouds. Beyond the lake lay another stretch of blue-green forest. To each side of the lake was all open beaver meadow and widely scattered Ponderosas.

Kentucky was walking back toward the other three men along the water's edge, casting his gaze along the ground. The wool-lined collar of his mackinaw was pulled up to his jaws against the breeze that had a knife-edge to it at these high climes.

Glancing up at Hunter, he said, "No tracks this way."

Hunter stared down at the tracks that ended at the waterline. He looked to his right, along the lake's north shore. Nothing there either. He walked along that edge of the lake, growing more and more confounded.

He turned back to Red Otter, scowling. "What'd he do—swim across the lake?"

Red Otter turned his stony face to the lake again, gazing across the water to the low, forested ridge rising on the opposite shore. Hunter and Kentucky, standing to either side of Red Otter, did the same thing.

"Maybe he walked along the water's edge to cover his tracks." The statement had come from behind Hunter, in soft, Spanish-accented English.

Hunter glanced at Noble Sanchez flanking them. Sanchez stared warily across the lake, but when he saw Hunter turned to him, he feigned a lighthearted smile and shrugged. "Just a thought."

"Damn smart animal, then," Hunter mused aloud.

Hunter glanced at the chief again. A chill rose in him when the man just continued staring with a dark forbidding in his long, slanted, Indian-dark eyes beneath the brim of his bullet-crowned hat, his features set in a cold indifference that masked the trepidation in the man's heart. Hunter knew it was there. He could sense it. He remembered their conversation last evening. He felt a cloying sense of annoyance.

"Let's split up," he said. "Kentucky, you and Noble head around that side of the lake. The chief and I will walk around this side, meet on the opposite shore."

"You got it, boss," Kentucky said.

"Hold on," Hunter said. When Wade and Sanchez turned back to him, he said, "Either of you ever hunt a grizzly before?"

Kentucky shook his head.

Sanchez said, "My father and I hunted one in Sonora. It killed thirty of our sheep in two nights. We never found it; it disappeared in the mountains."

"When you shoot a buffalo," Hunter said, "the buff either drops or runs away. When you shoot a grizzly, they either drop or run at you—like a freight train screaming downhill without brakes. We should have larger caliber rifles, but the repeater should suffice. When you get a shot, take it and keep throwing lead at the bruin until he drops. A .44 round should break its neck."

Wade grinned wryly, pulling up one side of his handle-bar mustache. "What if the bruin doesn't drop even after you've pumped him full of lead?"

"Pray," Hunter said.

Wade and Sanchez exchanged dubious glances.

Sanchez stared across the lake and crossed himself.

The group split up, Wade and Sanchez walking along the south shore, Hunter and Red Otter walking along the north shore. The Indian's stony silence continued to annoy Hunter. He didn't know why, but it did. He kept his wolf on its leash, though, and ignored the man.

Leave him to his superstitions I'm a practical man, one of this world, not the unseen world. Because there is no unseen world. At least none involving demon bears carrying out curses from the other side.

His resolve was not complete, and that nettled him. Earlier that morning, he'd urged Bobby Lee to accompany the hunting party after the grizzly bear, for Bobby could track the bear by scent. Bobby had helped Hunter track several dangerous wildcats over the years. This morning, however, Bobby had mewled, pulled his ears back, drawn his tail between his legs, and slunk off behind the barn.

That hadn't been like Bobby at all. He and Hunter were normally joined at the hip even on a dangerous hunt.

The coyote's reaction to the bear the previous night and this morning had stuck in Hunter's craw, giving voice to irrational fears.

Hunter and Red Otter walked along the shoreline, spread out a good thirty feet apart, the chief walking along the water's edge, Hunter out away from it. Both men scoured the ground. No sign. Nothing showed the recent passing of a thousand-pound bear.

Hunter's frustration grew. He pinned the blame on the stoic, annoyingly silent Red Otter, though he knew it made no sense. The Indian was not to blame for the bear having given them the slip.

They entered the forest and walked through the trees and rocks along the water's edge. Wade and Sanchez came into view ahead. Hunter cursed under his breath. He could tell by the expressions on the men's faces that they'd spied no sign.

The four men reunited wordlessly, their silence speaking volumes.

Sanchez's face was pale, his eyes dark. He looked darkly into the forest rising beyond the water's edge to the west. "He's in there, isn't he? Waiting for us."

He turned to Red Otter, as if he believed the Indian would know the answer to the question. That annoyed Hunter too. Of course, the Mexican would be as superstitious as the Indian. Hunter didn't know where these angry thoughts came from. He was normally an understanding, rational man. Other men's superstitions shouldn't bother him.

But they did.

Because, like Bobby Lee's behavior earlier that morning, they gave voice to Hunter's own irrational fears. He supposed he came by them honestly though. There were few places more superstitious than his native Appalachia.

"Let's spread out and move ahead," Hunter said authoritatively.

But he felt the short hairs prick along the back of his neck.

Chapter 11

They spread out and moved north through the forest.

The sun brightly dappled the soft, fragrant forest duff between the pines and firs. The air was cool enough that Hunter's breath frosted before his face as he moved slowly, steadily north, stepping over deadfalls and weaving his way around trees.

Gradually, the ground sloped upward, likely toward an unseen ridge.

As he moved, he could occasionally see Red Otter roughly fifty feet to his left, holding his Winchester up high across his chest in his gloved hands, salt-and-pepper braids hanging down over his raised collar and the back of his coat. Less often, he saw Kentucky Wade moving steadily ahead another fifty feet beyond Red Otter.

Hunter couldn't see Noble Sanchez at all.

As Hunter walked forward, the tension in his body made him squeeze the Henry almost savagely at times. He kept expecting the big bruin to suddenly appear before him, stepping out from behind the broad bole of a pine or spruce, rise onto his back feet, and tower over him, roaring.

His heart thudded with the expectation. The day was cool, but he was sweating.

When they'd walked steadily for fifteen or twenty minutes, a rifle crack rended the forest's ethereal silence.

Hunter stopped abruptly as did Red Otter to his left.

Another crack and then another.

Hunter's heartbeat quickened. It fairly raced when a man's scream followed the rifle's third report.

Hunter swung left and ran, quickly overtaking the older and slower Red Otter.

"No!" came an agonized cry. It was Noble Sanchez. "*¡Dios mío, ayúdame!*" Oh God, help me!

Ahead, Kentucky Wade came into view, running wildly and looking around in desperation.

"Where is he?" Hunter said, having to pause to climb over two spruce trees fallen across each other.

"I don't know," Wade yelled, running west and down the slope at an angle, weaving around trees. "The screams came from that way!" He pointed in the direction he was running.

Moving fleetly but heart still shuddering as the echoing screams continued, Hunter overtook Wade and then, dead ahead, he saw the mouth of a side canyon, a fifty-foot gap in an uneven stone wall tufted with evergreen shrubs and cedars. Hunter ran into the opening and down the dimly lit corridor abutted on both sides by rock walls in places streaked with moisture from runout springs.

Ahead, a man ran toward him. Hunter could see only his silhouette, but it was Sanchez. The man had lost his hat and rifle and was running wildly, looking over his shoulder, screaming, "Help! *Dios*—help me, boss!"

Hunter ran forward as Sanchez stopped suddenly. He jerked violently backward, as though lassoed from behind.

Then Hunter saw the broad, dark bulk of the bear obscure Sanchez's smaller shadow. The bear and Sanchez were moving away now, farther up the canyon. They were moving fast, too, because Hunter was running as fast as he could, and he wasn't gaining on them.

Sanchez sobbed and whimpered as the bear appeared to be dragging him with one paw hooked around the man's arm. Sanchez's feet bounced along the ground, his entire body flopping like that of a rag doll.

"*Christ!*" Hunter gritted out, trying to increase his pace.

A rock appeared from nowhere. He hooked his boot on it. That foot came out from under him and he flew forward, hit the ground hard on his chest and belly, getting a mouthful of dirt and pine needles. He lost his hat and rifle.

He cursed, dazed, stretching his lips back from his teeth and shaking his head to clear the cobwebs. He reached for his rifle, swept it up off the ground, heaved himself to his feet and continued running, mindless of the grit clinging to his mouth.

Ahead, the canyon narrowed down to an arrowhead tip—a gap that was maybe ten feet wide. He couldn't quite believe what he was seeing in that gap at the end of the canyon —the bear vaulting almost gracefully up a sheer stone wall, dragging the kicking and screaming Noble Sanchez behind him.

Hunter's heart did a somersault; his guts tied themselves in knots.

What he saw threatened to turn his feet to lead, but he kept running.

"Noble!" he bellowed as he drew to within twenty feet of the man now being pulled up out of the canyon, the bear roaring and snarling madly.

Sanchez's flailing boots were six feet up off the canyon floor.

Seven feet . . .

Hunter reached up with one hand to grab the man's right foot, and pulled. The boot came off in his hand. He looked up. Sanchez stared down at him, brown eyes opaque with holy terror, his face as white as flour and bathed in sweat.

He wailed, "*Jefe—ayúdame!*"

Hunter levered a round into the Henry's action and raised the rifle to his shoulder. Just then the bear slipped out of sight at the top of the canyon, ten feet above the canyon floor. The bear pulled the still-kicking and wailing Sanchez up out of the canyon and out of sight. The man's other boot had come off at the canyon's lip and dropped back down into the canyon to land at Hunter's feet.

The man's screams and the bear's roars dwindled into the distance, echoing.

Hunter leaped, reaching for the canyon lip, but it was two feet higher than he could jump. He cursed in frustration.

Running footsteps sounded behind him. He turned to see Kentucky Wade sprinting toward him. Red Otter was right behind him.

"My God—what happened?" Kentucky yelled. "I heard the screams an'—"

"Give me a boost!"

"What?"

"Give me a boost! Lace your fingers together!"

Kentucky set his rifle down, crouched, and laced his hands together. Hunter poked his right boot through the makeshift step, and as Wade lifted from below, Hunter lunged for the lip above with one hand, tossing the rifle out ahead of him. He grabbed the canyon lip with both hands and, grunting and cursing, hoisted himself up out of the arrowhead notch.

He swept up his rifle and found himself in a rocky area, the rocks picture-painted by ancient Indians, a common find in the Black Hills. He strode forward, looking around desperately. He no longer heard Noble's pleas or the bear's roars.

He found the erratic scuff marks left by Noble's kicking feet and followed them through a gap in the rocks. He ran for maybe a hundred yards down the gradual slope. He weaved around a spruce and stopped suddenly, looking ahead and down at some grisly thing on the ground.

No. Not some thing.

Noble Sanchez.

What was left of him.

Beyond, already a quarter mile away, the bear raced off to the northeast, fast as a racehorse—a blur of jostling cinnamon that disappeared once it busted through a heavy stand of spruce lining the edge of another small lake. Trees jostled violently, making way for the giant beast.

Gone.

Hunter looked down at the carnage of Noble Sanchez. About all he recognized were two brown eyes staring up in glassy, silent pleading.

He dropped to his knees and buried his head in his hands.

An hour later, Hunter plunged the blade of his folding saddle shovel into the sod and gravel near where he and

Kentucky Wade and Red Otter had gathered what remained of Sanchez and wrapped the poor man in his saddle blanket. Now the blanket lay near where Hunter scooped out a few lumpy chunks of sod and tossed them aside.

Again, wincing, he stomped the blade into the cold, hardening ground, grateful for the labor to distract him from his grief and anger.

Kentucky and Red Otter sat nearby, around a small fire on which they'd hung a coffeepot over a tripod. They sat glumly, side by side on the same log, sipping coffee and watching Hunter work.

Their four horses, which they'd retrieved earlier, stood ground-reined and unsaddled behind them.

Hunter had no idea how much time had passed when someone poked his shoulder and he glanced up to see Red Otter standing over him, the man's brick-red hand extended toward the shovel. Hunter had been so lost in contemplation that he was surprised to see that he'd dug a roughly rectangular hole nearly three feet deep. He hadn't realized until now, either, that he was bathed in sweat.

"I'll take a turn, boss."

Hunter shook his head. "He worked for me, so he died for me. I'm the one who has to bury him."

"Horse manure, Hunter!" Hunter looked up at the broad-shouldered, severely featured Indian in surprise. He'd never heard the man give voice to such a white man's epithet. "He was our friend. Let us help you bury him."

Hunter looked down at the grave, sighed. He handed the shovel to the chief. He stepped up out of the hole and, while Red Otter continued digging, accepted a cup of coffee from Kentucky, and sat down on the log beside him.

Hunter stared off for a time in the direction the bear

had disappeared, pondering. For some reason, he felt like talking.

Turning to Kentucky, he said, "Do you know what the chief thinks about the bear?"

"That it's an *otshee-monetoo*?" Kentucky spread his broad, mustached mouth in a smile.

"Do you believe it?"

"Hell, no—that's crazy Injun stuff!"

Kentucky threw a rock at Red Otter. It bounced off the ground and struck the chief lightly in the right thigh.

The chief cast a wry, slit-eyed grin over his right shoulder at his assailant. "Don't make me come over there, top hand, or I'll show you some Sioux torture tricks."

"Ouch!" Kentucky said, glancing at Hunter. "He will too."

Hunter and Kentucky chuckled and sipped their coffee. Red Otter chuckled, shook his head, and continued digging.

After a half hour, Kentucky got up and walked over to relieve Red Otter, who returned to the fire and accepted a fresh cup of coffee from Hunter.

"Obliged," the Indian said with a nod, and took Kentucky's place on the log with a sigh.

"Thanks for the help," Hunter said, blowing on his own fresh coffee, then taking a sip.

Red Otter shrugged. "He was our friend, boss."

They watched Kentucky work for a time and then Hunter, after more frustrated pondering, turned to the chief again and said, "Let's say that I was sort of halfway leaning toward believing your theory about the bear. That it is a *otshee-monetoo*."

Red Otter turned to him, one brow raised skeptically.

"Can you kill an *otshee-monetoo*?"

The chief sipped his coffee, swallowed, and said, "If they've taken earthly form, yes. Aside from that he's driven by the curse to get even with you for whatever spirit sent him, that bear is like any other griz . . . in body."

"Awfully big."

The chief nodded. "He's a big one."

"And powerful. He dragged Noble damn near fifty yards faster than I can run, and carried him up a sheer stone wall."

Red Otter looked at him again. "He's still a griz. A big griz can do that. Hell, even a small one can outrun a horse."

"A bullet will kill him, you think?"

"Placed right, and you pump enough into him."

"Hmm."

"It would help if I smudged you with sweetgrass and said a prayer over you."

Hunter scowled. "That really necessary?"

"It couldn't hurt. And if you're going up against a bruin that size, and with that size of a mad on, you're gonna need all the help you can get."

Hunter looked at Kentucky, who glanced over his shoulder at Hunter, pulled a wry mouth corner up, and shrugged.

"That can wait," Hunter said, and sipped his coffee. "First, I'll try it my way." It wasn't that he took umbrage with Indian ceremony. It was just that he wasn't ready to believe he'd had a demon sicced on him from the other side. That wasn't an easy thing for a white man to wrap his mind around.

It was too frightening to believe. Frightening for himself and Anna and all the other people around him. Already, Hec was badly injured and Noble was dead.

Was it all because of him? Because of his own bloody past?

He didn't want to believe it.

Red Otter smiled his understanding. "All right. You let me know when you're ready."

Chapter 12

"Sit up tall in the saddle," Annabelle called. "Keep your back straight but loose. Firm up your legs. Very good . . . very, very good, Nathan!"

Now in the mid-afternoon, they'd graduated from riding around the corral to riding around the yard. Annabelle followed Nathan closely as he rode a small buckskin pony toward the barn, sitting up straight and tall in the saddle. He rolled his shoulders with the horse's movements.

Bobby Lee watched with keen interest from the house's front porch. The coyote had been staying close to the house since the bear attack the night before.

Annabelle stopped her own mount, a dun named Chester, and said, "All right, now, stop him. Remember how to stop him?"

"I think so!" Nathan pulled back on the buckskin's reins.

"Easy, easy," Annabelle called. "Remember, the bit's in his mouth, and his mouth is sensitive. He can feel even the slightest pressure."

"All right, sorry," Nathan said, turning a sheepish look toward Annabelle.

"No, no, you're doing fine," Annabelle called. "Now turn him this way and ride back the way you came."

Nathan licked his lips, then, holding the buckskin's reins in both hands, gently tugged them to the left. The buckskin turned.

"Keep turning him," Annabelle called.

When Nathan had the buckskin pointed in the opposite direction, he looked over at Annabelle, nervously awaiting instruction. "Remember how to get him moving?"

"I gently squeeze with my legs."

"Exactly. If he's a little sluggish, you can give him a little nudge with your . . . that's it . . . there you go," Annabelle said, clapping softly as Nathan, having lightly touched the buckskin's loins with the heels of his boots, rode back in the direction of the house.

He glanced back at Annabelle and smiled.

That warmed her heart. He was not only learning, and learning quickly, but he was having fun. At first, he'd been a little afraid of the sheer size and height of a horse, just as most folks were the first time they climbed aboard one. But now, after nearly three hours of steady work in the corral and then in the yard, he was gaining confidence.

"Want to trot him?" Annabelle called, having turned her mare to slowly follow him, in case he needed her help.

He grinned back over his shoulder at her. "Can I?"

"You know how to do it."

Nathan stiffened his back, raised his elbows, and clucked, lightly touching the buckskin's flanks with his boot heels. The buckskin arched his tail and picked up his pace until he was in a full trot.

"Go ahead and let your upper body move with the horse but try not to bounce— there you go! Don't be afraid to grab the horn—there's no shame in grabbing the horn. That's it! Let your legs keep you in place the way the girth keeps the saddle in place—that's it, Nathan, you got it! Way to go!"

Nathan stopped the horse in front of the house and then turned him back to Annabelle. Again, he clucked the horse into motion, and the buckskin clomped toward her in a fast walk, his head held high, dust churning up around his shod hooves. Annabelle could tell the pony was getting as used to and confident in the boy as Nathan was getting accustomed to the horse and confident in his own skills. Nothing made a horse more nervous than a nervous rider.

Nathan gently tugged back on the reins, stopping the horse near Annabelle. He leaned forward and patted the horse's right wither. "Atta boy," he said, grinning at Annabelle, his cheeks touched with the rose of sunburn. "Atta boy, Reno!"

"There you go," Annabelle said, having taught the boy that just as people do, horses respond to affection. "What do you think, Nathan? Enough for one day?"

"I reckon it best be," Nathan said with a glance at the sky. "I best get to work in the barn before I'm working in the dark!"

The agreement was Annabelle would teach him how to ride, and he'd take over for Hec Prather mucking out the barn and tending the horses, including feeding and grooming them and cutting burrs from their tails. Earlier, she'd shown him what to do and how to go about doing it. He'd seemed eager to get to work and earn his keep.

"Let's see you dismount," Annabelle called to him.

The boy deftly put the buckskin over to the mounting block, which was a makeshift pile of shipping crates that Annabelle had set up near the corral to help the boy climb in and out of the saddle. Just as he got the buckskin stopped, Annabelle saw the horse glance sidelong at the boy on his back. She saw the devilish glint in the horse's eye, and, having been around horses all her life, knew right away what Reno was going to do.

Oh no!

The horse's tail went up, his head down, and both feet came straight out and up in a brief but violent buck-kick. Nathan, who'd just started to pull his right boot free from its stirrup, gave a wild yell as he went flying up and out in a long arc over the buckskin's right wither.

Arms and legs pinwheeling, Nathan hit the ground on his chest and belly a good twelve feet beyond the horse. He rolled up against the corral in a tan cloud of billowing dust.

"Ohh!" he cried, lifting his now hatless head, hair hanging down over his dusty forehead.

Bobby Lee gave a little sorrowful yip, then lay down and placed his snout between his paws.

"Nathan!" Annabelle cried.

Anna galloped over, swung down, and dropped to a knee beside the boy, who sat up looking around in taut-faced, wide-eyed shock. "Nathan, are you all right?"

Nathan turned to face her, blinking slowly, his face beginning to crease with emotion, his upper lip trembling.

Raucous laughter filled the yard.

Nathan tucked his lip down over his teeth as he and Annabelle swung their gazes toward the bunkhouse. Hec Prather stood in the open bunkhouse door in his longhandles and stocking feet, several thick, white, slightly bloodstained bandages wrapped around his chest. He wore his battered butternut Stetson. He laughed around the quirley drooping from the right corner of his mouth, then removed the quirley, exhaled a thick cloud of smoke, and looked at Nathan.

"Now what are you gonna do?" Open challenge lay heavy in the old hostler's gravelly voice.

Nathan blinked at him several times. With each blink, he seemed to regain more of his composure. He swallowed, brushed a sleeve across his lips, and turned to Annabelle who knelt beside him, her arms loosely draped around his shoulders.

"Excuse me, Annabelle," Nathan said, shrugging out of the young woman's embrace.

He got up, dusted himself off, walked over, and picked up his hat. He batted the hat against his knee several times, dislodging dust, then carefully set the topper on his head. He looked at the buckskin that had pranced off away from the corral and now stood, reins drooping, head down, staring back at the boy, a little of that devilish glint remaining in the buck's liquid-brown eyes.

"That's the way you're gonna play it, eh, Reno?" Nathan asked.

Still down on one knee, Anna watched the boy walk over to the horse. The horse regarded him skeptically. As Nathan approached, the horse lifted his head and twitched an ear, incredulous.

Nathan walked calmly up to the horse, stooped to pick up the reins, then clucked as he led the horse back over to the shipping crates. He stopped the horse by the crates, mounted the block, poked his left boot into the left stirrup, and swung his right leg over the cantle. He adjusted his weight in the saddle, raised the reins, and turned them to the right, against the left side of the buckskin's neck.

When he got the horse turned, he clucked to him, lightly touching his boots to the buck's flanks. The horse broke into a trot and then, as Nathan said, *"Hy-yahh!"* and batted his boots against the horse's flanks once more, a little harder this time, the horse broke into a gallop.

Annabelle's heart thudded. She placed a hand to her chest and found herself holding her breath as the boy galloped the buckskin straight out through the ranch portal and into the pasture beyond. Nathan rode maybe a hundred yards beyond the barn, and just when Annabelle started to worry he might not be able to slow and turn the horse back around, he did just that.

When he got the buckskin turned, he leaned forward and yelled, *"Hy-yahhh!"*

Horse and rider galloped back through the ranch portal, the boy sitting straight and tall in the saddle, legs firmly curving around the horse's barrel. Nathan drew back on the reins, stopping the horse in the middle of the yard. Dust billowed around him, sifting slowly in the copper sunlight of the late afternoon.

Sitting up, Bobby Lee lifted his long, pointed snout, and howled.

Looking at neither Anna nor Hec Prather, who remained in the doorway, leaning against the frame and smoking, Nathan put the horse back over to the shipping crates. He stopped the pony, leaned forward to give him an affectionate pat on his left wither, then, a little haltingly at first, pulled his right boot from its stirrup.

Gaining confidence, he swung down from the horse's back and onto the crates

Still on one knee, Anna started breathing again. She and Hec exchanged smiles.

Nathan leaped down off the crates, led the horse forward, opened the corral gate, and led the horse inside. He promptly removed the saddle, slung it over the top rail with a fierce grunt, and rubbed the sweaty buck down with a scrap of burlap sack hanging from a nail.

He looked at neither Anna nor old Hec but kept his attention on his work. However, a proud flush had crept high into his cheeks and was working its way to his ears.

Annabelle looked at Hec again. The old man was watching the boy, grinning proudly around his quirley.

Feeling buoyant as a proud mother, Anna pushed to her feet and led her own horse into the corral to unsaddle her.

Anna had unsaddled her horse and turned the mare over to Nathan to rub down and groom and was walking back to the house to get supper started, when the rattle of a wagon drew her attention to the trail angling around the pine-peppered northern ridge. She held her hand up to shade her eyes against the west-angling sun.

Angus was approaching on the buckboard.

Relief washed over Anna. The oldster had been gone longer than a trip to town usually took, so she'd grown worried but was glad to have the distraction of giving Nathan his first riding lesson. She'd suspected that Angus had stopped at his old friend Homer Calhoun's place on Willow Creek to sample Calhoun's homemade wine.

Still, she'd been worried.

The old man looked fine, however, as he swung the big gray and the buckboard through the ranch portal and into the yard. She smiled. Sure enough, a rosy glow touched his bearded, craggy cheeks, and there was a distinct sparkle in his pale blue eyes.

"Hello there!" Anna hailed.

"Aft'noon, Miss Annabelle," Angus said, drawing back on the gray's reins. His Southern accent always seemed to get more pronounced when he'd been drinking. "Right fine day, is it not?" He glanced skyward, then returned his sparkling gaze to his daughter-in-law, and grinned.

"You know what, Angus? It is a right fine day. And *I* didn't even stop over at Homer Calhoun's for a sample of that chokecherry wine of his!"

Angus smiled a little sheepishly and rolled his eyes. "Ah, hell—you know me too well! I didn't have you too worried, then?"

"Yes, you did, but teaching Nathan how to ride took my mind off you. Everything went all right in town, I take it?"

"Fine as frog hair cut four ways!" the old man crowed. "I had to hand Royce his hat, but that taught him. He won't be no problem."

Annabelle frowned. "You handed *who* his hat?"

"Like I said, he won't be a problem. How'd the ridin' lesson go?"

Hec Prather yelled from the bunkhouse's open doorway, "By sixteen that boy's gonna make a top hand!"

Angus turned to Annabelle. "That well?"

"Pretty dang well," Annabelle said with pride. "Nathan's had a hard life, but he's made of strong stuff."

"That's what it takes," Angus said, turning and heading toward the house. "Time for a nap."

Anna followed the old man. She stopped when in the periphery of her vision she spotted movement on the ridge rising south of the compound. Two riders up there, at the very top of the ridge. Anna scrutinized them more closely, but they were far enough away that they were mainly in silhouette—though she could make out a brown hat and a red neckerchief on one of the riders.

They both sat facing the ranch. One held something up to his face. Whatever was in the man's raised hand cast a fleeting reflection of golden sunlight.

A spy glass?

The man lowered his hand. The two reined their horses around and rode south, dwindling quickly from view.

Anna stood staring after them, one hand raised to shade her eyes. Uneasiness touched her. She cast her gaze toward the house's front door and through which Angus had disappeared.

"You're sure everything went all right in town, Angus?" she called, striding forward.

Chapter 13

It was a grim and silent trio of riders that rode in through the 4-Box-B portal after ten o'clock that night.

None of the three said anything as they stripped the tack from their horses and turned the mounts into the corral. They parted just as silently, Hunter heading for the house, Kentucky Wade and Red Otter striding wearily off in the direction of the bunkhouse.

Wan lamplight shone in the bunkhouse windows. Hec had been waiting up.

Now as Hunter walked toward the house, he heard the bunkhouse's front door click, the hinges groan faintly. The old man's voice came as raspy as the scratching of two dry leaves together in the night's heavy silence: "Where's the bean-eater?"

Kentucky Wade said something too softly for Hunter to make out. Hec gave a loud, anguished wail, "*Ah, hell!*"

Hunter squeezed his eyes closed and mounted the porch steps. He'd just gained the porch when the front door came open and Anna stepped out in her white night-gown, raising a hurricane lamp. Her recently brushed hair spilled across her shoulders, glistening in the lamplight.

She studied Hunter's face, and her own face fell with worry, eyes widening.

"What happened?"

"Noble's dead."

Anna opened her mouth, but she didn't say anything for several seconds. "How 'bout the rest of you?"

"We made it."

She turned and walked back into the house. "Come in. I've kept a plate on the warming rack."

Following her, Hunter said, "Pa, the boy in bed?"

"Angus tried to stay awake but couldn't manage it. He and Homer Calhoun got into the chokecherry wine earlier. Nathan's in the bunkhouse."

"Why?"

Annabelle shrugged. "He had a good day, and he wants to be one of the men, I reckon."

"Well, I'm glad he had a good day."

Hunter followed Anna into the kitchen. He leaned his rifle against the wall and pegged his hat. He stood near his hat and ran his hand through his hair in frustration, the pain of losing Sanchez still a rusty nail prodding his insides.

Anna pulled a cloth-covered plate off the range's warming rack and set it on the table. She filled a cup from the coffeepot and set it down beside the plate, looking at Hunter, who stood statue-still, chin down, his right hand clutching a handful of blond hair. His face was frozen in a grimace.

"Come," Anna said, patting the oilcloth-covered table. "Sit and eat. You look beat."

"I'll sit, but I'm not sure I can eat."

Hunter sat heavily down. Anna sat across from him, gazing directly into his eyes. "Tell me."

Hunter rested his arms on the table, on either side of the plate. "It was bad, Anna. That's as far as I'll go."

She reached across the table and took his left hand in both of hers.

"On the way back home," he continued, "we rode up to Blue Meadow and found four dead steers, all only partly eaten. The herd was spread out. We gathered them and herded them down closer to home, where we can keep an eye on them." He paused, gazed darkly back at Annabelle. "That bruin has been busy. Some of those kills were a couple of weeks old. He's not a traveler. He's a stayer. And now he's a man-killer."

"You'll get him."

"I have to get him."

"You will." Anna gave his hand an urgent squeeze. "Eat."

Hunter kept his eyes on hers. "Red Otter thinks the bear is a curse from the other side."

"From what other side?"

Hunter pressed his hands to his eyes. "God knows."

Anna frowned, puzzled.

"He thinks it's an *otshee-monetoo*, evil spirit, and that it's been sent after me by someone I killed."

Anna frowned skeptically. "For what? To get even?"

"I reckon."

Again, she took his hand in hers. "Look, Hunter, I love the chief. But that's Indian talk. We don't believe the way he does. Let him believe it. You don't. That bear is nothing but a bear unless you believe it's an *otshee-monetoo*. If you believe it's an evil spirit sent here to get even with you, then it's liable to be true. Do you know what I mean?"

Hunter nodded. "I know exactly what you mean. I tried not to let him get into my head."

"And you didn't."

"No, I didn't."

"Eat."

"I can't."

"Eat!"

Hunter gave a wry chuckle. He sighed and picked up his fork and knife and reluctantly carved into the steak sitting in a pool of its own butter beside a fist-size baked potato.

"Here—maybe this will help with your appetite." Anna had gotten up, stepped onto a chair, and pulled a bottle of good labeled whiskey down from a shelf over the range.

"That's Pa's good Spanish brandy. If we get into that, I'm liable to get the strappin' I haven't had in years."

"We need it worse than Angus does." Annabelle smiled devilishly as she stepped down from the chair, her shining hair bouncing on her shoulders and snaking down to caress her sides beneath her arms. "Besides, I'll hide the bottle and he'll forget he even has it."

"That's nasty—messin' with an old man's memory."

Anna grabbed two clean water glasses off a shelf and set them on the table. "Desperate times call for desperate measures."

She filled a glass, slid it over to where Hunter was working with a little more interest on his meal. She filled the other glass and sat down.

Hunter looked up at her as he ate. "I'm lucky to have you. I'd hate to go through somethin' like this without you."

"Me too."

Anna raised her glass. Hunter picked up his glass and clinked it against hers.

"To Noble," he said, a hitch in his voice. He threw back the entire shot of brandy and squeezed his eyes closed in silent prayer.

"To Noble." Anna threw hers back as well.

When Hunter had finished his meal, Anna slid his plate aside, set his glass back in front of him, and refilled it before refilling her own. She took his hand in hers once more and looked him in the eye, her right one slightly crossed with significance. "Tell me about it."

Hunter grimaced. He sipped the brandy, set the glass back down on the table, and looked at her. "Are you sure you want to know?"

"I don't want to know, but I need to know what you men went through up there."

"It was terrible."

"I can take it."

He told her. When he finished, she lifted her glass in her trembling hand and threw back the rest of the shot.

Hunter woke suddenly, snapping his eyelids up in the dark.

He pricked his ears, listening. Something had awakened him.

Annabelle snored very softly beside him, where she rested her head on his shoulder. He could hear the louder but more muffled snores of his father in the room across the hall. A faint night breeze whispered through the pines in the backyard.

Still, something had alarmed him as he'd slept. His heart had quickened.

Then he heard it—the nervous whicker of a horse. Then another.

Another horse whickered loudly. The whicker grew into a whinny. That made Hunter's heart beat faster, thudding in his ears.

He quickly but gently slid his shoulder out from under Anna's head. She fluttered her eyelids and moaned but did not awaken. She snugged her head down against the side of Hunter's pillow and continued snoring faintly, a lock of her copper hair sliding down to cover her cheek.

He quietly stepped into his boots, donned his hat, and left the room, drawing the door quietly closed behind him. He hurried downstairs, walking on the balls of his feet. He shrugged into his buckskin coat, grabbed his rifle, and stepped out onto the porch, holding the rifle up high across his chest and pricking his ears, listening, as he cast his gaze toward the two corrals left of the barn.

The horses were milling edgily, a couple running in circles around the corral, whickering. Several stood staring toward the west, switching their tails.

Hunter hurried down off the porch and crossed the yard at an angle toward the two corrals, pumping a cartridge into the Henry's action. The bear was here. He could tell by the horses' wide eyes and arched tails and fearful whickers. By the three running in circles. He moved along the front of the corral to the west.

It was probably around three in the morning, and the red moon was obscured by high clouds. Very dark out here. He could see only a few feet in front of him.

He came to the far western end of the second corral

and stood staring into the darkness toward the ranch portal. Nothing. He walked north along the side of the corral. The northern ridge was a dark velvet hulk looming before him, totally black, obscuring everything between Hunter and the ridge.

Heart thudding, squeezing the rifle stock with both hands, Hunter came to the end of the corral. He stopped, looked right, back in the direction of the bunkhouse and barn.

Nothing.

Nothing to his left either.

He started forward, toward the black hulking mass of the ridge, his racing heart shrinking with fear. He stopped suddenly. A warm wave of fetid air washed over him. It reeked of pepper and the sour smell of rot.

Two red eyes shone in the darkness, moving toward him, rising . . . rising . . . growing larger until the bear stood over him, dwarfing him, opening its mouth to show its white teeth, roaring.

The roar filled Hunter's head. He froze, his limbs going heavy and numb, as he stared up at the roaring, reeking bruin glaring down at him, already tasting his flesh in its jaws.

"No!"

That snapped him out of his stupor. He raised the Henry, angling it up toward the bear's head, and fired.

He fired again, again, and again . . .

The bullets had no effect. He might as well have been throwing spitballs.

The bear stepped forward, lowering its head and those savage, white teeth toward Hunter's neck. Hunter tried to fire again, but the bear swatted the rifle out of his hands.

Men's shouts sounded beneath the bear's roars. Old Hec Prather leaped up onto the bear's back from behind. Gritting his teeth and scrunching up his face in desperation, the old graybeard wrapped his arms around the bruin's thick neck as though to strangle the beast.

The bear merely jerked its head and shoulders forward, and old Hec went flying head over heels off the bear's right shoulder, his shrill scream fading quickly.

Kentucky Wade leaped onto the bear's left shoulder, a pistol in his hand. He jutted the revolver toward the bear's neck, but the bear swatted Kentucky away in the darkness as though he were merely swatting a fly. As Chief Red Otter ran up on the bear's right side, aiming his Winchester at the bear's head, the bear lunged toward him, and with one swat of a long, hairy arm and paw with claws extended, sent the Indian flying off into the night, screaming and shooting his rifle skyward.

Hunter lay on the ground, gazing up in shock at the bruin looming over him. He tried to climb to his feet . . . to run . . . but it was as though he were glued to the ground. As the bear dropped to all fours and flung itself atop its prey, Hunter felt the powerful, hairy legs wrap around him in a deadly embrace. He felt the long teeth rip into his neck.

Hunter tried to struggle, to scream, but he couldn't move, couldn't seem to get his breath past his vocal cords.

"Hunter!" Annabelle cried.

Hunter opened his eyes to find himself sitting up in bed, propped on his elbows, panting. His entire body was bathed in cold sweat.

"It was just a dream, honey," Annabelle said, encircling

her arms around his neck and sliding her face up close to his right cheek. "Just a dream, just a dream," she soothed.

Hunter shook his head, sweat-damp hair jostling about his sweat-soaked shoulders. "Lordy me . . ."

"You were dreaming about the bear, weren't you?"

His heart only now beginning to slow, Hunter nodded. The images were still hurling around in his brain. He kept seeing old Hec Prather's red, scrunched-up face as the old man wrapped his arms around the bruin's neck as though to strangle him.

That made him chuckle, at least.

He brushed his arm across his sweaty upper lip.

"Just a dream, honey," Annabelle said, massaging his shoulders. She kissed his cheek. "Just a dream."

He'd had the dream . . . or nightmare, rather . . . because he'd been worried about the bruin returning to the ranch. If it had followed him, Kentucky, and Red Otter, to the 4-Box-B once, it could do it again.

He should have stayed up and kept watch.

Hunter flung his covers aside. "I'm gonna check the horses."

Chapter 14

All was well in the ranch yard. All was quiet.

Some of the horses slept standing, some lying down. They all awoke as Hunter approached. He set them at ease with a soothing voice, then returned to the house. He sank into a chair on the porch and rested the rifle across his thighs.

After the nightmare, he'd get no more sleep tonight.

Might as well sit out here and keep watch.

Time passed slowly. After the moon had set, the stars grew clearer for a brief time before the false dawn made them fade. The still night had a knife-edge chill, his breath pluming frostily in it.

Annabelle came out at five, carrying two steaming coffee mugs. She had her hair up and was wearing one of Hunter's old, falling-apart mackinaws. She sat on his lap, and they sipped their coffee together in silence until she'd finished her coffee and emptied the grounds over the porch rail.

"Don't go back out after him today," she said. "You didn't sleep. Stay home and rest."

"Can't do that, honey." Hunter pecked her cheek. "The

more time he's on the loose, the more cattle he'll kill. He tracks in a wide range. Soon, he'll find the herds on the winter pastures."

"He's not a demon from the other side." She shoved her face up close to his, sliding his long, blond hair back from his cheek. Her eyes crossed prettily, a little flirtatiously. "All right?"

Hunter smiled sheepishly. "I know, honey." But then he remembered that in the dream his bullets wouldn't pierce the bruin's hide.

He also remembered in the dream staring into the bruin's eyes. Only, when he looked deep into them, they were not the eyes of a bear. They were the eyes of a young man. They were the eyes of a young Union picket he'd gutted with his bowie knife.

It had been late—one or two in the morning—and he'd been sent out to blow up several supply wagons along the Tennessee River, using the Union's own Ketchum grenades.

The young man he'd killed had been one of those guarding the wagons.

But he hadn't died right away. He'd sobbed and pleaded for his life, horrified by the end that was fast approaching. Hunter had killed so many almost without thinking about it. That's what you had to do as a soldier. You had to numb yourself against killing. You killed for the greater good. You killed for the freedom of the Confederacy, to stamp out the uppity Yankee aggressors.

But as much as he'd wanted to ignore the innocent eyes staring up at him that moonlit night along the Tennessee, he found his mind recoiling in horror and revulsion at the fear he'd inflicted, the life he'd just taken.

The boy whispered so softly that Hunter could barely hear him.

"Ma an' Pa . . . never gonna . . . see 'em again. My lovely May!" The boy's eyes filled with tears. "We was gonna be married as soon as I went home!"

Hunter felt as though it were his own heart that had been pierced with the knife he kept honed to a razor's edge. He looked at the blood glistening low on the young soldier's blue-clad belly, wishing that he could take back what he'd just done, return this horrified soldier's life to him. Return Ma and Pa to him, and the girl, May, whom the boy had loved and intended to marry.

But Hunter hadn't been able to do that. The boy had died, sobbing and wailing for his family in Hunter's arms.

It had been that young soldier's eyes that Hunter had seen deep in the eyes of the killer grizzly.

Was it the young Union soldier who'd sent the bear from the other side?

The demon bear?

He jerked his head almost violently, blinking, ran his fingers over his eyes.

"I'd best get ready," he said. "We're pullin' out at six."

Annabelle wrapped her arms around his neck. "There's nothing I can do to make you stay?"

Hunter smiled.

"Are you sure?" she said, teasing, pressing her nose against his and gazing coquettishly into his eyes.

"No. I'm sorry, honey."

Annabelle pulled her head back and frowned. "I don't think I like what's happening to you, Hunter. I think you're getting obsessed. I think you've let the chief's *monetoo* theory get under your skin."

"No, I haven't," he said again sheepishly as he climbed up out of the chair.

Annabelle gazed up at him, not believing him. She took his coffee cup.

Hunter kissed her, then turned to the door. "Time to wash up."

"I'll fry some eggs," she said behind him, her voice troubled.

An hour later, in the chill morning with the sun just rising, Hunter took up the lead rope of the packhorse he'd outfitted to carry extra supplies.

As he did, Kentucky and Chief Red Otter led their own mounts, each from his own rough string—a blue roan and a steeldust stallion, respectively—out of the barn. The boy, Nathan, was forking hay into the corral's crib for the other horses, glancing longingly over at the men now congregating in the middle of the yard.

"Hunter?" the boy called over the fence, lowering his three-tined fork.

Hunter looked at him.

"I know how to ride now myself. Just ask Annabelle." Nathan jerked his chin toward Annabelle standing on the porch, still wearing Hunter's old coat and holding a fresh mug of coffee in both hands up close to her mouth.

She smiled.

"Need an extra hand today?" Nathan said. "I think I'd make a right reliable bear hunter."

Hunter glanced at Anna and then at Kentucky and Red Otter, both of whom were grinning.

Hunter rode over to the corral and said, "Already set your hat for a promotion, eh?"

The boy shrugged. He wore an overlarge wool coat and a green knit hat Hunter had seen Hec Prather wearing. Hunter made a mental note to buy the kid a proper coat and hat and a good pair of winter gloves on his next trip to town. A new pair of boots too. Hell, a whole new outfit for the long winter ahead.

"I hear from your teacher you make a right fine rider," he told the boy. "Tell you what—you cut your teeth on hostling for old Hec, give it a year or two, and I'll give you a horse and a saddle. In the meantime, work on your roping skills. Next year, I'll start you off on a rifle and we'll get you target practicing."

The boy's eyes widened. "Really?"

"A range rider needs to know how to shoot," Hunter said. "Especially in this country."

He pinched his hat brim to the boy, then reined Nasty Pete toward the ranch portal, putting the horse and the packhorse behind him into trots. He waved to Annabelle and she returned the gesture, lazily waving her arm high over her head. She was a hard woman to leave. Kentucky and Red Otter trotted through the portal behind Hunter. They as well as Hunter owned an air of solemnity in the wake of Noble Sanchez's death, as was to be expected.

They'd lived and worked and ate and slept in the same bunkhouse with the man for nearly a year. That made men as close as family.

Now both Kentucky and Red Otter wanted their share of the bear, even if Red Otter believed in his heart he'd thrown in to fight a demon from the other side.

Hunter didn't believe that. Well, maybe he partly did,

or he wouldn't have had the nightmare. But the rational part of his brain did not believe it, and he was going to cling to that.

It was far easier to kill a bear than a demon.

He put his mind to hunting the bear, deciding that if they didn't cut sign before they reached Devil's Rock, where they'd last seen the bruin, they'd continue to Devil's Rock and into the valley below it. If it hadn't rained or snowed up there overnight, they should be able to cut the grizzly's trail.

They followed Big Sandy Creek for several miles, then left the creek at a divide and followed Moony's Coulee straight north before swinging west through Big Yellow Gulch, so named for all the aspens carpeting the ridges to either side and which turned a bright golden yellow every fall.

They were just passing an old, moldering trapper's cabin on their left when Hunter spied movement on the ridge ahead and to his right, amidst the autumn-barren aspens. He and Kentucky and Red Otter checked their mounts down.

Hunter scrutinized the two riders, unable to make out distinguishing features until they were nearly to the bottom of the slope. The two riders, both middle-aged men, one tall and lean, the other shorter and with a potbelly, both wore winter wool coats and broadcloth trousers. The taller man wore a black, high crowned Stetson, while the shorter man, who also appeared a few years older and grayer than the other one, wore a gray felt *sombrero*.

He was also bespectacled, the silver frames of his glasses glinting in the late morning sunshine. They weren't rustlers, or Hunter missed his guess. Not market hunters either. There was something too polished, too civilized about them. Possibly stock detectives.

Hunter didn't know who they were, but he felt the tension leave his body. In these parts, when you ran into other riders you didn't know, a man just naturally got his blood a little up, and he kept his hand near his hogleg. But these men didn't look like a threat to either him or his herd.

As the two men approached Hunter's party, Hunter noted the moon-and-star badges pinned to their coats and was further put at ease, though his curiosity grew.

"Afternoon," Hunter said.

"Afternoon," said the taller, slightly younger fella with a cordial dip of his chin. As he and the other man drew rein just beyond Hunter, Kentucky, and Red Otter, the tall man said, "I'm Bill Talon and this is my partner, Ted Revis. Deputy U.S. Marshals out of Bismarck."

Hunter introduced him and his own small party, and said, "You're a little off the beaten path out here, aren't you?"

"Just a little," said the older federal, Ted Revis, with a wry smile. "We're on the trail of the men who robbed several banks south of Bismarck nigh on three weeks ago now. We trailed 'em into the Black Hills just north of Deadwood. They seem to know the mountains. At least, a whole lot better than we do."

"We lost their trail three days ago," Talon said, leaning forward and crossing his wrists on his saddle horn. "We're short on supplies, so we're heading back to Tigerville. Gonna send a telegram to the home office and wait for instructions."

"You're sure they're still here?" Kentucky asked the

two federals. "Maybe they've headed over to Wyoming. Most owlhoots do, sooner or later."

Revis shook his head. "We heard they hole up in the hills, in some isolated spot—nobody knows where—till their trail cools. Then they head over to Wyoming and into Colorado and New Mexico for the winter and spend the loot they stole. They're the Axel Hingham Gang out of Wyoming.

"Five of 'em. Been around awhile. Notorious bunch. Mean and wily. Really cover their tracks. They prey on little prairie banks that can't do much to defend themselves. Rob a whole string of 'em, one town after another, generally after harvest and beef sales have been made, then head into the hills and then, like I said, south to Colorado and New Mexico for the winter."

"Where you men headed?" Talon asked.

"We're hunting a rogue griz. He's been preying on my beef, turned man-killer yesterday."

"Sorry to hear that," Revis said.

"So am I, Marshal. So am I."

"Watch your backs," Talon said, glancing from Hunter to Red Otter to Kentucky sitting his roan to Hunter's right. "Hingham and his boys know they're being hunted, so if they spy you on their trail, they're likely to shoot first and ask questions later."

"Fair warning," Hunter said. "We'll keep our eyes skinned."

"You do that," Talon said, pinching his hat brim and reining his big calico to his left. "And good luck with the bear."

Hunter nodded.

When the two marshals had ridden on, Hunter, Kentucky, and Red Otter shared dubious glances.

Chapter 15

Annabelle reined her horse up in front of the old miner's cabin and smiled in fond remembrance.

The cabin hunched here in the spruces and pines just south of the mine shaft in which Hunter had hidden his gold cache before it had been stolen by Annabelle's brother, Cass. The outlaw sheriff, Frank Stillwell, had collapsed the mine on Hunter and Annabelle, and they'd been trapped in the shaft for a torturous albeit brief time before they'd discovered a way out through a ceiling flue.

That had been a close one. Annabelle had thought for sure that she and Hunter were going to die there inside that mountain, before they'd even gotten a chance to get married. Of course, Annabelle could think of no one she'd rather die with than Hunter Buchanon, but she'd preferred it be long after they'd raised a passel of healthy children and lived out their lives together. Not when they were still young and unmarried, not at the hands of the evil Stillwell, in a mountain where no one would ever find them.

Now she studied the cabin and remembered a far better time than the collapse of that shaft. She recalled all the afternoons and early evenings that she and Hunter had met here in secret. It had been their hideout, so to speak. Their trysting place. Since her father had disapproved of Hunter because he'd fought for the Confederacy, they'd had to meet on the sly. In a way, she'd liked it better that way. It had lent an air of mystery and derring-do to their burgeoning romance.

She hadn't been out here for two years. She'd been too busy helping rebuild the Buchanon ranch. The place hadn't changed much. Maybe a little more moss on the slumping, shake-shingled roof, a little less chinking between the weathered-gray, hand-adzed logs. The little front stoop, carpeted with red and yellow leaves, had a pronounced list to it, more than Annabelle remembered.

Still pretty much the same though.

While she had many fond memories here of the beginning of her and Hunter's romance, times were better now. Now, after the old trouble, they'd been married and they'd rebuilt the ranch. Of course, Shep and Tye were dead, and old Angus was worse for the wear, but, despite the bear, the future looked bright.

She turned to gaze off along the valley floor to the north. The good memories faded under the cloud of what she was doing out here in the first place. She hadn't ridden out here only to visit the cabin. She was on her way home.

She shook her head.

No, not home. She would never again see her father's Broken Heart Ranch as her home. Her home was the 4-Box-B. The Broken Heart was where her father, the man who had Buchanon blood on his hands, resided with her brother Cass. For some reason she felt compelled to journey back there, to see her father one last time. If he wasn't already dead, that was. Cass had sounded as if the old reprobate had one foot in the grave.

Anna swung the mare around and booted her north along the valley floor, along a shaggy, two-track wagon trail nearly covered with aspen leaves fallen from the forest lining both sides of the trail. As she rode, she wondered why, after all this time, she was finally returning to the Broken Heart. Especially when she'd vowed to never see the place or her father ever again. To not even think of Graham Ludlow as her own blood.

Was it because of Cass?

When he'd visited the previous morning, he'd seemed lonely and wayward. Maybe it was for Cass she was visiting.

She shook her head, making the horsehair thong of her hat jostle across her face along with the long wavelets of thick copper hair tumbling down the shoulders of her blue plaid winter coat.

No, it wasn't for Cass. Partly for Cass. But deep inside her she felt compelled to see her father one last time. She had no idea why. He was not her father anymore. Still, when Cass had told her he was dying, she'd felt the urge, suppressed from her consciousness at first, to see him one last time.

That urge made her feel guilty. The man had burned the 4-Box-B and killed Hunter's brothers. At least, he'd ordered it done, and he'd had a hand in most of it too.

Ludlow had Buchanon blood on his hands. Which meant he also had her, Annabelle's, blood on his hands. She felt as though she were betraying Hunter and Angus by visiting the old killer again.

Still, she found herself continuing to ride north and

then west, picking up the old ranch trail she knew so well. A half hour later she reined up on the hill just south of the ranch and stared down into the yard spread out before her.

She gasped at the startling sight.

The place looked abandoned. Of course it didn't help that the barn she'd inadvertently burned when she'd been fighting off her brother, who'd threatened to bullwhip her, still lay in a large, charred mound on the yard's near side, facing the house that lay up a low rise to the east.

Weeds had grown up around the buildings. Boardwalks fronting the buildings looked half-rotten and were covered with leaves and dust. Pig's ear had grown up as high as the highest rails of all three corrals. One barn door hung askew from its metal track, the top boards pulling free of the rest.

Even the house, a sprawling white frame building with a wrap-around porch and several gables as well as two large, fieldstone hearths abutting both sides of the place, needed paint, as did the white picket fence ringing it. Some storm had ripped away shingles, leaving bare patches. Around the lodge, the grass was tall and brown, curling over on itself now after several frosts, and speckled with wild rye and thistle.

No one was about the place. A few horses stood languidly in one corral. Otherwise, there was no sign of life.

Cass had led Annabelle to believe he'd been keeping up the place, since their father had run off nearly all the hired hands. Obviously, Cass had been lying. No one appeared to be keeping up anything at the Broken Heart headquarters.

Now she realized how aptly named the place had been

by the rancher, stricken with a broken heart after his wife
and two daughters had died from diphtheria, who'd originally homesteaded here before selling the place to
Ludlow, who'd tripled his holdings in his first three years.

Obviously, that Graham Ludlow was dead.

Annabelle wondered if the current one was as well.

She booted the mare down the hill and through the
rotting portal and into the yard. Looking around, she felt
heartbroken herself by the dilapidated condition of the
place she'd for nineteen years called home. The ranch may
no longer be her home, but she couldn't deny having
grown up here and having some fond memories of that
privileged childhood. As she put the horse up to the house,
she shook her head to clear the emotion beginning to swell
in her throat.

*This is no longer your home. This is that killer's home.
Your home is the 4-Box-B.*

She swung down from the calico's back, slipped the
cinch and the bit, and tied the bridle reins to one of the
two wrought-iron hitchracks fronting the cobbled walk
stretching beyond the gate in the picket fence. The gate
wasn't latched, and when she shoved it aside, she saw that
it hung loose on its rusty hinges.

She shook her head, and, frowning curiously, strode up
the walk, which had buckled in places from last winter's
cold and had not been repaired. She mounted the porch,
tripped the latch, and shoved open the heavy, iron-banded
front door with a brass doorknob in the shape of a horse's
head, the unoiled hinges squawking like angry birds.

Again, she gasped.

The parlor lay before her. It was no longer the neat and

tidy sitting room she remembered. The furniture had been rearranged, and it was covered with clothes and newspapers and bits of tack and plates and cups and empty vegetable tins. Also, whiskey and beer bottles, and several over-flowing ashtrays, one overturned on the Persian rug on the floor.

Where was her father's longtime and very loyal house-keeper, Chang? Besides cooking and doing laundry, Chang had always kept the place neat and tidy, disdaining a mess or even a single grain of dust anywhere in the house!

The air smelled sour, downright putrid in fact. As well as musty and heavily laced with the lingering tang of pent-up tobacco smoke.

More debris littered the fireplace hearth, including two mismatched revolvers and a box of cartridges. A pair of boots lay on the floor in front of the big, leather chair that had been pulled up close to the fireplace and was, appar-ently, much in use. The cracked and moisture-stained leather seat was bowed inward by the rump that had parked there, likely for hours on end, alone. The rest of the furni-ture was so covered with miscellaneous clutter, it would have been impossible for anyone to occupy it.

Annabelle looked through the parlor toward the kitchen, which she could see enough of to conclude that it, too, was a wreck.

"Cass?" she called.

Only the house's eerie, sepulchral silence responded.

She wanted to call to her father, but she didn't want to call him "Father." Not knowing what else to call him—Ludlow?—she called for Cass again.

She moved through the parlor to the stairs, placed a

hand on the newel post, and called up the stairwell for her brother. Her voice echoed in the silence.

The silence was relieved by a thudding sound coming from the second story.

"Cass?" she called again, and started climbing the stairs, which were littered with dust and grime, the grime overlaid with footprints. No one had swept the staircase in months.

She stopped at the top of the stairs and gazed straight down the dim hall. Six doors faced each other from both sides of the hall. The first door on the left was partly open. That was Graham Ludlow's room. That was the room from which the thudding was coming from. Grunts sounded from inside as well. Grunting and heavy, raspy breaths.

She moved forward, angling toward the door. She stopped and slowly slid the door open, canting her head to see inside.

Graham Ludlow stood on the other side of the room, in grimy longhandle bottoms without a top. He held a shotgun butt-down against the floor. He was crouched over the double boars of the weapon, apparently trying to stick the end of the barrel inside his mouth while attempting to use his bare right toe to trip the triggers.

"Pa!" Annabelle reacted automatically, stepping into the room. "What in blazes do you think you're doing?"

He got the end of the barrel inside his mouth, then gagged and, unable to hook his toe through the trigger guard, fell back against the window, red-faced and breathless, his gray hair long and greasy. His face was so bloated that for a moment Annabelle didn't even recognize him. His torso was as white as flour, the flesh sagging down toward his bulbous belly, as round and nearly as hard as that of a woman eight months pregnant.

Annabelle grabbed the shotgun out of his hand, broke it open, and removed the shells. "What on earth, Pa? You're trying to *kill* yourself?"

Ludlow was still breathing as though he'd run a mile barefoot. He shook his sagging head, his eyes pouchy and bloodshot. "I'd rather . . . be dead . . . than let you . . . see me like . . . *this!*"

"*Good Lord!*" Annabelle lowered the shotgun and studied her father, her mouth twisting a sour expression. She hadn't expected to find him in a good way, but certainly not as bad as this. A mere shadow of the man he'd once been. A pathetic one at that—so pathetic that he wanted to annihilate himself.

But, then, why had she stopped him?

She looked from his wretched, self-tortured gaze to the shotgun in her hand.

Yes, why stop him?

She tossed the shotgun and shells on the bed and glanced around the room, wrinkling her nose at the putrid stench. It smelled like rancid sweat and urine. The room was even more of a wreck than the parlor, the rumpled bed sheets and quilts twisted and lying askew, half the sweat-stained mattress showing, clothes strewn everywhere, medicine and whiskey bottles cluttering the dresser along with glasses and an ashtray overflowing with the brown fat worms of Ludlow's cigars.

Anna turned back to her father. Her horror and disgust must have been plain on her face, for the decrepit old man averted his gaze and brushed an arthritic fist across his nose.

"Where's Cass?" she asked him.

Chapter 16

"Haven't seen him since last night," Ludlow said.

Annabelle turned to leave the room, then stopped and looked at the shotgun on the bed. She looked at her father. For the life of her, she did not know why she plucked the shotgun off the bed and took it with her as she walked down the hall toward Cass's room.

She certainly didn't care if the man killed himself.

Did she?

She knocked on Cass's closed door. "Cass?"

Nothing.

"Are you in there?"

From behind the door came a muffled groan.

Annabelle opened the door. She winced. Cass's room was in much the same state as the rest of the house. A mess. Cass lay on the bed, buried under sheets and quilts. He lay belly-down, arms thrown out to each side. All she could see of his head was the burlap sack he wore over it.

A half-empty bottle stood on a chair beside the bed. A cigarette butt lay on the chair beside the bottle. It had burned a two-inch-long worm of gray ash before going out.

"Cass? For God's sakes!"

Annabelle walked into the room. She leaned the shotgun against the wall, then sat on the edge of the bed and placed her hand on her brother's back and jostled him. "What on earth is going on here, Cass? I thought you were keeping the place up."

"I do my best, Annabelle," he said, keeping his eyes closed. "I'm all alone. Just me now."

"Where's Chang?"

"Gone. Pa ran him off with most of the others, except for Ernie Sneed. Chang bought a train ticket for Frisco, left the premises cussing in Chinese." Cass laughed miserably. "Pa—miserable, contrary cuss!"

"Is drinking all you do?"

"What the hell else is there to do?"

Annabelle just stared in shock at her brother, shaking her head slowly. "You need to get out of here, Cass. If you stay here, you're going to die. Along with him." She canted her head to indicate their father's room.

Cass turned his masked face to her. His eyes shown red through the holes cut in the sack. "Look at me. Where am I gonna go?"

"Why don't you look at you, Cass? When's the last time you looked at yourself without the mask?"

"I don't look at myself without the mask, Annabelle. Why do that to myself? You know how I look! You know what that fire did to me!"

"No, I don't." Annabelle reached over and tugged the mask off his head.

"Dammit, Anna—stop!" Cass reached for the mask but, hungover as he was, he was too slow. Annabelle let it drop to the floor.

"It was a long time ago, Cass. Look there. You don't look all that bad at all. Why, you're nearly healed!"

It wasn't quite true, but Cass looked considerably better than he obviously imagined he did. There was considerable scarring around his face, but it wasn't hideous scarring at all. Cass looked more like how Annabelle remembered than she would have suspected. More than he probably suspected as well.

"Look here"—she reached out to touch an oily, unkept but full lock of his curly brown hair—"your hair has grown back." It was thin in only a few places.

Cass blinked up at her, frowning uncertainly, as though wondering if she were toying with him. He raised his right hand, brushed fingers across his cheek.

Annabelle rose from the bed, walked over to the door, and plucked the mirror off the wall above the washstand. She brought it back to the bed and gave it to Cass.

"See for yourself."

Reluctantly, Cass accepted the mirror. He raised it slowly, regarding it as though it were an evil talisman. He glanced at Annabelle once more, then slid his gaze to the mirror.

He frowned as though puzzled. Again, he raised his hand to his face, touched his forehead above his left eye, and ran two fingers down his nose.

"I'll be," he said, an optimistic light entering his eyes. "Nothin' like . . . nothin' like"—he shifted his gaze to Annabelle—"I expected."

"What'd I tell you?"

"I'll be damned. I mean, I'm nothin' to write home about . . . a far cry from what I was, but . . . not bad. Least-ways, not as bad as I thought." Cass looked at Annabelle again, his mouth shaping a smile. "I don't look like some kinda circus freak anymore. I healed!"

Annabelle smiled. "Darn right you healed."

Cass rolled onto his back, propped himself on his elbows, and brushed both hands up and down his face again, smiling. "I'll be damned!"

Annabelle glanced at the shotgun and then turned to Cass, frowning. "Cass, I found Pa trying to stick the end of that greener in his mouth."

"Yeah, he does that from time to time. I've had to wrestle it away from him a couple of times myself." Cass arched a brow at Annabelle. "I'm surprised you went to the trouble."

"I am too. Not sure what came over me."

"Annabelle, we both know what he's done. But he's still your father. Deny it all you want, but it's true."

"I suppose it is, but it doesn't mean I don't hate him for who he is. I thought you said he was dying. It appears to me he only wishes he were dead."

"He had a bad spell the other night. I fetched the doc from town. He thinks Pa had a stroke. He's probably had several. Pa couldn't move for two days. I had to spoon-feed him. Then, just this morning, I went in there and saw him rummaging around in his closet for a picture of Ma. I saw he'd even gone downstairs to fetch a bottle." Cass chuckled, shook his head.

Annabelle patted his knee and rose from the bed. "Come on. Get up."

"Huh? Why?"

"We're gonna get this place cleaned up, you and me."

* * *

They started on the parlor, which took them well over an hour to shovel out and straighten up and clean.

Next, they tackled the kitchen, Cass washing dishes while Anna threw out, straightened up, organized, swept, sponged, and mopped.

From there, they went to Cass's room and stripped the bed. They went to Ludlow's room and stripped his bed as well. While Cass straightened up both rooms, Annabelle hauled the sour bedding out to the wash shack flanking the house, heated water, and boiled the linen in lye soap a good, long time, stirring it with a broom handle.

By the time she got the bedding rung out and hung up to dry, she was exhausted. She turned to start back to the house and stopped. Cass stood on the porch, near the house's open back door. How strange it was to see him without his mask. His hair was as long and curly as a girl's. He smiled as he held two cups of coffee. He raised one.

"Join me for a cup o' mud."

"Why not?"

Anna walked up the porch steps and accepted the cup from Cass. They sat in wicker chairs and sipped the coffee, staring out over the rolling, pine-peppered hills to the southeast, taking in the depth and breadth of their father's holdings. So much wasted land now, peppered with untended cattle.

"What are your plans, Cass?" she asked.

Cass grimaced, shook his head. "I don't reckon I made any." He raised a hand to his face. "I reckon I was a prisoner of that mask. Haven't looked at myself once without it on since . . . you know . . . since it happened."

"You're still a good-looking man, Cass. A few scars give a man seasoning. You'll find a woman and settle down, raise a family. Give it time."

Cass leaned forward, holding his coffee cup in both hands between his legs. He sighed and stretched his neck likely kinked up from all of his idle hours. "We sure could use a woman around here. I didn't realize that till you showed up."

Annabelle looked at him. "Leave here," she said solemnly. "This place is a losing proposition. He's ruined it. He's ruined himself. Don't let him ruin you."

"It's my home, Annabelle."

"Come over to the 4-Box-B. We'd love to have—"

Annabelle stopped when shuffling footsteps sounded from inside the house.

The footsteps grew louder, along with the creaking of floorboards, until Graham Ludlow appeared in the doorway. He'd pulled a robe on over his longhandles, and he'd put socks on.

He stood there in the doorway, a stoop-shouldered, wasted, gray, unshaven monster-like figure staring straight out into space. In his trembling right hand, he held a cup of coffee.

Cass stood. "Pa, you take my chair. I was just about to go into the kitchen and see if I can find something for my sweet tooth."

Cass walked over to the door and patted the old man on the shoulder as he sidled past him into the house.

Annabelle turned away from Ludlow. She wished Cass hadn't left her alone with him. She had nothing to say to him, as she knew he had nothing to say to her.

In the corner of her eye, she saw him turn to her, stare at her for a time. Then in his slow, shuffling way, using the cane in his left hand, came over and sat heavily down in the chair Cass had vacated.

Annabelle felt her shoulders tighten.

She stared straight ahead, saying nothing, hoping he would do the same.

He sipped his coffee for a time and then he turned slowly to her and said, "It's good to see you, Daughter."

"Please don't call me that," she said tightly.

He turned his head forward again and gave a long, ragged sigh.

She turned to him, then, anger brewing in her, said, "What do you expect?"

He closed his eyes, drew a breath. When he opened his eyes again, he said in a low, raspy voice, "I was hoping you might forgive me before I die."

"Don't count on it," she said.

He arched his brows. "Might do us both some good."

"Like I said," she replied, turning her head forward again and hardening her jaws in anger, feeling a flush rising in her cheeks, "don't count on it."

"I know what I did, Anna. Lord knows since my ticker started giving out, I've had plenty of time to think about it." Ludlow closed a hand around his cup, squeezing. "I don't really know who that man was . . . the man who started that war. I don't think . . . at least, I don't want to believe . . . that I am that man anymore."

Anna sneered at him, smiling coldly and shaking her head. "You are. Oh, you still are, Pa."

"A man can change, Anna."

"A man can feel guilty for what he's done, but it doesn't change the fact of what you did. You murdered two young men and burned their ranch, leaving their father and brother homeless while they rebuilt. A man can want his daughter to forgive him, but it doesn't change the fact of what that man did to her and the man she loves. What you did can never be forgiven."

Ludlow drew his mouth corners down, nodded his head twice, and stared off into the southeastern distance once more.

"With that," Anna said, rising from the chair, her voice quavering with barely bridled rage, "I will take my leave."

"Thank you for coming. For all your hard work."

"I did it for my brother."

"Just the same." Ludlow looked up at her and gave a thin smile. "It was good to see you. I hope you'll stop by again soon."

"No." Anna shook her head resolutely and started for the door. "This is the last time you'll see me. I've encouraged Cass to leave this ruin of a place, and that's all I can do, so I'm done here."

She moved through the door into the kitchen. Cass stood at the food preparation table, his coffee on the table before him. He looked at her solemnly.

Annabelle set her still half-full cup on the table and looked at her brother. "I hope you'll come to your senses and leave here, Cass. You have a standing invitation to the 4-Box-B. We've had bear trouble. We lost a hand. You could take his place."

Cass didn't say anything.

Anna turned and walked back through the house and outside.

Earlier, when she'd realized she'd be here longer than she'd intended, she'd stripped the saddle from the mare and turned her into the corral. Now she crossed the yard, swung open the corral gate, roped and saddled Ruthie, and rode her out of the ranch yard.

As she passed out through the portal, she found herself crying like a baby. It made her hatred for her father even keener.

Chapter 17

Hunter, Kentucky Wade, and Chief Red Otter scoured the hills around Crow's Nest Peak for two and a half days before they finally came upon bear sign—a pile of relatively fresh scat, cake-size and tubular, with hair and bits of bone woven through it.

Cow hair, no doubt. Hunter's party had come across three more dead cows over the past couple of days. The cows had been dead for weeks, which meant the bruin was moving closer to the ranch to feed because it was following the herds that Hunter and his men had gradually moved down to the winter pastures.

They found the scat at the mouth of a side canyon and followed the paw prints into the canyon. Hunter had stalked deer in the canyon and knew it to be a box canyon, a steep stone ridge rising at the other end, beyond a dogleg and roughly a quarter mile from the entrance.

Hunter's heart quickened. The hair beneath his shirt collar bristled. The bruin was close. He could sense it. The scat had been so fresh he could smell the pepper in his nose.

They rode northeast, a shallow creek rippling through

barren cottonwoods and aspens on their right. A pine-peppered ridge rose on their left. It was late in the afternoon, and the light angling over them from over the riders' left shoulders owned a copper cast.

The creek made a musical tinkling sound where it rippled over its stony bed to the right. The stones and stream edges were rimmed with frost from previous cold nights. Blackbirds cawed in the spidery branches over the water. Not ominous in and of themselves; under the circumstances the creek and the birds filled Hunter with a dark foreboding.

He unsheathed his Henry, said just above a whisper, "This is a box canyon, gentlemen. If he's in here, we have him."

Riding his steeldust stallion to Hunter's right, Red Otter kept his stony features aimed straight ahead. To Hunter's left, Kentucky, forking a blue roan, cast him a nervous grin beneath his heavy, drooping mustache.

"Remember," Hunter said as they rounded the dogleg, "get as many into him as you can."

As he continued riding, the peak at the canyon's far end loomed ahead, very close and roughly arrow-shaped and painted bright, lens-clear gold by the westering sun. Boulders and shrubs pocking its face cast lengthening purple shadows in sharp contrast to the sun's brightness.

The riders had just cleared the dogleg when Kentucky grunted and grabbed his right shoulder, jerking back in his saddle. A rifle report followed a second later, screeching its echo around the canyon. Casting his glance ahead, Hunter saw pale smoke puff about a quarter-distance up the ridge from the bottom, atop a pile of loosely strewn boulders and stunt pines and cedars.

Kentucky rolled off his roan's right hip to hit the ground with a grunt on his back, the roan jerking forward with a start. He rolled onto his side, cursing.

"Ambush!" Hunter said, and whipped his right leg over his saddle horn, dropping to the ground and ramming the Henry's butt plate against Nasty Pete's rear end. "Drift, Pete!"

As Red Otter reined his stallion off the trail's right side and behind a stone outcropping rising among the cottonwoods lining the stream, Hunter ran back to where Kentucky lay groaning on the trail, clutching his right shoulder with his gloved left hand. Blood oozed up between his elk skin-clad fingers.

Another bullet plumed dust to Kentucky's left, narrowly missing Hunter's right calf.

Red Otter dismounted his steeldust, turned the horse, and slapped it back the way it had come. He dropped to a knee, raised his Winchester, and sent two rounds screeching toward the top of the boulder pile.

"Come on, Kentucky!" Hunter thrust his hand down to the ailing cowboy. "Getting you to cover!"

Kentucky held up his left hand. Hunter grabbed it, heaved the man to his feet, then wrapped his arm around him, ushering him quickly off the trail's right side and behind a broad-boled Ponderosa pine. Kentucky gave his back to the tree and slid down to his butt, grimacing with pain.

Hunter edged a look around the pine toward the boulder pile just as another round buzzed eerily and thwacked the front of the tree, spraying bark into Hunter's eyes.

As Red Otter returned fire, Hunter lowered his head and fingered grit from his eyes, blinking. Hunter turned to Red Otter. "I got a feelin' that's them bandits those two marshals warned us about!"

Red Otter triggered another round toward the boulder pile and glanced over his shoulder at Hunter. "I got a feelin' you're right, boss!"

"Damn!" Hunter turned to Kentucky slouched to his right. "How bad you hit?"

Kentucky winced. He'd lost his hat, and his dark brown hair was sweat-matted to his head, showing the marks of his topper. "I think it's just a flesh wound."

"Let me take a look."

"I'll be all right. Why don't you fellas give them bush-whackin' sons of Satan the what-for for me?" Kentucky coughed and spat trail grit from his lips.

Hunter untied the billowy red neckerchief from around his neck and folded it into squares. "Don't you worry, partner—we're gonna do just that. Nobody ambushes one of my men and gets away with it!"

He pressed the neckerchief against the bloody wound in Kentucky's shoulder, up close to the top, and placed Kentucky's left hand over it. "Keep pressing down on that."

He edged another look around the pine toward the top of the boulder pile. The shooting had stopped—the bush-whackers' as well as Red Otter's. The Indian knelt on the far side of the trail and forward a few feet from Hunter, keeping his Winchester taut against his shoulder, waiting for a target to show itself.

"Did you see how many?" Hunter asked him.

"Five, I think."

"It's them, then."

"Yeah." Red Otter glanced over his shoulder at Hunter

again, his heavy-lidded eyes slitted seriously. "How do you want to play it?"

Hunter cast his gaze toward the boulder pile again. A man's hatted head moved between two of the rocks near the top of the pile. He glimpsed the bespectacled face of another bushwhacker a second later, between two other boulders, before the man drew his head back out of sight.

Hunter turned to Red Otter. "There's an old mine up there. That must be what the bank robbers are using for a hideout. Hardly anyone knows about this canyon or the mine. I think me and my brothers are the only ones to have hunted in here over the past ten years. But they found it, all right, and now they've got the high ground."

"High ground, steep odds," Red Otter warned.

Steep odds, maybe, but those bandits had made it Hunter's fight when they'd shot one of his men.

"Maybe, but we'll work around them. You head over to the other side of the stream and work up along the water. I'm gonna take to the ridge over yonder"—Hunter jerked his head to indicate the ridge behind him— "and work my way around from there."

He sleeved sweat from his forehead. "One thing we have in our favor."

Red Otter glanced at them again. "What's that?"

"The light's behind us, facing *them*."

"Still steep odds."

"You're your customary cheery self today, Chief—you know that?"

Red Otter cast a wry grin at Hunter over his left shoulder.

"Let's do it!"

As Red Otter ran crouching out from behind his boulder

and into the cottonwoods, drawing the bandits' fire, Hunter turned to Kentucky. "You gonna be all right, partner?"

"I'll be just fine if you scrub the kitchen floor with those scoundrels!"

"All right." Hunter patted the man's left shoulder, then, rising, stepped over Kentucky and ran into the trees and rocks, heading for the forested ridge beyond.

Red Otter crossed the creek via a shallow, rocky ford.

As he did, he glanced toward the end of the canyon, but the cottonwoods blocked his view of the shooters, and thus their view of him as well. He stepped into the thick evergreen forest just up the slope from the creek and began moving northeast, toward where the robbers were holed up atop the boulder pile.

He moved deliberately, quietly, pausing every few steps to look around and listen. He was well aware that danger could come from any quarter—be it man danger or bear danger. He had not forgotten for even a minute that their real quarry was the *otshee-monetoo*—a demon needing to be sent back to the otherworldly hell it had been spawned in.

Red Otter cared for the big Southern Rebel, Hunter Buchanon, more than he'd ever cared for another white man. He was old enough to be Hunter's father, and maybe that's why he felt fatherly toward the young man, who still had some boy in him. You could see it when he was with his woman, Annabelle. Like a boy, he could never mask his intense feelings for his wife. You could see a bit of the child in him when he joked and teased with her and his men and his father, who was much like Hunter.

Hunter and Angus took an Indian-like, child-like delight in humor.

You could also see the boy in the big rancher when you tried to convince him he was endangered by something he had had no previous experience with or had been taught about. He did, however, have respect for the ancient beliefs. Red Otter sensed this in him. Hunter had been raised among ancient folk beliefs in the mountains of the Old South. For that reason, being told that he'd been targeted by something as slippery as an evil spirit made him angry and sullen, like a boy parrying with his own fears.

Deep down, he suspected what Red Otter had told him was true. However, the rational man in him—and the fearful man—would not let him fully accept it.

Red Otter walked along the edge of the forest and then left the forest to walk among the boulders that had likely rolled down from the top of the main pile. Now, weaving his way among these large granite rocks, he could approach the crest of the boulder pile without being seen.

Unless the robbers had suspected his and Hunter's ploy to steal around them and were patrolling the rocks . . .

Red Otter slowed his pace and moved even more deliberately, looking around him and listening, sniffing the air for the smell of man sweat. Slowly, he climbed the rise, stepping out from the concealment of one boulder and into the concealment of another, climbing steadily toward the top of the pile and, presumably, the mine Hunter had mentioned.

He stepped along the side of a boulder, brushing his right fingers across the cracked and crenelated face. He held his Winchester snug against his right hip and angled upward, his thumb on the hammer. He came to the edge of the boulder and stopped suddenly.

Having glanced along the very edge of the rock, he'd seen something dark. Part of a man's hat?

He held very still, listening, caressing the rifle's hammer with his thumb. When the grinding gravel of a footstep did not come, and he saw no shadow slide along the ground to his right, he stepped out from the boulder quickly, aiming the Winchester straight out from his right hip, index finger drawn taut against the trigger.

A raucous screeching assaulted his ears, freezing him and making his blood run cold.

He increased the pressure on the trigger but held fire when he saw the blackbird sitting atop the rock just ahead of him, maybe ten feet away, the bird as large as a small dog, regarding him boldly, angrily, giving another *caw-caw-caw*, then spreading its wings and taking flight.

Red Otter drew a calming breath, feeling his heart slow.

It picked up again when a man stepped suddenly out from the opposite side of the boulder he himself had just left the protection of. The man was as surprised to see Red Otter as Red Otter was surprised to see him.

He was a broad-shouldered white man with blue eyes beneath a shabby brown slouch hat, and a thin blond beard. He, too, held a Winchester. It took him a second or two longer to recover from the shock of seeing Red Otter than it took Red Otter to recover from the shock of seeing him.

That extra second gave Red Otter time to take the man soundlessly by sweeping up his big bowie knife from the sheath on his left hip and slashing it across the bearded man's throat. Blood spurted as the man staggered back-ward, dropping his rifle, clutching his throat, and staring at Red Otter in horror. He half-turned, opened his mouth to scream, but only gagging sounds issued.

The chief sheathed his bowie, then slammed the butt of his Winchester atop the dying man's head, laying him out in a fast-dying, quivering mass.

"Good night, White Eyes."

Red Otter continued forward.

Chapter 18

Hunter had gained the side of the boulder pile and was climbing.

He was ten feet up from the base when a shadow slid over him from above. He ducked into a niche in the boulders and waited, holding the Henry straight up and down in his hands.

The sun was sliding lower, and thick shadows were overtaking the canyon. The light that reflected off the canyon's back wall, a towering bastion of granite, was fading by the second.

The man's fading shadow slid down the boulders. Hunter heard a boot kick a stone. The man stopped and cursed under his breath. Hunter saw the stone roll down through a path between the rocks ahead and to his right.

The shadow continued sliding until the man himself, a slender figure in a bullet-crowned cream hat, caught up to it. He'd just stepped into Hunter's view when he stopped suddenly, maybe sensing Hunter's presence.

He whipped around, his long, black duster fanning out around him.

He cocked the Henry rifle in his hands but fired a full

second after Hunter's bullet had cut into the man's belly, knocking him backward into the rocks. His own bullet flew wide and to Hunter's left, spanging shrilly off a boulder and kicking up a ringing in Hunter's ears.

Hunter stepped out of his niche in time to see another man running toward him down a corridor in the rocks.

"Down here!" the man called over his shoulder, unsheathing the two matched Colts on his hips as he turned his head back forward.

The man stopped when he saw Hunter, his eyes widening. He had the Colts half raised.

Hunter snugged the Henry firmly against his shoulder and aimed down the barrel at the man's face. He was a thickset gent with a salt-and-pepper beard and sagging belly. His eyes flashed challengingly as he eyed Hunter's Henry.

"Drop 'em," Hunter chewed out.

The man's eyes flickered doubtfully. He glanced down at the Colts in his hands, then turned his head to gaze back up toward the top of the boulder pile behind him.

"You got him, Axel?"

Hunter's gut tightened. A man stood atop the boulder pile, aiming a rifle straight out from his right shoulder, angling the barrel down toward Hunter. Another man stood a little lower down on the rocks, crouched over the rifle he was aiming out from his right hip, grinning.

Axel Hingham, a big, bearded man in a buffalo fur coat and black slouch hat, and with a quirley dangling from one corner of his mouth, smiled then too. The glasses on his nose winked in the fading sunlight.

"Yep, I done have him dead to rights," Hingham said.

Hunter knew it was true. A cold stone dropped in his belly.

A loud animal wail sounded suddenly, filling the canyon with its tooth-gnashing din. The sound had come from behind Hingham, who wheeled suddenly and screamed as something tall and broad and cinnamon brown loomed over him, lifting its head and casting another roar at the fading sky. The outlaw leader was so frightened that instead of firing his rifle, he screamed again in terror and raised it to swing like a club.

The bear merely batted it aside, then engulfed Hingham in his long, shaggy arms, backing away with the screaming and kicking Hingham pressed up snug to the bruin's chest, hugging him in a sadistic lover's embrace.

"Good Lord!" yelled the man standing lower down on the rocks, having swung around to see what Hunter had just seen.

A young man with long, blond hair, he fired his rifle, then ran up the rocks, hopscotching boulders and bellowing.

Hunter turned back to the man before him. Just then the man, having been staring at the unlikely spectacle above, remembered Hunter and turned back toward him, eyes wide. He started to raise the Colts again, then, seeing the Henry trained on his forehead, dropped them as though they were hot potatoes.

His features were doughy pale, and, glancing back over his shoulder, half-raised his hands palm out. "What the hell . . . what the hell . . . was *that*?" He acted as though he thought maybe Hunter had something to do with the bruin's sudden appearance.

Hunter sprang forward, whipped the Henry's barrel across the man's right temple, laying him out cold. Then he ran up the rocks, leaping from one boulder to another, his heart racing now as he continued to hear the bear's roars and now two men's screams.

Hunter had the bruin!

He leaped a gap between two boulders, then another. He misjudged the distance. His left boot slipped off the edge of the opposite rock. Down he plunged, losing the Henry into the gap and catching himself at the last second by the very tips of his fingers. He heard the Henry clatter to the gap's bottom.

Hunter looked down. It was a twenty-foot drop.

Grunting and groaning, he dug his fingers into the rock, pulling up with the bulging muscles in his biceps and fore-arms, gritting his teeth with the effort.

"Come on!" he encouraged himself, hoisting slowly upward against the face of the rock.

Above, the din was dying.

"Come on!" he shouted, and then got himself far enough up to snake his elbows out before him and to set them against the lip of the rock. He used them to lever the rest of his body out of the gap. He rolled onto his shoulder.

A rifle cracked somewhere among the boulders at the top of the pile.

It cracked again . . . again . . . again . . .

The bear's roars were quickly dwindling but still echo-ing. The shots echoed as well.

Hunter heaved himself to his feet and started forward. He stopped suddenly. The man who'd been standing lower down on the rocks now knelt facing Hunter. He was young, early twenties, lean and blond. His brown eyes were wide and round and glassy, and his face was bleached with shock.

"No," he said, slowly shaking his head. "No . . . no . . . Axel's dead . . ."

Hunter hurried up to the kid. He saw no sign of the kid's rifle. He grabbed the two Remingtons from the kid's holsters and tossed them into the gap in which he'd lost the Henry. Then he continued running forward until he gained the top of the boulder pile, which was even with a sloping forest floor, the forest stretching upward to the base of the great bastion of granite, which was purple now, most of the light having left it.

Red Otter was walking toward Hunter through the darkening pines, holding his Winchester on one shoulder.

Hunter stopped. Red Otter stopped ten feet away from him, the man's brick-red face sweaty and flushed from exertion.

"I took some shots, don't know if I landed any. As soon as the bruin finished this fella, he took off up through the trees." Red Otter had turned to gaze down at the badly bloodied carcass of the gang's leader, Axel Hingham. The man's face had nearly been clawed off, the nose dangling. One arm appeared to have been wrenched from its socket. His mangled corpse was bizarrely twisted, his wool pants nearly torn off his legs, his gun belt hanging askew.

Though dead, his buffalo coat open wide, revealing the checked shirt and suspenders beneath it, Hingham lay staring upward in wide-eyed terror, as though he'd seen the devil there at the end.

Maybe he had.

Hunter bent forward and pounded the ends of his fists against his thighs. "Damn!"

"We'll get another chance at him."

Hunter stared wide-eyed up through the forest. Again, he'd been so damn close.

"Maybe, maybe not," he said in frustration. "I was fool enough to take two of those outlaws alive. Best fetch 'em and get back down to Kentucky. I dropped my damn rifle."

He walked over to where the kid still knelt, staring and muttering. His back was quivering.

Hunter drew his LeMat, clicked the hammer back, and aimed at the kid's forehead. "Get up, junior." He had no time for bushwhackers, frightened or not.

The kid looked up at him. His long, yellow hair framed his pale face and fear-bright eyes. He wore a brown leather coat, a red, Spanish-style shirt with a red silk neckerchief, and black denims.

"Did you see it?" he asked. "Its eyes . . . its eyes . . . they were . . ." He let his voice trail off, shaking his head.

"What about its eyes?"

"They were . . . the strangest . . . most *awful* pair of eyes I ever seen. It looked at me. Looked right *through* me. Real deep. Like clear to my soul. I thought it was gonna come fer me . . . but it was too busy with Axel. Then"—he glanced at Red Otter—"the Injun come and started shootin' at it."

"What about its eyes?" Red Otter asked the kid.

The kid's own eyes widened. "They were the devil's eyes!"

Red Otter glanced at Hunter. Hunter merely shrugged, though he was thinking about that young Union picket he'd killed. In his dream, far back in the bear's eyes, he'd seen the eyes of that young soldier. They hadn't been a devil's eyes. They'd been sad, lonely eyes.

Obviously, it had just been a dream and the bear had

nothing to do with the Union picket Hunter had killed so long ago. That had just been Indian superstition getting into Hunter's head.

Hunter grabbed the kid by his shirt collar, jerked him to his feet.

"Get movin'," he ordered. "Let's check on your pard."

"Dietrich?" the kid said as they approached the big, salt-and-pepper-bearded man, who had risen to his hands and knees and was shaking his head as if to clear the cobwebs courtesy of the butt of Hunter's brother's Henry. "You all right, Dietrich?"

The big man looked up at Hunter standing over him, extending the cocked LeMat at him. "No thanks to your friend here, Danny."

"Oh, he ain't my friend, Dietrich," the kid said. He gave another shudder as he looked down at the big man. "Did you see the bear? I never seen such a thing. It killed Axel!"

"Dead, eh?" the big man said, his eyes dark. He winced.

"They're all dead," Red Otter said, holding his Winchester on the two. "All but you two bushwhacking sidewinders." He glanced at Hunter. "I don't see any reason to keep them alive, boss."

The big man cursed and fingered his forehead, where Hunter's rifle had laid open a four-inch gash that dripped blood down toward the bridge of his nose.

"Get up and get movin'," Hunter ordered, ignoring the chief's more practical suggestion. "We're taking you two into Tigerville tomorrow."

The big man heaved himself to his feet, stooped to collect his hat, and set it tenderly on his head. He glared at Hunter. "Think you can get us there, big boy? You and the rock worshipper?"

Red Otter cut his dark eyes at Hunter, then smiled shrewdly at the man called Dietrich. "If you don't make it, it will be your fault, not ours." He quickly, threateningly levered a cartridge into his Winchester's action, aiming the barrel at the man's sagging gut. "Get moving."

Grumbling, casting glares back over his shoulder, Dietrich started walking down off the rocks, the kid stumbling along behind him, still pale and washed out and fearful.

Hunter turned to Red Otter. "Take them down to Kentucky, will you? We'd best set up camp for the night. We're gonna have to tend that wound of Kentucky's before we move him. I'm gonna retrieve my rifle and check the mine for the loot those savages stole from the banks. Hard winter comin' on, and I figure those prairie folks are gonna need their hard-earned money back to help get 'em through."

"Like I said, if they don't make it, it will be their fault, not mine." The taciturn Red Otter stepped into line behind the owlhoots, aiming the Winchester out from his right hip.

Hunter made his way back to the gap between boulders into which he'd dropped the Henry. He found a route down that wouldn't kill him, even with it as dark as it was getting to be, and descended, using rocky ledges for hand-and footholds. He reached the ground between the boulders and saw the Henry lying propped on a rock, its butt partly concealed by an evergreen shrub.

Hunter winced. Lousy way to tree Shep's rifle.

He picked it up carefully and inspected it. He could see in the fast-dying light that there were a few nicks and scrapes, but he was relieved to find no significant damage. He cocked and depressed the hammer, also relieved that the action wasn't compromised. He'd fix the abrasions with boiled root oil and the long gun would look as good as new.

He walked up to the mine and lit a lamp.

He found the money strewn around the makeshift camp the outlaws had set up in the mine shaft. They'd apparently been gambling with the greenbacks and coins before they'd heard Hunter's party approaching and exchanged the pasteboards for their rifles. Five horses were picketed between trees just outside the mine, their tack piled nearby.

Hunter found a pair of empty saddlebags and stuffed the money inside. There was enough loot that both bags bulged a little. Hunter figured there were several thousand dollars' worth of stolen bank money in those bags. The prairie farmers would be happy to get it back.

Hunter slung the bags over his shoulder, blew out the lamp, and went out and freed three of the outlaws' horses. He saddled two and rode one, leading the other one, around the boulder pile, following a deer trail back to where he and Red Otter had left Kentucky.

It was dark, and the bear was on his mind, so he kept an eye skinned on his backtrail.

The bear might have saved his life when it had killed Axel Hingham, but Hunter doubted saving his life had been the bear's intention.

"Did you see 'em?" he asked. *"Its eyes . . . its eyes . . . they were . . . devil's eyes!"*

Chapter 19

Earlier that afternoon, young Nathan helped Angus carry the fifth and last keg of beer out of Angus's brew shed and set it with the four others in the back of Angus's buckboard wagon.

"Thanks for the help there, Mr. Jones," Angus said, breathing a little heavily under the strain of carrying the beer. "Much obliged to ya."

"Don't mention it, Mr. Buchanon."

"You're a good kid and a durn hard worker. You tend the hosses like you been tendin' 'em all your life."

Nathan gave a self-effacing shrug, though his cheeks turned a little red. "Miss Annabelle showed me how it's done, introduced me to the whole remuda. She's right—each one has his own personality." He smiled.

"Ha! They sure do at that." Angus frowned and glanced around the yard. "Say, I wonder where Annabelle is, anyway. I seen her ride out mid-morning but haven't seen hide nor hair of her since." He glanced at Nathan. "Have you seen her ride back into the yard, boy?"

Nathan shook his head. "She gave me my riding lesson early because she said she was going to visit a neighbor."

"A neighbor, eh? Hmm." Angus thumbed his jaw, thoughtful. "She often heads out on a solo ride, but she's never been gone this long. Probably got to jawin' with Miss Brandon or that schoolteacher over to the Skully Creek schoolhouse, an' time got away from 'em. Well, anyway, I'm off my ownself. You'll be all right here. Hunter and the fellas likely got that bear on his heels. You need anything, just go roust old Hec in the bunkhouse. He needs to be up and movin' around, anyway, before he gets bedsores."

Angus cackled a laugh as he walked up to the wagon's front wheel and climbed aboard with a grunt. He sat down and glanced over his shoulder at Bobby Lee sitting on the house's porch steps, looking at Angus speculatively, both ears cocked. Angus patted the seat beside him and said, "Come on, Bobby Lee. Let's take us a trip to town! No bears in town!"

The coyote turned its head to give the north a wary sniff. He still wasn't right after he'd gone after that bruin. Damned confounding. It really was as if he'd seen a ghost, or worse.

He turned back to Angus, gave a soft little yip, ran across the yard, and leaped up into the wagon and then onto the seat, sitting down and curling his tail around himself. Bobby Lee was a country coyote, but he often enjoyed a trip to town for much the same reason Angus often did— a change of scenery.

Still, he'd had the starch taken out of him. He was worried about Hunter . . . and the bear.

"Who you sellin' your beer to, Mr. Buchanon?" Nathan asked.

"I'm gonna sell that beer there to a hog pen in . . . er, uh . . . I mean a *saloon* in Tigerville—the Three-Legged

Dog," Angus quickly corrected himself. "Long John's the proprietor and his customers, mostly miners, favor my ale, don't ya know? I make a killin' off Long John an' his whor . . . I mean, *saloon girls* . . . alone!"

He winked over his shoulder at Nathan, who smiled knowingly. "If Annabelle's back before me, let her know I'm gettin' a late start. If I'm not back for supper, ask her to keep a plate warm for me— will you, son?"

"You got it, Mr. Buchanon."

"Call me Angus, boy. I ain't much into that formal stuff."

"All right, Angus."

"Good day to you, boy."

"Good day to you," Nathan said, and kicked a rock.

He hiked his trousers up on his hips and headed back to his chores in the barn while Angus rattled on out through the ranch portal before turning onto the northern trail that would take him into Tigerville.

He entered town roughly forty minutes later and turned onto the north-and-south lying main track, Dakota Avenue, heading north. It was another busy day in the still-booming town, with men of every stripe, including Indians and Chinese, crossing the street or palavering on boardwalks fronting the dozen or so watering holes and hurdy-gurdy houses. This time of the year, many of those men wore skins or furs against the autumn cold.

Angus smiled at that.

The older he got, with his creaky and arthritic bones, he enjoyed summer more and more but still always welcomed a break in the heat and humidity. This was a red-letter day, cool and crisp with a bright blue sky, large, low-lying puffy white clouds that glowed like pearls, and bright autumn leaves being shepherded to and fro along the street by the breeze.

Blackbirds wheeled in large flocks over the false-fronted wood frame buildings, log cabins, and tent shacks standing on each side of the avenue.

Halfway through town, Angus pulled the gray up at the Three-Legged Dog Saloon, a long and narrow log building with a large false front painted with a black, white-spotted three-legged dog. Bobby Lee stared up at the dog, mewling deep in his throat, lifting his upper lip above his teeth.

"Easy, Bobby Lee," Angus said, chuckling as he set the wagon's brake. "It's just a picture. It ain't a real dog." He chuckled again as he patted his companion's head. Bobby Lee had no time for dogs.

Angus clambered down from the wagon seat and turned to the saloon where a big half-breed Indian in baggy denims, blue work shirt, a braided leather headband, and knee-length moccasins sat on a half-log loafer's bench beside the Three-Legged Dog's batwing doors. The big man was crouched forward over his knees, smoking a cigarette. This was Long John's barkeep and bouncer, Luther Three Wolves.

"Fresh batch of beer for you, Luther," Angus said, hooking a thumb at the wagon behind him.

The fleshy-faced Indian gave a slit-eyed smile. Even Luther liked Angus's ale.

Angus mounted the saloon's wooden stoop, stopped in front of the batwings, and turned back to Bobby Lee. Luther had mashed out his cigarette and was sauntering over to the wagon, his tall, heavy frame shifting from one hip to the other, to off-load the beer. Bobby Lee sat up, growling at him softly and showing his teeth the way he'd shown his teeth to the three-legged dog.

Bobby Lee was right protective. He'd give his life to protect what was his, and that included Hunter and Angus Buchanon. Annabelle now as well.

Angus pointed an admonishing finger at him. "Bobby, you give Luther free passage. This is a business transaction, you scrubby old brush wolf!"

Bobby Lee lowered his lip and turned to Angus with an innocent cock of his head, one ear tilted forward, the other ear tilted backward.

Angus chuckled again and pushed through the batwings. He stopped just inside and looked around.

The place had few windows. The late-day light was growing dim in the few it did have. It was so dark and smoky that Angus couldn't see much but the silhouettes of three groups of men, likely miners, sitting around several tables before him, sending up a low roar of conversation and ribald laughter. Angus heard several different brogues and one man speaking broken English in a Chinese accent.

The bar ran along the wall to the left. Behind the bar stood the short, swarthy Scot, Long John Stevenson, who wore his thick, bushy gray hair in a roach cut atop his large, square head. He was severely featured, with broad, chiseled cheekbones, and a thick wedge of a nose above his gray handlebar mustache. He was the sort of gent who looked as though he had a mad on even when he was happy.

Now he looked up from the newspaper he was reading atop the bar, shedding ashes from the cigarette dangling from the left corner of his mouth. "Well, now," he said in his heavy Scottish brogue. "Look what the cat dragged in. What're you doin' in our fair city, Angus Buchanon, you bloody nasty old cur from the backwater hills!"

Angus laughed. That was how the ironically nicknamed Long John greeted his best friends, so Angus took no offense.

"I'm here to hock my magic elixir," Angus said, stepping aside as Luther pushed through the batwings beside him, a keg of beer on each shoulder. "Though why I waste it on you and your miners is anyone's guess. Just feelin' charitable, I reckon. I woulda hauled it in here myself, but I figure why wear myself out when you got this big, strappin' Injun on your roll?"

As Angus headed for the bar, in the corner of his eye he saw a man rise from one of the three occupied tables. The man disappeared for a moment in the room's deep shadows, but then, as Angus neared the bar, he saw the man again, in the corner of his other eye, just as the gent stepped into the light angling in from over the batwings.

The man glanced quickly over his right shoulder at Angus, jerked his head forward again, and pushed on out through the louvered doors.

Angus was too preoccupied with business to give the man much thought, though he vaguely noted the man's features had favored the Pipers, which meant there was a distinctive rodent quality about him.

As Luther set each of the two kegs down atop the bar to Angus's right and Long John's left, Angus said, "My best batch yet! So good, in fact, Long John, I'm raisin' my price to fifty cents a gallon!"

Angus slapped the bar with a sharp crack of his hand. It was always best to start the dickering right away and knock the old skinflint from the Outer Hebrides back on his heels.

Long John's mouth opened, his lower jaw sagging in shock. "Fifty cents a gallon. Bloody hell, Buchanon, I can't even sell it for that!"

"Ha, you old swindler!" Angus smiled shrewdly, turning his head to one side, and pointed his crooked index finger at the barman. "You know you get top dollar for my beer. You get a whole dollar a gallon. Even the miners are willin' to pay that much for the sorta ale they used to drink back home and they can't find anywhere but here and only a few other places in town!"

Again, he slapped his hand down on the bar.

"I'll give you your usual thirty-nine cents and not a penny more!"

"It's fifty or nothin'!"

"Forty!"

Angus swung around as Luther hauled the last keg through the batwings. "Stop, Luther! Back to the wagon with it! Each and every one of these sweet fine lads and lasses! They're goin' to the Dancing Bear!"

Again, he slapped the bar.

He jutted his devilishly grinning mug across the bar at the sour-looking old Scot. "Just imagine all the sweet, dark ale sloshing around in them kegs. Made from the finest malt shipped straight from Scotland and flavored with my own homegrown hops from seeds that came straight from merry old England!"

The one-armed old Scot by way of the Rebel South dropped his voice to an enticing growl, lowering his head and looking up at his fellow, scowling Scot from beneath his brows. "Imagine how that dark ale will cream up at the top of the mug, Long John. Go ahead and take a whiff—molasses and peat! Go ahead, imagine it but wipe your lip—you're droolin', you old dog!" Again, he slapped the bar. "Ha!"

It was Long John's turn to slap the bar. "Forty-one!"

Whack! "Forty-nine or nothin'!"

Whack! "Forty-two!"

Whack! "Forty-eight or load it up, Luther!"

"Stand down, Luther." *Whack!* "Forty-three!"

Angus turned and started toward the batwings. "Load it back up, Luther! It's goin' to the Dancin' Bear where them game hunters will appreciate it proper!"

Long John grabbed Angus's lone arm and pulled him back, slapping the bar with his other hand. "Forty-eight it is, you mangy old grayback!" His swollen red face broke into a grin of sorts. "But only if you'll stay and sample it with me."

He winked.

"You drive a hard bargain, you old mossyhorn. As if I got time to stand here and chin with the lowly likes of you. Biggest skinflint on the whole western frontier!" Angus returned Long John's wink, and they shook hands like long-lost brothers.

The two oldsters stood at the bar for nearly forty-five minutes, gossiping about the doings about Tigerville like a couple of old church women over coffee and crumb cake, and reliving the old days when both of them had settled here when Tigerville wasn't much more than a half dozen tents and prospectors' huts along Tigerville Creek, pillaged and plundered regularly by white outlaws or the local Sioux.

For Angus, the old days and building up the ranch for

the first time and acquiring a herd had been hard. Damned hard. And Indians had always been a threat. Long John hadn't had it much easier establishing Tigerville's first saloon, what with the violence that often came from competitors and there being no law within five hundred square miles.

Still, somehow, reliving those days still seemed like a worthwhile thing to do. A fun thing to do maybe because when you relived them with an old friend they didn't seem nearly as hard as they seemed fulfilling, looking back at them. And, too, both men had survived those years. They wore those hard times now like a badge of honor.

The two oldsters drained their mugs, shook hands, insulted each other up one side and down the other, and reluctantly parted, Angus heading for the batwings

Angus stepped outside and cursed. It was nearly dark. He saw that Bobby Lee was no longer in the wagon. The coyote had likely gotten restless or maybe spied a cat or a rabbit, and run off for a little of his own coyote brand of fun. That was all right. Bobby Lee never wandered far. Besides, he knew his own way back to the ranch.

Angus stepped down off the stoop and stopped suddenly.

A man had just stepped out from behind the wagon. He was a hulking silhouette in a broad-brimmed hat. He stopped near the back of the wagon, standing a little uncertainly, as though drunk. Light from the saloon behind Angus limned the figure of Rolly Piper's red-haired, big-gutted, and thuggish cousin, Royce.

Another man stood in the shadows beyond Piper— likely the rodent who'd summoned Royce.

Piper held his hands straight down at his sides. In his

right hand he held something that reflected the light angling over Angus.

"I told you it wasn't over, now, didn't I, old man?" he bellowed as he jerked up his right hand.

The gun roared.

Angus felt the hot fist of the bullet tear into his right side.

He groaned as he fell back against the front of the Three-Legged Dog.

The gun boomed again.

Another hot fist of pain slammed into Angus's right thigh, jerked him around to half-face the saloon wall.

Boom!

One more hot fist punched the side of his head, and he dropped on the boardwalk like wet wash from a clothes-line, the darkness of unconsciousness washing over him.

Before he was all the way out, he heard the drumming of four padded feet, and snarling. Bobby Lee gave an angry bark. The bark was followed by a man's wail.

"Oh—*ow!*" the man bellowed. "Let go of me, you mangy cur!"

A gun barked. Bobby Lee yelped.

"No," was Angus's last, fleeting thought as the clinging hands of slumber pulled him deeper into their warm, dark well. "Don't kill . . . don't kill Bobby . . ."

And then he was gone.

Chapter 20

Red Otter probed the wound in Kentucky Wade's right shoulder with his own right index finger. "I can't feel it in there."

"Oh God, Oh God," Kentucky groaned, taking another pull from the whiskey bottle in his hand. "That hurts like holy blazes!"

"Sorry, partner," Red Otter said quietly.

Kentucky lay by the fire Red Otter had built in a small clearing surrounded by firs and boulders near the creek and near where Kentucky had been so brutally ambushed. Kentucky's shirt had been removed, and his chest was bathed in sweat painted gold by the fire's dancing light.

The two prisoners, Dietrich and the young string-bean, Danny, sat side by side, each tethered to a separate tree. Danny sat staring off into the darkness with that dazed, frightened look still on his long, narrow face with close-set eyes and a long hawk's nose. Dietrich sat grinning at Red Otter's tending of Kentucky, as though he were thoroughly enjoying the show.

"I didn't see an exit wound so the bullet must be in there," Hunter said. He knelt on the other side of Kentucky from Red Otter, holding another bottle of whiskey with which he frequently poured over the wound as Red Otter probed it with his finger or a narrow-bladed skinning knife.

"It's in there, all right. Must be deep." Red Otter pondered the bloody wound, troubled. Finally, he glanced at Hunter. "Let's turn him over."

Kentucky really kicked up a fuss when they turned him over so that he lay facedown against his blanket roll. Kicked up a fuss, that is, until, seconds after they'd rolled him over, he gave a long, ragged groan before passing out, his muscles slackening instantly.

Hunter grabbed the bottle out of the wounded man's hand and set it aside.

"I'll take some of that," Dietrich said.

"Shut up," Hunter said without looking at the man.

Red Otter ran his hands gently over Kentucky's right shoulder blade. Finally, he stopped and probed one spot in particular, at the very bottom edge of the blade, where it humped up wing-like from the man's back.

"Here it is," Red Otter said. "I can feel it. Must have bounced around in there, looking for a way out but didn't quite make it."

"Can you get it?"

"Should be able to. It's just beneath the skin." Red Otter looked at Hunter darkly. "Probably tore him up pretty good inside though."

"We'll get him back to the ranch and I'll fetch the sawbones from Tigerville."

Hunter heard Dietrich chuckling softly behind him. Fury boiling up in him, he turned, rose to his feet, and shucked the LeMat from the holster thonged on his right thigh. He walked up to Dietrich, who kept the sneer on his face as he gazed up at Hunter, one eye narrowed.

Hunter raised the LeMat and cocked it, aimed down from his right shoulder at an angle. "You want one in the same spot?"

"Stand down, big boy. I didn't put that bullet into your friend." Dietrich slid his eyes to the kid sitting to his left and gave a crooked smile. "That was Danny's bullet. He don't look like much, but he's the only one of the five of us who could make a shot like that from that distance."

Hunter looked at Danny. The kid was still in shock. He didn't appear as though he'd heard the conversation. He just sat gazing, stricken-eyed, into the darkness beyond the crackling fire.

Hunter turned back to Dietrich. "Just the same, if you don't wipe that stupid smile off your face, I'm going to give you one hell of a sore shoulder. And, believe me, we won't be digging the bullet out but making you ride all the way back to Tigerville with it bouncing around in there. Understand?"

Dietrich glared up at Hunter, one nostril flared.

"I asked you if you understood?" Hunter said, narrowing one eye down the LeMat's barrel as he took closer aim at Dietrich's right shoulder.

To Hunter's satisfaction, that wiped the snarl from the man's lips and put some genuine fear in his eyes. "I understand. Holster the hogleg, big boy."

"It's *Mister Buchanon* to you, you low-down dirty son of a back alley cur! I realize I made a mistake taking you alive. Don't quite know why I did that. It's only caused us more trouble. It will not take any coaxing at all to make me rectify the problem. In fact, one more nasty look is liable to do it. Tell me you understand that too."

Dietrich blinked, swallowed apprehensively. "I understand," he muttered, and glanced away.

"I got it!" This from Red Otter.

Hunter turned to him. Red Otter held up the bloody bullet while holding a whiskey-soaked neckerchief over the incision he'd cut in Kentucky's back, at the edge of the man's shoulder blade.

"Nice job." Hunter holstered the LeMat, then set his bowie knife in the fire.

When the blade was glowing red, he used it to cauterize first the wound in Kentucky's back and then, after rolling the still unconscious man over, the one in his shoulder. Kentucky stiffened and groaned each time the red-hot blade was pressed, smoking, against the wounds but did not regain consciousness.

They pulled the man's covers up tight over and around him and draped Kentucky's mackinaw over his chest for added warmth against the night's growing chill.

Hunter looked at Red Otter, who'd learned a few doctoring skills from his mother, who'd been a Sioux medicine woman. "What do you think?" Hunter asked.

Red Otter shook his head, shrugged. "Anyone's guess. If he's going to die, he'll likely go tonight. Tomorrow his chances will be better as long as we can keep his fever down and keep those wounds closed on the ride back to the ranch."

Hunter nodded. "I'll rig a travois and pad it out good first thing in the morning."

Their administrations to their wounded friend complete, at least for now, the two men cooked beans, sowbelly, and corncakes. They were both famished and ate heartily around the fire, giving their leavings to the suddenly mannerly

Dietrich. Hunter offered a bowl to the kid, as well, but it was as though Danny had gone into a state of catatonia.

He stared out into the darkness beyond the fire, widening his eyes often and whipping his head around as though he'd heard something moving out there.

Later, when Hunter and Red Otter had cleaned their dishes and poured themselves a fresh cup of coffee to which they added a liberal jigger of nerve-settling whiskey, Hunter himself heard something moving out in the darkness beyond the fire.

There'd been the snap of a twig and a low chuffing sound.

He'd just taken a sip of whiskey-laced coffee. He lowered the cup, peered into the darkness over his right shoulder, and glanced across the fire at Red Otter.

"Did you hear that?"

Red Otter had. The Indian was gazing off into the night beyond Hunter. He nodded slowly. With one hand, he reached up to his neck, grabbed a leather thong, and pulled his medicine pouch out from inside his coat, letting it hang down over his chest.

Hunter set his coffee down. He rose, grabbed his Henry, quietly racked a cartridge into the action, and stepped slowly out into the periphery of the fire's flickering light, which cast eerie shadows upon the ground.

He pricked his ears, listening.

He leaped back with a terrible fright when a loud roar charged out of the darkness at him. It was so loud and sudden that it was like the bear itself bulling into him. Hunter got his feet set again, raised the Henry to his shoulder, and fired into the darkness.

On the heels of the shot came the heavy thuds of the big beast moving around in the brush and shrubs, tramping low-down branches and dead leaves. It snarled and mewled and growled, more brush thrashing, more branches breaking.

"Where is it? Do you see it?" Red Otter was standing to Hunter's left, his own rifle in his hands.

Hunter aimed the Henry into the darkness, trying to track the sounds but having trouble. The beast seemed to be moving in all directions at once, sometimes lunging forward, toward the camp, other times moving back away, the sounds of its passing dwindling quickly before rising once more.

Again, the beast roared from off to Hunter's left. He and Red Otter each fired a shot toward the source of the roar.

The thuds of the bear's heavy feet followed, dwindling as the beast moved off again into the distance.

Hunter turned to Red Otter. "What the hell?"

Red Otter gazed into the darkness, saying nothing. His eyes were wide and alert.

"Christ almighty—you gotta untie us!" came Dietrich's plea from behind Hunter and Red Otter. "You can't leave us tied up like this! Not with that beast runnin' off its leash out there!"

"He's over here!" Danny cried. "He's behind me!"

Hunter wheeled and ran back into the camp, Red Otter following close on his heels. Dietrich glared up at him and Red Otter, gritting his teeth.

Danny looked at Hunter, eyes wide and round and bright with fear. He was digging the heels of his boots into the ground. He jerked his chin to indicate behind him. "Back there! Behind me!"

Hunter and Red Otter ran between the kid and Dietrich

and again stopped at the edge of the firelight. They listened closely, both men holding their breath. Again, they heard the grunting and thrashing. The bear was now moving around in the darkness on this side of the camp. Farther away than before. Likely out of rifle range even if Hunter and Red Otter had been able to draw a bead on him.

The bear roared and mewled and growled. More thrashing. Then it roared again, the roars echoing and then came the softer but just as menacing mewling and growling.

Hunter started forward. "I'm going after it."

Red Otter grabbed his arm, gazed at him darkly. "That's what it wants you to do. It's trying to draw you out beyond the firelight."

"Right," Hunter said, nodding. "And I'm gonna kill it."

Red Otter shook his head slowly. "It's tricky. Trickier than you, boss. Take it from me."

"There you go again with that demon stuff."

"Say it's not a demon. Just a very smart, man-killing bear. It's likely killed men before. Maybe got a sporting sense about it. Or a taste for human flesh. There are bears like that too. I know. I've hunted them."

Hunter studied the Indian's flinty dark eyes set above the broad, copper planes of his chiseled cheeks. Hunter turned to stare out into the darkness where the bear was still moving around, just out of rifle range, caterwauling like some demon fresh out of hell.

Only it wasn't.

Like Red Otter admitted, it was likely just a very smart bear that had acquired a taste for man flesh. That's why it had tracked him and the other men back to the ranch. To sate its hunger.

Hunter nodded slowly, glanced at Red Otter. "All right. We'll wait him out till morning."

He turned and walked back into the camp.

"For the love of God, man," Dietrich said, gazing fearfully up at Hunter. "You gotta untie me. You can't leave me trussed up like this with that bear runnin' off his damn leash. It ain't human!"

Hunter leaned his rifle against a tree, then walked over to Dietrich, unsheathed the LeMat again, cocked it, and aimed it at him. "One more word out of you, and I'm gonna drill one through your head. Tell me you understand."

"But, dammit, man, it ain't—"

He stopped and gazed up at Hunter's implacable features and the double maws of the LeMat aimed at his head. He gave a ragged sigh, chest contracting, shoulders slumping. "Yeah, yeah, I understand."

Hunter lowered the LeMat and looked at Danny, who sat as before, gazing in terror into the darkness over his right shoulder. His eyes were wide, lips parted, his pale features bathed in sweat.

"Easy, kid," Hunter told him. "He won't come into the camp as long as we keep the fire built up."

If Danny heard, he gave no indication.

Meanwhile, the bear continued its menacing high jinks. Judging by the changing direction of the sounds, it was slowly circling the camp.

Hunter turned to Red Otter who was down on one knee beside Kentucky, holding his hand over the wounded man's forehead, checking for a temperature. Red Otter stared back at Hunter.

They exchanged the same message in silence.

It was going to be one long damn night.

Chapter 21

Hunter picked up a cottonwood branch from the pile of mixed pine and cottonwood he'd gleaned from the woods and set it in the fire. The dry wood instantly flamed, the fire building, snapping, and crackling as the orange flames chewed at the seasoned wood.

He sat back against his saddle and picked up his coffee cup, held it up in front of his mouth but did not sip. The bear was still circling the camp, giving its occasional roar punctuated with mewls and snarls and threatening growls.

Dietrich sat on the far side of the fire, wrists tied behind him, ropes binding him to the tree. He stared at the ground, his features tense and sweating.

The kid, Danny, sat with his back straight up against the tree, staring forward at nothing, eyes as wide and bright as before, lips drawn slightly back from his crooked, white teeth. Sweat shone on his pale cheeks.

Hunter glanced at Red Otter sitting on the other side of Kentucky from Hunter. The Indian lay back against the wool underside of his saddle, hat pulled down over his eyes. His broad chest rose and fell slowly, but Hunter knew the man was not sleeping. Maybe semi-dozing. There would be no sleep for either of them tonight.

Hunter finished his coffee and tried to ease the tension in his bones and muscles. With that bear out there trying and doing an admirable job of scaring the holy hell out of him, it was not easy. But he did manage to relax enough that he found himself in a doze until a sudden cry pulled him up out of the semi-slumber like a baited hook impaling and dragging a trout from a weed bed into the startling air above a creek.

He snapped his eyes open and looked up to see Danny bolting to his feet and casting away the shredded ends of the rope that had bound his wrists and his body to the tree. Dropping a six-inch knife he must have sequestered in a hidden sheath, the kid bolted forward, leaped the fire that had burned down to three dancing orange flames. His boots struck the ground to Hunter's left. As he ran past Hunter, on Hunter's left, Hunter rolled that way and lunged for the kid's ankles.

His fingers brushed one of the kid's pounding feet, but then the kid, screaming incoherently and sobbing, was gone, sprinting off into the darkness beyond the fire.

"Dammit, kid," Dietrich wailed. "Why didn't you cut me loose, you *yaller dog*!"

Lying belly-down beside his mussed blanket roll, Hunter looked up to stare into the darkness where the kid had disappeared. The pounding of the kid's feet and the kid's agonized cries dwindled gradually.

Silence save for the soft crackling and snapping of the fire.

Hunter turned to where Red Otter sat against his own saddle, staring back at him incredulously.

"How in the hell did he manage that?" the chief asked Hunter.

"Hideout knife."

"Fool move."

As if to corroborate the Indian's assessment of the kid's ploy, a great roar vaulted across the night. It was followed by a scream of otherworldly terror.

The bear roared again, louder.

Again, Danny screamed.

The bear snarled and growled and there were distant thrashing and thumping sounds. The kid grunted and wailed and cried out and sobbed hopelessly and begged for mercy.

The bear continued its snarling and growling.

The kid's cries dwindled until there were only the bear's contented grunts and groans and grisly tearing and chewing sounds as it sated its taste for human flesh.

"Good God!" Dietrich said, glaring up at Hunter. "*Good God!*"

"You're wrong there, partner," Hunter said. "God's got nothin' to do with it."

He looked at Red Otter who stared back at him, the Indian's face customarily expressionless.

One torn boot stood upright in the clearing, limned by dawn's pearl light.

The shaft and instep had been shredded down to the heel, so that the leather hung like the skin on a peeled banana. Every inch of the boot was crusted with dried blood.

Staring down at it, holding the Henry in both hands,

his coat collar drawn up against the morning's frosty chill, Hunter felt a witch's bloodless hand press itself against the middle of his back.

The bear was gone. It had stopped its infernal cater-wauling not long after the kid's screams had dwindled to eerie silence, turning the forest so quiet that Hunter had imagined he'd heard the stars burning in the velvet sky for the rest of the long, sleepless night, until just a few minutes ago when the dawn stretched a gray shawl across the eastern horizon, fading the stars.

There was nothing left of the kid much larger than the boot. Not enough to bury, certainly, even if Hunter had been of a mind to bury him, which he was not.

He could have tracked the bear from here, but he didn't have the stomach for it now. He hadn't slept in two nights, and his stomach was still sour from Noble's hideous fate. Now he had to help Red Otter get Kentucky Wade and their prisoner, Dietrich, back to the ranch. Then he'd continue on with Dietrich to town and turn the outlaw over to Sheriff Lodge and fetch the local sawbones out to the 4-Box-B to tend Kentucky.

After a good night's sleep for both him and Nasty Pete, and with a meal or two of Annabelle's savory grub in his belly, he'd light out again for the bear. This time he'd go alone. He wouldn't get another man killed when . . .

What?

When the bear was really targeting him?

No, that's not what he believed. The bear wasn't after him. That was Indian superstition. He just didn't want to get another man injured or killed working for him. Red Otter had not signed on to hunt a man-killing bear.

This was Hunter's business now. His alone.

He swung around and tramped back in the direction of his camp.

When he reached it, Red Otter was finishing strapping the pack to the packhorse's back. Unable to sleep, Hunter had fashioned a travois from aspen branches and rope and padded it out with saddle blankets and Kentucky's own bedroll. Kentucky lay against his saddle, still sound asleep, though earlier Hunter had without luck tried to get a little coffee and griddle cake into him.

"Did you find the kid?" Red Otter asked.

"What was left of him."

"The bear?"

"Plenty of sign. I'll be back."

Red Otter turned back to the pack he was strapping to the horse's back. "Not alone you won't."

That was an argument for another time.

Hunter shucked his bowie knife and walked over and cut through Dietrich's ropes. When he'd freed the man, he straightened, sheathed the bowie, and aimed the LeMat at the man's head.

"Get mounted." Hunter jerked his head toward the man's saddled horse.

Dietrich scowled at him. "Why trouble with me, big boy? You got an injured man there. Wouldn't you rather concentrate on him and not have to worry about me braining you or the dirt worshipper there with a rock or slipping a hidcout knife between your ribs?"

He curled one half of his upper lip in a sardonic smile.

"Oh boy," Red Otter said fatefully.

Hunter smiled at Dietrich. He smashed the LeMat against the man's right temple, laying him out cold.

Hunter glanced at Red Otter. "Should be a quiet trip now."

The Indian smiled and shook his head.

It was an agonizingly slow ride back down to the 4-Box-B.

Normally, the trip wouldn't have taken much over ninety minutes. But with Kentucky and the travois in tow, Hunter and Red Otter had to move slowly. They stopped often to check on the wounded man. Kentucky remained unconscious, though he half-woke from time to time, talking gibberish and sweating with a fever.

He kept muttering the name "Nancy" several times, and Hunter and Red Otter shared glances of silent speculation.

Several times they stopped just so that Red Otter could bathe Kentucky's face with cool water from the several springs and creeks they crossed, trying to keep the fever low enough that they wouldn't be dragging a dead man back to the headquarters.

As for Dietrich, the outlaw rode tied belly-down over his horse's saddle. He was quiet for half the trip. He regained consciousness around the halfway mark and began cursing and snarling and demanding to be allowed to ride upright *like a living man and not a dead one, big boy!*

He fell into sullen silence under threat of another braining.

They rode into the ranch yard well after noon. As he rode through the portal, trailing the travois, Hunter was surprised to not see Bobby Lee running out to greet them. He hoped the coyote was not still so fear-struck by what had happened the other night with the bear that he was still cowering under Angus's bed.

As Hunter and Red Otter rode into the yard drenched with crisp autumn sunshine, young Nathan came running out of the barn in his over-large hat and green knit cap, holding a pitchfork. Hay and straw clung to his coat and sack trousers. He regarded the riders in wide-eyed silence, taking in the travois and the horse with Dietrich slung over the saddle.

"Good God—what happened now?" Hec Prather was sitting on the bench to the right of the bunkhouse door. He had a wool blanket wrapped around his shoulders, his battered Stetson stuffed down on his head. He wore only longhandles from the waist down, and the old, black leather mule-eared boots that must have been purchased as long ago as his hat, most likely back before the start of the Little Misunderstanding Between the States.

As the oldster heaved himself stiffly to his feet, Annabelle came out of the house. She stopped on the porch and, turning to see the raggedy-heeled quartet of riders—one on a travois, another riding belly-down over his saddle— opened her mouth in silent shock and slowly lifted a hand to cover it.

"What happened?" Hec asked, limping over to the house where Hunter's party was just drawing rein at the base of the porch steps.

"Kentucky took a bullet from that buzzard's bunch," Hunter said, glancing at the silent figure of Dietrich riding belly-down across his saddle to the right of Hunter and Nasty Pete. Looking up at Annabelle, who stood staring down in shock from the top of the porch steps, Hunter said, "Honey, would you get a bed ready upstairs for

Kentucky? We're gonna need to keep him close. And maybe boil some water? It's a shoulder wound. Red Otter dug the bullet out and we seared shut the wounds so I don't know what else we can do except keep them clean. I'm gonna run to town for the sawbones just as soon as I can switch hosses."

Annabelle glanced at Dietrich. "You ran into the bank robbers, didn't you?"

Hunter frowned up at her curiously.

"Those two marshals stopped here for water, and I gave them some pie and coffee. They told me about the bank robbers haunting the area around Crow's Nest. The same general area where they ran into you."

Hunter could tell by her eyes and slightly drawn features she'd been worried. He hated when she worried, but how could she not worry? He hated himself for it, but at such times he often wondered if she would not have done better for herself marrying the moneyed popinjay, Kenneth Earnshaw.

"Yeah, we found 'em, all right," Hunter said, swinging his right boot over his saddle horn and dropping wearily to the ground. "Or they found us, more like. Shot Kentucky right out of his saddle."

He cast a glare over his horse toward Dietrich, then started walking back to where Red Otter was already crouched over Kentucky, uncapping his canteen.

"It wasn't me that shot him," Dietrich said tightly from where his head hung down against his horse's belly. "I told you Danny shot him. Now, will you kindly—and I'm askin' politely now though I feel as though I'm about to split apart in several pieces—cut me down from here!"

"You keep your bloomers on," Hunter said.

"How bad?" Hec wanted to know.

He was standing near the travois. Nathan stood beside the old man, staring down in speculative silence at where Kentucky lay, breathing heavily through parted lips, sweating, eyelids fluttering, his hair sweat-matted to his head. Even the man's mustache was soaked with sweat.

"Not good," Red Otter told the old hostler, draping his arm around the older man's spindly shoulders. "We got the bullet out, but it was in deep and might've torn him up pretty bad. We'll know better when the doctor gets a look at him."

"That quack?" harped Hec.

Nathan stared up at him.

"Don't mind him, boy," Hunter said. "He's just off his feed of late." He crouched over Kentucky and glanced at Red Otter. "You ready, Chief?"

"Yes."

"Here, I'll help," Nathan said.

As Hunter and Red Otter picked Kentucky up by his shoulders and ankles, respectively, Nathan wrapped his arms under the man's back, offering support that, despite his diminutive stature, he was able to give, keeping Kentucky from sagging too uncomfortably.

The three carried Kentucky up the porch steps and then up the more problematic, narrow staircase. They were all red-faced and breathing hard when they got him onto the second story. Annabelle stood in the open doorway of her and Hunter's bedroom.

"In here," she said, nudging the door wider and then backing into the room. "He'll be more comfortable in here."

Hunter said, "Good thinkin', honey," as he and Nathan

and Red Otter carried Kentucky into the room and then gentled him onto the bed.

Kentucky's eyes had fluttered and he'd gritted his teeth in pain as they carried him into the house and up the stairs, but Hunter wasn't sure if he was conscious until, lying on the bed, he reached up and wrapped his right hand around Hunter's left one.

He stared up at Hunter through pain-murky eyes. "How bad, boss?"

"Ah, hell," Hunter said, closing his hand around Kentucky's and giving it a reassuring squeeze. "I've cut myself worse shaving."

Kentucky wasn't having any of it. He stared up at Hunter, waiting for an honest answer.

Hunter leaned down again and gave the man's hand another squeeze. "Not good. It went in your shoulder and Red Otter had to cut it out of your back."

Kentucky sucked a sharp breath through gritted teeth. "That chills me right down to my toes."

"The wound?" Annabelle asked, standing to Hunter's right, looking down at their patient.

"No." Kentucky shook his head and turned to Red Otter standing at the foot of the bed with his hands resting on the shoulders of Nathan standing in front of him. "Havin' a redskin cuttin' on me."

They all chuckled at that, even Red Otter, the tension easing if only a little.

"I'm off to fetch the sawbones," Hunter told Kentucky.

"Let him be," Kentucky said. "I'll heal with some rest."

Hunter didn't respond to that. He just ushered everybody out of the room and closed the door behind him. As Red Otter and Nathan headed down the stairs, Annabelle drew up close to Hunter and said, "I'll clean the wounds and see if he'll eat or drink something. He feels awful hot."

Hunter nodded grimly. "He has a fever, all right."

"I'll try to bring it down."

"Thanks, honey. I'd best saddle a fresh—"

She was following Hunter down the stairs. "Hunter?"

He stopped at the bottom of the stairs and turned to her, one brow arched.

She stopped two steps above him on the stairs and gazed down at him. He could see that more than Kentucky was on her mind. She didn't say anything but seemed to be searching for words.

Hunter reached up and gently caressed her cheek, tucking a lock of red hair back behind her ear. "What is it, honey?"

"Angus . . ."

"Pa? What about him?" Hunter glanced around her as though he thought he might see the one-armed old Confederate at the top of the stairs. "Where is he, anyway? I'd expected to . . ."

Annabelle squeezed his wrist. "He went to town yesterday, late in the afternoon. He didn't come home last night. In fact, he's still not home."

Chapter 22

Cass Ludlow gazed into the mirror above his washstand as he ran the razor down his right cheek and then made the slow curve over his jawline to his neck.

He stopped when he reached the collarbone and stared at the white soap that had rolled up over the blade, peppered with the last of his brown beard stubble. He wanted to raise his eyes and take in his entire reflected image now that the beard was gone, but something kept his eyes glued to the soapy blade.

It was he himself who was keeping his gaze on the blade.

Don't do it. Don't look up. Keep your eyes down here. No, close them. Close your eyes. Grab the towel and wipe the soap from your face without looking at it, then grab the sack and pull it down over your face. Business as usual, Charlie. Your sister only saw you with the beard. The scarring under the beard was what she didn't see. You don't want to look at your hideous face without the beard to disguise the ugliness, to mask the horrific, monster-like countenance that is you—Cass Ludlow!

His heart pounded. The hand squeezing the pearl grip of the razor grew slick against the handle.

His heart increased its pace until he could hear the drumroll in his ears, the wash of blood rising to a deafening roar.

Don't do it. Your sister saw only what she wanted to see. She felt guilty about what happened.

Wait.

You saw it, though, too. You saw your face.

True, you were still wearing the beard that you hacked off every few months with a sewing shears, with your eyes closed. You hacked it off to a comfortable length, so your face didn't get so hot and itchy under the mask. You kept your eyes closed through the entire process and, when accomplished, you grabbed the mask and pulled it down over the hideous thing that is you.

Only then, did you open your eyes.

"Go ahead—open your eyes. What do you have to lose?"

His father's stentorian voice made him drop the razor in the washbasin with a plop. He gasped, jerked with a start. He looked up into the mirror to see his father's own ghostly, hunched figure standing in the doorway behind Cass. Ludlow wore his shabby robe over his longhandles. He had a half-filled whiskey goblet in his gnarled left hand, his cane in the other.

However, he appeared to be standing a little straighter than usual, and for the first time in months, he'd combed his hair. Might've even washed it, for it didn't look nearly as greasy as it had before—when?

Before Annabelle had made her visit. The return of the prodigal daughter.

Cass kept his eyes on his father. He felt himself trembling.

He stared at his father who gazed back at him in the mirror.

Ludlow's chapped lips and craggy, patch-bearded cheeks spread a rare smile. "Go ahead, son," he rasped, raising his chin a little. "Go ahead and look."

Cass looked.

He stared into the mirror.

At first, he saw the hideous old scars. But then the scars faded just like they must have gradually faded under the mask, leaving no monster or midnight specter. Not even a particularly ugly version of himself. A scarred one, still, of course. He'd been severely burned. His face looked like a wax figure that had been shoved too close to a fire. But only around one side of his mouth, on his nose, and in a few spots on both cheeks. His neck was pitted as though from a light case of smallpox or teenage pimples.

There was a ragged stretch of skin stretching down from his right temple to the corner of that eye.

But . . . not bad. Not bad at all. He did not make himself want to vomit, which he'd wanted to do the last time, nearly two years ago now, he'd last looked at himself in a looking glass. He recognized the face in the mirror as his own. Not one that belonged to the monster the fire had turned him into.

"No," he said, slowly shaking his head.

He looked at his father in the mirror. He probed the old man's face as though for corroboration of his own assessment, hoping desperately that he wasn't fooling himself.

"No," he said again, looking into his father's eyes. "Not . . . too . . . bad . . . Right . . . Pa?"

Ludlow ambled forward. He stopped behind his son and raised his glass in salute. "I'll be damned," he said, shaking his head. "I thought I'd seen the last of you."

"I thought I'd seen the last of myself." Cass frowned. "Can you live with what you see here, Pa?"

Ludlow grunted, jerking his head. "That's nothin'. I've seen men who've been pitched into barbed wire. Hell, they live with themselves. You're no worse than that. In fact, better than some. Besides, it's not really what you look like, Cass. It's how you feel about who you see in the mirror."

Cass was a little taken aback by Ludlow's words of wisdom. Cass had thought Ludlow already buried that gentler and rarely seen side of himself. What had caused it to surface again after a heart stroke, heartbreak, and two years of drink and brooding isolation?

Seeing Annabelle again, maybe.

Cass studied his image in the mirror. He smiled, nodded slowly. "I can live with that fella. Only thing is . . ."

"What?"

Cass stretched his smile a little broader, shook his head. "Never mind."

He grabbed a towel and wiped it across his new countenance, for that's what it felt like. It felt like a whole new face. Certainly not a pretty face. Not like before. He'd been damned pretty before. All the girls had told him so. But the face staring back at him was not so hideously different from before. Not how he'd imagined, at least. He saw no reason to hide away here in his room, draining bottle after bottle to assuage his self-pity, his self-loathing.

"Pa, I'm gonna make a supply run."

"Oh?" Ludlow looked surprised. Usually it had taken

several days' worth of cajoling to get his son to ride to town for supplies. Sometimes Ludlow had to send the last man remaining on his roll, the quiet but loyal Ernie Sneed, who'd stayed on to take care of the horses, though he lived alone now in the all-but-derelict bunkhouse.

Sneed had likely remained as much because, climbing into his late sixties, he had nowhere else to go. Still, the man was loyal and a good hostler, and Cass was grateful indeed that he'd stayed, though he'd been little help in keeping the buildings up.

Like Cass and Ludlow himself, Sneed had a weakness for the redeye. That was likely another reason why he'd hung around, though Cass knew he loved the horses as well.

Ludlow, as though suddenly understanding his son's actual reason for going to town, smiled. He winked at Cass, turned away, sipped his drink, and shuffled back toward the door. "Don't be long, now, boy." He glanced over his shoulder, a not so mock look of reproof in his eyes. "Mind yourself. I will not be sending bail money. Those days are over. Remember that."

Cass chuckled and began looking around his not-so-messy room, thanks to Annabelle, for a decent pair of clothes to wear to town.

Cass wasn't worried about keeping his wolf on its leash.

He wasn't going into town to celebrate. At least, not yet. He was going to town, his first time without wearing his mask since the accident, to have his and his father's opinion of how he looked corroborated. He wouldn't have any confidence in himself until he looked a person in the eye and have them return the favor and not turn away in revulsion.

Just in case that happened, he left the house with the flour sack mask stuffed into a pocket of his quilted elk hide mackinaw.

As he roped and hitched a stocky sorrel named Titan to the ranch supply wagon, he glanced around the yard. Revulsion nearly overcame him. He felt as though he were looking at the Broken Heart yard with new eyes as well as a new face, which suddenly felt overly exposed, since this was the first time he'd not worn the mask in nearly two years.

The cool autumn air felt good against his cheeks though. He welcomed that. He used to dream of shedding the mask for good, but vanity hadn't allowed him to leave his room without it or even peer into his mirror bare-faced while shaving.

What did not give him a warm feeling at all was the shabby state of disrepair he'd allowed the yard to tumble into. His new face and his new eyes were no longer revolted by his own appearance as much as the appearance of the yard.

Good Lord, he hadn't even realized how shabby the buildings had become, how overgrown the yard had become with uncut brush and weeds. No wonder Annabelle had seemed so mortified by the disrepair of the place. Several corral rails were down, and one of the stable doors was falling off its iron track. Casting his gaze to the house, his self-recrimination grew even more intense.

My God, the house hadn't been painted in years and it had never shown it so much as it did now. Apparently, one of the several recent wind storms had ripped shingles off the roof as well. If they weren't replaced, the roof would soon spring a leak.

Weeds had grown high along both wrought-iron hitchracks fronting the porch's front steps. Chang, knowing that a visitor's first impression of a place mattered most, had always trimmed the grass and brush from the hitchracks with a scythe, working fussily and muttering in his native tongue out there in his straw hat and traditional red silk Hanfu robe with sparring dragons stitched on the back.

Chang.

Damn, Cass missed the persnickety Chinaman. Not only for his cooking skills, either, though there was certainly that. Cass's mother hadn't even been able to cook a pork roast with all the trimmings as well as Chang had.

Cass hadn't realized how much he missed the man until now. He wondered if he'd ever be able to track him down and get him back. Probably not. But if all went as planned and he finally got both oars back in the water, so to speak, he was going to try. He was going to get the yard back into tip-top shape; he was going to paint the house and repair the roof. He was going to get a lot of it done before year's end too. The Broken Heart Ranch was no longer going to be such an unsightly spectacle of mental and physical dissolution.

He should stay home, roll up his sleeves, and get started right now.

But he couldn't. First, he had to make an offering to the old witch that had haunted him from the time he was fourteen years old and had started realizing how easily he turned young women's heads.

The old witch—Vanity.

It was not to his credit that he needed to make such an offering, but there it was.

"Giddyup, there, Titan," he said to the horse, shaking the reins over the sorrel's back.

Roughly an hour later, he rode into Tigerville.

As he did, he kept his head down, his hat pulled low, the collar of his mackinaw raised high against his jaws. He didn't want to be seen until he was ready to be seen.

As he and Titan rolled along Dakota Avenue, negotiating their way through traffic, he spied several familiar faces along both sides of the street glance in his direction. Though he was driving the traditional supply wagon with BROKEN HEART RANCH stenciled in red letters along both sides of the box, no one seemed to recognize him. Or that much interested in who was driving the wagon. Maybe they thought he was a new hand Graham Ludlow had somehow lured into his wretched lair.

Of course, Ludlow's run of hard luck was known far and wide. No rancher once as prosperous as the Ludlows could take such a dramatic fall from grace with no one noticing. Not only noticing but gloating about it. Especially Ludlow's ranch rivals, who, while no allies of the still much-maligned Buchanon clan, still celebrated Ludlow's drop in fortune and were probably wringing their bejeweled hands in eager anticipation of the ranch going up on the auction block for cheap to offset the past two years of unpaid taxes that had accompanied the non-existent sale of any beef to the Belle Fourche slaughterhouse.

Cass was angling toward H.C. Duffy's Mercantile, where he and his father traditionally did business and where he hoped he could find a little more extended credit, when he stopped the sorrel suddenly.

"Whoa, boy—whoa, there!"

He gazed up at a second-floor balcony on the street's left side. More specifically, he gazed at the pretty, willowy blonde leaning forward against the pink-painted balcony rail, smoking a cigarette. She wore a powder-blue velvet robe that concealed most of her, but she'd rolled the collar down to expose her bare shoulders to the sun. She'd tipped her face up to the sun, as well, and leaned there, smoking and smiling dreamily while the autumn sun caressed her.

"Jane Sweet," Cass muttered to himself.

He hadn't paid her a visit in two years. When he'd still been visiting any of the parlor houses in town, he'd visited the mostly Mexican cribs on Poverty Row. Those girls were so desperate for *dinero* they didn't care what a man looked like. Of course, Cass had always kept his mask on so as not to overly frighten or—indeed—horrify them.

But then he'd become so despondent of his condition that he'd ceased enjoying even the talented Mex gals' ministrations and started staying home and using alcohol to sooth his misery. He hadn't visited Jane Sweet since the accident. He wouldn't have even considered it. Just thinking about visiting Jane, the most popular whore in Tigerville, sent a rush of hot humiliation rising in his exposed cheeks.

Once upon a time, he'd visited her every Friday night. Would she recognize him now?

Did he dare . . .

He sucked a sharp breath through gritted teeth. The pretty, blond doxie turned to him suddenly, as though she'd felt the caress of his gaze. She frowned down at him, deep lines corrugating her otherwise smooth, pale forehead.

Cass gave a sheepish smile and averted his gaze.

She didn't recognize him.

Shame blazing up from his cheeks and into his ears, he started to boot his horse forward when Jane stopped him with "Cass? Cass Ludlow, is that you?"

Drawing back on his reins, Cass gave his gaze to the balcony once more.

Jane smiled down at him. The smile turned coquettish when she cocked one foot forward and placed her fist on her hip, canting her head to one side. "Where on earth have you been?"

Cass's heart fairly leaped into his throat with joy. He opened his mouth to speak but could find no words.

Jane shook her head with mock accusing, then beckoned to him with the hand holding the cigarette. "Get up here, you handsome devil. We have some catching up to do!"

Chapter 23

He didn't come home last night. In fact, he's still not home.

Annabelle's words echoed around inside Hunter's head as he unsaddled Nasty Pete and Dietrich's horse and turned them both into the corral to be rubbed down, watered, and grained by Nathan. He saddled a black gelding named Barney for himself and a zebra dun named Banjo for Dietrich.

He decided to let the outlaw ride upright on the trip to Tigerville. At least, he'd try it out, though Dietrich was under threat of being turned belly-down again with so much as a whispered oath or a mere expression that rattled Hunter's cage.

Hunter's cage was easily rattled. Angus had been late driving his old buckboard back to town before. When he sold his beer to a handful of local saloon owners, he usually stayed and "sampled a keg." Sometimes he and his crony or cronies would do more than sample, and Angus would sometimes arrive back at the headquarters three sheets to the wind and under cover of darkness.

But he'd never remained in town overnight.

Hunter hoped that he'd find the old man passed out and in some buxom doxie's care at one of the several hurdy-gurdy houses everyone knew he was not beneath cavorting in from to time. Even an old, one-armed ex-Confederate needed to stomp with his tail up now and then. The man's wife, Hunter's beloved mother, had been dead for over twenty years. It was only natural that Angus got lonely and in need of a woman's caress from time to time.

Hunter prayed that was all that was holding him up. He'd likely find the man passed out and sawing logs in the crib of some buxom doxie named Polly, Hattie, or Madam Dora.

Wisely, Dietrich didn't test Hunter's patience. It was a sullen prisoner, indeed, who, hands tied to his saddle horn and feet tied to his stirrups, his horse being led by Hunter, rode up in front of the sheriff's office in Tigerville one hour after leaving the ranch.

Dietrich glanced at the bulging saddlebags of Dakota Territory bank loot draped across the black's hindquarters, atop Hunter's own saddlebags and blanket roll. He slid his gaze to Hunter and gave a wolfish grin. "Ain't too late to change your mind. What do you say we split it, have us a wild time in town? In fact, I'll give you two-thirds. Hell, I'll even buy the first round! What do you say?"

Hunter shucked his bowie knife, cut the man's left foot free of its stirrup, walked around to the other side of his horse, and cut the other boot free from the other stirrup. Then he reached up with the bowie knife, which Dietrich eyed cautiously, a little fear in his eyes. He looked at Hunter.

"Easy, now . . ."

Hunter smiled up at him, then sawed through the ropes

that tied the man's wrists to his saddle horn. He sheathed the knife, stepped back, and said, "Get down. Slow. No sudden moves."

Dietrich glowered at him. With a weary sigh, he swung his left leg over his horse's rump. He glanced again at Hunter with a vaguely challenging smile on his thick lips, then stepped down to the ground. Slowly, he turned to face his captor.

"I'm down."

"Inside."

Dietrich turned to the sheriff's office. He winced no doubt at the prospect of the several years he had facing him in the Dakota Territorial pen outside Yankton, then stepped forward. He started up the three porch steps. Hunter stepped up behind him.

Dietrich stopped, swung around suddenly.

Hunter was ready for him. He'd been ready for men like Dietrich for most of his life but especially since the war and the trouble that had followed his family here. He deflected the doughy man's fist easily and rammed his own right fist into Dietrich's soft belly.

"Oh!"

Dietrich jackknifed and stumbled off the step to the ground, his forehead connecting soundly with Hunter's left, raised knee.

"*Oh!*" the man said again, and flew back to land atop the stoop with a bang.

The office door opened suddenly, and Ben Lodge stepped into the doorway, scowling. "Good Lord—what in holy hell is going on . . . ?" He looked at the man groaning on the stoop before him to Hunter standing at the bottom of the steps, angrily grinding his right fist into his left palm.

Hunter wanted to pick up Dietrich and start it all over again for Kentucky Wade, but the man looked down for the count.

"Buchanon?" The vaguely familiar voice had come from behind Lodge.

Hunter watched as Deputy U.S. Marshal Ted Revis nudged Lodge aside and stepped out onto the stoop. He held a whiskey bottle in one hand, an empty goblet in his other hand. His partner, the taller and younger Deputy U.S. Marshal Bill Talon stepped out behind him, and they stopped to the right of Lodge, scowling incredulously down at the man all but passed out at their feet. They lifted their gazes to the still fuming Southerner flanking the prisoner.

Hunter looked at the bottle and goblet that Revis was holding, then at the half-empty goblet Talon was holding. He looked at Lodge, then, and saw a ruddy flush in the sheriff's face. All three had ruddy flushes.

The three lawmen had been sitting around drinking while Hunter had led the bank robber into town—after the tough-nuts had ambushed his top hand.

"There's one of your Dakota bank robbers," Hunter said testily, turning to pull the bulging saddlebags down from Barney's back. "Don't worry about the other four. They aren't in any condition to rob the farmers up on the wheat flats anymore." He tossed the saddlebags onto the stoop beside Dietrich who now lay groaning and holding his head. "That's their money. And for doing your job for you—you're welcome!"

He didn't bother waiting for a response from the two

skeptically staring, half-stewed lawmen but turned to Lodge. "Ben, have you seen Angus? Annabelle said he . . ."

"Oh yeah," Lodge said with a sheepish look. "He's . . . uh . . . Hunter, he's over at Doc Dahl's. I'll be damned if he wasn't ambushed comin' out of the Three-Legged—"

"What? *Ambushed?* And I'm just now finding out about it?"

Lodge stepped forward, holding out his hand. "Hunter—wait! I was going to . . . Hunter, hold on!"

But Hunter had already forked leather. He reined Barney around and booted him into a gallop down Dakota Avenue, heading back the way he'd come just a minute ago. He didn't worry about Banjo, the horse Dietrich had rode in on, knowing the deputies would see to him.

Doctor Norton Dahl's office lay next door to the Purple Garter whorehouse on the south end of town. The hurdy-gurdy house served as a hospital when Dahl had more than two or three patients. His office was on the second story of an unpainted, wood frame building whose first floor housed a law office.

Angus's buckboard was parked outside the office, Angus's beefy gray gelding standing hang-headed in the traces. The doctor's black-canopied, leather-seated buggy sat there, as well, hitched to the sawbones' chestnut sorrel. As Hunter reined up at the hitchrack, a loud yammering sounded. He lifted his gaze to see Bobby Lee standing atop the outside stairs that rose to the door of Dahl's second-story office.

"Bobby!"

Hunter rushed up the stairs, taking the steps two at a time. As he approached the coyote yipping and yammering in his excitement to see his master, Hunter saw a gash running across Bobby's left hip. Hunter stopped a few steps below the coyote and scrutinized the cut and the dried brown blood matting the coyote's fur—obviously a bullet burn. No doubt, like he'd tried to do for Hunter in the past, Bobby Lee had tried to defend Angus last night and taken a nasty graze for his trouble.

"I'll check you out after we get home," he said, giving the coyote's head a pat, then moving up onto the top of the stairs and reaching for the knob of Dahl's door. "In the meantime, I gotta see what kind of condition Pa is in."

He opened the door and stepped into the office.

"Dahl? You here, Dahl?"

Two doors flanked the doctor's cluttered desk outfitted with a green-shaded lamp, bottles of all shapes, sizes, and colors, medical paraphernalia, and an ashtray overflowing with black Mexican *cigarillos*. Behind the door flanking the doctor's desk to its left, Dahl called, "In here!"

Hunter hurried forward. He stopped in front of the door, his hand on the knob.

He stared at the door, heart thudding, feeling a rusty pig-sticker of raw worry prodding his insides. Angus ambushed. What kind of condition would he find the old man in? Angus had taken a bullet two years ago, during the old trouble with Ludlow and Chaney, and he'd damn near died. He couldn't take another bullet like that.

He drew a deep breath, stealing himself, then twisted the knob and stepped into the examining room. Again, he froze, eyes snapping wide in shock. Angus sat bare-chested on the examining table, legs clad in baggy, faded denims dangling to the floor. He was just then lighting a fat stogie, turning the cigar inside the flame, the flame leaping and dancing, smoke billowing around Angus's head.

The doctor, Dahl, was just then wrapping a white felt bandage around Angus's belly.

"Pa!" Hunter said, not quite able to believe his eyes. He'd expected Angus to be on his deathbed. Instead, the old scudder sat up smoking a fat cigar, which Dahl had warned him several times in the past he had to give up or they'd be the death of him.

"Lodge said you were ambushed!"

"I was!" Angus bellowed, blue eyes sparking fire, craggy face turning red. "Comin' out of the Three-Legged Dog after selling my beer to Long John! Dirty devil flung three shots at me"—suddenly, Angus grinned devilishly through the cloud of billowing blue smoke—"but he was so damn drunk, each one only grazed my rancid old hide. Practically kisses. Hell, I been cut worse shavin'!"

Hunter looked at Dahl, the thirtyish, somewhat be-draggled and bespectacled *medico* with untrimmed red hair. The doctor, known for both his penchant for drink and cheap women as well as being a fairly sound *medico*, wore a wrinkled white shirt whose sleeves were rolled up his forearms, suspenders, and age-coppered broadcloth trousers. "Is he right, Doc? The bullets only grazed him?"

Smoking a long, black *cigarillo*, Dahl kept his eyes on his work. "He took a minor graze across his forearm, an-other minor one in the leg. The one here on his side is a might deeper, but"—the sawbones turned to Hunter now—"I held your father overnight to keep an eye on it, and the bleeding's stopped and it's already starting to scab."

He smiled at Angus. "I think your old man's gonna be

all right—as long as he doesn't rattle the cage of Royce Piper again anytime soon."

Hunter turned to his father, his own face flushing with anger now. "Royce Piper? He's the one who bushwhacked you, Pa?"

"Sure as hell!"

"You don't know that for sure, Angus." The voice had come from behind Hunter, who'd vaguely noted the tread of booted feet climbing the office's outside stairs. "You yourself said it was too dark to get a good look at the man."

Hunter turned as Sheriff Ben Lodge, wearing his crisp cream Stetson and blue wool coat and black gloves, stepped into the office.

"I may not have gotten a good look at him," Angus said, "but it was Royce, all right. Who else would it be?"

"We both know you've made your share of enemies around Tigerville, Angus."

Hunter said, "Why would Royce ambush you, Pa? I mean, why you and not me?"

Angus stared back at Hunter, slowly puffing the stogie. His eyes acquired a vaguely sheepish cast.

"Tell the boy, Angus. I mean, if it was Royce Piper, which I still contend you don't know for sure, so I don't want either of you going off half-cocked." The sheriff shuttled his admonishing gaze from Angus to Hunter. "Tell your son why it *might* be Royce."

"No point," Angus said. "You about done there, Doc? I need to get home."

"I don't understand," Hunter said, scowling curiously. "Why would Royce Piper bushwhack you in the dark?"

Lodge said, "Because Angus told him it was him who killed his cousin Rolly." The sheriff gazed at Hunter pointedly. "Is that true, Hunter? Did the old man kill those three?" He turned his incriminating gaze back to Angus. "When he was riding horseback out on the range, which I don't think he's done in years."

Dahl, who'd finished with the bandage, stepped back, snorted a laugh as he nudged his spectacles up on his nose, and shook his head.

"Don't laugh at me, sawbones," Angus said. "You ain't been paid yet."

"Really, Pa?" Hunter said incredulously. "That's what you told Royce?"

"That's what he told a whole crowd, so it's likely gotten back to all the other Pipers and Gilpins in the county by now," Lodge said. The Gilpins were cousins of the Pipers. "Then, to add insult to injury, the old scudder slapped Royce down in the street!"

Chapter 24

"And I saved your life doin' it!" Angus pointed out to the sheriff.

"I didn't need your help, Angus," Lodge said, indignant. "I'm the sheriff here in town, and I don't need some . . ."

He let his voice trail off, giving a sheepish wince.

"What?" Angus said. "Some stove-up, old one-armed ex-Confederate? Looked to me like you did!"

Lodge only scowled, the look of indignance back on his face.

"I can't believe you, Pa," Hunter said. "First telling the Pipers you shot their cousin, then *slappin' Royce down in the street*?"

He believed that Angus would have tried to take the blame for killing Rolly. But at Angus's age, with a logy heart and every bone in his withered frame ransacked by arthritis, Hunter had trouble imagining the one-armed old man slapping anyone down in the street or anywhere else. Especially a thickset, broad-shouldered ranny like Royce Piper.

"He had it comin'," Angus said, smiling around the stogie from which he took another puff.

"Anyway," Lodge said, "we don't know for sure it was Royce Piper who ambushed you. I looked around town for him earlier, and couldn't find him. He probably lit out. I'm going to send out my two deputies, have 'em bring Royce in for questioning."

"No need," Angus said. "We Buchanons have a way of settlin' our own scores."

Lodge acquired a pained expression. "Now, galldangit, Angus—that is just what I don't need. This is not twenty years ago. It's not even *two* years ago. Times are changing. When I pinned that badge on my chest last year, I aimed to bring law and order to Tigerville. So far, so good. Now"—he shuttled his beseeching gaze to Hunter—"I don't need you two riding out for vigilante justice. If you do, I'm gonna have to arrest you, and I mean it!"

He slid his threatening gaze between father and son once more.

"Don't worry, Ben," Hunter said. "I have bigger fish to fry. At least, for now. I have a bear feedin' on my cattle and"—he turned to Doc Dahl—"I need you to ride out to the 4-Box-B with me, Doc. Kentucky took a bullet to his shoulder. Red Otter and I cauterized the wound, but I'd like you to take a look at it, make sure infection hasn't set in."

"Kentucky took a bullet?" Angus had been pulling up his longhandle top. Now he stopped and turned his surprised look at his son, the stogie poking out one corner of his mouth.

"I'll tell you later, Pa," Hunter said, turning back to Dahl. "Can you come, Doc?"

"Sure, sure." Dahl stubbed out his *cigarillo* in an ashtray and turned toward the examination room's open door. "I was going to drive your father out there, anyway, as my buggy's a lot more comfortable than his buckboard. I'll wash up and grab my kit. I had my buggy hitched, so we can head out right away."

The doctor left the room.

Hunter turned to his father, gave his head an admonishing wag. "You crazy ole grayback."

Angus snorted around the cigar in his teeth.

Hunter helped his father down the outside stairs to the street and into the doctor's buggy.

Bobby Lee followed close on their heels, mewling his obvious concern for Angus. The coyote didn't appear to be bothered overmuch by the graze he'd taken across his hip last night. Bobby had been grazed before—probably the only coyote who'd ever thrown himself so heedlessly into his master's affairs.

But then, most coyotes didn't have masters. At least, not human ones. Hunter really didn't consider himself Bobby's master. It was hard to be the master of a wild animal. Bobby had found a good home at the 4-Box-B with Hunter, Angus, and Annabelle, but he spent as much time hunting out on the range as he did at headquarters.

Over the summer he'd been gone long enough, several days at a time, that Hunter had suspected Bobby might have found himself a gal on the side. Who knew—he might even have a passel of yammering coyote pups tucked away in a den somewhere with their ma.

Bobby was still wild, all right. At least, half-wild. Then, again, Hunter Buchanon himself was half-wild. Always had been, always would be. It figured his bosom companion would be as well.

"I got me a feelin' Royce Piper is sportin' a sore hand this mornin'," Angus said as he settled himself in the buggy.

"How's that, Pa?"

Angus glanced at Bobby Lee standing beside Hunter. "Last thing I heard before I passed out—I thought I was dead for sure, but I reckon the fall knocked me out—was Bobby snarlin' like a wolf with one helluva mad on. Royce screamed just before he sent that bullet against Bobby's hip, the infernal reprobate."

"Good," Hunter said. "I'm glad you got at least one lick in, Bobby Lee."

Gazing up at him, Bobby Lee widened his eyes, tilted his head, and jerked his tail as though in acknowledgment.

Lodge had stepped up close to the carriage and then gave Angus's arm a reassuring squeeze. "I'm glad you're all right, Angus."

"Yeah, well, no thanks to . . ." Angus looked off and let his voice trail away, flaring his nostrils angrily.

Lodge looked at Hunter. "I'm glad you decided to keep your wolf on its leash. I appreciate it, Hunter."

"Just run him in, Ben," Hunter said pointedly, "and there won't be any problem."

Lodge grimaced. "All right, all right. I'm going to try. Take it easy, both of you. Good luck with your bear problem. I'm gonna head back on over to my office."

When Lodge had tramped north along the busy street, Hunter looked at Bobby Lee. "You ride with Pa and the doc, Bobby."

Bobby Lee gave an acknowledging chortling yowl, then leaped up onto the buggy seat, stepping over Angus to sit down between the old man and Doctor Dahl, who'd taken his seat on the buggy's left side. He wore a wool coat, muffler, gloves, and bowler hat. He glanced distastefully at the coyote sitting beside him

"Are you . . . sure . . . he's not . . . *dangerous* . . . ?" the doctor asked.

"It helps if you give him jerky treats," Hunter said. "He tends to nip if he thinks someone's holding out on him. But Bobby Lee's nearly as smart as his namesake, Doc. He knows you've doctored Angus, so he'll leave you with all your fingers, most like."

Hunter grinned.

The doctor sighed, turned his head stiffly forward, took up the reins, and released the brake.

"I'll ride behind you in the buckboard," he told his father and Dahl. "Glad you're all right, Pa."

Angus turned to his son and narrowed one eye. "I don't care what Ben says, Royce Piper's got him a comeuppance comin' to him. You know how it is, boy. If you let them Yankees whip you and do nothin' to make it right, they'll just keep comin' an' comin'. Just like Ludlow, Chaney, and Stillwell."

Hunter nodded grimly, drew a fateful breath. "I know how it is," Hunter said. He really did. They had to handle the matter eventually; not doing so would only bring more trouble down on their heads. "Believe me, I know how it is. Especially with the Piper clan."

He'd handle it after he'd settled up with the bruin haunting his range.

Hunter patted his father's shoulder, then stepped back as Doc Dahl shook the reins over his horse's back and turned it out into the street, heading south. Hunter walked over to Barney who stood with his reins dangling to the ground. Hunter tied the reins to an iron ring at the back of the buckboard, then leaped up onto the buckboard and untied the reins from the brake handle.

He waited for an ore wagon hauled by a six-mule hitch to rumble past in a heavy dust cloud, the burly driver popping a blacksnake over the team's backs, then turned the gray gelding south along the avenue.

He'd ridden only a half a block and was nearing the edge of town when he cast his gaze to a second-floor balcony of the Old Union Saloon & Gambling Parlor (as well as whorehouse) on the street's right side. Three men stood out there, sipping beer.

Hunter wouldn't have paid much attention to the men except that he'd heard them laughing especially loudly and mockingly. One looked down into the street at Hunter, and the man—stocky, thick-shouldered, big-gutted, and red-bearded—froze for maybe two seconds before stepping back out of sight between the two other men on the balcony.

Hunter drew back on the gray's reins, frowning.

Royce Piper?

The man had sure looked like Piper. And Hunter thought he'd spied a bandage on the man's right hand. Maybe Piper hadn't lit out of town but had decided to stay and look into the handiwork he'd done on Angus.

Or finish the job . . .

Hunter had no doubt that Piper had tried to kill Angus last night from ambush. That bandage confirmed it. And in the dark, to boot. About as cowardly a way to go about a killing as you'd find.

Piper hadn't tried to miss or just give Angus a warning. He'd wanted revenge for what Angus had done to Piper on the street. Maybe Royce was even stupid and gullible enough to believe that Angus had really killed Piper's cousin. Hard to say.

But he'd tried to kill Angus, all right. And if he got the chance, he'd probably try the same trick again.

Let it go, Hunter told himself, glowering up at the balcony. *You heard Lodge. He's trying to make Tigerville a law-abiding town. Don't ruin it for him. Best of all, don't get yourself thrown into the hoosegow. You have a bruin to hunt.*

Hunter swallowed down his rage and flicked the reins over the gray's back. Several wagon drivers had given him dirty looks for having stopped in the middle of the avenue, causing them to have to swerve around him, but Hunter wasn't thinking about them.

He was thinking about Royce Piper and those bullets he'd flung at Angus last night. Only by accident he hadn't killed the old man.

Anyway, Hunter kept riding. He'd just passed the balcony when a squealing, snickering laugh rose above the din on the street.

"There he goes," the voice said above and behind Hunter now. "Hot-footing it away just like the grayback cowardly heathens he and all the other Buchanons are!"

Royce Piper and the other two men laughed.

That cut it.

Before he even knew what he was doing, Hunter reined the gray over to the street's right side, set the brake, and swung down from the seat. He tossed the reins over a hitchrack, stepped up onto the boardwalk, and walked back north.

There was a high-pitched but quiet, steady ringing in his ears.

A hot orange flame burned in his belly.

His boots thumped on the boardwalk, tattooing a deadly, purposeful rhythm.

The balcony was just above him now. As he looked up, Royce Piper gazed down over the railing at him. Royce had both hands closed over the rail before him. Sure enough, the right one had been wrapped.

The man's dung-brown eyes widened in surprise. He gulped and jerked back.

"I'm comin', Piper."

Chapter 25

Hunter pushed on into the large, darkly sprawling building, which contained as much shadow as crisp autumn light filtering through the large, dirty windows.

A long bar ran along the wall to the left. A good-sized crowd for this early in the day sat at tables between Hunter and the stairs at the end of the dark room—mostly big, bearded men in miners' hobnailed boots nursing beers and partaking of the free lunch counter. Crumbs and bits of ham and egg clung to beards and fat lower lips as all heads swung toward the newcomer.

An inked sign had been tacked to the flowered wall in front of Hunter:

NO INJUNS, HALF-BREEDS, NEGROES, CHINESE, FOOLS, DOGS, OR GRAYBACKS

Ignoring the placard, Hunter walked through the crowded room, all heads turning to follow him, to the stairs rising at the room's far end.

"You're not allowed in here, Buchanon!" a man's burly voice called from behind the bar. In the corner of his left eye, Hunter saw a fat man in a black bow tie point a chubby pink finger at him.

Ignoring the admonishment, Hunter swung around it and climbed the stairs, taking the steps two at a time. He gained the top of the stairs, took one more step forward, and stopped.

This was sort of a gambling and lounging area up here, with card tables scattered among arrangements of comfortable if shabby chairs, sofas, and fainting couches, with tables strategically placed to hold a glass or two.

Only a few of the tables were being occupied, just as only a few of the comfortable chairs, sofas, and fainting couches were being occupied by rugged-looking, slightly pie-eyed men in serious or flirtatious discussion with a scantily clad doxie or two. Straight out ahead of Hunter, Royce Piper now stood on the balcony, just outside two open and curtained French doors.

He was alone out there now. The two other men who'd been at his side earlier now sat at a table to Hunter's left, ignoring a hand of poker laid out between them. Their wary, expectant, mildly amused gazes were on Hunter himself.

Hunter stared stone-faced at his opponent. The bearded, dumpy Royce Piper stood in front of the balcony rail, gazing at Hunter, trying to put some steel into his own look, too, but his eyes were unable to carry that kind of water. He held his right hand down over the worn holster sagging low on his stout, right thigh, the twin handles of a Remington .44 jutting up above the leather.

A blood-spotted bandage was wrapped around it.

Hunter smiled to himself. Bobby Lee had chomped into him, all right.

Royce licked his lips. "Wha . . . what do you want . . . B-Buchanon?"

"You know why I'm here, Royce."

"Uh-uh." Royce shook his head slowly, tried a smile, though his eyes weren't having any part of that either. "No, I don't." He cast a weak little smirk toward his raggedy-assed partners sitting to Hunter's left. This was a Union saloon, so he thought he could play the lone gray-back however he wanted.

Only, at the same time, he knew he was treading into dangerous water. Thus, the twitch off the corner of his right eye, and the sweat that had popped out across his freckled forehead.

"Draw," Hunter said, very quietly.

Royce's gaze returned to Hunter, and his eyes widened a little. His eyes were shiny from drink. Hunter could smell the rotgut on him from fifteen feet away. He'd likely been drinking before he'd ambushed Angus and then resumed, trying to keep his nerve up, knowing very well what would come to him sooner or later.

"Draw!" Hunter said again, keeping his voice low but leaning forward a little to spit the words out with menace.

Royce flinched. He slid his hand down toward the Remington but jerked it back up again. His back was ramrod straight, and he stared at Hunter with those wide, fearful, drink-shiny eyes that glowed in the light angling over the balcony rail around him.

The room around him as well as the one below had gone as quiet as a church on Friday night.

Piper made a little strangling sound in his throat. Just barely loud enough to be heard. He opened his mouth a little, twisted it. His eyes grew wet and his face crumpled as he lowered both hands to his sides in defeat, and bellowed, "*Damn you!*" He raised his right, bandaged hand. "I got a sore hand!"

In the periphery of his vision, Hunter saw every other man and woman in the room look at each other in hushed silence. He heard a few snickers.

Hunter walked slowly forward. He stopped in front of Piper who gazed up at him, face set in a horrified snarl, lips parted. He was nearly as tall as Hunter but considerably wider.

Hunter ripped the Remington from the man's holster. The sudden move startled Royce, and he gave a frightened yelp. Hunter tossed the gun over the balcony rail but kept his eyes on Piper.

"Don't ever let me catch you anywhere near my family again. I hope you understand what will happen if you ever do."

He swung around and left Piper quaking there in his boots.

He started down the stairs toward the main drinking hall and stopped.

Two big men stood facing him at the bottom of the steps. Hunter could see mostly only their silhouettes, but he knew who they were, all right. Everyone in Tigerville knew who they were.

Shaggy Willis and Blane Millbrook. Bouncers. Bare-knuckle fighters in their free time.

Hunter continued down the stairs. He stepped onto the main floor and stood facing the two thick hardtails.

"How can I help you?"

Blane Millbrook was large and blond with two cauli-flowered ears and one milky white eye that wandered unmoored in its socket. His thick lips were badly scarred inside his thick, blond mustache. He spoke in barely literate, guttural English. "You ain't supposed to be in here, bub!"

With "bub," he rammed his index finger into Hunter's belly.

Hunter saw no point in prolonging the inevitable. Or in letting these two bruisers draw first blood. He knew from great experience that when a fight was inevitable, there was no point in giving your opponent the advantage of the first move. That was for tinhorns.

He slammed his right fist into Millbrook's face, sending the big man flying heavily backward. As Shaggy Willis stepped up, gritting his teeth, Hunter slammed a left across the man's stout jaw. That didn't do much, so Hunter stepped forward and head butted the big-gutted Shaggy, who smelled like he'd just climbed out of a hog wallow.

Shaggy lurched back with a wail.

Hunter followed him, smashing him once with a left cross then with a right until the man was falling toward a table that had just been hastily vacated by three miners and a doxie clad in little more than a faux pearl necklace.

A shadow slid across the floor to Hunter's right.

He wheeled and instinctively crouched so that Millbrook's sledge-size fist merely glanced off the side of his head. Hunter buried his left fist in the big man's hard stomach.

He buried his right, his left, his right again, his left until he had Millbrook up against the wall. Then he brought a haymaker up from his ankles and slammed his own maul-like fist against Millbrook's left ear.

"*Ay-eeeee!*" the big man screamed as he fell like a dropped fifty-pound sack of cracked corn to the floor.

Hunter turned again to see Shaggy coming up off the floor with a chair in his hands and fury curling his ruined lips. He gave a great bellowing wail and threw the chair.

Hunter ducked, and the chair smashed against the wall behind him to fall in pieces onto the groaning Millbrook who lay clutching his ribs.

Shaggy came running up to Hunter, bellowing and raising his right arm, club-like. The man moved like a sixty-year-old fat woman, so Hunter easily avoided the windmilling fist and clubbed Shaggy on both ears, then smashed his mouth and drove him back onto the recently vacated table. The shaggy-headed bouncer promptly broke the table in half and continued to the floor bathed in liquor bottles, glasses, pasteboards, cigar stubs, and scrip and specie.

Fists still raised, Hunter turned toward Millbrook. He lowered his fists. The big man was down on one shoulder, looking at Hunter miserably, blood trickling down from both freshly torn ears. Hunter lowered his fists.

He looked around the room. All eyes were on him. Three men standing at the bar had turned to watch the festivities. The barman, Bilge Kroger, stood out front of them, his stout arms crossed on his chest, a scowl on his walrus-mustached face.

Hunter crouched to retrieve his hat.

He batted the sawdust off it against his left leg, set it on his head, and turned toward the front of the room.

One of the big miners—big-bearded and wearing an eye patch—rose to his feet, glaring through his lone eye at the big ex-Confederate. "Hold on, grayback! This ain't over!"

He looked around the room at the other big, bearded men of the pick-and-shovel trade—raw-boned men with fists every bit as big as Hunter's and layered thick with callouses. They were a rowdy, Union-sympathizing bunch, and Hunter could see that it was going to be a long walk to the front door.

Another man, short but as wide as he was high, rose from his own chair and glared out from under his black knit, leather-billed, moth-eaten immigrant cap at Hunter. A quirley stub dangled from the left corner of his mouth. He pointed angrily at the big ex-Confederate.

"You Buchanons kick way too high around here for nothin' more than Georgia hillbillies who fought fer the Rebel South. For years now, you been needed takin' down a notch." He glanced around at the other miners in the room. "Boys, I think it's time we finished what Ludlow and Chaney started. What do you say?"

A roar went up around the room, and every man in the place was suddenly on his feet. The girls scuttled away like mice after a lamp had been lit in a dark room.

Hunter sighed. Yep, it was going to be a long walk to the front door . . .

As the men kicked their chairs back and started moving away from their tables, glaring at Hunter like dogs at a particularly meaty bone, sudden thunder filled the room. The floor bucked beneath Hunter's boots. Everybody in the room jerked with starts and looked around wildly.

Hunter followed the source of the blast to the far end of the bar, at the front of the saloon, where bits of wood and pressed tin were sifting down from the ceiling onto the bar itself. The wood struck the bar with ticking and thudding sounds. The bits of tin tinkled like stream water over rocks.

A stranger stood there at the end of the bar, just then breaking open the sawed-off shotgun in his hands and re-placing the spent shell from the now-empty tube with a shell he'd laid out on the bar. He snapped the greener closed, cast a mild, toothy smile across the room, and said, "Now, why in the world would you fellas wanna make my dear sister dress in widder's weeds so early in her union? Annabelle never did look good in black!"

Hunter scrutinized the stranger. He blinked a couple of times as though to clear his vision. "Cass?" he said.

No . . .

He didn't know the man holding the shotgun.

No, wait.

In Hunter's mind, the facial disfigurations of the young man standing behind the bar retreated into the man's face, and he saw the old Cass Ludlow standing there, his freshly barbered, curly, chestnut hair hanging down to his shirt collar in back and combed straight back over his head in front. His cheeks dimpled with the winning grin his strik-ingly handsome if somewhat effeminate features had once owned . . . before the fire.

No, it wasn't the same Cass that Hunter remembered standing there. But this Cass much more resembled the Ludlow son whom Hunter remembered than the bizarre, unlikely specter who'd for the last two years never been seen without his flour sack mask. In fact, the resemblance between this Cass and the old one, the more Hunter favored the young man with his gaze, was really not all that striking, when you got accustomed to a few minor scars, blemishes, and furrows of still-healing flesh.

This face owned more seasoning and ruggedness, the character that comes from weathering and age. It was the face of an older, more mature man—not as confident, perhaps, but aged and tempered by experience. By his own mistakes . . .

Everyone in the room seemed to marvel at this newly revealed visage of Cass Ludlow. The man, and the women lined up behind the bar where they'd sought refuge, gazed uncertainly at the man in his mid-twenties holding the greener on the room.

"Cass Ludlow?" a bandy-legged old pick-and-shoveler wheezed, leaning forward at the waist and squinting his eyes for a better look. "That *you*?"

"How you been, Ernie? Turnin' up anymore color in Emma Gulch or you spend all your time in here now?"

The old buzzard just stared, blinking his eyes and running knotted hands in wonder down his linsey shirt.

"Cass Ludlow?" one of the girls flanking Cass said in hushed awe.

Cass turned toward her. "Ain't as purty as I used to be, Fannie, but the ladies still seem to enjoy my company!"

He turned back to the room and said, "Just came in fer a little whiskey and High Five just like the old days. What do I see but my brother-in-law about to get the bum's rush? So I just moseyed up here all quiet-like an', rememberin' where Bilge always kept his sawed-off twelve-gauge"—he cast a wink to the barman standing in front of the bar, also staring at young Ludlow in shock—"an' sure enough it was still there."

"You throwin' in with this grayback now, Cass?" asked

one of the other tough-nuts standing around the room, jerking a thumb in Hunter's direction. "What about the old trouble? What about what become of your ranch . . . your pa? What about what become of *you*?"

"That was our fault," Cass said quietly, sincerely, nodding his head to give his words weight. "Yessir, every part of it. What became of the appropriately named Broken Heart. What became of Pa. What became of *me*. We own all of it."

He said that last while looking at Hunter standing at the other end of the room from him.

"Now," Cass said, returning his gaze to the tough old miners around him, "I'm sure you fellas can understand how I'd side with my brother-in-law, since Annabelle sets right store by him, an' all." He chuckled. "I reckon we're family now, me an' Hunter Buchanon. Blood's blood. So . . . make way, boys. I sure don't need to get crossways with any of you—pards of mine, all—over a family matter."

They all turned their heads dumbly between Hunter and Cass.

Hunter walked forward, sidling between tables and the unwashed, wool-clad men around him, half-expecting to have an Arkansas toothpick slipped between his ribs or a .45 blasted into his guts.

But neither came.

He made his way to the door and stopped to see Cass sauntering carelessly toward him, smiling, the greener now on the bar, Cass's right hand closed in vague warning to the room over the grips of his holstered Colt.

Hunter turned and walked out onto the stoop. Cass followed him and stopped beside him.

"Well, I'll be," Hunter said. "You did some healing behind that sack."

"I'd like to say it's all my clean living over the past two years, but, well, we both know that ain't true. I was quite the regular at Poverty Gulch."

"Thanks for the help in there. If you hadn't shown up, I'd have been carried out feet-first."

"Nah, they'd most likely have left you to rot on the floor. Leastways, till you got to stinkin' too bad."

Hunter chuckled. "Buy you a drink?" He canted his head toward the Union. "Uh . . . anywhere but here?"

Cass pursed his lips, shook his head. "Nah. I just came to town to pick up supplies and try out my new face."

"How'd it go?"

"That she didn't run to a slop bucket I figure is a plus in my column," Cass said, smiling broadly, proudly rising up and down on the toes of his freshly polished boots. "Now I'd best get back home. The wagon should be loaded by now. I got me a ranch to rebuild, don't ya know?"

Cass turned to walk away. He turned around and, walking backward, called to Hunter, "You're about to get some Ludlow competition again, Buchanon! Just business competition this time." He grinned.

"Good to hear, Cass," Hunter said with a smile, meaning it.

Chapter 26

Chief Red Otter had found Annabelle a nice, flat fieldstone out in the pasture not far from the ranch portal. She was working carefully with hammer and chisel now, with the stone propped up against the front wall of the 4-Box-B ranch house.

So far, she'd managed to carve NOBLE SAN and part of the C, the long gradual curve of which was giving her trouble. She'd never worked with a stone chisel before. She probably should have left the task up to someone handier, but she wasn't sure if any of the men about the place were any handier than she.

Besides, she didn't like the idea of Noble lying up there on that cold mountain in an unmarked grave. Somehow, an unmarked grave seemed even colder than a marked one. A marked one seemed cold enough.

Besides, she needed to keep busy. She had supper in the oven. She'd laid cool compresses on Kentucky Wade's forehead and shoulders, and Nathan was up there now, keeping an eye on the poor man. Nathan was to let Annabelle know if there was any change in the man's condition.

She had nothing to do now but wait for the doctor to arrive.

Also, she was worried sick about Angus. What on God's green earth could have kept him away from home all night long? The only thing Annabelle could come up with was a percentage gal. The thought made her upper lip curl as she worked.

Sure, that was it. Angus had gotten drunk on his own beer with one of his cronies, and he'd decided to stay in town and snuggle up to a warm, bosomy whore. He'd been too drunk to think overmuch about how worried his family would be.

"The old devil," she said aloud, and ran a sleeve across her forehead, mopping some of the perspiration. The day was cool but she'd worked up a sweat with the hammer and chisel.

She could hear the chief working with one of the half-broke broncs in the breaking corral. She could hear the chief's flat but gentle voice, the quiet clucks and clicks of his tongue, the soothing grunts and coos, the thuds of the nervous horse's hooves.

Annabelle knew the chief was nervous too. He was heartbroken about Noble, worried about Kentucky, probably even worried about Angus too. While the crew hadn't been together here all that long, they'd become family. They looked out for each other, worried about each other.

Suffered the loss of one as they would the loss of one of their own.

Just as Annabelle finished the c, carving a downward, decorative notch into the very bottom of the arc, just as she'd done up where the arc had started, footsteps sounded on the stairs and then in the foyer, growing louder until

Nathan pushed out the door Annabelle had propped open with a brick to let out some of the stove heat.

She'd baked two pies, biscuits, and had a big stew bubbling on the range. She was cooking now for the men in the bunkhouse, because Hec Prather, who normally did the cooking for the hands, was still laid up from the bear attack.

Annabelle looked up at Nathan, worried. "What is it, boy?"

Nathan glanced away with a queer expression, then looked back at Annabelle frowning befuddledly. "He keeps going on about some gal named . . . Nancy."

Annabelle tucked back a smile. "Hallucinating. Does he ever say anything about this Nancy?"

Nathan bunched his lips and shook his head. "Not so far."

"Well, if he does," Annabelle said, "you cover your ears, hear?"

Nathan blushed, then turned to start back into the house. He stopped when the clatter of wheels sounded to the north of the yard. Annabelle turned to see Doc Dahl's small, canopied surrey roll around a bend in the northern trail, heading for the portal. Shielding her eyes against the sun's glare, Annabelle saw Angus sitting beside Dr. Dahl, and Bobby Lee sitting between the two men.

"Thank God!"

Annabelle set the hammer and chisel aside, rose, and hurried down the porch steps. She walked out into the yard, meeting the buggy and then walking along beside as Doc Dahl kept it rolling toward the house.

"Where in blue blazes have you been, Angus Buchanon? Where's your wagon?" She glanced back through the portal. "For that matter, where's my husband? I hope I haven't gone and exchanged one for the other. I'd just as soon have you both here at the ranch, though don't ask me why after all the misery you both cause me!"

As Dahl braked the wagon in front of the hitchrack, Angus turned to the pill-roller and said, "Now, you see there, Doc? That there is exactly the reason why I never got married a second time around. Peck, peck, peck—that's all they do till a man don't know if he's comin' or goin'!"

"I never did marry for that very reason," Dahl said, hooking a quick, teasing grin at Annabelle.

"Come here, you old mossy-horn," Annabelle said, leaning into the buggy and sandwiching the old man's wizened, gray-bearded head in her hands. "As nasty as you are, I'm glad you're safe. Where've you been? Wait." She scrutinized him closely, "Something's wrong. What's wrong?"

He was pale and his features looked a little tight, his eyes a little strained.

"You're in pain," Annabelle said, an accusatory tone entering her voice. "What happened? Did you get drunk and get into trouble last night, you old Rebel scalawag?" she demanded, placing one gloved fist on her hip.

"See there, Doc! They always expect the worst!"

Dahl stepped out of the buggy and grabbed his medical kit off the floor.

Annabelle said, "Kentucky's upstairs, Doc. First door on the right. I'll be there in a minute."

Dahl nodded and climbed the steps to the porch.

Bobby Lee grew bored with the palavering and, likely spying a mouse, gave a yowl, leaped out of the buggy, and ran in a mad dash across the yard toward the hay crib fronting the main corral right of the barn where a half dozen horses stood gazing with typical equestrian curiosity toward the buggy.

No longer having the sawbones for a sympathetic ear, Angus turned to young Nathan standing as though in attendance beside Annabelle, an amused smile on the boy's mouth and in his eyes. "See there, boy!" Angus said, mock-glaring at Annabelle. "See how they are!"

"Stop filling the boy's head with your foolishness, old man," Annabelle said, no longer kidding. There was a time and a place for Angus's high jinks, and this was not one of them. The old fool had gotten himself hurt—doing what was anyone's guess. "What did you do and how bad are you hurt? If you think I'm going to cart your meals upstairs three times a day, and—"

"Annabelle, honey, I was shot!" Angus cried, regarding her self-pityingly now, rolling his hips uncomfortably on the buggy seat.

Annabelle frowned. "You *were*?"

"Yes!" Angus glanced quickly at Nathan before returning his gaze to Annabelle.

Annabelle noted the quick look. She glanced at Nathan, then, too, and said, "Nathan, why don't you go inside and see if the doctor needs help?"

"Yes, ma'am," Nathan said with understandable reluctance, and strode back to the house.

Annabelle glanced behind to make sure the boy was inside, then turned to Angus. "It was the Pipers, wasn't it?"

"One of 'em."

"One of Rolly's brothers?"

"His cousin Royce."

"Why did he go after you?" Annabelle cast her gaze

with more worry than before toward the trail angling northward toward Tigerville. "Where's Hunter?"

"Don't worry, honey—he'll be along shortly. Must've gotten sidetracked, is all."

"Did he start out behind you?"

"Yeah, but you know Hunter." Angus glanced toward the ranch portal, then shuttled a falsely reassuringly smile to his daughter-in-law. "Probably saw a nice-size buck along the trail, decided to fill the keeper shed. Not that your steaks and roasts ain't prime!"

Angus laughed, but Annabelle could tell from his wooden tone that he was concerned too.

"Want me to go after him, Annabelle?"

She looked toward the bunkhouse out in front of which both Chief Red Otter and Hec Prather, wrapped in his usual blankets over boots and longhandles, stood with skeptical expressions showing beneath their hat brims.

"Would you, Chief?"

"You got it."

Red Otter reached inside the bunkhouse door for his coat and rifle and headed for the corral to rope a horse.

Annabelle returned her attention to her father-in-law. "Why did Royce Piper attack you, Angus?"

"Oh, I don't know—I reckon I was the only Buchanon handy at the time."

"Because you were the only one handy at the time?" Annabelle exclaimed. "What's that supposed to mean?"

"It means he's lying."

Annabelle gasped as she lifted her chin sharply to peer toward the north once more. Just then she heard the thuds of hooves and the clatter of wheels as Hunter, driving

Angus's buckboard, trotted around the last bend in the northern trail. Barney trotted along behind the wagon.

The cool air was so still he'd apparently been able to overhear at least the tail end of Annabelle and Angus's conversation.

"Hunter!"

She glanced at Red Otter, who'd just then dropped a noose over a piebald mare but now turned to look toward where Hunter was riding through the ranch portal. The chief glanced at Annabelle, nodded once, and slipped the noose from the mare's head and walked back toward the gate.

Annabelle stepped back as her husband rode up to her, grinning.

"I hope I didn't worry you, honey," he said in his winning way. In maybe an overly winning way, trying a little too hard to butter her up. "I got distracted by a fat doe along the trail."

"See—I told ya that's what happened!" Angus crowed at Annabelle. Turning to Hunter, Angus said, "Thank God you're here to rescue me from this wildcat, son. You sure landed a game one, all right. Why, she hasn't given me a minute's peace since I done rolled into the yard!"

Ignoring the old man, Annabelle kept her critical, skeptical gaze on her big husband. Annabelle's eyes had already picked out the blood leaking through the torn seams of Hunter's gloves, over the knuckles. She'd already picked out the bloody top of his right ear not quite covered by his Stetson, and a faint bruise beneath his right eye.

"A fat doe, eh?" Annabelle hardened her jaws in anger fueled by worry.

She was beginning to entertain the uneasy feeling that things were slipping away from her here, that the good luck that she and Hunter and Angus had enjoyed for the past two years, rebuilding the ranch and restocking the range, was beginning to head south. As good luck . . . such hard-fought and appreciated good luck . . . often did. As, she supposed, it was bound to—mortals being mortals and life being what it was. A mixed bag. Fortunes racing along like autumn leaves in a strong breeze . . .

No. God, no. She just wanted a good life for her and Hunter and their children. That shouldn't be too much to ask!

"Where is this fat doe?" Annabelle wanted to know.

There was no deer in the buckboard.

"Plumb missed!"

"You're full of malarkey, Hunter Buchanon!"

"See how she is!" Angus said. "Would someone please help me down out of this infernal contraption? How do you get out of these leather seats is what I'd like to know. This is why I prefer my buckboard. Thanks for driving it home for me, Hunt. You're a good boy. You don't deserve this catamount of a wife," he added with a mock snarl at his daughter-in-law.

Annabelle snorted as she and Hunter helped Angus down out of the buggy.

One arm around the unsteady Angus, Hunter glanced at Annabelle. "Has the doc said anything about Kentucky's condition yet, honey?"

Don't honey me, Hunter Buchanon! she silently fumed. She'd keep her anger on its leash for Angus's benefit. Maybe for her own benefit too. She wasn't entirely sure what she was mad about. Or maybe she was mainly worried. Frightened.

No, horrified. If so, she didn't want Hunter to know. He had enough to handle the way it was.

"He just went inside a few minutes ago," Annabelle said, giving her head a dismissive shake.

"Come on, Pa—I'll help you into the house. That's it. There you go. Not feelin' too poorly, are you?" As Hunter led Angus gingerly toward the porch steps, he turned his head to one side. "Comin', honey?"

Annabelle remained back with the buggy, scowling at the old man and her husband who dwarfed him. She was half-lost in thought and wanted to stand here awhile and sort the myriad of preoccupations running amok in her head.

"Be along in a minute."

"Here we go, Pa," Hunter said as they gained the porch steps. "One step at a time, Pa."

Chapter 27

Later that night, after dark and everyone else had turned in, Hunter stood outside the main corral, running his hand gently down the snout of a handsome, young piebald gelding whom he'd put at number two in his own string, behind Nasty Pete. The horse had belonged to his younger brother Tyrell, who'd still been gentling the horse two years ago when he and Shep had been killed right here in the yard.

Fortunately, before they'd died, one or maybe both of Hunter's brothers had opened the corral gates so the entire remuda could flee the bullets of Ludlow's and Chaney's marauders. For all Hunter knew, Shep and Tye might have even died saving the lives of their beloved horses, which would be in keeping with the two young men Hunter had known and loved.

The pie dipped his head and half-closed his eyes as Hunter caressed the long, fine snout with a slender S blazed into the snout just beneath its eyes.

"Good horse," Hunter said, sliding his hand up to caress each ear in turn. "Good, good horse."

Suddenly, the horse lifted its snout and blew quietly. Its

eyes had come alive, reflecting the milky light of the moon half-hidden behind high, scudding clouds.

Hunter's heart quickened. "What is it, boy? What'd you sense?"

He looked around.

Several of the other mounts had turned to stare off across the yard to the north, as had Pie. Hunter reached for the Henry he'd leaned against the corral. He lifted the gun, turning slowly and quietly levering a round into the action, hoping despite his bone-deep fear of the beast that maybe the rogue griz had returned.

Maybe, Hunter could finish the hunt right here and now, tonight.

The darkness shifted over there on the far side of the yard, right of the house and back near the far end of it. Hunter raised the Henry, then forestalled the motion when a small four-legged creature took shape in the murky light shed by the high-flying moon, ears pricked into twin V's. Some unfortunate creature, probably a rabbit, flopped down from Bobby Lee's jaws as the coyote trotted proudly across the ranch yard to show his trophy to his master.

Hunter realized that the sigh he'd just expelled had been one of relief.

Damn tinhorn, he told himself. *Sooner or later, you're gonna have to face that beast.*

Still, he was glad it was not tonight. At least, not so far tonight. He was too tired. He'd gone nearly three nights without sleep. He needed a good night's rest tonight before getting after the beast again first thing in the morning.

Bobby walked up to Hunter and dropped the beast— yep, a rabbit—in the dust four feet in front of Hunter, then looked up with the eyes of an acolyte wanting the preacher to pat him on the head for not letting his candle go out.

"Hello, Bobby Lee," Hunter said, chuckling, depressing the Henry's hammer and lowering the rifle to his side. "Nice rabbit you have there. Very nice. Good on ya. Now, why don't you . . ."

He let his voice trail off when he heard the house's front door open and close. He shifted his gaze and saw a slender figure in a long, bulky coat step out across the porch and start down the steps. At first, Hunter thought it was his father. But this visitor moved far more fluidly for Angus, and, besides, Angus didn't have a thick tangle of copper-red hair tumbling about his shoulders and glinting in the ragged moonlight now as Annabelle angled toward the corral and her husband.

The steam billowing up from the two mugs in her hands also shone in the vagrant strands of moonlight angling down between scudding clouds. Hunter heard the soft, deerskin slippers slapping quietly against her heels as she approached.

"I thought you'd gone to bed," he told her, speaking quietly in the almost eerily quiet night.

She was wearing Angus's old, moth-eaten buffalo robe, which was always hanging by the front door. It was big and bulky and a little ripe-smelling, but it was also warm and apparently otherwise comfortable. It must have been, for she wore it often on quick chore runs. Angus never wore it anymore; or maybe he'd silently bequeathed it to his daughter-in-law, who he knew favored it.

"Not a chance, bucko." Annabelle thrust one of the mugs at him and gave her back to the corral, as he had. "You're not gonna get out of this night without having to talk to your wife. No such luck, so there." She shouldered up close beside him, stuck her tongue out at him, and sipped from her chipped stone mug.

Hunter's ears warmed a little. There was getting nothing past his wife, as smart and shrewd as she was easy on the eyes. He had been trying to avoid Annabelle, if only in a vague sort of way, because he hadn't wanted to talk about what had happened in town. Through all the commotion of earlier, avoiding a deep discussion hadn't been too difficult.

The doctor had sewn some sutures in Kentucky's wounds and provided medicines and bandages as well as instructions on how to keep his fever down and the wounds free of infection. Annabelle had invited Dahl to stay for supper, and they'd had a kitchen full, with the doctor, Nathan, Hec Prather, and Red Otter in addition to Hunter and Angus, who'd felt well enough to sit up for the meal, though he'd retired soon afterward.

Dessert and cleanup had followed. Hunter and Annabelle had seen the doctor off, and then Hunter, as per Annabelle's instructions, had helped Nathan heat water in the bunkhouse for a bath, and Hunter had stayed to make sure the boy had had a thorough soak.

Afterward, he had his own soak in the house, also at Annabelle's insistence, and then, when Annabelle was checking on Kentucky again, he'd slipped out here to ponder the sundry complications that had visited his life of late—namely, the bear as well as his dead and injured men, and, of course, the Pipers.

Now Annabelle looked up at him and gave her brow a schoolmarmish arch. "I want to know what happened in town." Her tone announced that she knew very well that it was the question he'd spent the night tiptoeing around, and that she was having no more of it.

Hunter sighed. As he opened his mouth to parry the topic, which must have been obvious by his expression, she grabbed his left hand with her right one and brushed her thumb across the bruised and swollen knuckles. "I've already seen your hands, Hunter."

Again, he sighed. He resigned himself to the fact that she wasn't going to let him slip away. She rarely did.

"When Pa took Rolly and his two dead pards to town day before yesterday, he told Lodge, and several other people on the street, including Royce Piper, that he'd taken them down."

That didn't seem to surprise Annabelle. "And Lodge and Piper believed him?"

"Lodge didn't. Hard to tell if Piper's gullible enough. Don't matter, though, because Angus added insult to injury—or, should I say injury to *insult*?—when he slapped Royce down in the street."

"Angus slapped Royce Piper down in the street!?"

"Sure enough."

"I didn't think the old man had it in him anymore."

"Neither did I. I doubt even Pa did. A wicked temper has Angus Buchanon. I can't figure on how it hasn't got him killed by now, though it sure as hell has come close a few times."

Annabelle kept staring up at her husband in astonishment, the moon scudding behind the ragged-edged clouds in her wide eyes. "Royce Piper must weigh twice as much as Angus dripping wet!"

"Lodge was there. Angus surprised him, most like.

And he had his shotgun. He and Lodge filed Piper's horns for him."

"But he got his revenge last night. Or came close, anyway."

"The only reason he's still kickin' is because Royce was too drunk to shoot straight."

Looking up at Hunter, Annabelle arched both brows. "Now, what was it that held you up in town earlier this afternoon? And please keep in mind, Hunter Buchanon, I will not abide a husband who lies to me." Annabelle reached up and snapped her finger against the underside of his hat brim.

Hunter rolled his shoulders. "Hell, honey—it wasn't like I was seein' a hurdy-gurdy girl!"

"That's probably next. Yessir, I will nip these lies in the butt right here and now!"

Hunter laughed, wrapped his arm around her shoulders, and planted a kiss on her mouth.

She was having none of that either. She kept her lips stiff and crossed her arms on her breasts, gazing levelly up at him.

The message was clear. It was time to get serious.

He kept his arms around her. "All right, honey."

"I want the whole story."

"You'll get it."

"Always."

"Always, right. As I was riding out of town, I saw Royce Piper in the Union Saloon."

"Oh dear."

"I tried to ride on by. Really, I did. But . . ."

"Of course, being who you are, a proud and stubborn Buchanon, you couldn't."

"Don't worry. I didn't touch him. Didn't touch a hair on his head. Turned out I didn't need to."

Annabelle turned her mouth corners down and nodded knowingly. "He didn't have the stomach for it. Figures. That's a bushwhacker for you." She turned her head to press her lips to the swollen knuckles of his left hand resting on her right shoulder. "If you didn't fight Piper, what happened to your hands?"

"Union bouncers."

Annabelle sighed.

"Would have had a helluva lot more trouble getting out of there if I hadn't run into an old friend."

Annabelle frowned, curious.

"Cass."

"My brother?"

"Cass without a mask isn't all that hard to look at. Doesn't look all that different from how he looked two years ago. Can still wield a gut-shredder too."

"Cass backed you in the Union?"

Hunter smiled. "Seems your brother's an ally now. Though he assured me he was going to be competition in the marketplace again soon."

Annabelle looked away, vaguely sheepish.

Hunter brushed his thumb across her chin. "What is it, honey?"

Annabelle bunched her lips, shook her head, looked down guiltily. "I . . ."

"Yes?"

She shook her head, obviously troubled.

Hunter cupped her chin in his hand, lifted her face to his. "What is it, honey?"

She drew a breath. "I rode over there the other day."

"Where?"

"To the Broken Heart."

"You did?" Hunter was genuinely surprised.

"I did." She gazed up at him guiltily. "Cass rode over and said that my father was on his last legs, so I rode over . . . well . . . I guess I rode over to see him one last time."

"I see. Why didn't you tell me?"

"I guess I was afraid to. I felt guilty."

"Why on earth would you feel guilty about visiting your home ranch, Anna?"

"Well, because . . . of all that happened. Of all that my father did."

"The Broken Heart is still your home. I never asked you to disavow your home. For that matter, I never asked you to disavow your father or your brother."

"I know." Annabelle frowned up at him. "Why didn't you?"

Hunter shrugged. "It wasn't my place. Family's complicated."

"They . . . he . . . killed your brothers. Burned your ranch."

"Honey, if I'd wanted to kill your father, I'd have killed him a long time ago. He's still your father."

"Is that why you didn't kill him?"

Again, Hunter shrugged. "I guess I didn't see the point. He was a wretched old soul. I don't think I or anyone else could have made him suffer more for his sins than he himself could."

"Well, you're right. He is suffering."

"I don't doubt it."

Again, Annabelle looked down and shook her head as though trying to organize the chaos of her thoughts. She looked up at Hunter again, wrinkling the skin above the bridge of her nose. "You don't feel any resentment toward me at all for feeling compelled to go back to the Broken Heart, to see him again?"

"Honey, like I said— he's your father. The Broken Heart is where you grew up. It's your home. As far as I'm concerned you can ride back there whenever you feel like it. No need to feel guilty. Like I said, the man is still your father. Families are complicated.

"I know what you must be feeling. You're feeling a strong connection to him. To the ranch too. Of course, you do. It's only natural. Don't hate yourself for it. Make peace with the man, if you need to." Hunter leaned forward and pressed his lips to Annabelle's forehead. "Make peace with yourself."

She smiled up at him for a long time. The smile grew brighter. She wrapped her arms around his neck and leaned against him. "I love you, Hunter."

"You know how I feel about you—now, don't you?"

"Yes." Again, she looked off, once again troubled.

"Now what's wrong? What else can I help you with, young lady?"

She turned back to him. "You're going after it again tomorrow—aren't you? The bear."

"Yes."

"You don't think you should rest up a day? My God, Hunter, how long have you gone without sleep?"

"I've gone longer than this." Hunter looked off across the dark land to the north from where the yammering of several distant coyotes came. Bobby Lee either didn't hear or wasn't interested. He lay nearby, busily tearing and devouring the rabbit. "Every day that bruin runs free on our range is another day he could potentially kill another ten, fifteen cows."

Annabelle reached up to slide a lock of hair from his eye. "You're obsessed, darling."

"I reckon I am."

She gazed up at him, studying him closely, lines of deep concern spoking her lovely eyes.

"What is it, Anna?"

Abruptly, she turned away and lifted her hands to the sides of her neck, bowing her head and massaging. "Nothing."

"No. Please." Hunter placed his hand on her shoulder. "What is it?"

She lifted her chin to stare toward the house. "I have a deep dread inside of me, Hunter."

"Because of the bear?"

"Because of the bear, the Pipers . . . what happened to Angus, so close to being killed and the only reason he wasn't was because Royce Piper was three sheets to the wind." She turned to gaze up at Hunter again. "Your obsession with the bear, most of all."

"Honey, what would you have me do?"

"Do what my father did when he had bear trouble or cat trouble. Do what other ranchers do. They bring in a professional hunter. Men who earn their livings hunting such beasts."

Hunter shook his head defiantly. "No. I can't. Anna, I've done this before. Black bears in Georgia, grizzlies up here."

"You're too close to this bear, Hunter. You believe the chief's superstitions. You believe this bruin is your own personal enemy. That only you can kill him . . . before he kills you. You're obsessed. Obsession . . . going after him without adequate sleep and everything else that goes with obsession . . . will get you killed."

Hunter laid his hand along her cheek. "I won't let him kill me, Anna. I promise."

She gave a weak half smile. "I'll never forgive you if you do." She rose up on the toes of her slippers and placed a tender kiss on his lips. Pulling away from him, she said, "We can continue to build up a nice life for ourselves here, Hunter. To fulfill the dream we've entertained for years. Right now, though, I feel it being threatened."

"The bear will be dead in two days. Three, tops."

"It's not only the bear, it's the Pipers . . ."

"Don't worry about the Pipers, honey." Hunter gave a dry snort. "I don't think we're gonna have to worry about any of them ever again. The Piper clan has learned its lesson. Believe me."

Again, Anna smiled, but the gesture was even more halfhearted than before. "Come to bed soon. You need at least a few hours' sleep."

"I'll be along in a minute."

Anna turned and, head down, shoulders bowed as though under the burden of a great weight, began treading back toward the house. Neither she nor Hunter saw young Nathan standing in the heavy shadows of the partly open doorway, gazing toward them.

Nor did they see the door slowly close, hear the latching bolt quietly click into place.

Chapter 28

Two days later, high on the north side of Crow's Nest Peak, Hunter held a steaming cup of coffee in his hands. Gazing through the steam, he said quietly, "He's calling me, isn't he?"

As if in edgy agreement, Nasty Pete whickered in the trees behind Hunter, on the south side of his camp.

"Sure enough," Hunter said, hearing the guttural groans and wails issuing from that distant valley, nervously tapping his thumb against the rim of his hot tin cup. "He's callin' me."

It was early, and large, downy snowflakes fell from a goose-down sky that hovered low over the trees, fogging the spruce and pine crowns. The air was nearly still and so quiet that even from a mile away, Hunter could hear the bear's aimless rampage, the guttural echoes of its savage, mindless fury.

No, not mindless. The beast knew Hunter was here.

It was calling him.

Hunter mulled over the reflection and scoffed at the thought, giving a dry chuff. "Get the chief out of your head, old son. Listen to Anna. It's just a bear like another."

Hunter was alone. He'd elected to come alone this time. The chief hadn't put up much resistance. Red Otter knew that Hunter's war was nearly as much with the old warrior's superstitions as it was with the bear.

"You're stayin', Chief," he'd said on the way to the stable the previous morning, his rifle on his shoulder. "I'm goin'."

Red Chief had been standing outside with Hec Prather and young Nathan, drinking coffee and enjoying probably one of the last temperate mornings of the year. The chief hadn't said anything. He hadn't nodded or even blinked. He'd merely watched Hunter enter the stable and then lead out into the yard Pete and a beefy sorrel for packing.

While Hunter had adjusted the saddle and bridle straps, Annabelle had walked out onto the house's front stoop, wearing that old buffalo robe she'd appropriated from Angus, sort of crouched over the thick stone coffee mug she held in both fingerless gloved hands up high against her chest. Bobby Lee sat at her feet, gazing toward Hunter, whining, shifting his weight between his front feet.

When Hunter had mounted up and rode over to the porch to lean out to kiss his wife good-bye, he'd felt for the first time, in the slight stiffness of her lips and in the cast of her gaze, that something had come between them. Between him and his darling bride.

The bear.

It had broken his heart. He still felt it. The wretched ache had followed him throughout the day yesterday and throughout the night and into now.

Of course, things had come between them before. Namely, when Hunter had wanted to hold off on getting married until after he'd built up a stake again with which to rebuild the ranch. This was before Cass had returned the gold he'd stolen from Hunter's secret cache. Annabelle had gotten a job as a saloon girl to make him jealous and, while seeing her parade around in her skimpy costumes had done just that, it had also made him dig his heels in all the deeper.

Because, gallblastit, that was the kind of man he was.

Now as then he'd dug in his heels. The bear was his problem. His alone. Whether it was of this world or some other world, he was going to kill it. He was going to rid his range and his life of the dangerous interloper.

One after another, if need be.

One was more or less another. The threats interchangeable, almost. First there was the War of Northern Aggression. Then there was Ludlow and Chaney and Frank Stillwell.

Now, the bear . . .

Sure as hell, it was as though some evil thing, some curse originating from his own dark past, was dogging his heels, trying to make him pay for his own wicked ways . . .

The thing of it was—how long could he hold it off?

How long could he delay payment for all the men he'd killed? Anna didn't deserve this—to be married to such a man who could attract such danger into his life and the lives of those he loved.

"There you go again," he said, finishing off his coffee, then tossing the dregs in the fire, "letting your thoughts drift. Stay with the bear," he told himself, raking the words out bitterly through clenched teeth. "Just stay with the damn bear!"

He stowed the cup in his saddlebag, shook the snow from his blankets, and struck camp. Five minutes later, he swung up onto Pete's back and, trailing the sorrel to which his camp supplies were strapped, dropped down the long, gradual slope, dead heading toward the bear's furies boiling up from the dark spruce forest tucked into the snowy seam between haystack hills below.

It was a little like riding toward hell while hearing the screams of the forever-sufferers caroming out of the smoking open gates.

He rode down into the crease between hills, burr oaks and shrubs and Ponderosa pines closing around him. A partly frozen creek ran along the bottom of the crease— barely wider than a freshet. Hunter put Pete and the packhorse along a deer trail that followed the creek's meandering course.

He'd easily picked up the bear's trail, the paw prints clearly delineated in the half inch of fresh snow. Ahead, the bear continued its intermittent roars, which echoed over the ermine hills.

Hunter followed the bear's trail up and over a low divide and into a broader valley than the one he'd just traversed, with fewer trees and only pines and firs and a few spruces standing on the higher ridges to either side.

The valley floor rose gradually.

He'd ridden maybe twenty minutes along this incline when the bear's tantrum-like bellowing ceased abruptly.

Occasionally along the game trail he tracked, following the bear, he paused to inspect the deep scuff marks the bear had scratched out as though in a frenzy in the snow and dirt, before moving on. More and more frequently along the trail, he came upon trees in which the bruin had scratched long, deep, vertical lines with its razor-edged claws.

As he climbed and descended yet another divide, he

came upon partly devoured cow and deer carcasses and strewn bones half-buried by the snow. The air was sickly sweet with the odor of death.

Hunter looked around warily.

Where in hell was the beast leading him anyway?

It was leading him, wasn't it? It knew he was back here. It had called for him after all.

But now it was eerily, ominously silent.

Hunter and Pete and the beefy packhorse climbed, feathery snow falling around them from the low, pearl sky. It was so quiet that Hunter thought he could hear each downy flake tumbling onto the conifer and spidery autumn deciduous branches around him.

He imagined that God was holding His breath in dark anticipation about what was about to happen.

And then it happened. Pete stopped so abruptly that Hunter was jarred forward over the horse's poll. The packhorse stopped at the same time, taking up the slack in its lead rope.

Pete swung his head to the left. Hunter could feel the horse's heart pumping faster and faster between his legs, its lungs expanding and contracting. Just as the packhorse whickered and drew back against the rope in Hunter's left hand, a hoarse cry as loud as God's own agonized wail blasted the snowy, silent morning wide open.

Hunter watched in momentary awe as the big bruin bounded out from behind a granite outcropping fifty feet up the slope to Hunter's left. In a blur of motion, snarling and shaking its head, it lunged into a dead run downhill toward Hunter and the horses.

Hunter's heart leaped into his chest. "Holy—!"

The beast's stentorian roar was like a physical blow.

Hunter had started to raise the Henry from the saddle bows, but he didn't get it a foot high before Nasty Pete reared sharply, screaming. Hunter had dropped the pack-horse's lead line, and the sorrel also reared, adding its own horrified scream to that of the grullo.

Hunter dropped the rifle and reached for the horn. His fingers merely brushed it before he was flying backward, leaving the saddle and going airborne over the horse's tail. As Pete dropped down to all fours and wasted no time in breaking into a dead run up the trail, on the heels of the screaming sorrel, Hunter struck the ground on his back and shoulders.

He rolled, came up on his right hip and shoulder, cast-ing his own wide-eyed gaze toward the bruin. It was thirty feet away—so close Hunter could see the rage glinting like small bayonets in its dark, almond-shaped eyes. The bear's long, cinnamon fur buffeted in the wind as it ran, its slab-like muscles rippling down across its stout hump and neck and heavy, powerful shoulders.

The drumming of its platter-size paws kicked up a near deafening din as it approached, kicking gouts of snow and dirt out behind it.

Twenty feet away, jaws clacking . . .

Ten feet away, so close that Hunter could see the spittle bathing its teeth and foaming inside its lower lip.

The beast's sour smell making his eyes water, Hunter hurled himself into a backward somersault. One of the bear's front paws brushed the tip of his left boot, the sharp claw ripping through the leather and into Hunter's foot. He expected to roll onto solid ground behind him.

He did not.

He dropped like a stone through air, straight down a

crenelated stone wall pocked with damp snow sliding in a blur just inches beyond his face. He reached out. As he did, something came up to smack against the undersides of his arms.

"*Ohhh!*" he cried as the air was sucked from his lungs and he felt as though his arms were going to be wrenched from their sockets.

He'd caught a heavy root curling out of the side of the cliff. The root bent slightly, bouncing beneath his weight. It made a cracking sound, shedding bits of wood and bark.

Hunter looked down. The ground dropped a hundred feet away below him.

Rocks and gravel slid down from the lip of the ridge, and Hunter looked up to see the bear glaring down at him. It snarled, opening and closing its mouth, showing all those long, sharp teeth. It shook its head in fury and primal frustration.

Heart racing, again, Hunter looked down, raking his eyes across the cliff wall. It was a sheer drop—straight down to the ground with no apparent hand- or footholds. Which meant he wouldn't escape the bear by going down.

On the other hand, he had even less chance of escaping the bruin by going up. Going up, he surmised, his eyes fixed on those slashing and clacking teeth, smelling the bear's hot, musky breath, would be sure suicide.

The bear lunged forward, kicking more rocks and gravel over the ledge. The debris smacked Hunter's head and peppered his face. He dipped his chin and blinked against it. When he looked up again, a fresh wave of terror rolled through him. The bear was hunkered nearly flat against the lip of the cliff, stretching its right front leg and huge, round, black-padded paw down against the cliff wall, waving it back and forth, trying desperately to slash the face of its prey with its extended claws.

Hunter stared in horror, feeling the wind as the big paw whipped through the air maybe six to eight feet above him. The paw smelled like sour leather.

The bear edged its head and shoulders over the side of the cliff, thrusting its paw lower . . . lower . . . the paw and the black pads and the stiletto-like claws sliding ever closer to Hunter's head, whipping back and forth. The bear slid even farther over the cliff's edge, whipping that enormous paw, one thrust of which, Hunter absently opined, would rip his head clean off his shoulders.

He jerked his face down as the paw drew even nearer.

He winced as one of those claws ripped a lock of hair from his head.

"Ah, hell," Hunter said aloud, drawing his head and shoulders down as far as he could, knowing it was only a matter of seconds before he'd look mighty funny with his head tumbling down into the canyon below, separate from the rest of him. "Just . . . ah . . . *hell!*"

Chapter 29

Hunter's loins twisted into knots when he felt the root jounce beneath him, giving a little more, and beneath the bear's infernal roaring heard the wood crack, saw more bark slither down into the canyon beneath him.

He glanced up once more.

The bear's head was eight feet from his own, hanging well over the edge of the ridge. The bruin glared down at Hunter, eyes as large and black as eight-balls cast with a soul-numbing malevolence. Again, the beast thrust one of its giant paws down toward its quarry, curving claws extended to nearly the length of bowie knives.

As those scissoring claws plunged toward him, Hunter started to release his hold on the root. Better to fall to his death than have his head ripped off. He renewed his hold when the paw stopped its descent a foot above Hunter's face.

The bear roared even louder than before, and withdrew its paw, turning its head as though distracted by something on top of the ridge, approaching from its right, Hunter's left.

The bear roared again, and in the relative silence that

followed, a rifle thundered distantly. Another shot followed, and another. Beneath the shots came the thunder of pounding hooves.

The bear roared and pulled away from the edge of the ridge.

The hooves stopped pounding. There was another shot and then a man yelled, though Hunter couldn't make out what he said. He seemed to be yelling in a foreign tongue.

There was another shot . . . and another With each shot, the bear roared louder, angrier . . . the roars dwindling as the bear moved away from Hunter's position. The bear was running off to Hunter's left, toward the man on the horse.

Hunter stared up the ridge wall before him, puzzled.

The man continued shouting in the foreign tongue. It was accompanied by a yammering, coyote-like wail.

The man was chanting in Lakhota. At least, it sounded like a Lakhota chant to Hunter's ears.

Chief Red Otter . . .

What in the hell was he doing out here? Hunter had told him in no uncertain terms that he was hunting the bear alone. He wanted no more men endangered by the formidable bruin. This was his fight now. His fight alone.

A horse screamed shrilly. The chief gave a bellowing wail. The rifle thundered. The bear roared, and then there was a great din, as though bear and man and horse had smashed into each other. The coyote wailed, yipped, yammered hysterically.

Bobby Lee.

"Chief," Hunter spat out through taut jaws, trying to push himself up higher on the root and reaching for the stone wall before him.

A silence had settled over the ridge. An eerie one. A deathlike silence.

"Chief?" Hunter shouted. "You all right, Chief?"

More silence save for the rushing sound of the chill breeze against stone and the cawing of distant crows.

Gritting his teeth, Hunter again hoisted himself up higher on the root, intending to climb over it and onto the wall, though he could see few hand- or footholds there.

He had no choice. The root was continuing to sag lower and lower, shedding wood and bits of bark where it pushed out of the cliff. Where the root emerged from stone was where it was weakening. Deciding he couldn't climb over it without ripping it out of the cliff, he considered a move to his left or his right.

Choosing left, he shoved his left hand out toward a very shallow ledge about five feet in that direction.

He ground his fingers into the ledge. When he thought he had a firm hold on it, he removed his right arm from the sagging root. Just as he did, his left hand slipped off the ledge. He pitched hard to his left, automatically grabbing the sagging root again with his right hand. It was the only way to save himself.

Now he hung sideways, clinging to the root with one hand, staring in horror at the canyon floor below him.

The root sagged again, and again, jerking violently downward. It was ripping out of the cliff!

Hunter's heart raced. His blood ran cold.

He had only seconds left. Staring at the narrow, rocky canyon below him, he thought of Anna, the family they might have had . . .

A rope appeared before him, between his face and the

stone wall. The slip-knotted loop opened wider as more hemp was paid out from above.

Hunter looked up. Chief Red Otter knelt on one knee atop the cliff, the rope in his hands. His hat was gone, his almond-shaped eyes were black, and his brick-red face was badly creased with misery.

Bobby Lee stood beside him, staring worriedly down toward Hunter dangling against the cliff. The coyote dipped his head low, yipping softly but frantically.

"Take . . . it . . ." Red Otter said too softly for Hunter to hear. He could only read the man's lips.

Hunter grabbed the loop with his left hand, slipped it over his head and shoulders. He looked up the ridge again.

Red Otter was gone. Hunter was still clinging to the root, but now, with a suddenness that sent his heart into his throat, the root tore loose from the rock wall. Hunter gave a terrified grunt as he fell headfirst, staring down at the root tumbling down away from him, bouncing twice off the side of the cliff before plunging to the canyon floor and busting into several pieces.

The loop drew taut around Hunter's chest, sliding up beneath his arms and squeezing the air from his lungs. It jerked him upright and smashed him hard against the cliff face.

"*Ohh!*" he said with a loud exhalation, taking the brunt of the blow with his head.

The rope ground even more tightly against him as it began to pull him up the wall. He grabbed it where it angled up before him with both hands, grunting against the pain and pressure, and kicked away from the wall. Slowly, steadily, he was pulled upward, raking the toes of his boots against the stone wall before him.

As he neared the lip of the ridge, he heard a distant roaring. A feral, enraged roaring. Roars of deep anger and frustration.

The bruin's roars echoed hollowly.

Hunter watched the lip of the ridge slide down toward him as he slid up toward it. Bobby Lee watched him, lifting his long snout and howling skyward.

When his head had cleared the ridge crest, Hunter used his hands to hoist himself up and over the edge and was dragged a few inches along the ground before, glancing back over his shoulder at Hunter, the chief drew back on his horse's reins. The other end of the rope was dallied around his saddle horn.

Red Otter stared back at Hunter. His shoulders were bowed, his face slack. He backed the horse a step, putting some slack in the hemp, then uncoiled his end from around his horn and dropped it.

He blinked a couple of times, heavily. His eyes rolled back in his head and he sagged to one side before tumbling down his left stirrup to strike the ground with a thud.

"Chief!"

Bobby Lee was raking his rough tongue across Hunter's mouth and chin, yipping joyously.

"Not now, Bobby," Hunter grunted, tossing the rope up and over his head.

He scrambled to his feet and ran over and dropped to a knee beside the chief, who lay belly-down, unmoving.

"Chief, what happened?" he said as he rolled the man over on his back.

Red Otter's pain-racked eyes snapped wide, and he groaned, clutching his belly. He writhed from side to side. "Ribs! Bear bulled into my hoss . . . knocked us over!"

"You're damned lucky to be alive, Chief. What the hell are you doing out here, anyway? Did Anna send you?"

"Hell, no." The Indian snorted a rare laugh as he rose onto his elbows, breathing heavily, painfully, stretching his lips back from his teeth. "I don't think your woman wants me around you. She was giving me the wooly eyeball for the past two days."

"Sorry about that."

"Nah—hell, she's probably right to." The chief shook his head. "You shouldn't listen to me. My ways are not your ways. I should have realized that."

"Well, I'm glad we finally have that cleared up." Hunter's ironic chuckle belied his doubts. He'd seen the beast's eyes up close. In them, he'd seen what that outlaw kid had seen, what had sent him running off to a grisly death in the chill darkness.

Pure evil. Not an earthly kind of evil either. An evil straight from hell.

He still felt the snowy chill of it deep in the marrow of his bones.

"I gotta admit, Chief, hearing your voice picked my mood up a tad. If not for you, I'd likely be lyin' at the bottom of that canyon in several bloody pieces about now." Hunter spat grit from his lips.

"You can thank Anna's wooly eyeball. If not for her, I'd have likely stayed on the ranch. Warmer down there. Damn chilly up here." The chief, still looking agonized, shivered.

Hunter looked at Bobby Lee sitting beside him. He patted the coyote's head, which seemed to satisfy the brush wolf to no end. "How in the world did you get this scared boy out here?"

Bobby Lee gave an incredulous yip at his master.

"He seemed to know where I was headed and insisted on going. He led the way, in fact. Good tracker, Bobby Lee. Almost as good as we Sioux." Red Otter gave a dry snort.

Bobby Lee cocked his head sideways at the Indian, shifting his weight from one front foot to the other.

Red Otter said, "A couple miles back, I heard the bear singing that song of his. Figured it was you he was serenading. Bobby did too."

As if on cue, the bear roared somewhere off in the distance. It was hard to say where the beast was exactly, for the roars echoed off the high, pine-covered ridges and roiled up out of the canyon that had nearly swallowed Hunter. The cold, breezy air was stitched with granular snowflakes.

Bobby Lee sniffed the breeze and showed his teeth, growling from very deep in his chest.

Hunter and the chief stared in the same direction as the coyote, and shared meaningful glances.

"He'll be back," the chief said.

"Can you get up?"

"I'm gonna have to." The chief threw a hand up to Hunter. "We'd best head for higher ground."

Straightening, Hunter pulled on the man's hand. Red Otter came halfway up, then groaned deeply, turned nearly white behind his natural tan, and sagged back down on his butt.

"Damn!" he said, clutching his right side and bowing his head miserably.

"Let me see them ribs."

Red Otter lifted his head, shook it. "No time."

"We're gonna have to take time. Sit back."

Red Otter groaned again as he leaned back on the heels of his hands.

Hunter opened the man's coat and pulled the right flap back. Hunter sucked a breath through gritted teeth. Blood stained the man's blue shirt over his ribs, roughly halfway between his cartridge belt and his shoulder.

"Damn!" Hunter reached out and gently touched the blood stain. It wasn't only blood he felt. He also felt a broken bone protruding slightly from the bloody tear in the shirt.

Red Otter threw his head back and moaned.

Bobby Lee, sitting beside Hunter, threw his head back and yapped toward the leaden sky.

"We're not goin' anywhere till I've set them ribs," Hunter said.

"No choice," Red Otter insisted. "That bruin's gonna be back. We need higher ground. He's a stubborn beast, that one. I think I put five shots into him. Hardly phased him. Never seen the like."

"I have Angus's .56 Spencer. If I can place a shot right, it should penetrate that thick hide."

Hunter looked at the gauzy sky. It had grown more and more leaden over the past couple of hours. More snow was falling. The air was no longer merely stitched with it. The white stuff was falling at a forty-five-degree angle in a continuous billowing curtain, and the flakes were larger than before. The time was likely only noon, but it was as dark as four or five on a late-autumn afternoon.

Hunter looked at Red Otter. "Weather's getting worse. Storm moving in. We don't have any choice but to camp here." He looked around, saw some trees and rocks back along the trail and on the opposite side of the trail from the canyon. "Cover over there. I'm gonna help you to your feet, Chief."

Hunter crouched low and draped the chief's left arm over his shoulders. The chief groaned, muttered what Hunter assumed were Lakhota curse words under his breath.

Hunter got the man on his feet, though Red Otter was so weak that Hunter practically had to hold him up. The man could put very little weight on his feet. It was too much strain for his broken ribs sliding around like bayonet blades in his chest.

Cursing now himself, Hunter began very slowly and gently leading the man into the trees and rocks. Bobby Lee ran nervously around them, mewling, casting terrified looks around each time the bear sent out its caterwauling roar.

"I sure wish you'd stayed put, Chief," Hunter said as he eased the man down on the ground, in front of a blowdown pine. "I purely wish you'd stayed at the ranch."

Red Otter looked up at him, grimacing. "If I'd stayed at the ranch, you'd be dead. You said so yourself."

"I'd rather die than have more men die for me."

"Balderdash!"

Straightening, Hunter arched a brow at the man. "Not very Injun of you, Chief."

"You're too independent."

"How can a man be too independent?"

"The Sioux have a saying that it's an insult to not accept help from those who care about you. To my people, being too independent is a sin. It gives men meaning to help other men, even if it means dying for them."

Red Otter grimaced again as he sank back against the log. "It's called brotherhood. There is nothing more important in this world."

Hunter stood pondering that for a moment.

Maybe the chief was right. He'd never thought of it that way before. Hadn't he himself fought in the war, gaining meaning and purpose at the possibility of him dying for others?

He was amazed at the notion, however, that a red man would feel that way toward a white man. It brought him up short for a moment but there was no time for sentimentality.

"Yeah, well, just the same, Chief," he said, dropping to a knee beside the man again, opening his coat to inspect the wound where the rib bone was poking through the skin and the torn shirt. "You're not gonna die for me or anyone else today. Not if I have anything to say about it."

Just then the bear's roar caromed around them, echoing once more.

Red Otter looked wryly at Hunter, narrowing one eye. "Yeah, but what about him?"

"He can go to hell."

Bobby Lee groaned skeptically and lay down and planted his long snout between his paws.

Chapter 30

Sheriff Ben Lodge reined his horse to a halt along the trail east of Tigerville.

He slipped his Colt Lightning .44 from its holster and opened the loading gate. He turned the wheel until the cylinder he normally kept empty beneath the hammer gaped up at him. He removed a shell from his cartridge belt, thumbed it into the cylinder, closed the gate, and spun the wheel.

He slid the Colt back into its holster and secured the keeper thong over the hammer.

He gazed ahead now through the aspens to which only a few remaining yellow leaves clung to the spidery branches. Forsythe's Saloon lay ahead of him—a low-slung, brush-roofed, mud-brick affair flanked by an old mine dug into the side of a haystack butte, a small barn, and corral. Half a dozen horses stood tied to the two hitchracks fronting the saloon.

A light snow had fallen during the night but had started melting after the sun had come up. Only a little remained glistening in the brush atop the saloon and in the yard around it, the rest having melted, leaving a few muddy puddles in its place. Steam snakes hovered low upon the ground.

Lodge drew a breath and booted his horse ahead, not liking the apprehension that always visited him when he rode out here. Forsythe's could be an unpredictable place.

He usually rode here once a month for a beer and to make his presence known, so Forsythe and the ne'er-do-wells—mostly small-time criminals including stock and hay thieves the saloon catered to didn't get too comfortable. That they were aware that unlike previous lawmen in and around Tigerville, Lodge was not afraid to ride out here and make sure the raggedy-heeled tough-nuts were keeping their wolves on their leashes and that they would be remiss in considering Forsythe's a safe haven from the law.

If they stole stock or robbed prospectors or jumped mining claims, he would find them here.

Earlier today, he'd been told by a Piper extended family member in town that he'd likely find Royce Piper here. The man had made the confession under threat of being arrested for drunk and disorderly and cutting a whore.

Piper was why Lodge was here, though if he saw any of the men he knew were wanted in the area for petty crimes, he'd throw the cuffs on them. That included two men—a Negro, George Washington Winslow, and a Canadian, LeRoy Sleighbough —he suspected of hanging a young Indian hostler from a ceiling beam in one of the local livery barns for no other reason than they'd been drunk and wanting to see the Indian dance the mid-air two-step. Now Lodge feared he was going to have trouble keeping the local Indian population on its leash.

One damn thing after another.

As Lodge followed the trail through the trees limned by brassy sunshine angling down through high winter clouds, he had to admit he hoped he didn't find the Negro and the Canadian here today. One of his deputies was sick at home so he'd felt compelled to leave the other one in town to man the office and in case the Negro and the Canadian showed up in Tigerville.

Which meant Lodge was riding solo today, no one to back his play.

That shouldn't matter, he knew. But he hadn't been a lawman all that long. Also, he wasn't a young man anymore. While he liked to believe he was up to the job despite how challenging it could become in this relatively lawless region, the truth was he was often scared to death—though he'd die before he'd ever let anyone know that.

Scared for himself as well as for his dear wife, Syvvie. That good woman had worked too hard on their ranch after his first wife, Em, died to have to take a job cooking in some back alley grub tent for a living, which would likely be the case if Lodge ever discovered he was indeed not up to the task and didn't make it home one evening.

He knew, however, that the best way to prevent trouble was to head it off at the pass, as it were. That's just what he intended to do here today. He'd heard grumblings in town from Piper relatives about exacting revenge on Hunter Buchanon and his father not only for the death of Rolly Piper but for what Angus and Hunter had done to Royce.

Namely, humiliating him.

You might be able to kill a Piper and get away with it. But humiliating one was another matter. When you humiliated one Piper, you humiliated them all. They were a cowardly lot, but they were a proud, cowardly lot.

Lodge knew there would be several Pipers here today. Where you found one Piper, you usually found several. They were like a pack of unwashed, underfed curs that way.

Lodge drew up in front of a hitchrack and studied the crude building before him. A man in a ragged wool coat and dungarees lay passed out on a bench to the right of the closed door, atop the dilapidated stoop fronting the place. A tattered red scarf encircled his neck. A battered bowler hat and an empty bottle lay on the floor near the bench.

Lodge gave a sardonic snort, then eased his fattening, middle-aged bulk out of the saddle. He looped his horse's reins over the hitchrack, turned to face the saloon, and unsnapped the keeper thong from over his Colt's hammer.

He clomped up onto the stoop and walked over to the bench and stared down at the ugly, black-bearded face of Arnie Piper, brother of Royce.

The man had vomited on himself. He must have lain out here a good long time, because the filth on his beard, scarf, and ragged buckskin shirt and on his open coat was partly frozen. He sat with both feet on the floor, slumped to one side, one arm hanging off the bench. His long, greasy hair also hung toward the floor. His lips and mustache fluttered as he snored.

Lodge wrinkled his nose. The man smelled like an overfilled privy pit.

Placing his hand over his holstered Colt, Lodge tripped the rickety latch and pushed open the door, stepping cautiously inside and looking around quickly. The men out here, like most men with guilty consciences, were easily startled. Easily startled men, especially those with too much of Forsythe's unholy water coursing through their veins, were known to slap iron and shoot and save the questions for later.

A pair of deputy U.S. Marshals looking for men selling whiskey to the Sioux were said to have been killed that way a few years ago, though their bodies had never shown up. Still, Lodge and most other men who'd lived in the Hills a number of years had heard the story, which was entirely believable given the nature of Forsythe's.

Lodge would have closed the place down if he hadn't known that another place, like a bad weed, would spring up to fill the void. At least, he had a handle on Forsythe's. Or so he told himself . . .

Several heads swung toward him in the room's deep shadows, hands reaching for iron.

"Uh-uh." Lodge quickly closed the door so the opening no longer outlined him, and turned to face the room.

Three men sat at a table roughly ten feet away from him, to the left of a ceiling support post and potbellied stove leaking smoke around its door and through gaps in its chimney pipe pushing up through the low ceiling. All three men had turned to Lodge, two with their hands on their holstered six-shooters, another with his hand on the sawed-off shotgun angled across the table before him.

Three more men sat at a table against the wall to Lodge's right. One had been sitting with his head down on the table when Lodge had entered. That man lifted his head slowly now, blinking his eyes as if to clear the cobwebs, and turning his face to the sheriff.

Royce Piper.

The other two men sitting at the same table, first cousins of his, were playing cards. They'd dropped their cards and reached for their own holstered hoglegs but so far had kept the shooting irons leathered.

His eyes apparently just then focusing, Royce slid his own right hand to the pistol on the table near an empty bowl, a small plate with a scrap of bread on it, and an open gold pocket watch he'd likely stolen from some prospector he'd rolled behind a Black Hills saloon.

Lodge kept his hand on his holstered Colt as he stared at Royce, who, apparently having second thoughts about reaching for his own pistol, lowered his hand to the edge of the table. He hardened his jaws and flared a nostril.

Lodge smiled and turned to the other men, who also removed their hands from their weapons.

"A friendly visit," Lodge said to the room in general.

"A friendly visit?" This from Royce Piper, who looked as though he'd been ridden hard and put up wet. The thin red hair atop his head was badly mussed, and the longer stuff that hung to his shoulders lay in greasy tangles.

"A friendly visit," Lodge said.

When the other customers' attention had drifted away from him, Lodge turned to the fat young man sitting in an ancient brocade rocking chair in the shadows at the rear of the room, at the far end of the bar. This was Dana Forsythe, grandson of the watering hole's owner, Matthew Forsythe.

A young woman sat near Forsythe, in a ladder-back chair. She wore a black and wine-red corset and bustier, and gawdy feathers in her hair. Her legs were bare. She had a purple birthmark just below her left knee. She had one pale, bare foot up on the edge of the chair, and she was crouched over it, picking at a nail.

She was too skinny, and that's likely why she was down here instead of upstairs on her back, but she had a heart-shaped face that was almost pretty in a crude sort of way. She eyed Lodge skeptically.

The jowly Dana Forsythe squinted his eyes, set too close to either side of his large, doughy nose, at Lodge, feigned an affable smile, and said, "Buy you a beer, Sheriff?" His smile widened and his eyes hooded. "As long as you're not here to make trouble . . ."

"Like I said, just a friendly visit," Lodge said, turning to the plank bar on his left.

There were three fly-specked mirrors on the wall behind the bar, amidst the shelves holding dusty bottles and glasses, and with their aid Lodge could keep an eye on the room. Syvvie didn't need him getting a bullet in his back; though he figured his chances of that had gone down when he'd noted silently but not unenthusiastically that the Negro, G.W. Winslow, and the Canadian, LeRoy Sleighbough, were not on the premises.

Dana Forsythe glanced at the girl sitting to his left and said, "In that case . . . Wynona, draw the man a beer."

Wynona scowled at him. "Why should I do it?"

Forsythe hardened his fat jaws as well as his voice, his jowls pinkening with anger. "Because I said so. You ain't doin' nothin' else but pickin' at your dirty feet."

"My feet ain't dirty!"

Wynona dropped her foot to the floor and, scowling nastily at Forsythe, rose and slapped angrily around behind the bar, grabbed a cracked mug off a shelf, blew a dead fly and at least some of the dust out of it, and drew beer from the lone keg between two of the mirrors behind the bar.

She set the mug down so hard in front of Lodge that a good inch of vanilla-colored foam spilled down the edges to pool at its base. "There you are, Lodge. Big spender says it's on the house!"

Still lounging back in his chair, thick arms crossed on his lumpy chest, Dana gave a girlish laugh.

Lodge smiled over his beer at the girl glaring at him. "Wynona, you aren't still sore about having to spend a few nights in my fine little hotel in Tigerville, now, are you?"

"You go to hell!" She slapped the bar, swung around, and stomped back to resume her perch on the chair.

The previous year she'd stolen the poke from a customer, a horse buyer from Cheyenne; she'd brained him with a beer bottle in a crib in town, and Lodge had arrested her trying to board the stage for Lusk.

Again, Dana gave a girlish laugh.

The others in the room chuckled. Lodge saw that as a good sign that the tension inherent in his presence had broken. Now was as good a time as any to fulfill the purpose of his visit. He sipped the foam from his beer and, swallowing, turned casually to face Royce Piper, whose hard eyes were on him.

Chapter 31

"Friendly visit, my ass," Royce groused.

He slid his chair back, gained his feet, and thrust an arm and pointing finger at Lodge. "I was assaulted by Hunter Buchanon the other day, Lodge! At the Union Saloon, an' he ain't even allowed in there. An' you came here to give *me* hell 'cause for some reason you've thrown in with them hillbilly graybacks!"

The three men playing cards near the potbellied stove chuckled, one casting a jeering grin at Royce. Royce turned to the other table, glowering. His two cousins sitting around him—Elden and Donny Gilpin—also turned toward the other three. Lodge recognized the others as local woodcutters who also occasionally illegally sold the whiskey they distilled in secret stills to the Indians, though Lodge had never been able to catch them red-handed. Neither Gilpin brother took kindly to the woodcutters' making light of Royce's humiliation, which, since they were kin, shone badly on them as well.

"He got the drop on me!" Royce yelled, cheeks flushing angrily above his tangled beard. He held up his bandaged hand. "And I gotta bum paw!"

"Yeah," said one of the woodcutters, looking at the others and giving a crooked grin. "We heard all about what happened in the Union." He chuckled and shook his head.

"Let it go, Royce," Lodge said, stepping up to his and his cousins' table. "Never mind them. I'm not here to rub your nose in it. I just wanted to talk to you . . . real friendly like . . . about pulling your horns in." He glanced at the cousins. "You an' the rest of your family."

"Meanin' what?" Royce wanted to know.

"Meanin' I know you're gonna push against the Buchanons. Somewhere . . . somehow . . . you're gonna make a move. You're not gonna be able to resist. They're an itch you can't help but scratch. They're like that for a lot of you Union boys. I'm just here to help stay the urge."

Lodge smiled with equanimity and took another sip of his beer.

"What?" Royce said, his indignance growing. "You think they're too much for us?"

"Obviously," said another one of the woodcutters, hooking a sardonic smile at his accomplices, "they are."

"Even the one-armed old Rebel," said another.

Royce whipped his crazed eyes at the woodcutters. "You shut up, Horton! I bet you never had a go at 'em!"

"No, I ain't that stupid," Horton said. "Only a Piper would be that stupid, to get crossways with Hunter Buchanon."

The other two men at Horton's table laughed.

"You're startin' to chafe," said Elden Gilpin. He was tall and bald on top but with long, sandy hair tumbling down from a band above his ears. He wore a tattoo of a naked woman above the band of hair above his right ear. "You're startin' to chafe real good!"

"What're you gonna do about it, Elden!"

This was going south real fast.

Lodge held up his free hand. "Rein in, fellas! Rein in!! I didn't come out here to throw coal oil on a bonfire. I came out here to talk reason with you, Royce. I am not saying the Buchanons are or are not *too much* for you. I am saying that if you start anything with them—anything at all—I will arrest you and turn the key on you. Now, don't you think you've seen the inside of my jail enough times over the past two years?"

It was Elden's turn to chuckle at his cousin.

"Shut up, Elden," Royce raked out, keeping his eyes on Lodge.

He didn't say anything to the sheriff. He just stared back at him, hard.

Lodge saw that wielding a feather duster wasn't quite going to cut it. He strode slowly forward, his beer in his left hand, his right hand free in case he needed to pull the Colt, though he hoped he didn't have to. Royce was mostly colic and tallow, but it was said he was fast with his six-gun. Lodge had never witnessed that speed in person, so he didn't know if there was any truth to it or not, but if he backed down to every man he thought might be faster than he, he might as well chuck his badge down the privy and go home and starve with Syvvie.

Besides, Royce's Colt was on the table, a farther reach than his holster.

Lodge had to admit that fact emboldened him. He stopped four feet away from Royce, dropped his chin, hardened his eyes, and pitched his voice with cool authority. "Let me grind it up a little finer. If you start trouble with the Buchanons . . . and if you by some miracle of nature survive a run-in with either one of them . . . I will run you out of the county on a long, greased pole!"

The chuckling had resumed at the woodcutters' table before Lodge had finished the sentence.

Royce slid his hard, indignant eyes from Lodge to the woodcutters, then back again. He pursed his lips. His chest rose and fell heavily as he breathed.

As the seconds ticked past, Lodge grew more certain what Royce was going to do. He kept his own hard gaze on Royce's eyes, but he could see in the lower periphery of his vision Royce's right hand dropping slowly toward the holster thonged on the fat firebrand's beefy right thigh.

Toward the empty holster on that thigh . . .

Inwardly, Lodge smiled.

"I've had enough of you, Lodge. You're nothin' but an old dried-up cowman, and I'm done listenin' to you, you old *duffer*!" Royce slapped the empty holster, closing his hand around where the gun butt would have been if the gun had not been on the table. Instantly realizing his mistake, his mouth and eyes widened.

Lodge closed his own hand around his Colt's handle, whipped it up, and smashed it down at an angle, laying the barrel against Royce's left temple. Royce screeched and stumbled backward into his chair, throwing his arms out to both sides like the wings of a bird taking flight . . . or trying to take flight, rather.

Instead, Royce and the chair went down with a clamoring thunder, and for a few seconds it was as though the man and chair were wrestling until Royce whipped the chair aside with a frustrated wail and slapped his left hand to his darkening temple and the two-inch gash Lodge's gun sight had ripped in the flesh.

Lodge stepped back away from the table, holding the Colt on both Gilpins, who remained seated but looking like they were about to spring to their feet, their backs taut, lips compressed, eyes hard.

"Pull your horns in, fellas," Lodge advised.

"You damn old tinhorn!" Royce bit out, looking at the blood smeared on his palm, then glaring at Lodge. "You cut me!"

Lodge stepped forward. He plucked Royce's gun off the table and threw the Colt into a corner. He pulled the six-shooters of each of the Gilpins and tossed them into the corner as well. "Leave them there until I've ridden out of here, or I'll gut-shoot the lot of you."

Yep, he was done wielding a feather duster. He should have known it wouldn't work. The Pipers and Gilpins respected only a hammer. Even then, Lodge doubted they'd stay under rein.

Big mistake, riding out here. He should have let Hunter and Angus finish them off once and for all. His problem was he took too much pride in trying to maintain peace in the county—the first sheriff to ever do so.

Or the first one to try so hard. Maybe he figured it was the one legacy he'd leave, since he and Em, then Syvvie, never had children.

Big mistake. Oh well.

He lowered the Colt and was vaguely surprised to see that he still held his beer in his left fist. He hadn't spilled a drop. He chuckled inwardly at this, impressed, then polished off half of the beer. He set the mug on a table, thanked Dana and the girl for the beer.

They just stared at him, expressionless.

The woodcutters had stopped playing cards to watch him with bemused expressions twisting their mouths.

Lodge nodded to them, walked to the door.

He opened it, started to step out but froze when he saw two men just then riding up to the hitchrack fronting Forsythe's. A chill washed through his belly like the ripple on a dark lake at midnight.

One of the newcomers was a tall, shaggy-bearded white man wearing a red knit cap and a wolf fur coat. The other was a rangy black man in a blue wool coat and black Stetson, a spruce green muffler wrapped around his jaws sporting several days' worth of beard stubble. He wore the striped-blue slacks of the U.S. Cavalry, and high-topped, mule-eared, low-heeled cavalry boots. The two men were talking and glancing back over their shoulders as though they were checking to see if they'd been shadowed.

The white man spoke in the unmistakable lilts of a French Canadian.

As George Washington Winslow and LeRoy Sleighbough—yep, had to be them, gallblastit!—drew rein at the hitchrack, Lodge ignored the thudding of his heart and raised the Colt. "Hold it right there."

The two hardtails jerked their heads toward him.

"Sheriff Lodge," the black man said, glancing at his partner. "Fancy meetin' you here."

Sleighbough spat chew over the side of his saddle and leaned forward against his saddle horn. "Well, now, en't this a surprise!"

"Throw your guns down," Lodge ordered, stepping out onto the stoop and drawing the door closed behind him so he didn't get a bullet in the back. He slid his Colt between the two men before him.

"What's this all about?" Sleighbough asked.

"Yeah," Washington said. "What's got your drawers in a twist, Sheriff?"

"You know what it's about. One dead Injun. Throw your guns down. I won't tell you again." Lodge enunciated slowly, clearly: "Nice and slow. No sudden moves."

"No sudden moves, eh?" asked the black man, an infuriating, mocking smile on his mouth, a jeer in his black eyes beneath the brim of his black hat.

"No sudden moves," Lodge said. "Come on—get on with it!"

"Don't get nervous, Sheriff," Sleighbough said. "We heard you the first time."

The two men shared a glance. Straightening in their saddles a bit, each drew up the flap of his Colt, pulled a six-shooter from a holster, and tossed it onto the ground.

"Now the rifles," Lodge said, glancing at the scabbards strapped to each man's saddle.

"Them, too, eh?" Washington said.

"Get on with it!" Lodge was nervous. He didn't like the feeling. He was facing two wildcats with three more in the saloon behind him.

He should never have ridden out here alone.

"All right," Sleighbough said in his clip-voweled Canadian accent. "Don't get nervous, hey, Sheriff. You're not a young man. Liable to die right there."

He and Washington shared another annoying glance.

"Throw those rifles down!" Lodge barked, trying to keep his anger and his nerves under control. Neither feeling would do him a damn bit of good.

"All right." Sleighbough reached forward with his gloved right hand, slowly slid a Henry repeating rifle from his saddle scabbard. He held it out to his side, smiling. He just held it there, three feet out from his right knee, smiling.

Lodge wished his heart would stop beating so fast. Anger throbbed in his temples.

"Drop it," he ordered through taut jaws.

Sleighbough broadened his smile. Suddenly, he opened his hand. The quick move made Lodge start a little, draw a quick breath into his throat. The rifle fell straight down from the Canadian's open hand to clatter onto the ground.

Lodge slid his Colt toward the black man. "Now, you."

"Patience, my friend," Washington said. He leaned forward and slid his right hand toward the walnut stock of the rifle jutting up from the scabbard on that side of his coal-black horse. Keeping his eyes on Lodge, he closed his hand around the stock and slowly slid the rifle from the scabbard.

Lodge darted his gaze between the man's suddenly cold, hard eyes to the rifle inching up out of the leather. His heart thudded. He could feel his pulse in his knees.

"Get on with it," he spat out through gritted teeth.

"You said to go slow," Washington said. "I'm goin' slow." He smiled, showing a crooked, chipped front tooth.

Lodge watched the barrel clear the leather. "Drop the damn thing!" Lodge barked.

"All right, all right," Washington said in a mock reasonable tone. "Don't get impatient, Sheriff."

But he didn't drop it. Instead, he whipped up the barrel of the Winchester '80 and thrust his hand up around the neck, poking his index finger through the trigger guard and around the trigger just as the octagonal, black maw came level with Lodge.

Lodge's Colt spoke first. The black man's Winchester

spat smoke and flames. The bullet thudded into the frame of the door flanking the sheriff as Washington jerked back in his saddle, shocked eyes bulging.

Lodge cocked the Colt and slid it toward Sleighbough as the Canadian brought up a second pistol from the left pocket of his coat.

Lodge's Colt bucked and roared once more.

The Canadian's eyes bulged in much the same way Washington's had. He fell back over his dun's right hip, throwing the hideout high in the air as he did. He fell down that side of the horse, which pitched with a start and then swerved hard left to pass in front of Lodge. As it did, Lodge saw that Sleighbough's right foot was hung up in the stirrup.

The Canadian stared up at Lodge as the horse dragged him along the ground, Sleighbough's arms thrust up above his head, the blood stain on the front of the man's coat quickly growing as the precious fluid oozed out of his ticker. The man's eyes had turned opaque by the time the dun had dragged him out away from the cabin, then stopped and turned to look at its rider, twitching its ears curiously.

Lodge returned his attention to Washington.

The man remained seated in his saddle, shoulders hunched, both hands drawing back firmly on the black's reins. The black man's wide, shocked, black eyes remained on Lodge. His mouth was sort of bunched, as though he were trying to withhold a laugh. But Lodge knew the man viewed the situation of his life ebbing away quickly as no laughing matter.

Washington opened his mouth and tried to say something, but then he rolled down the left side of his horse and flopped onto the ground. His horse lurched forward with a start and broke into a run, shaking its head and trailing its reins.

Lodge sighed. He sleeved the cold sweat from his brow and lowered the still-smoking Colt to his side. He'd be glad to get home to Syvvie.

The thought had no sooner passed through his brain than something large and hot slammed into him from behind. No, not large. Likely the size of a .44- or .45-caliber bullet. It just felt large. Definitely hot though.

A bullet, for sure. Lodge could still hear the reverberation of the blast rocketing around inside the saloon behind him.

He stumbled forward and down into the yard. His knees weakening, he turned clumsily just as the door showing a single bullet hole in the middle of it opened and Royce Piper stepped into the opening, grinning.

"Thanks for the warning about the Buchanons, old man," Royce said, aiming his own smoking Colt at Lodge's belly. "Here's what I think of it."

Again, the Colt roared.

Chapter 32

"I know Injuns an' firewater don't mix, but here, have a drink."

Hunter held the bottle out to Chief Red Otter.

The snow was coming down harder now, sizzling in the fire Hunter had built in the small clearing in the trees and rocks. He'd retrieved both his horse and the chief's mount and the pack animal, and picketed them nearby, where he could keep an eye on them. He didn't need the bear getting them, leaving him and the chief afoot out here.

His father's old Spencer repeating rifle leaned against a tree within an easy reach. He thought the larger caliber gun would work better on the bear, but he knew that by wielding it instead of the Henry he was giving up speed and a magazine that held sixteen shots. The Spencer was heavier, slower, and held only seven rounds.

Red Otter took the bottle, winked at Hunter. "Salute."

He took a deep pull, then another, then extended the bottle to Hunter. "Your turn."

"I'd best stay clear." Hunter had a feeling it was going to be a long night out here. The snow was coming down too hard to make retreating back to the ranch a practical option. He knew this section of the Black Hills like the back of his hand, but when an autumn storm blew down from northern Dakota, and the snow came down so heavy you could barely see the hand in front of your face, a man could get hopelessly lost even on his own range.

Even in his own ranch yard, for that matter.

He didn't know if this was going to be that kind of storm, but they were better off sitting right here and waiting until this norther blew itself out before heading back to the 4-Box-B. Because of the chief's condition, they'd have to take their time.

"Here we go."

Hunter wrapped a spare shirt he'd found in his saddlebags around Red Otter's waist, over where that rib was tearing through the skin and oozing more blood onto the Indian's flannel shirt. Hunter knotted it loosely, then held both ends of the shirt in his hands.

Red Otter stiffened, closed his eyes. "Go ahead."

"Hold on." Hunter pinched a .44-caliber bullet from his cartridge belt, held it out to his patient. "Bite down on that."

"I don't need it."

"You're gonna need it, Chief. Even a tough old Sioux."

"You know how many times I've been wounded?"

"How many times you had a rib poking through that thick hide of yours?"

Red Otter drew his mouth corners down. He plucked the bullet out of Hunter's hand and stuck it in his mouth, tucking it back along his right jaw. "All right. Go ahead."

Red Otter still passed out when Hunter, grunting with the effort, tightened the shirt around the man's waist, drawing the broken rib back inside his chest cavity and sliding the two ends together. He held the passed-out Indian upright by the shirt, then took one hand off the shirt and used that arm to cradle the man's head and ease him gently back against the wooly underside of his saddle. The bullet tumbled out of Red Otter's mouth.

"Easy does it . . ."

Red Otter groaned, shook his head as if in defiance of the pain.

Hunter gazed down at him. "Tough old warrior, just the same." *Ridin' out here with a storm comin' on to save this white man's hide. One of the white men who drove his people out, helped changed the course of their history, the way they lived . . .*

How many white men had that brand of forgiveness in their hearts?

Hunter didn't like the shallow way the man was breathing. He had to save him. He owed the man his life. He drew the man's blankets up to his chin, tucked them tightly around him, making a warm, soft bundle. Then he added more wood to the fire.

As he did, Bobby's Lee's eyes glowed more brightly over where he sat on the fire's other side, in front of a broad-boled, lightning-topped fir, regarding the passed-out Indian with mute interest. Maybe even concern.

The coyote had become close with every man in the bunkhouse, even Red Otter and Hec Prather who at least outwardly regarded him as vermin. But, then, most Indians didn't consider most dogs worthy of more than a stew pot.

Bobby Lee suddenly turned his head to stare up the gentle, forested rise to the north, ears pricked. Nasty Pete did, as well, and whickered. The grullo stomped a hoof and snorted, whickered again.

"What is it, fellas?" Hunter asked, moving around the fire to kneel on one knee beside Bobby and placing a hand on the coyote's head.

He'd just realized that it had been a good half hour since he'd heard the bear. He'd heard him in the distance but had seen nothing but a few of the bruin's tracks when Hunter had been fetching the horses back to where the bruin had scared them. It had taken considerable doing to lure the three horses back to the area where the bear had been. The only thing horses feared as much as grizzlies was wildcats.

All three mounts had been trained well, and they were naturally loyal. That's why Hunter had added them to his remuda, and why Nasty Pete had been the first horse in his own prized string. Every rancher worth his salt knew to take a good horse to the job.

Red Otter's mount and the pack mount turned their heads now to stare in the same direction Nasty Pete and Bobby Lee were staring. Then Hunter heard it too.

The bear.

It was a distant bugling sound. Gradually, it grew louder, like the caterwauling of some phantom born out of the storm.

Hunter had hoped the bruin had taken shelter from the storm, as he and the chief had done. That hope had been in vain. It was back to wreak more havoc. It was back to kill the man it had been sent here to kill.

By soul of the young Union picket?

Hunter shook his head.

No. It was just a bear like a million others that stalked the West. This one had acquired a taste for human blood in addition to the taste for cattle. That's why it was back.

It now needed to satisfy that hunger for the rare delicacy that was man-flesh. It was driven by a need maybe as potent as the need of an addict for opium.

Hunter thought he could hear that need in the bear's growing cries that rose quickly now to angry wails and echoing roars muffled only partly by the wind and swirling snow.

Hunter added yet another couple of chunks of blow-down wood to the fire, then reached for Angus's Spencer .56. He was sure a .56 round could penetrate this bruin's uncommonly thick hide. If a .56 couldn't do it, likely nothing could.

Apprehension shuddered through him. What if, unlike what Red Otter had opined, the bear couldn't be killed? What if it really was a—

Again, Hunter shook his head and hardened his jaws against the thought.

No. Just a bear, you superstitious fool!

He stepped out away from the fire and around a tree, then dropped to a knee and worked the Spencer's trigger guard cocking mechanism, sliding a long, brass round up from the tube in the rifle's stock into the action, then dropping the trigger guard back into place beneath the breech.

He gazed into the storm. The snow seemed to be lightening a little. He could see maybe fifty feet out away from him, but all he noticed at the moment were the dark stems of the pines and winter-naked aspens, occasional rocks and boulders, all silhouetted against the knife-blade gray of the falling snow.

To his right, the horses whickered and stomped in place, occasionally shaking their heads. Bobby Lee came up to sit beside Hunter and stare off into the storm, mewling softly in his throat.

The roaring grew. There was the cracking of a heavy foot coming down on a branch.

Bobby Lee rose to all fours and raised his hackles and showed his teeth, growling.

The bear bugled again, louder this time.

Bobby flinched, then looked up at Hunter as though embarrassed.

"You're right to be scared, Bobby," Hunter said quietly, gazing into the storm along the barrel of Angus's .56. "Only a fool wouldn't be afraid of that thing." He caressed the Spencer's heavy, cocked hammer with his gloved thumb. "I just need one shot at him. One shot. A .56 should break the weasel's neck."

He watched. He waited.

The wailing continued but it stopped growing louder. It did, however, start swirling around the camp.

"He's going to play it like he did the other night," Hunter grumbled to himself, turning his head to scan the entire area around the darkening camp and the brightening fire. "He's gonna try to scare me into making a move, into leaving the safety of the fire."

The fire.

Hunter looked at the flames burning inside the stone ring he'd set for it. He had only a few dead branches left, piled beside the leaping orange flames. He'd need more. Many more, as it was likely to be a long night with that bruin circling, hoping to lure Hunter out away from the fire or to watch and wait for his own entrance.

"Smart beast. He knows fire . . . and he knows rifles. He's either been hunted before, or . . ."

Again, he let the thought go.

He off-cocked the Spencer, leaned the rifle against a tree, checked on the still unconscious Red Otter, then slipped off away from the fire to gather more wood while there was still some showing above the snow. He'd make short forays and keep his eyes skinned for the bear. He wouldn't venture any farther from the fire than a few yards so if he needed to, he could run back quickly and grab the rifle.

Earlier, he'd spied plenty of seasoned wood near where a pine had been wrenched up out of the earth a few years ago. He could break off the dead branches. They'd be fast-burning fuel, but fuel just the same. And there were plenty of them.

He quickly broke off several branches, having to stomp on some of them to break them, and, looking around warily, hauled them back into the sphere of reassuring firelight.

Bobby Lee sat at the edge of the light—a yellow-eyed sentinel. The coyote had met up with the bear a few nights ago, and knew how dangerous it was. How *otherworldly* it was, maybe. He'd likely only narrowly avoided certain death. He knew to be afraid.

Still, he'd been worried about his master. That's why he'd joined Red Otter on his journey out here to check on Hunter.

Hunter gave a fleeting smile at that. He wished both the coyote and the Indian had remained at the ranch. On the other hand, if they had, the bear would likely be stripping Hunter's bones of their flesh at this very moment at the bottom of that cliff he'd nearly tumbled off of.

He broke more branches off the pine until he had a

good-size pile of dry wood stacked beside the fire. It was going to be a cold night, and he needed to keep Red Otter warm. He'd checked on the Indian several times and found him shivering inside his blankets. Since that broken rib had torn through the man's flesh, there was a good chance of infection. Hunter had to get the Indian back down to the ranch as fast as he could.

More work for the sawbones.

He knelt beside Red Otter, leaning on his rifle. He placed his hand on the man's forehead. Warm.

Hunter winced, shook his head.

The horses whickered again, uneasily.

Sitting on the opposite side of the fire from where he'd been sitting before, Bobby Lee lifted his long snout and loosed a mournful wail at the gauzy sky.

The bear's roar came again, this time from the south, the direction Bobby was facing.

Anger rolled through Hunter. He rose from his knee, took the old Spencer in both hands, and walked over to stand beside Bobby, facing south. The bear roared again, the sound being ripped and swirled by the howling wind.

"Come on, you lily-livered snake!" Hunter yelled. "Come on!"

Behind him, Red Otter coughed. He said something in what Hunter assumed was the Lakhota tongue. Hunter turned toward the man. He lay as before, his head resting back against his saddle, blankets pulled up to his chin.

The chief's severely lined face was drawn taut. He shook his head slightly from side to side, and his lips twitched. He muttered in Lakhota, tightly, as though he were arguing in his sleep.

Suddenly, he opened his eyes and lifted his head and

shoulders from the saddle. He opened his eyes wide and yelled in Sioux. He stared wild-eyed into the storm, the snow catching like down in his gray-streaked black hair.

"Easy, Chief," Hunter said. He walked over and knelt again beside the man, placing a hand on his shoulder. "Easy."

The chief's eyes focused. He turned to Hunter. His face relaxed a little, acquired a vaguely sheepish expression. Slowly, he lay back against the saddle, wincing against the pain in his broken rib.

"What was it you said?" Hunter asked the man. "What was it you said just now? In Lakhota."

The chief shook his head. "Never mind."

"Tell me."

Red Otter looked at Hunter again, his liquid black eyes grave. At the same time, that sheepish expression tugged at his broad mouth. "I told *otshee-monetoo* to go back to where it came from, to leave this good man alone."

Chapter 33

Hunter shuddered.

Then, he, too, felt chagrined. He wasn't supposed to believe in that Injun mumbo jumbo.

The chief reached out and placed his large, copper-skinned hand on Hunter's forearm. "Those are my beliefs. Not yours."

Hunter smiled. "You can say that again."

The Indian returned the smile. The smile did not reach his eyes.

Again, the bear roared distantly. Bobby Lee showed his teeth and growled.

"He's toying with us," Hunter told the Indian. "Just like the other night."

"He's trying to terrorize us. It's all a part of his game."

"It's a game to him?"

The chief shrugged a shoulder. Hunter thought he understood. Sure, a demon would want to terrorize before it killed. The terror was part of the fun. Whoever heard of a demon that didn't take satisfaction . . . pure joy . . . in scaring the bejesus out of its prey?

Hunter snorted a wry laugh. "That Injun stuff again."

Red Otter nodded once but kept his grave eyes on the sky.

"How you feeling?"

"Don't worry about me. Worry about . . . that." He jerked his chin in the direction from which the bear's roars emerged from the snow and the wind.

"I have enough worry for both of you."

"I could use a cup of coffee. Maybe some whiskey in it."

"Comin' right up."

Hunter set the rifle aside but kept it near as he rummaged through his pack gear for his coffeepot and bag of Arbuckle's. He erected an iron tripod over the fire and hung the filled pot from the hook. While the water heated, he sat on a log near Bobby Lee, the rifle across his thighs, staring into the storm. The bear's roars came distantly and intermittently.

"Why isn't he hibernating?" he asked the chief.

But then he turned to see that the man had fallen into another uneasy sleep.

Why isn't he hibernating? Hunter asked himself.

Bobby Lee looked at him, shifted his weight uneasily, and whined.

"Just trying to get good and fat first . . . for the long sleep ahead," Hunter said out loud as he used a leather swatch to lift the lid and drop a heaping handful of the ground coffee into the boiling water.

When the water had returned to a boil, he removed the pot from the hook, added a little cool water from his canteen to settle the grounds, then filled two cups to which he added a liberal jigger of whiskey and stirred the whiskey into the hot, black brew with a spoon.

He looked at Red Otter. The man was awake. His coal-black eyes were on Hunter, their expression inscrutable. What was the man thinking?

That the bear was here because of him—Hunter? Because of his bloody past?

A good man had died and now three others were badly injured, Annabelle terrorized, because of Hunter's bloody past . . .

Hunter stared back at the chief, his own guilty gaze meeting the Indian's dark, inscrutable one head-on. *Was that what he was thinking?*

In his mind flashed the Union picket's sad, terrified eyes, and he gave another involuntary shudder.

"You going to drink both of those or is one for me?" the Indian asked finally, his expression unchanging, though his tone was edged with his customary dry humor.

Hunter brought the cup over to him, set it down beside him. "Careful, it's hot."

He fed Bobby Lee a few strips of deer jerky. The coyote ate without his customary relish, keeping his eyes skinned on the snow and the wind that turned darker now as the day waned. Hunter reclaimed his seat on the log, rifle resting across his thighs, and slowly sipped his coffee, so slowly that it was cold before he'd finished even half.

Quickly, it grew darker.

Hunter kept the fire built up. The snow stopped falling and the wind lightened a little, but the temperature was dropping so that Hunter huddled lower inside his coat and hunkered close to the fire, as did Bobby Lee, who lay down and curled into a tight ball though he did not sleep but kept his eyes open, ears pricked with alertness.

Hunter wasn't sure how much time had passed since the last of the light had oozed out of the storm when he realized he hadn't heard the bear now for a long time. Not five minutes after the thought had swept through his brain, all three horses stirred and one of them gave an ear-rattling whinny.

Hunter jerked with a start. To his left, the chief stopped snoring to grunt his own surprise. Hunter saw first two red eyes glowing like hot coals, moving in the darkness straight out away from him and from the upwind side of the camp. The eyes shifted from side to side and then rose, and then the bulk of the bear took shape in the darkness illuminated by the freshly fallen snow and starlight peeking out from between ragged clouds.

Bobby Lee barked angrily and ran up between Hunter and the bear, hackles raised, tail up, barking furiously.

As the bear lumbered toward the camp, thirty feet away and closing fast, eyes glinting in the firelight, Hunter leaped to his feet, cocked and raised the Spencer.

"Get out of the way, Bobby!" he yelled as the coyote ran toward the bruin.

Hunter leaped up and drew a bead on the bear but held fire when Bobby leaped up into the bear, snarling savagely. The bear swatted Bobby away. Bobby yipped as he tumbled into the brush to Hunter's left.

Hunter aimed and fired.

The bear kept coming, flailing its front legs and roaring, showing its hooked, white teeth, eyes blazing atavistic fury.

Hunter cocked the Spencer again, fired.

The bear faltered as the bullet punched into its chest, parting the fur, but kept coming.

Vaguely, Hunter was aware of the chief half-chanting, half-singing over where he'd been lying against his saddle.

Again, Hunter ejected the smoking cartridge, which sailed back over his right shoulder to clink off a stone behind him. He racked another round and raised the Spencer to his shoulder.

He paused as he stared into the bruin's eyes. The beast was fifteen feet away and closing. He tried to pull the trigger but it was as though his finger had turned to stone.

Behind him, Red Otter's singing and chanting grew louder, shriller.

Bobby Lee was circling the bruin but staying beyond its reach, leaping forward and backward, growling and barking, kicking up the fresh snow that now glinted in the firelight.

Finally, Hunter's right index finger drew back against the trigger but nothing happened.

Misfire!

Red Otter stumbled up between Hunter and the bear, his blankets draped over his shoulders, waving a burning log high above his head and singing and chanting like some demented warlock. The bruin stopped, looked at the burning logs, its eyes blazing brighter. It lifted its head and cast a deafening wail toward the sky.

Suddenly, it dropped, turning, and ran on all fours into the darkness, gone as fast as it had appeared. Bobby gave halfhearted chase but did not go far before he wheeled and returned to the firelight, snarling, whimpering, and quivering.

The chief stopped chanting and dropped to his knees. The burning log fell from his hand to snuff out in a cloud of steam in the snow. Red Otter bent forward over his broken rib.

"Chief!"

Hunter set the rifle down and dropped to a knee beside the ailing Indian, wrapping his right arm over the man's bowed shoulders. "Let's get you back by the fire, Chief!"

Hunter eased the man to his feet. Red Otter shuddered from the pain and the cold. Hunter could feel the fever sweat on him through the blankets.

He helped him back to his saddle and eased him down against it, the Indian scrunching his face up against the waves of agony rolling through him. Hunter retrieved the whiskey bottle. As he did, he saw his own hand shaking.

The bear had rattled him. Rattled him in a way he never *got* rattled.

He knew he'd struck the bear with one shot, but now, seeing how he was shaking, he couldn't be certain he'd hit it with any of the other ones. Likely, he hadn't. There was no way the bruin's hide could be thick enough that a .56-caliber round wouldn't punch through it.

He popped the cork and tipped the bottle to Red Otter's lips. The man drank thirstily. Hunter pulled the bottle back down and looked at the shirt wrapped taut over the broken rib.

He thought he could see some red spotting the edges of it. He'd at least partway opened up the wound.

"Now you've done it, Chief," he said, grimacing and wagging his head.

"The horses!"

"What?"

Red Otter sagged back against his saddle, breathless,

sweating, his heavy lids drooping down over his eyes. "They're gone. They busted loose."

Hunter whipped around. Sure enough, the horses no longer stood just beyond the edge of the firelight, where he'd tied them. All three rope halters lay on the ground, the lead ropes still tied to the picket line that Hunter had strung between two aspens. Now Hunter remembered hearing the horses screaming and dancing when he'd been confronting the bear.

He cursed loudly and ran over to where the picket rope sagged over the snowy ground. All three mounts had run off toward the east. They'd likely been scared to death— the way only a wildcat or a grizzly could scare them. All three would likely run all the way home, to the safety of the ranch.

Again, Hunter cursed. The worst had happened. He and Red Otter were stranded out here on foot.

No, something even worse than that could happen. If they did run all the way back to the 4-Box-B headquarters, someone else might ride out looking for Hunter and the chief. The only one capable of doing that now would be Annabelle.

"Don't do it, honey," Hunter silently prayed. "Just stay there. Don't come out here. This is my fight. Mine alone. I never should have involved anyone else."

Gazing south toward home, he clenched his hands into tight fists at his sides.

"Stay home, Anna. Stay home."

Sitting close beside him, Bobby Lee mewled.

Hunter leaned down to give the coyote's head a reassuring pat, then walked back into the camp. Red Otter lay with his eyes squeezed shut, mouth open, raking deep breaths in and out of his lungs, his broad chest rising and falling sharply.

Hunter wasn't sure if the man was awake until Red Otter, keeping his eyes closed, said, "Going to be a long night. You should catch a few winks. He'll likely be back but not for a while."

"You don't think we discouraged him?" he asked hopefully.

Keeping his eyes closed, Red Otter gave a grim smile and shook his head.

Then his muscles relaxed and his head sagged to one side, chin dipping toward his shoulder. Out again.

The man had a point.

It was going to be a long night. Hunter should try to take a brief nap. He wasn't sure he could. In fact, he was relatively certain he couldn't, but he decided to try.

He built the fire up again, lay down against his saddle, and drew the blankets up. He rolled onto his side, snuggling up in the blankets, facing the blazing heat of the fire.

Bobby Lee curled up in a tight ball in the V between Hunter's knees and his chest.

Soon the coyote was snoring. Soon Hunter was too. No one would have been more surprised than himself. He was even more surprised when he opened his eyes to see gray light washing through the snow-trimmed spruce boughs.

He jerked his head up off his saddle and looked around.

He jerked with another start when he spied movement in the trees silhouetted against the dark gray sky. He breathed a sigh of relief when he saw Bobby Lee standing ten feet away, a dead rabbit hanging slack in his jaws.

Hunter hacked phlegm from his throat and looked at Bobby again. "At least one of us has been busy."

The coyote made a noise in his throat, then lay down with the rabbit beneath a spruce and began ripping and tearing, taking his breakfast.

Hunter turned his head to look across the cold fire at the chief. Red Otter lay as Hunter had last seen him, beneath his blankets. He didn't appear to be moving. His craggy face shone above the covers. His face sagged slack across his severely sculpted cheekbones.

"No," Hunter heard himself mutter.

Red Otter lay as still as death.

Chapter 34

"Nathan, Belle didn't kick you harder than you let on this afternoon, did she?"

Nathan looked up from his plate. "Nah. My leg's just a little sore is all, but that's to be expected. Like you said, takin' your bruises is how you learn about horses."

Earlier while tending his chores in the stable, he'd walked up behind a temperamental mare named Belle, who'd spooked and kicked him.

"You're sure?" It was suppertime, they were alone at the kitchen table, and Anna held a bite of roasted venison up in front of her mouth as she closely studied the boy sitting across from her. "You're not just trying to be tough, are you? I know all about men."

A smile flicked across the boy's mouth and a blush rose in his cheeks at being called a man. "Don't worry, Annabelle," he said, poking at the food on his own plate. "It hardly even colored up. It's just a little scrape is all."

Anna forked the food into her mouth and chewed but kept her curious gaze on the boy. "How come you're being so quiet, then? It's not like you."

No, it wasn't like him. He'd quickly taken to the 4-Box-B. Most days, he hopped and skipped around the place, whistling while he worked. With most of the men having gone down due to the bear or to the outlaws they'd run into while tracking the bear, the boy had gladly accepted more responsibilities. As his horsemanship skills grew and he gained confidence, more and more he walked around with a proud male strut that Anna couldn't help feeling good about.

Today, however, he'd resembled more the shy boy whom she'd first introduced to the ranch.

Again, Nathan lowered his gaze to his plate and twisted his fork in his mashed potatoes liberally covered in Anna's rich, dark venison gravy flavored with garden onions and wild mushrooms. "Uh   I don't know," he said, half-heartedly. "I reckon I didn't realize I was bein' quiet."

Annabelle watched him as she continued eating. Something was bothering him, all right. But she didn't want to badger him. What had likely happened was that Hec Prather or Angus had chewed him out about something, or been typically brusque, hurting his feelings. He'd placed a lot of stock in both oldsters and wanted so much to please them that on the rare occasions he'd fallen short, Anna had noticed that he visibly grimaced and his shoulders sagged.

The two older men weren't used to being around a more sensitive boy than those Angus himself had raised so had not yet learned to moderate their tones. On the other hand, maybe they shouldn't. Maybe the boy needed to take his bruises from the older men in the same way he needed to take them from the saddle stock.

It was the only way to learn and to gain a thicker hide in the bargain.

Anna was sopping her plate with a half piece of sourdough biscuit when the boy looked up at her suddenly, deep lines slicing across his nicely tanned forehead—at least, nicely tanned beneath where his hat sat. "Anna . . . ?"

Anna set the biscuit back down on her plate. "Yes?"

Nathan studied her for a moment, his mouth half-open, wanting to speak. He winced, closed his mouth, and looked down at his plate again. He'd eaten only about half of his food. That wasn't like him either. Something was chewing at him, all right.

"Nathan, what is it? Look, if old Angus or Hec came down too hard on you, I'll talk—"

"No!" Nathan had looked up at her suddenly. "It ain't them. I mean, they do keep sendin' me to fetch a two-handled hammer an' such and to set traps for the jackalope that comes around at night, but . . ." He let his voice trail and the puzzled frown cut more deeply across his forehead. "Anna, there really isn't such a thing as a jackalope, is there?"

Annabelle choked back a laugh. "No, there's not. Any more than there is such a thing as a two-handled hammer, a three-wheeled buckboard, or a nail with two heads."

"I didn't think so!"

"Well, you were right."

He studied her again, again with a deeply troubled expression. "Anna?"

"Do you want me to take those two old devils to the woodshed? Just give me the word and I will!"

"Nah, that's not it." Nathan paused again, glanced down

at his plate, then looked up at Anna once more, finally getting out the words he'd been looking for: "I come from bad people, don't I?"

"What?"

"I come from bad people."

"What makes you say that, Nathan?" Annabelle asked, feeling guilty for the disingenuousness of her tone if not her entire attitude. His uncle had been rustling 4-Box-B cattle, after all. He had bushwhacked Hunter, after all . . .

"I heard you and Hunter talkin' the other night. Out in the yard. I wasn't meanin' to eavesdrop. Honest, I wasn't! It's just that I heard you talkin' about the Pipers. And, well . . . I'm a Piper."

"Nathan, you are a Piper, but you are not like the others. If you were, don't you think I'd know by now? Since the first time I met you, and even knowing who your uncle was, I never once have judged you based on who your family is."

"But I do," Nathan insisted. "I come from bad people. I never really thought about it before . . . or seen me that way, but . . . I come from bad stock. Some of the worst around. My ma, you know . . ." He looked down at his hands in his lap. "She was a—"

"I have never once judged a woman by what her circumstances have made her do to survive. Just as I have never judged a person by their fa . . ." She paused for a moment, frowning, before finishing the word. ". . . Family."

She hadn't realized it before, but what she'd just said was true. She didn't judge others by their families. So, why should she judge herself by who her father was?

"It's true, Nathan. You are your own person. Separate

and apart from those whose blood you carry around in your veins."

"What if I turn out to be like them? Ma, she used to say the apple don't fall far from the tree. She was talkin' about men who came to visit her, but . . . I reckon the same could be said of me, couldn't it?"

"If you were to judge your mother separate and apart from what she had to do to feed both you and herself, would you say she was a good person?"

Nathan smiled. "One of the best around."

"Well, there you go." Annabelle slapped the table. "Case settled!"

Nathan wrinkled the skin above the bridge of his nose again. "Annabelle?"

"Yes?"

"Just in case . . . if I hang around here . . . an' I start to seem like I'm turnin' out bad . . . will you turn me back around?"

It was Anna's turn to smile. "You can bet on it." She winked.

Again, a warm smile sparkled in the boy's eyes. "Thanks."

"Don't mention it." Annabelle straightened in her chair. "Are you going to finish that plate of food or do I have to throw it out? Bobby Lee isn't here to finish it for you, you know. He swallowed down his fear of the bear enough to go looking for Hunter with Red Otter."

"I'll finish it!" Nathan picked up fork and knife and got back to work on the plate.

Anna rose and took her plate over to the wreck pan in the dry sink beside the stove. "When you're done, I'll have you take a plate out to Hec in the bunkhouse. I'll take one to Angus upstairs . . . see if he's awake from his nap yet. I hope Kentucky feels like eating a bite as well. He won't heal without food in his belly."

"You got it," Nathan said, shoveling venison drenched with gravy into his mouth. He added with a wag of his head, "Boy, we sure have us a load of laid-up menfolk—don't we?"

Annabelle smiled grimly as she pumped water into a pot for dish washing. "We certainly do. I've never seen the like." She peered out the window above the dry sink, at the light snow that had been tumbling out of a low, gray sky all day.

Her worry about Hunter intensified. If it was snowing like this down here in the lowlands, it was probably snowing even harder up where her husband was likely hunting the bear. She hoped that Chief Red Otter had found him by now. Even better, she hoped the chief had convinced him to come home. This was no weather for bear hunting. Besides, the beast would likely hibernate soon, and Hunter could resume the hunt in the spring.

She set the pan of dishwater to heat on the stove, then prepared a couple of plates of food—one for Hec out in the bunkhouse and one for Angus who she'd last seen asleep upstairs in his room. His wounds weren't serious, and they seemed to be healing all right, but they'd taken more out of the old man than he'd at first thought. She fixed another small plate for Kentucky, just in case he could manage a bite or two, and left it on the warming rack.

Nathan finished his own supper, deposited his dishes into the wreck pan, then headed off to the bunkhouse with the oilcloth-covered plate that Annabelle had prepared for

Prather. Annabelle covered the second plate with oilcloth and took it upstairs.

Angus's door was partway open. Through the two-foot gap between the door and the frame, she saw Angus standing near the room's single window, clad in a ratty robe and gazing down into the yard onto which snow continued to fall out of the darkening sky of early evening.

To the right lay his rumpled bed with a puma skin comforter.

Annabelle lightly tapped her knuckles against the back of the door. "Watching for your son?"

Angus turned to her. Right away, she saw the worry in his eyes. Hunter had been gone for two days and though a storm had descended on the higher elevations, he had not returned to the ranch.

Angus drew his mouth corners down inside his patchy, gray-brown beard. "Just like you've been doin', I'm sure."

"Yep." Annabelle pushed into the room. "I brought you a plate."

The old man grimaced. "You didn't have to do that, honey. I was about to head downstairs."

Annabelle set the plate on a small table beside the bed. "You shouldn't move around so much. Give those wounds time to heal."

"Heck, they ain't wounds. They're grazes!" Angus chuckled. "Royce was so drunk, he couldn't have hit the broad side of a barn from inside the barn!"

"Just the same, you listen to your daughter-in-law." Annabelle walked up to him and flicked her thumb against his chin. "And stop sendin' that boy out to trap jackalopes."

Angus laughed again, sheepishly this time.

"He told you about that, did he?"

Annabelle smiled, nodded. She stepped over to the window to gaze down at the bunkhouse in which wan lamplight shone behind a curtained window, the other windows being dark. She'd invited Hec into the house. After all, with Kentucky in Anna and Hunter's room, and the chief out looking for Hunter, the old hostler was alone out there. That was how he seemed to prefer it, however.

Old Prather was not a man comfortable amidst the niceties and comforts of a house, even an only half-furnished house. He preferred the crudities of a bunkhouse, with its man smells. Also, Anna suspected he wanted to be alone to sip whiskey to his heart's content and without the possibility of scrutiny or judgment.

She didn't blame him. Those deep wounds of his were painful.

"It's not easy being married to a Buchanon—is it, Annabelle?"

Her old father-in-law's question surprised her.

She turned to him, frowning. "What's that?"

"To a stubborn SOB like my son."

Anna gave a wry snort. "Like father, like son—eh, Angus? I knew what I was getting into. It wasn't like it was a rushed marriage or anything."

"No, you didn't. Any regrets?"

Anna looked back out the window. "Nope."

Angus stepped up beside her and peered out the window with her. "He's lucky to have you. Not too many women would put up with his headstrong ways. His peculiar ways. He's always been notional, Hunter has. Solitary in a way too."

"By peculiar, you mean his obsession with the bear?"

Angus nodded.

"By peculiar," Anna asked again, "do you mean his notion the bear was sent here as a curse on him?"

Angus's grim expression did not change as he gazed out the window. He hiked a shoulder.

Remembering something Nathan had just said down in the kitchen, Annabelle said, "Well, in that regard, I reckon the apple didn't fall far from the tree—did it?"

Angus stretched his lips back from his teeth, shook his head. "I've seen some peculiar things in this world, Anna." He turned to her. "Not to worry you though. Red Otter will help. If it's anything but a bear, I mean. The chief will help."

Anna stared at him. A bleak uneasiness had settled over her.

Good Lord, was Angus's peculiar notions getting to her, now, too? She shook her head against them.

She turned back to the window. "I'm sure he'll be home by morning."

"God willin'."

"God willing." Anna kissed the old man's cheek. "You eat, now. I'm going to check on Kentucky and then go back downstairs and wash dishes. Going to be a long night, I'm afraid."

Angus smiled again, grimly.

"You need anything else?"

Angus looked at the plate on the table. "No, I'm good. You treat this superstitious old fool too kindly, Anna."

"I enjoy spoiling superstitious old reprobates," she said, and kissed his cheek.

As she did, three soft knocks issued from the front door downstairs.

Angus had heard it too. He frowned at Anna. "Was that the front door?"

"I think so."

"Is it locked?"

"No. I'm expecting Hunter and Red Otter anytime."

"Well, it's not them, then."

"I'll see."

Anna left the room and headed downstairs. She slid the curtain aside from the long, rectangular window left of the door, and peered out. A man in an animal hide coat and broad-brimmed black hat stood to her right, in front of the door. Behind him, a horse stood at the hitchrack, wearily hanging its head.

Anna released the curtain and picked up the double-barrel shotgun that she and Hunter always kept leaning against the foyer wall, in case of unexpected trouble.

Maybe not so unexpected in this still-half-wild country . . .

At least, whoever was out there respected the fact that the door was not locked and didn't come barging in, guns blasting. Still, Anna opened the door and stepped back quickly, lifting the double bore across her chest and caressing the hammers with her thumb, ready to pull them back at a moment's notice.

In his winter coat and with a muffler wrapped around his neck, the visitor was silhouetted against the night, so

Anna didn't recognize him by appearance. She recognized his voice, however.

"Anna?"

"*Cass?*" She lowered the shotgun slightly. "What are you doing out in this weather?"

"Pa's dead."

She didn't say anything for a moment.

Then, lowering the shotgun to her side, she said, "Come in."

Chapter 35

"Pull that bottle down, you damn fool. We get any drunker, we're gonna get both of us killed!"

"If I don't get any drunker, Royce, I'm gonna turn around and ride back home!"

Royce Piper scowled at his cousin, Elden Gilpin, who sat a horse to Royce's left, at the very edge of the 4-Box-B ranch yard. Donny had decided to head back to town and not pursue this foolhardy scheme. Elden held a near-empty whiskey bottle in his gloved right hand on that thigh.

"You ain't goin' anywhere, you damn fool," Royce stammered. "You threw in with me. Once you throw in with Royce Piper, there's no turnin' back . . . less'n you want a bullet in your guts!"

"Tough talker," Elden muttered, sort of half-turning away and hunching his head down low in his ragged wool coat sewn together from trade blankets.

"What's that?" Royce said.

"Nothin'."

"No, I want you to say it to my face, Elden. Don't turn away from me, coward. Tell it to me straight-on."

Elden turned back to his larger, beefier cousin, Elden

being a scrawny little rat-faced man with a flat-tipped nose and red pimples showing through his thin, dark brown beard cut through on the right cheek with an old, knotted, pink knife scar. Elden opened his mouth to speak but thought better of it and averted his gaze and pulled his mouth corners down instead.

"You don't think I'll go through with it?" Royce asked. He kept his voice low. The wind had died and the snow had stopped falling, leaving only two or three downy inches on the ground, so he didn't have to speak above the wind anymore to be heard. "That horse's ass—hell, *both* them Buchanons—made me look the fool, an' they're gonna pay for it."

"What're you gonna do—waltz in there, gun blasting?" Elden canted his head toward the large lodge house, nearly all of whose lower story windows—at least, those that could be seen from this angle—were lit behind drawn curtains with glittering lamp- and firelight.

Royce raked a mittened hand across his furry jaw. "Ain't thought about that yet." He pondered it shortly, then turned back to his scrawny, cowardly cousin. Hell, Royce thought he himself was a coward. He had nothing on Elden! "Yeah, why the hell not?" he said.

"Huh?"

"We're gonna waltz right in there, *guns* blasting. Why not? They won't be expecting trouble on a cold, stormy night like this one here."

Just then, Royce's chestnut whickered and turned his head to peer behind him. Royce turned, then, too, and his heart thudded inside his own heavy coat when he saw the silhouette of a horse and rider moving along the trail behind him and Elden.

"Someone's coming!" he hissed, and put the buckskin off the trail and behind a large Ponderosa and a small cluster of cedar brush.

Elden followed suit, batting his heels frantically against his coyote dun's ribs.

"Hurry up, dammit!" Royce raked out.

"Shut up—I'm tryin'. Stubborn damn hoss!"

When they were both safely separated from the trail by the pine and the brush, Royce leaned forward to peer through a small gap in the brush and around the pine, toward the trail. As he did, he slid his carbine from his saddle sheath and rested the barrel across his pommel. The rider's hoof thuds rose gradually and then the man and the horse passed along the trail, following the curve through the open portal and into the ranch yard.

Elden turned to Royce. "If that was him, you blew your chance!"

"I don't think it was him!" Royce returned, angry. "If I thought it was, he'd be bleedin' out on the ground by now. You can be double-dee-damn sure of that!"

"Tough talker," Elden grumbled again, half-turning away.

"What'd you say?"

"Nothin'," Elden said, sheepish.

Royce let it go. He had more important fish to fry than his cousin's smart mouth.

The whiskey he'd drank—and the stewing he'd done while drinking—had stoked the stoves of fury inside him to a raging fireball. Those stoves would not cool until Hunter and Angus Buchanon were dead. He didn't care if he had to shoot them through a window like the coward he was.

At least, they'd no longer have the satisfaction of having humiliated Royce Piper. No. Dead men didn't feel satisfaction. They didn't feel anything at all.

"What're we gonna do about the visitor?" Elden asked, watching the newcomer pull his horse up in front of the house, tie the reins to the hitchrack, and mount the porch steps.

Again, Royce raked his mittened hand across his bearded jaw. "We'll use him. As a distraction. Yeah . . . yeah. This is good."

"Hold on—wait a minute."

"What is it?"

"Look there." Royce pointed toward the yard. More specifically, toward where a diminutive figure in a bulky coat was walking from the barn toward the house.

Elden looked at his cousin. "A kid? I didn't think the Buchanons had no kids."

"Must be that kid Rolly had livin' with 'em. His whore sister's kid. I heard Angus tell the sheriff that the Buchanons took him in." Royce pitched his voice with sarcasm. "They was gonna be all charitable and take the boy in because they didn't think his blood kin could raise him up proper!"

"Hoity-toity hillbilly jackals!"

"Yeah." Angrily stretching his lips back from his teeth, Royce neck-reined his horse around and said, "Come on."

"Where we goin'?"

"Change of plans. I just got me a whole new idea—one that will keep us from havin' to go into the house, see? We're gonna make Buchanon come to *us*!"

"What?"

"Shut up and follow me!" Royce said as he put his buckskin onto the trail.

He put the steel to the mount, and the buckskin stretched its stride into a hard gallop. It thumped through the ranch portal and into the yard. The kid was now about halfway between the barn and the house. He swung around as he heard the two horses galloping toward him.

Royce reined up about ten feet away from the boy who had stiffened in fear and, keeping his eyes on the two strangers, started to back toward the house.

Royce held up his left hand, palm out. He kept his voice low so no one in the house or the bunkhouse heard him. "Hold on, kid, hold on. We're friendly. In fact, we're *family*!"

"Huh?"

Royce chuckled. "Kid, I'm a Piper, same as you. What're you doin' here with these Buchanons, anyway? They ain't kin. You belong with kin!"

"No!" the boy yelled suddenly, spooking Elden's horse. The dun whinnied and nearly bucked Elden off.

As the boy swung around and started to run for the house, he slipped in the fresh snow and fell. Royce gigged his horse forward, leaned far out from his saddle, and grabbed the boy's arm just as the kid regained his feet.

"You're comin' with me, you little traitor!"

With a loud grunt, Royce pulled the boy up and laid him belly-down across his saddle, wedged painfully between Royce's broad hips and the horn.

"Ow—*no*!" the kid cried. "Ann . . . *Annabelle*!"

Just a few minutes earlier, Anna closed the lodge's front door and turned to her unexpected visitor.

"How?" she asked. "How . . . did . . ."

"Don't worry—he didn't shoot himself. He died earlier this afternoon. In his sleep, I think. He laid down for a nap . . . downstairs, in the parlor. I was in the kitchen and heard him stop snoring. I went into the parlor to try and rouse him, and . . ." Cass shook his head.

He looked drawn and pale, his eyes haunted.

"I see," Annabelle said, her hollow tone belying what she felt.

She wanted to feel nothing. No. Maybe what she really wanted to feel was relief at the old sidewinder's passing. But relief was not what she felt. No, she felt . . . what?

Sad.

Imagine that.

Maybe even a little regret that she had not last left him on better terms. But she had left on her terms. At least, what she'd believed at the time were her terms. Not having forgiven him.

Maybe she should have, after all. Maybe Cass had been right. Maybe it would have done them both some good.

But she hadn't and now it was too late, and now she could get down to the business of forgetting him.

"What are you thinking?" Cass asked, staring down at her from beneath the brim of his hat.

Anna shrugged. "I don't know. A strange mix of things."

"Yeah." Cass nodded. "Me too."

"You could have waited until tomorrow, Cass. It's cold . . . dark outside."

"I was going to wait, but . . . I needed to get out. He's still in there. I put him in his bed, cleaned him up. Tomorrow, I'll build a coffin." Cass looked down at the toes of his boots. "I just . . . I just needed to get away . . . take a ride." He looked at his sister again. "I needed to tell you."

Suddenly, tears glazed his eyes. "I hope," he said, haltingly. "I hope you and me . . . I hope we can . . . you know . . ."

"No, I'm not sure what you mean, Cass."

"I hope we can be like sister and brother again. You know—be closer than we've been in a long time."

Annabelle's heart warmed. She smiled and placed her hand on her brother's arm. "I'd like that too." She paused. "I tell you what—why don't you stay here tonight? You don't want to ride all the way back to the Broken Heart. Not with . . . you know . . . him lying—"

"I think you're right, Anna. I'd like to accept your off—"

A shrill yell from outside cut him off.

It came again, louder: *"Annabelle!"*

"Nathan?"

Anna grabbed the shotgun again, brushed past Cass, opened the door, and stepped out onto the porch. Two silhouetted figures—one large, one small—were skirmishing in the middle of the ranch yard, to the left of the windmill and stock trough. Another man sat a horse to the left of the skirmishers, trying to hold the nervously prancing mount steady.

"Nathan!" Anna shouted, hurrying across the porch.

"Now you've done it, you little—"

The smaller of the two figures, which was obviously Nathan, just then wrenched free of the big man's grasp, twisted around, and dropped to a knee.

"Damn you, kid!" the big man bellowed, lunging toward Nathan once more in the slippery snow.

Himself falling to a knee, the big man wrapped his beefy left arm around the boy's neck. It was Royce Piper. Had to be. Most folks who'd spent any time in and around Tigerville knew who most of the Pipers were.

"Piper, get your hands off him!" Anna cried, stopping at the bottom of the porch steps and raising the two-bore to her shoulder.

Holding Nathan taut against him, Piper glared at Annabelle, showing the off-white line of his teeth between his lips in the darkness. "Put the greener down, or so help me, I'll snap the boy's neck!"

"What in holy blazes . . ." Annabelle heard Cass mutter as he came down the steps to stand beside her.

Anna clicked the shotgun's hammer back. "Let the boy go or so help me, Royce Piper, I'll blow you in little bitty pieces through the smoking gates of hell!"

"I'll snap his neck! I will! I swear it!"

"Anna!" Nathan cried.

Meanwhile, the man on the horse had chewed off his right mitten and fumbled a revolver out of his coat pocket. Holding his horse's reins with his left hand, he aimed the gun at Anna with his right hand, yelling, "He means it! He means it! Drop the greener, little girl!"

He turned to Royce. "Should I shoot her, cousin?"

A gun blasted to Annabelle's left, setting up a ringing in that ear. The crashing report had nearly made her leap out of her slippers. The horseback rider was quickly horseback no more. He yelped and tumbled back over his horse's left hip as the horse pitched, wheeled, and fled back toward the portal, trailing its reins. The former rider lay in a twisted heap, unmoving, dead.

"Bad idea!" Cass said, sliding his smoking Colt toward Royce Piper. "You're next if you don't let the boy go, Piper!"

Royce switched his startled gaze from his motionless cousin to Cass. "Who the hell are you?"

"That's my big brother," Annabelle said through gritted teeth. She glanced at Cass, curled a quick half smile, then returned her gaze to Piper and the boy.

"Cass?" Piper said, incredulous.

"That's right."

Royce opened and closed his mouth several times before he got any words out. "I . . . I didn't . . . I didn't . . ."

"Recognize me? Yeah, I get that a lot these days."

"I didn't know . . . I didn't know you was here . . ." Piper's voice was pitched with wariness. "Where's . . . Buchanon . . . ?"

"So that's what this is about."

Anna stepped slowly forward, keeping the shotgun aimed at Royce's head. She wasn't about to take the shot, because there was no way the buckshot spread wouldn't include Nathan, but she didn't want Piper to know that. "Let the boy go, and we'll talk about my husband."

Piper tightened his crooked arm around Nathan's neck. "Stop there, or so help me, I'll kill him! I'll kill the boy! Wouldn't want me to do that, would ya?"

Again, Cass stepped up beside his sister, keeping his Colt aimed at Piper. "Do what Sis says, Royce. There's no way out for you. You hurt the boy, and she'll blow your head clean off your shoulders."

"Drop the hogleg, Cass!" To Anna, he said, "Send your husband out here, and I'll let the boy go."

"He's not here."

Royce considered that, cocking his head skeptically to one side. "Sure, he is. Where else would he be on a night like this?"

"He's hunting a bear."

"A bear? My butt, he's huntin' a bear on a night like this! What—is he hidin' from me?" Piper grinned, slitting his drink-bleary eyes jeeringly. "Is he hidin' from Royce Piper?"

"Yeah, that's it," Annabelle said. "He's hiding from you, Royce. You're not gonna see him tonight. So, you either let the boy go or die. The choice is yours."

To the boy, Anna said, "Hold on, Nathan. He's going to let you go. You'll be all right. He's not a total fool!"

Royce looked at his dead cousin. Then he looked around for his horse, but the buckskin had run off through the portal with the dun. Turning back to Anna, his voice growing shrill with desperation, he said, "I'm either takin' the boy . . . on a fresh hoss . . . or I'm gonna *kill him!*"

He gained his feet with a savage grunt, pulling Nathan to his feet also. Again, Royce tightened his hold on the boy's neck.

Nathan screamed and danced in place, trying in vain to pry the big man's stout arm from his neck. "I swear I'll kill him. Put them guns down and saddle me a hoss!"

From above and behind Anna, she heard a familiar, raspy voice say almost casually, "You damn fool, Piper."

A rifle barked.

Again, Anna jumped. So did Cass.

At the same time, Royce snapped his head back sharply as viscera blew out the back of it. The man's arms fell to his sides. He staggered backward several steps before tripping over his own feet, half-turning, then falling in the snow with a dull, crunching thud.

He lay as still as his cousin in death.

Sobbing, Nathan gained his feet, glanced back at Royce Piper, then ran to Anna. She lowered the shotgun, dropped to a knee, and wrapped her free arm around the boy, drawing him taut against her. As she did, she glanced up at the half-open second-story window from which Angus's Winchester still protruded, as did the old man's wizened, bearded face.

Angus shook his head in disgust. "That damn Yankee has been needin' a bullet since the day he was born. The boy all right?"

"I don't know." Anna looked at Nathan. "Are you all right, Nathan?"

Nathan nodded, sleeved tears from his cheek. "More of my kin, ain't they? My blood." His tone was fateful, bleak.

"No." Anna shook her head. She glanced up at Angus and then at Cass and smiled as she said, "We're your blood now."

"And no one messes with a Buchanon!" Angus added.

Cass looked up at the old man. "Nice shootin', Mr. Buchanon."

"Yes, it was." Angus pulled in his head and rifle and closed the window.

Hoof thuds sounded in the north. Anna turned to see two horses trotting along the northern trail, heading toward the headquarters. She started to turn away, deciding they were Piper's and Gilpin's mounts, but turned back when she saw a third horse behind the first two.

All three horses trotted through the portal and into the yard.

Anna's heart hiccupped.

One of the horses was Nasty Pete. The other was the chief's horse. The third one was the sorrel packhorse that Hunter had led out of the yard three days ago.

Chapter 36

"Chief?" Hunter called again, staring worriedly over at where the Indian lay unmoving in his blankets.

He thought the man's eyes were partway open. His lips were parted as well. There was no breeze, and the birds were strangely quiet.

Still, Hunter couldn't hear Red Otter breathing.

"Chief?" Hunter tossed his blankets aside. As he did, Bobby Lee abandoned his breakfast and gained his feet, looking toward Red Otter and whining softly.

Hunter rose stiffly, walked stiffly over to the Indian.

He dropped to a knee. His gut rolled. The man's eyes were partway open all right. So was his mouth. But he didn't appear to be breathing. He made no sound and his chest was not rising and falling.

Not even a little.

Hunter nudged the man's shoulder. "Chief?"

The man's body was stiff. He did not respond. His sunken cheeks owned a death-like pallor behind the copper.

Sitting beside Hunter, staring down at the inert Indian,

Bobby whined again, tilting his head this way and that, obviously wondering why the man wasn't stirring.

Hunter lowered his head and turned an ear to the man's chest.

Silence.

He straightened, cursing, his guts twisting down low in his belly.

"Dead, Bobby Lee," he whispered.

He crossed the man's hands over the buckle of his belt and, squeezing the man's large, cold hands in both of his own, lowered his head in sorrow. He shut his eyes tightly, grimacing.

"I'm so sorry, Chief."

The broken rib must have torn him up inside. Likely, he'd bled to death during the night.

While Hunter had slept.

There would have been nothing Hunter could have done, not being a doctor and the man's blood draining away inside him. Still, guilt raked him. At least, he should have been awake. He should have been sitting with the man. The man had given his life for Hunter's, after all.

But, then, he remembered what Red Otter had told him the previous day:

To my people, being too independent is a sin. It gives men meaning to help other men, even if it means dying for them . . . It's called brotherhood. There is nothing more important in this world.

"Just the same," Hunter said. "You shouldn't have died for me. I don't deserve it."

Bobby lifted his long, pointed snout and gave a mournful howl. He turned his head sharply to stare off toward the north through the dark stems of the trees silhouetted against the gradually brightening sky.

"What is it?" Hunter whispered.

Bobby canted his head to each side, bent first one ear forward, then the other. He raised his lips to show his teeth, growled, then looked up at Hunter, a spooked cast to his gaze.

"Is he coming?"

Bobby turned his head to stare north again, growling softly and mewling warily.

Hunter rose and walked over to retrieve his Spencer .56 from where he'd leaned it against his saddle, where it had been within a quick reach during the night in case the bruin had come stalking. But it had not.

Why?

It might have been off licking its wounds. Hunter thought he had hit the beast at least once, possibly twice. Good. Maybe he'd weakened it.

He glanced at the chief, walked back over, and pulled the man's blankets up to conceal his face. He wished he could somehow secure the Indian's body from the bear, but there was no time to bury him or cache him in a tree.

Instead, he'd go out and try to intercept the beast before it gained the camp.

"You stay here, Bobby."

Bobby Lee sat down near the mounded gray ashes of the fire, drew his tail in a tight circle around him, and looked skeptically up at his master.

"Don't look at me like that," Hunter said. "I'm gonna go bear huntin'. Within an hour, we're gonna have us a nice new rug to lay down in front of the fireplace."

He liked the confidence he heard in his voice, though

it had taken quite the manufacturing. He worked the Spencer's trigger guard cocking mechanism, seating a live round in the chamber, then walked out away from the camp, leaving Bobby Lee gazing worriedly after him.

A cold hand was pressed tight against the back of his neck.

The truth was, he was scared. He didn't like the feeling. It made his legs and knees stiff, his hands clammy.

That's all right, he told himself. He'd felt the same way during the war, especially when he was on a clandestine mission behind Union lines, sent out by his commanding officers under cover of darkness to blow a bridge, a supply train, or an ammo dump, armed with only his bowie knife, one Griswold & Gunnison revolver holstered over his belly, and maybe a few Ketchum hand grenades he'd taken off Union soldiers to use against their own army.

He'd used the fear then as fuel. He would use it as fuel now.

From somewhere ahead, in the still dark but gradually lightening forest, the bear roared angrily. The roar echoed eerily, the echoes themselves like some living thing— giant prehistoric birds, say—winging threateningly around him but keeping out of sight.

The bear was calling him. Hunter knew it was. He knew it down in the murky depths of his own soul, and that knowledge further chilled him. Made his knees creak and cold sweat pop out on his back.

Slowly, purposefully, he moved through the forest, stepping carefully over blowdowns and around wild berry thickets mantled with fresh snow that glowed brighter by the minute.

He walked up to the top of a ridge slanting down from

a higher ridge to the north, on his left. The sun just then peeked out through clouds in the east, laying a burnished copper glow across the forest below and around him and on the narrow, southward-slanting stone ridge crest from which the wind had swept away yesterday's snow.

He stopped to catch his breath from the hard climb and to look around.

No sign of the bear.

No.

Wait.

He stepped forward several feet down the other side of the stony ridge and dropped to a knee. Four large tracks shone plainly in a wind-scalloped drift of feathery blue snow. Not only tracks but several small, pink teardrop blemishes.

Blood.

Hunter had, indeed, wounded the bruin.

There, you see—it can be killed! If it can bleed, it can die!

A demon sent from the other side. Pshaw!

Hunter's heart quickened. The scuffed tracks left the drift on the ridge's downhill side. Hunter spotted more prints in the moist soil beyond the drift, trailing off down the ridge and into pines at the bottom. The tracks were recent; the bear had passed through here within the last half hour.

His heart quickening even more, Hunter straightened, shouldered the rifle, and headed off down the ridge. He moved into the pines and stopped, taking the Spencer in both hands, resting his thumb on the hammer, and looking around carefully. Only pines around him pushing up from the soft, aromatic forest duff.

He picked up the tracks again and followed them down along the floor of the canyon, which doglegged to the east. They continued for maybe a quarter mile before turning from the floor of the canyon to climb the pine-stippled slope on Hunter's left.

Hunter followed the tracks. That cold hand remained pressed firmly against the back of his neck while his heart drummed anxiously. His hands, clammy inside his gloves, squeezed the Spencer tightly as he climbed the slope and followed the tracks as they weaved their way through the pines, firs, and spruce trees.

He remembered how suddenly the bear had appeared the night before. It could again. He had to be ready at a moment's notice to snap the Spencer's butt plate against his shoulder, aim for the bruin's neck, and fire.

Where are you, you devil? Show yourself.

No, not a devil. Just a bear like any other. But bigger and wilder than most. As deep as the bear pushed its track into the moist ground, it had to weigh well over a thousand pounds . . .

The trees fell back behind Hunter. The slope continued rising before him toward strewn granite boulders and a ragged-tipped granite ridge beyond. The wind moaned and howled against the rocks, blowing the fresh snow around so that it glittered like sequins in the intensifying sunshine.

Hunter crossed the open part of the slope and started walking through the boulders, moving slowly, breathing hard against the steep climb, keeping the rifle ready at port arms, his right index finger curled through the trigger guard and resting firmly against the trigger.

When he'd walked maybe fifty yards, the slope nearly

leveled out. He approached the windy crest, which was all blocks and lumps and thumbs of time-eroded rock. The powdery snow had collected in dimples, cracks, and bowls in the rock. The chill wind picked it up and blew it around in a pearl haze, sunlight flashing off the individual flakes, making it hard to see.

He stepped around a thumb of rock and froze.

He found himself staring through a mist of wind-blown snow buffeting like a white guidon at two glistening snow-flakes. Only, the flakes weren't moving. They were stationary and they were larger than the others.

They were not snowflakes.

Just then the bear bounded toward Hunter from twenty feet away.

Hunter gave a startled grunt as he snapped the Spencer to his shoulder. He fired, the rifle punching back against his shoulder, leaping and roaring against the howling wind.

He started to work the cocking lever, then stopped.

Too late.

The bear was too close.

Then it was on him, roaring, the head with laid-back ears and large, round amber eyes enormous in front of him, blocking out all the rest of the world. A mighty paw swung toward Hunter and knocked the rifle out of his hands.

He stumbled backward, lost his footing, twisted around, and fell. He rolled back down the steep part of the slope, the hard stone surface hammering his head and shoulders and hips. Grunts were punched out of him with every painful blow.

He rolled against the base of a boulder and looked up to see the bear stop only ten feet away, rise up onto its hind legs, lift its head, open its toothy jaws, and hurl a bugling wail toward the clear blue sky opening beyond the glistening, blowing snow.

"*Here!*" a voice called to Hunter's left.

He turned to see Chief Red Otter standing fifteen feet away, throwing the Spencer toward Hunter.

"You have to kill him!"

Hunter thrust his hands out and caught the rifle just before it would have brained him. His mind, numb with shock, was slow to accept Red Otter's presence. He'd left him dead in their camp, covered with his blankets.

Hunter gaped, speechless, at the Indian.

Red Otter pointed at the raging bear shuffling toward Hunter. "Kill it! Only you can!"

The Indian dropped to his knees, raised his hands high above his head, palms turned toward the bear, and began chanting loudly.

That seemed to distract the bear who stopped and turned toward him, a faint befuddlement passing like a cloud over his eyes.

Hunter aimed for the beast's neck and fired.

The bruin snapped its head back toward him, rage again glowing in its eyes.

The chief chanted more loudly.

Hunter ejected the Spencer's spent cartridge, seated fresh, aimed at the bruin's throat, and fired.

The beast stopped, waved its big paws at its throat, and shook its head. Startlement glinted in its eyes.

The chief chanted, waving his hands, singing the chants now, chin high, eyes closed, a solemn look on his severely sculpted features.

Hunter fired again. This time the bullet plunked into the beast's chest around where its heart would be.

That knocked the grizzly backward. Twisting to one side, it dropped to all fours, looked at Hunter once more, roared, and showed its long, white teeth. Hunter would be damned if the beast didn't look exasperated.

As the chief continued singing his chants at the tops of his lungs, Hunter fired again.

The beast jerked, shook its head, roared again furiously, then turned full around and took off running in its shambling, heavy-footed gait for the crest of the stony ridge.

Hunter smiled. He had him on the run.

But he needed to finish him.

He gained his feet, quickly pulled the magazine tube out of the Spencer's butt stock, and replaced his spent rounds with fresh from his cartridge belt. Aiming and firing another round, he hurried after the bear, the chief singing and chanting even louder behind him.

Hunter fired again at the retreating beast.

The bruin flinched and jerked its head around to snap at its left rear hip before it continued running.

At the top of the ridge, it stopped and turned back toward Hunter.

Hunter stopped fifteen feet away from the bruin.

He raised the Spencer again, fired again.

"Die, you devil!"

But it didn't die. Suddenly, it dropped to all fours and charged him. It came at Hunter like a quickly growing, cinnamon-colored cloud. So fast, it was a blur, the beast's stench filling his nose and lungs.

Suddenly it was on him and he was again dropping the Spencer and falling straight backward. The bear fell on his legs. Hunter looked down in horror to see the bear glaring up at him, snapping its jaws, clacking its sharp teeth together.

The beast thrust its head toward Hunter's, intending to rip out his throat.

Hunter gritted his teeth and closed his eyes, bracing himself for a certain, agonizing death. He just hoped the bear made it quick.

Nothing happened.

When four, maybe five seconds passed, he opened his eyes and looked down past his chest. The bear's head lay on the ground between Hunter's spread legs, the beast's paws sort of cradling Hunter's legs. The bruin lay with its chin against the ground, its flat, dull eyes staring up at Hunter.

Blood oozed from the beast's mouth, troughing down the long, dark pink tongue that hung down over its lower jaw to the stony ground.

Hunter stared into the bear's eyes.

He looked for the Union picket's eyes. For the fear and desperation he'd once seen in those eyes so long ago but could usually see in his mind's eye as if he'd killed the young soldier only yesterday.

But that look was not in the bear's eyes. There was only the bear's large, round, flat-brown orbs staring up sightlessly at his killer, looking a little befuddled by its demise.

Hunter shook his head.

No.

He shook his head again and gave a weak half smile.

No, that look wouldn't be there. "Only a bear," he said aloud. "Just a bear like any other. Bigger than most . . ."

"Hunter!"

He turned his head toward the source of the wonderfully familiar voice. Boots clacked on the rocks. Annabelle and her brother Cass came running around the side of a boulder, each holding a Winchester, the tails of their mufflers buffeting, cheeks burned raw by the sun and cold wind. Bobby Lee was running ahead of them, making a beeline for his master.

"Bobby!"

"Hunter!" Anna called again.

Hunter threw up an arm. "Here!"

Bobby Lee threw himself in Hunter's arms, whining and licking his face.

Anna and Cass jerked their heads toward where Hunter lay with the bear's head between his legs, and slightly adjusted their courses.

"Oh, Hunter!" Anna cried, her horrified gaze taking in the bear and then her husband lying in front of it, the beast's blood pooling between his legs. She dropped to both knees beside him and stared down at the hulking bruin. "My God!"

Bobby lowered his head to sniff the bear, growling.

"Don't worry—it's dead, Bobby."

Yes, it was dead. No sweeter word had he ever uttered. The beast was dead at last.

"How 'bout you?" Cass asked, standing beside his sister, gazing down with concern at his brother-in-law. "How're you doin'?"

"Never better." Hunter thrust a hand up.

Cass took it and pulled him to his feet.

Anna rose, too, and threw herself into her husband's arms, pressing her face against his chest and taking a long deep sniff as though she thought she'd never smell his wonderful, masculine scent ever again.

Which she'd come pretty damn close to not doing.

Hunter hugged her tightly and looked at Cass, frowning

curiously. "How in the world did you ever find me way up here?"

"Backtracked your horses from the ranch," Cass said. "They led us to your camp."

Anna looked up at him. "We saw the chief there." She shook her head sadly. "I'm so sorry, Hunt."

Hunter's frown deepened. "What're you talkin' about? He's right over . . ."

He turned his head and frowned. There was no sign of the chief. Just rocks and more rocks sloping down to the pine forest below.

"He *was* right over there," Hunter said, pointing.

Anna placed her hand on his cheek, turned his face back to hers. Deep lines of incredulity cut across her forehead. "Hunter, you left the chief in his blanket roll back at your camp. He's dead."

Hunter grunted a laugh. "No, no—he's . . ."

He stopped.

He looked down at the rifle lying on the rocks a few feet away. His stomach flipped.

The chief had tossed it to him. He was sure of it.

Or had he been hallucinating?

Hunter turned to see Bobby Lee sniffing the ground where he had last seen the chief. Or thought he had, anyway.

"Come on," Anna said, rising up on her toes to kiss his cheek. Then she hooked her arm around his. "Come on. Let's get you home."

"Yeah. Right." Hunter stopped and picked up the Spencer. He looked at it as though it were suddenly some forbidding totem.

He looked at Bobby Lee still sniffing the ground and whining.

He looked at the bear.

"You look awfully tired, *amigo*," Cass said, clamping a hand over Hunter's shoulder. "We brought a couple of fresh horses. We'll get you back home pronto. You'll feel good as new after a hot meal and a good night's sleep."

"Yeah," Hunter said dreamily, lost in thought, as Anna and Cass led him down the stony slope. "I reckon I will."

But he wasn't so sure.

Again, he looked back at the bear, then at the rifle in his hand.

Bobby Lee sat down and howled.

Hunter shuddered.

Turn the page for a special excerpt!

WILLIAM W. JOHNSTONE
and J. A. Johnstone

THE DEVIL YOU KNOW
✳ A STONEFACE FINNEGAN WESTERN ✳

As a Pinkerton agent, Stoneface Finnegan
faced the deadliest killers in the West.
But now that he runs a saloon, he serves them hard
liquor—with a shot of harder justice . . .

Stoneface Finnegan and his new partner are busy
renovating the Last Drop Saloon when a very unusual
stranger comes to town. He's nothing like the prairie rat
drifters, world-weary miners, and would-be outlaws who
normally pass through Boar Gulch. No, he's a big
handsome devil from San Francisco, Giacomo Valucci.
Valucci fancies himself an actor, but his
all-too-dramatic arrival is no act.
He's come to kill Stoneface Finnegan . . .
Finnegan's gut tells him that someone's put a price on
his head. Maybe one of his cutthroat enemies from his
Pinkerton days. Or maybe not.
Giacomo Valucci seems more interested in playing the
role of Jack the Ripper. He's carving a path of mayhem
and murder across the American West—
and saving Stoneface Finnegan for the last act . . .
and the final curtain.

Look for
THE DEVIL YOU KNOW
on sale September 2021!

Chapter 1

The sigh, long and low, leaked out of the big man's mouth. It could have come about because he had gulped a long-needed drink of cool water, or because he'd won the biggest hand of the night at the baize tables. But neither would be true. For this man wore spatters of blood on his face and chest, and on the twitching lids of his closed eyes. Runnels of gore dripped from his long fingers as he stood over two flopped bodies, people whose heads had been all but separated from their neck stalks.

Those necks bore telltale marks—wide, purple handprints that choked the life from the pair in that effortless squeeze that brought the big man such sweet, pleasing release. That pleasure was only topped by the final act of slicing the throats and feeling the warm gush of blood.

In the glow of his reverie, the big man thought he heard a tinkling bell. How nice, how soothing.

"Miss Tillis? Mr. Tillis? Yoo hoo . . . anybody here?"

The voice snapped his eyes open. It was not soothing. It was foul, the worst of interruptions, a harsh jag of light in an otherwise serene, shadowed moment.

More tinkling bell sounds, then bootsteps as the busy-body woman made her way through the store out front.

The big man let out a quick breath of disgust and, with a last glance down at his latest accomplishment that, had it not been for the interruption he might have considered one of his finest performances, he stepped toward the back door, eased it open, and slipped outside once more.

He set to his next tasks with measured motions, walking with long, sure strides across the rear loading deck of Tillis Mercantile, then down the six steps, his oversize, soft-sole brogans making no sound save for a shuffling whisper. He crossed the graveled yard and ducked low between the sagged rails of a weather-grayed fence and into the neighboring paddock, home of a sway-bellied pony.

"Good morning, sir," he whispered to the old beast, who had not yet committed to waking from its nighttime doze.

He crossed to the pony's water trough, which he knew from his foray through this way but hours before to be half-full. The man also knew that at any moment he would hear a scream that would likely rise to shriek pitch—women loved to draw attention to newly discovered horrors—and then haste would be required, lest he be caught by the screamer's goodly neighbors while rinsing blood from his hands.

He set to the task with vigor, a smile tugging up the right side of his wide mouth. Since it was still early dawn and gray light was all he had to work with, he didn't worry about the scrim of blood he knew would be under his nails, coloring the creases of his palms and fingers.

Satisfied his hands were clean enough, he once more bent low over the trough and splashed two handfuls of water on his face and throat, rubbing any flecks of blood that might still be there.

He unbuttoned the large, spattered shirt, peeled it off, and laid it on the ground, arms wide as if to welcome the rest of his ensemble.

He'd nudged his brown trousers down to his knees when the screams began. Despite his dicey situation, the big man could not help but smile. Standing on the shirt, he scuffed out of the large brogans and finished peeling off the trousers.

Beneath these clothes he wore black silk sleepwear, shirt and trousers, and black close-fitting house slippers. He bent over the soiled clothes, tied the sleeves and tails and collar into a tight bundle, and carried them with him as he bent low and left the still-drowsy pony's paddock.

The big man resisted the urge to whistle and instead hummed a nearly silent, low tune of sheer joy that only came to him when he'd completed a performance. They had been quite the couple, he mused. No, no, not yet. Don't give in to thoughts of the past few hours yet. Time a-plenty for that. First he must pass behind four backyards to return to the rear of the Starr Town Hotel and Rooming House, where he'd propped open the back door with a slender wedge of wood.

Halfway to the hotel, he heard commotion as people in other homes and businesses were roused by the screaming woman's unceasing cries.

"Ah," he said to himself. "The thrill of discovery."

He measured his steps, eyeing the outhouses and sagging sheds tucked at the rear of the properties until he saw the one he required, though not for usual reasons. This one, but one building from the rear of the hotel, had a widening hole behind it where earth had slumped beneath the privy. It exuded a pungent tang and he held his breath as he dropped the bundle and toed it into the reeking pit. It fetched up, so he squatted and poked a hand quick at it, lest something foul begrime him. It was enough and the bundle toppled into the drop, and out of his sight.

And sight was something he knew would work against him soon as more people woke to greet their day and to figure out who was screaming and why. What he had not counted on was being interrupted by that woman.

Why had the front door of the store been unlocked? Unless the woman had a key to the door. Perhaps she is an employee of the Tillis couple. Correct that, former employee. He indulged in a low chuckle and walked to the hotel's back door. It was still barely propped ajar by his trusty shim. He palmed the sliver of wood, swung the door open, and stepped inside.

A steep staircase rose to his right, the same set of stairs he'd used earlier to descend from the second floor where his room awaited him. He was about to ascend when he heard footsteps on the squeaking floorboards above and then approach the stairs. A light sleeper, no doubt, roused by the muffled shouts from down the street.

He had to give that intruding woman credit, even five buildings away, he could still make out her screams. Hers was a dogged personality.

The big man stepped back from the stairs, saw no alternative, but in true thespian fashion, he rose to the role thrust upon him by the moment. He glided down the hall that led to the front of the house, turned halfway down, and tucking his hands under his arms as if he were chilled, he hunched and faced the person on the stairs.

A woman, and she carried with her a lamp. He squinted as she raised it and peered down the hall. "Oh, Mr. Bardo, you startled me."

"And I by you, madam. Tell me, am I hearing shouts?"

She fell silent and they both cocked an ear. "Yes, as I thought. That's what roused me as well. It's early. Something must be wrong somewhere."

"Oh dear," he said, working up a shiver. "I sleep lightly and came down to investigate. You'll forgive me, madam, but I was afraid it might have been you I heard and I could not forgive myself had I not investigated."

His words produced the effect he expected—she half-smiled and looked askew and worked her face this way and that in a blushing moment. "Oh, Mr. Bardo, you are a thoughtful man. But no, I, too, sleep lightly—something else we have in common, eh, Mr. Bardo?—and had to find out what might be happening. Besides, my day should begin about now anyway. Those biscuits won't bake themselves."

"Ah, yes, your lovely cooking. But I wonder if you will excuse me just now? I fear I will catch a chill should I stand about in my sleepwear and little else for much longer."

"Oh, Mr. Bardo, please don't let me detain you. I will have a nice warm pot of coffee brewing in no time."

"Very good, madam. I look forward to it."

He moved to scoot by her, but she stepped to the side half the distance he'd wished, close enough that he had to brush her as he mounted the steps. Unfortunately, he thought as he climbed the steps, she is watching me. He sighed inward and had to admit that Mr. Bardo was perhaps not one of his better roles. He listened once more after he closed his room's door. The screaming had stopped, but he heard new voices, several, perhaps more, rising and falling like a barnyard of flustered geese.

"Let them flap and cackle," he said. "They will talk about this performance for years to come." Yes, he thought. *I have done this tiny town of Wilmotville a generous favor. I have brought world-class artistry to their dreary lives, and they shall not soon forget it.*

Ah well, he thought as he slipped out of his silk clothes. Not every role can be memorable. But they are all rewarding and, as he looked at his blood-crusted fingernails and smiled, he decided that frequently they were spectacular too.

He splashed cold water into his washbasin and stripped down. The frigid water raised goose bumps up and down his body. He smiled even as his teeth rattled slightly. Nothing like it, he thought. A pure, clean feeling gripping him and forcing his eyes wide open.

He scrubbed and scrubbed and allowed himself to indulge in the briefest of memories of the encounter that led him to this moment, to this feeling. He'd chosen the town almost without thought, one of any such annoying little bumps of settled humanity along the tracks of Western Lodestar's southwest run. It had been easy after that to fall in love with a woman on first sight, something he'd never had trouble with.

Their comeliness and interest and availability were always secondary matters. Fortunately for him Mrs. Tillis of Tillis Mercantile had been not only handsome and flattered by his flirtatious attentions of the previous afternoon, but she'd been a little more than willing to return his devilish darings by sliding her tongue across her lips, winking, and blushing fetchingly.

Her husband had caught sight once of her straying eyes and suitably reddened. The big man suspected this was not a first for the woman who, he noted, was obviously some years her spouse's junior. Mr. Tillis was a flea at best, someone undeserving of a pretty woman's devotions.

Now I, thought the big man, I am one who deserves them all. Was I not carved of marble myself, a god among men? Have women not regarded me as such my entire life? I, I alone am worthy. Also, it is my obligation, too, to return the lustful looks . . . and more, whenever possible.

But Mr. Tillis did not scold his wife forcefully, at least not in front of this stranger, a man who obviously had ample money, if his fine raiments and perfect black mustache and oiled hair and bejeweled fingers were of any indication. Even that black patch covering his left eye lent the man an air of daring that hinted at a treachery . . . and yet it also made him appear much more vulnerable and handsome to women, if his flirtatious wife was any indication.

And if that weren't enough, was not this stranger drawn to the most expensive two items in the store? A gold watch in a green velvet display case, and a nickel-plate revolver with bone handles etched with aces on each grip, and nested in an overly tooled black leather holster and belt studded with silver conchos.

And so the game unrolled for much of an hour late in the day. When the stranger had rubbed his perfect square jaw and smoothed his black mustache and regarded the items with his one good eye as if deciding something, only to suck in a breath through white, square teeth, Mr. Tillis had faltered, begun to reveal his frustration with the stranger and the situation.

That was when he had told the man he would sleep on the decisions. It was not a matter of money, oh heaven's no, he'd said with a chuckle and a smile, but of having to carry the items, gifts is what they would be, yes, all the way eastward on his journey, though he suspected he would make the purchases. He rarely in life refused to indulge himself in such matters. After all, he'd said with a shrug, why have money?

Knowing chuckles were exchanged between the two men. He would decide and tell the man on the morrow, before he left on the train. Would that be fair?

Oh yes, yes, Mr. Tillis had fawned. The big man had turned to leave the store, turned back, and bowed at the waist to Madam Tillis. Without taking his eyes from hers, he uttered one word . . . simply "Enchanted."

He turned and left the store, the tinkling of a bell and the memory of her fair blush carrying him down the street to a dining establishment. But return he did, though sooner than the pair had expected. In fact, it was well into the small hours when the big man turned up again at the mercantile, though this time through the back door.

He intentionally clunked into items in the store, making enough noise that, as he suspected, Mr. Tillis made his wary way downstairs from their living quarters, a shotgun barred across his chest. One quick knock to the head and the storekeeper was rendered unconscious. The wife, on hearing no response to her pleas, followed her husband's route and soon succumbed to the stranger's unforgiving intentions.

All he'd been after had been the blood, really. No, not even that, more the feeling of their lives letting go beneath his hands, though that took some hours of playfulness on his part. He'd dragged out the performance and then, with a flourish, had used a keen-edged shiny new blade from the store's display case to deliver the encore.

He scrubbed carefully above and below his false mustache—the theatrical glue worked well but its residue was a devil of a thing. He would deal with it once he returned home. The eye patch was a simpler prop to remove, and so he did, admiring himself in the mirror of the washing stand as he did each morning. Indeed, several times daily.

While he was pleased with having chosen the false mustache and eye patch as basic, useful items, in a simple yet straightforward theatrical ruse for this final fling before his grand outing, it did seem a true shame to dim the light of his own natural radiance and beauty with props and makeup and costumery. He sighed and patted dry his face. *Ah well, such are the tribulations I must endure.*

But well worth the trouble. Consider it a final rehearsal before opening night, he told himself. In fact, all of them through the years had been but rehearsals for his greatest show yet, the effort he would expend in seeking out, then rendering dead, the greatest foe of his life, one Rollie "Stoneface" Finnegan. The very beast responsible for every single bad thing that has ever happened to him, for robbing him of the happiness due him in life.

The big, handsome man glanced once more at his naked

self in the mirror and laid out his clothes for the day. He couldn't wait to hear the chatter at the breakfast table, and then up and down the street. The town would be abuzz with whispers of intrigue and thoughts of delicious terror. He giggled as he dressed himself.

Chapter 2

The first bullet chewed a hole in the privy door, right beside the crescent moon. A second shot chased it. On his knees inside, with his trousers around his boots, Rollie "Stoneface" Finnegan looked up at the new ventilation and decided they looked like stars around the moon. High shots, not aimed to kill, but to scare. A third joined them. Not like the thunder pit couldn't use more airflow, but there had to be a better way of going about it. He checked the wheel in his Schofield and thumbed back the hammer.

"Stoneface Finnegan! Come on out and I'll make this painless."

Rollie sighed. Here we go again. All he wanted to do was spend a night away from town, holed up with a bottle and his thoughts. It was the cabin and claim he and his business partner, Jubal "Pops" Tennyson, had taken in trade for a sizable bar tab from a back-East furniture maker who decided he was not cut out for life in the diggings.

They'd not had time to do much with either the cabin or claim yet, but each had used it off and on in the couple of months since owning it. It was an ideal spot to clear away the cobwebs and give each other a break from living cheek-to-jowl in the cramped quarters of the tent. At least they had a tent, propped as it was just behind where their saloon, the Last Drop, had stood, torched low by arsons looking for Rollie's head.

They were nearing the end of rebuilding the bar, and Rollie finally felt like he could take a day and a night off. But instead of peace and quiet, what did he get? Another moron looking to cash in on a bounty. It seemed they would never stop seeking him out, would never learn. He guessed it was the indomitable human spirit at play—never believing you might not succeed. Until you don't.

Rollie and Pops had laid low a sizable stack of men in the past few months. He figured he was about to add to that pile. On the other hand, it was as true that his luck would one day run out. Everybody's did eventually. Was it this day?

Rollie tugged up his trousers as he eyed through plank gaps in the front wall beside the door. His attacker, so far he'd detected only the one, stood behind a wide Ponderosa pine facing the outhouse. He looked out every few seconds, like a cuckoo clock. If he could time it right, Rollie might be able to drill him in the forehead.

"Oh, come on and answer me already. I saw you go in there. Heard tell there's a bounty on your head, Finnegan!" A ratty beard parted and a cackle burst out between two chaw-dripping lips.

"Where'd you hear that?"

"Now that's more like it!"

"I asked where you heard that."

"You saying it ain't true?"

"No."

"Well, I'll oblige you. I heard it from a fella on the trail, oh, Utah or somewhere . . ."

Rollie groaned. He didn't doubt the news was that widespread. What he didn't like was that he was still the target of undeserving hate by people he'd never met or wronged. It seemed that half the folks who'd come after him for being a Pinkerton agent once upon a time were just in it for the money. At least the other misguided souls had what they believed was reason enough to attack him. They were folks— or their vengeance-seeking relations— he'd sent to prison for various misdeeds over the years.

What was this fool's excuse? Had to be the money.

"Look. All I need's your head. The rest of you can stay put."

Rollie shook that wanted head. He had to give the man credit, at least he was forthright. Doesn't mean I won't kill him, though, thought Rollie. *But first things first, I am pinned down in the outhouse and that cannot stand.*

Getting out he'd have to raise a ruckus, and no way was he exiting through the hole below. Kick out a side wall? He'd have to do it fast, because the man would reposition himself. It was a risk, especially if the crusty hick wasn't alone.

Or . . . Rollie eyed the man again through the gap in the planks. Wait, wait . . . and there he was, peering around the tree once more. As quiet as he could, Rollie jimmied the tip of the Schofield's barrel between the planks and eyed down the sights.

"Come on, man!" said the ambusher. "I ain't got all day!"

"Hold on a second, I'm fixing my trousers—you caught me unawares . . ." That ought to buy time enough to watch the man give a couple more peeks around the tree. And he did.

Amazingly enough the rascal performed his funny little

head maneuver as if he were timed. One more and . . . Rollie squeezed a shot. The rough red bark of the tree burst in a ragged cloud. The man's screams told Rollie he'd not killed him, for a shot to the forehead would have snuffed any ability the man had to carry on so.

Within seconds the invader spun into view, holding his head and whipping in a dervish dance. He slammed into a knee-height granite boulder and flipped over it, collapsing on his back and flailing his legs.

By then Rollie had kicked open the privy door and stomped dead-on at the mewling man. The hot-nerved pulses always with him from too many old wounds prevented Rollie from a full-bore run.

He stood over him, though out of grabbing range, his revolver aimed down at the man's head. As he suspected, given the man's howls, his shot had blasted the tree and sent bark and jagged shards of wood into the man's leering face. From between his grubby, bloody hands poured gore, bubbling about the mouth as the man screamed.

Rollie glanced quickly up at the tree the man had been hiding behind. It was a huge Ponderosa and now sported a furrow of raw, honey-color wood chiseled up by the bullet into a ragged wound.

Rollie kicked him hard in the thigh. "Shut up."

Another two kicks and it worked, the man's noises tamped down to gasps and chesty sobs. "I . . . I can't see! Oh God, I can't see!"

"Take your hands away from your face, fool," said Rollie.

When the man did, it revealed the reason.

"I can't go through this life blind!"

"Aw, you won't be blind for long."

"Huh? You reckon? I don't understand."

Rollie shrugged. "Simple. You aimed to kill me, I figure that favor deserves one in kind."

"You're a devil! I heard about you . . . you're a devil!"

Rollie nodded. "Yep, and next time you decide to dance with one, you best be prepared for things to go against you."

"But . . . no!"

"Yep. Now, it's your choice, I can string you up here or I can drag you back to Boar Gulch. I was planning on spending the day up here doing nothing much at all, but you've ruined that for me. Thank you very much."

"What? What are you talking about? I don't understand."

"You were going to kill me, right?"

The blubbering man didn't answer.

"Right?"

"Yeah, yes, I guess . . ."

"So it's my turn."

"No!" The man howled again and snatched up a slender-bladed skinning knife from a sheath at his waist. Before Rollie could figure out what the fool intended to do with it, the man had driven it once, twice into his own gut . . . high, jamming the blade upward.

He got the two stabs in but lost steam. His hand, looking like a red-black glove of silk, trembled and released its shaky grip on the wood-handled knife. The hand dropped to the man's side, but the knife remained lodged in his breadbasket. Blood pumped and welled, pumped and welled from the fresh wounds.

Rollie wasn't certain the man had landed a heart wound, but he hadn't done himself any good. They were mortal wounds, to be sure. Rollie scratched his chin and looked down at the gurgling mess at his feet.

He couldn't recall ever seeing a man stab his own self to death. No, wait, there was that time in Alameda when he'd walked into that cabin to find that feral half-breed slicing on his own arms and legs for no earthly reason other than he'd been tetched. This fool didn't have that excuse. Well, maybe a little.

Rollie didn't like to all-but execute a man. This was rough. But the man was suffering mighty, his breathing was gaspy and ragged; blood bubbles rose and popped in succession up out of a mouth nested somewhere in the man's soaked, gore-matted beard.

Rollie crouched low, his knees popping, and held the revolver at the man's head, in case he decided to surprise them both and attack. Not likely though.

"I'll not shoot you to ease your passing, as you've done yourself in, mister. Your foolhardy ways are about over with. Any last words?"

"Da . . . da . . . devil!"

Rollie breathed deeply, pushed out the breath at about the same time the man's skinny frame shuddered, then seemed to collapse in on itself. That final, momentous act was a mystery Rollie had witnessed many times but never understood. Maybe one day he'd find out, but not today.

"I expect you'll meet the King of Devils himself, soon. Give ol' Scratch my best."

But the man would hear nothing ever again.

Rollie stood, knees popping once more, and looked around the clearing. Behind him, in the lean-to attached to the cabin, he heard Cap, short for Captain, his gray gelding, whicker.

"How in the hell did my day get off to such a start, Cap?" He turned to face the horse. "What next? What next for Rollie Finnegan?"

He heard no reply but a mountain jay and a far-off breeze through the tall trees. But something told Rollie he wouldn't have long to wait to find out the answer to his question.

Look for

THE DEVIL YOU KNOW

on sale September 2021!

Connect with 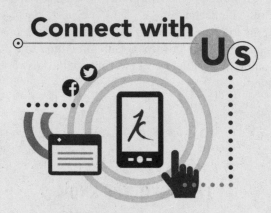Us

Visit us online at
KensingtonBooks.com
to read more from your favorite authors, see books
by series, view reading group guides, and more.

 Join us on social media

for sneak peeks, chances to win books and prize packs,
and to share your thoughts with other readers.

facebook.com/kensingtonpublishing
twitter.com/kensingtonbooks

Tell us what you think!

To share your thoughts, submit a review,
or sign up for our eNewsletters, please visit:
KensingtonBooks.com/TellUs.